SHERIDAN LEE

BROKEN SPIRIT

by Sheridan Lee

For my wonderful readers

Thank you for your support. I love receiving your messages (and I apologise for what you're about to read…).

GLOSSARY OF AUSTRALIAN WORDS AND PHRASES

Boot/car boot – car trunk

FSANZ – Food Standards Australia New Zealand

Grey nomad – a retiree who travels around Australia in a caravan or motorhome

Moccies [MOK-eez] – abbreviation for moccasins

Salvos – Salvation Army charity op shop/thrift store

STEM – the study of Science, Technology, Engineering and Mathematics

Toy boy – a younger man romantically involved with an older woman

Trolley – a wheeled metal basket/shopping cart

Ute – a vehicle with a car-like cabin and an open cargo area

VicRoads – State agency for road management and safety in Victoria

CHAPTER ONE
Playing with Fire

Thank God it's Friday. I closed the oversized classroom window, partitioning the late-afternoon summer heat behind streaky glass, and wiped my brow with a damp tea towel. February was my least favourite month on the school calendar. A new school year with inexperienced pre-teens bent on stressing me to death. Even a saint needed a break from fresh-faced Year Seven students determined to ignore safety measures and set off the fire alarm.

I trundled past the large pantry and tables topped with upturned chairs to my makeshift office—an oversized storage cupboard adjacent to the Tellarine Secondary College kitchen—tossed the tea towel in the laundry basket, and secured my cream-and-navy handbag over my shoulder. Maybe no one would try to burn down the school next week. One could dream.

My phone vibrated in my back pocket.

I closed my office door and surveyed the neat school kitchen. Aging white benchtops and grey linoleum floors gleamed under fluorescent lights. The quiet hum of refrigerators and an overworked dishwasher sang a familiar tune beside the silent study nook. I sniffed and wrinkled my nose. Charred chocolate chip cookies still tinged the air.

After adding "air freshener that doesn't smell like Impulse or Lynx body spray" to my mental shopping list, I switched off the Food Technology room lights, locked the door, and extracted my phone.

Two unread messages, one I had ignored at lunchtime. I clicked on the new message.

Tara Everton: ARE YOU AND MATT GOING TO BE AT THE JACOBSENS TONIGHT?

Envy slithered through my gut, and I clamped my palm over my stomach. Tara was great, but seeing her three-and-a-half-month-old daughter showcased my fertility deficiencies and tore at my battered heart.

When would it be my turn?

I leaned back against the warm hallway wall, closed my eyes, and uttered a prayer. *Help me, God, to get through tonight.* Heaviness slid over my shoulders and weighed my insides. I sagged. *And give me courage to read Alison's message.* I opened my eyes and contemplated my reply.

Me: YES, WE'LL BE THERE.

Brief, but to the point, like all of my text messages to Tara. Was it possible to nudge the door of my heart a little wider for Keanu's wife? My relationship with Victoria Jacobsen remained strong despite her easy pregnancies. I rubbed the back of my neck. Vicki had lost children in worse circumstances than me, so I fought the green-eyed monster to preserve our friendship. But for whatever reason, I failed to offer Tara the same courtesy. Maybe it was our age difference? I had no problem spending time with Vicki's stepdaughter, who was the same age as Tara, so maybe not.

I expelled a long breath and clicked on the infrequent text chain under my baby sister's name.

Alison Davies: HAPPY BIRTHDAY FOR TOMORROW, BINDY-BOO! 38? I KNOW YOUR ANNIVERSARY IS SOMETIME THIS MONTH TOO, SO HAPPY WHATEVER YEAR YOU'RE UP TO FOR YOU AND THE DEMI SEX GOD. I HOPE YOU GIVE IT TO HIM GOOD AND PROPER. STILL CAN'T

BELIEVE YOU BED THAT BLOKE ON THE NIGHTLY.

I clenched my fingers around my mobile phone and counted my breaths. Nice to know nothing had changed. "At least she remembered," I whispered through gritted teeth.

A dull thud and pop split the silent corridor.

I glanced across the hallway into the Textiles room, my old home away from home before I became the fulltime Food Tech teacher.

"Argh! Clucking trucks in muck!"

I stifled a laugh, pushing aside my mental weights, and approached the open doorway.

Cindy Wu hunkered over an ancient Brother sewing machine, her jet-black long bob obscuring her face. Her petite fingers were tangled in dark thread.

I padded into the carpeted room, placed my bag on what used to be my desk, and approached the young teacher. "Need some help?"

"Belinda Briggs, my saviour!" Cindy yanked her hand free and huffed a breath. "Stupid little sh—ugar babies."

I snorted a laugh and pointed to the sewing machine on a nearby table. "This need fixing too?"

"The little snots broke the needle and misaligned the foot."

What on earth were those kids doing? Practicing their tug of war skills?

Cindy balled the tangled threads and gestured toward two machines in the corner. "One's missing a spool cap, and someone stole a bobbin."

I grunted. "I'll fix this one while you tackle the other machines."

"Thanks." She sucked in a breath and stood. Her dark eyes widened. "Was it always like this? Or am I simply the worst Textiles teacher in the world?"

"It's not you." I inspected the broken needle, opened one of the supply cupboards, and grabbed a replacement. "You just need to keep a close eye on the Year Sevens, especially the boys."

"No one at University said it'd be this hard." Cindy carried the repaired bulky sewing machine to the shelf and slid it into place. "Those kids drive me insane and I haven't even worked twelve months on the job. Not sure I'll last out the year."

"Nah, you'll be fine. You still on probation?" I removed the broken needle and tossed its remains in the bin.

Principal Marsden had extended Cindy's probation period after the stressed textiles teacher lost her cool and swore at a student last year. From what I heard through the walls, Cindy was lucky to keep her job. Now she spent her days retraining her brain with creative replacements for the foul language she wished to spew.

A bitter laugh echoed across the room. "One more week. I've lasted almost six months without dropping an f-bomb in class. But I was close to strangling the f—luffing so and so after he damaged that machine today."

"Keep a close eye on the culprits and rely on the honest students to keep others in line." I locked in a new needle and straightened the sewing machine foot. "There's only so much you can do."

"I just don't know how you did this job for so many years." Cindy clipped in a new bobbin.

I lifted the fixed machine and carried it to the shelf. "I wasn't fulltime in here. Spent two days a week in the kitchen."

She perched a sewing machine on the shelf. "Maybe I should burn my frustration away in the kitchen. Care to swap a day with me?"

"Not on your life." I chuckled and grabbed the carpet sweeper.

Someone knocked on the doorframe.

I turned, leaned on the sweeper handle, and grinned at the sexiest forty-five-year-old man on the planet.

"Fancy seeing you here." Cindy's voice oozed with its usual mix of flirtation and awe.

I suppressed an eyeroll and stared into my husband's blue eyes.

"You done?"

"Almost." Matt ran his fingers through his cropped blond hair. "Was hoping to nab a pair of gloves from the kitchen."

"What's up?" I leaned the sweeper against a table, located my keys in my bag, and tossed them across the room.

Matt leaned forward and caught the clinking metal bundle. "Found some more colourful pills and punctured soft drink cans outside my computer room."

My heart stuttered.

"Again?" Cindy's voice squeaked. She trod to a cupboard and rifled in a drawer.

"Fourth time this year." Matt grimaced and flipped the keys between his hands. "I'd hoped this drug issue could be nipped in the bud."

I sucked in a breath and swallowed the lump in my throat. "Be careful."

"Always."

Cindy handed Matt a balled-up plastic bag. "Use this."

"Thanks." My husband pivoted and strode from the room.

I grabbed the sweeper with numb fingers and pushed it along the grey carpet. When had teaching in a rural town become so dangerous?

"Another reason to never have children." Cindy sprayed and wiped her desk.

What?

"You and Matt are one of the smartest couples I've ever met." She popped her cleaning items in a cupboard.

I stilled the sweeper and furrowed my brow.

"I mean, you're smart enough not to breed and add to Earth's overpopulation issues."

I squeezed the sweeper handle, my breaths short, and stared at the young woman. Was she for real?

"After working with teenage brats all day, I'm not surprised you'd decide to just enjoy that man of yours and keep him to yourself. Although, I'd be interested to see if two blonds produced blond babies or not." Cindy's cheeks flushed pink. "How long have you been together?"

I forced my lips into a cordial smile and thrust the sweeper forward. "We dated on and off for a few years, but it's our sixth wedding anniversary later this month."

"Congratulations! Any plans?"

Make a baby? I held my tongue and returned the carpet sweeper to storage. "None that I'm aware of."

Cindy passed me my handbag. "I'm sure your delectable husband will spoil you."

"I expect he will," Matt said from the doorway.

Cindy gurgled, and her blush deepened. "Th-thanks for your help, Belinda."

"Anytime. Have a great weekend." I approached Matt and walked down the corridor beside him. "Seems you still pull the young twenty-somethings."

Matt chuckled and retrieved my keys from his pants pocket. "But I only have eyes for you."

I accepted my keys, fisted them in my left hand, and glanced at his smiling face. "She was applauding us for not having children and overpopulating the earth."

Matt's eyes widened. "You okay?" He slipped his fingers along my arm and rubbed against the back of my hand.

"Yeah." What else could I be?

"Did you tell her—"

"No." My throat closed.

He intertwined his fingers with mine and squeezed my hand.

When was the last time we had touched each other like this? Walked hand in hand? Having a child had become the priority since my fourth miscarriage eleven months ago. I had focused on making and keeping a baby, and all that entailed, not the man beside me.

"Do you need anything in there?" Matt's voice pulled me from my thoughts.

"Huh?" I stared at the exit ahead. When had we stopped?

He nodded toward the corridor which led to the administration building.

"Oh. Don't think so." I could check my in-tray on Monday.

Matt released my hand, opened the external door, and guided me through the exit. He pressed his large, warm hand against my back, warming my lumbar region, and we descended the weathered concrete.

A tingle danced along my backbone, and I sucked in a sharp breath. When had I last reacted in this way to Matt's touch? Had distance crept into our marriage? Like a well-oiled machine, we were physically close at the right times of my menstrual cycle. But outside the slices of time together in bed, were we still connected? Was it possible to make love without intimacy?

"You still want to go to Vicki's?" Matt unlocked his car and opened the passenger door.

I stared up at him.

"I'm sure she'd understand if you're not up for it." He brushed my elbow with his fingers before fisting his hands at his sides.

Was I pushing him away? How had I not seen the shift in our relationship? *Because you spend more time obsessing over a potential baby than your actual flesh-and-blood husband.* Heat bloomed in my cheeks. I lowered my face, eased my tight jaw, and slid onto the front seat.

Matt closed the passenger door, walked around the car, and filled the driver's seat. "You'll see her tomorrow."

"No," my voice croaked. "I'm fine to go tonight."

Matt braced his hands on the steering wheel.

Was I being selfish wanting a baby? Would God think I was ungrateful for the things I *did* have? My heartbeat ratcheted. Maybe I should give the baby-making a break.

Matt settled his gaze on me. "If you're sure."

"I am." Despite the uncertainty vibrating in my gut regarding my baby agenda, I was sure this evening should go as planned.

He pressed Start and eased the car through the close to empty staff car park.

"Is my blue shirt clean?" Matt's voice echoed from his walk-in-robe, down the hallway, and into the family room where I stood.

I eyed my pink-and-white floral dress hanging from the clothes airer. Maybe wearing something bright and carefree would pull me from the heaviness still compressing my chest. I slid the garment from its hanger, desperate to escape the thoughts swirling inside my brain. What sort of wife treated her husband like a baby-making toy instead of a human? And what type of friend was I to envy Vicki and Tara because they could pop children so easily?

A selfish person.

"Bee?"

I gripped the dress collar and steadied my breaths. A selfish person who also happened to be a horrible sister.

"Bee? Can you see my blue shirt?" Strain coloured Matt's tone.

I shuffled toward our bedroom. "Which blue shirt?"

"The short-sleeved baby-blue one."

Baby blue. Was I experiencing a case of the baby blues? *Don't be ridiculous. You have to give birth before you can suffer the baby blues.* I scoffed at my stupidity, yanked the lightweight dress over my head, and plopped on the edge of our bed.

Matt stepped into the bedroom, shirtless. He met my gaze and froze. "Bee?"

I opened my mouth to speak, but my words evaporated on my tongue.

"You sure you're okay?" He furrowed his brow and stepped closer.

I clenched my fists in my lap, thoughts pummelling the walls of my mind. What *wasn't* wrong with me?

"Bee?"

Why was I such a drama queen today? Blasted Cindy and her overpopulation propaganda. I blinked away my blurry vision.

Matt's face loomed in front of me where he now kneeled on the carpet, his brow crumpled.

I stared into his clear blue eyes.

"I'll message Nick and cancel."

"No." My voice shook.

"But—"

"We're going to dinner."

Matt leaned closer and caressed my cheek.

A raspy sigh escaped my lungs, and my pulse quickened. I peeked at his bronzed chest before gazing at his tempting mouth. *Not now.* I lifted my chin, determined not to use Matt's embrace as an escape from my selfishness.

A dark glint flashed in his eyes, and he inched his fingers along my jaw and down my throat, one teeny, tempting step at a time.

My heartbeat accelerated, and I gasped a breath.

Matt brushed his fingertips along my collarbone, circling the thin strap of my dress, and kissed my exposed shoulder.

Heat infused my skin and radiated out of my body. "We mustn't be late," I whispered.

"They won't mind." His warm breath stroked my skin and ignited tingles along my back.

I shivered.

Matt's eyes darkened. He lowered his face and pressed lingering kisses against my clavicle.

I exhaled a loud breath and closed my eyes. *Five minutes won't hurt.*

His mouth heated my skin, trailing fire along my neck.

My pulse thundered under his lips. Could he feel my rapid heartbeat?

"You're not wearing lipstick yet."

I opened my eyes and stared at his mouth-watering face a

breath away from mine. My chest squeezed.

"Good." He leaned closer, eyes twinkling.

I pressed my hand against his firm chest and wished he wore a collared shirt so I could clutch him against me.

"Now you can't blame me for ruining your makeup." He brushed his lips over mine. Slow and soft, tentative kisses.

I mewled like the promiscuous teenagers I had caught making out in the girls' bathroom last week.

Matt's heart banged under my palm, and his breaths quickened with his kisses.

Five minutes would not be enough. I leaned back, lost my balance, and fell against the plush bedcovers.

He shot to his feet and bracketed me between his arms, his head shielding my eyes from the bright bedroom light.

Uh oh.

"I thought you said we mustn't be late." His gravelly voice dragged along my limbs, sparking goosebumps. He nuzzled the sensitive skin below my ear and nibbled my earlobe.

"Matt." His name sounded more like a whimper than a word.

"Yes, Bee?" He wielded his lips along my jaw, weapons to subdue the rational part of my brain.

My will languished in a pool of heady sensations.

Matt chuckled against my lips, mid-kiss.

What were we talking about?

He pulled away—stealing his warmth from my torso—and stood.

I furrowed my brow.

Matt extended his arm, grabbed my hand, and helped me upright. "Blue shirt?"

I glanced at my bedside clock and sprung from the edge of the bed. We were running behind schedule. I stepped toward the bedroom doorway. "I'll get it."

He clasped his fingers around my wrist and tugged me against his chest.

"Matt, we're going to be late."

He leaned closer and brushed his lips against my ear.

I sucked in a sharp breath.

"To be continued," he whispered before he released my arm and sauntered into the bathroom.

I rushed from the room, fixated on finding his shirt, not on the image of his corded back muscles and magnificent jean-clad behind which had burned into my brain.

CHAPTER TWO
Epiphany

"Honey, I'm home!" Matt shut the Jacobsens' heavy wooden front door behind us and linked his fingers with mine.

"About time!" Nick Jacobsen appeared in the entryway and embraced my husband with an enthusiastic, manly back slap.

I untangled my fingers from Matt's, clutched my handbag, and stepped toward the powder room. "I'll be there soon."

"Take your time." Nick gave me a quick one-armed hug and turned back to Matt.

I slipped into the powder room, closed the door, and glanced at myself in the mirror. My cheeks were too flushed. Why had I not reapplied my foundation when I touched up my lipstick? I fruitlessly scrounged through my bag. Lipstick and lip gloss were no help.

I hung my handbag on a hook on the door, patted cool water against my warm cheeks, and dabbed the dry hand towel against my damp skin. "Better," I whispered.

Someone knocked.

I shouldered my bag and opened the door.

"Ahneebee!" Elijah, Nick and Vicki's four-year-old son, grinned up at me and bounced on his toes.

Diana Harris, Vicki's stepdaughter, held her little brother's hand. "He's excited about dinner."

I chuckled and closed the powder room door behind me. "I'm

sorry you had to wait, Eli.”

“It’s okay.” He eyed his oldest sister. “Can I sit wiff you?”

“I think Jazzy already asked.” Diana ruffled Elijah’s hair. “Sorry, bud.”

“Oh well!” Elijah ran toward the dining room.

“You going well?” Diana nodded in the direction her little brother had disappeared.

“Yeah.” I ambled along the hallway beside her. “You?”

“I’m well. Jonathan’s had a lot of extra work the past week.” Diana’s husband was a respected Victoria Police officer stationed in Tellarine.

“Must be tough with a job like his.”

“It is what it is.” Diana gestured toward the dining room. “After you.”

“Hey, everyone.” I glanced around the room, smiled at all the familiar faces and abundant covered dishes spanning the table, and slipped into my seat beside Vicki. “Sorry we’re late.”

Matt ended his conversation with Jonathan Harris by the windows, occupied the chair on my left, and smirked at Keanu Everton near the table end. “My wife’s lips are quite the distraction.”

“Matt!” I slapped his biceps, heat stinging my cheeks. So much for splashing cool water on my face.

Deep chortles punctuated the air. Men.

Matt draped his arm across the back of my chair. “C’mon, you must know what a beautiful distraction you can be.”

“How can lips distract you, Uncle Matt?” Jasmine, Nick and Vicki’s almost-seven-year-old daughter, wrinkled her forehead where she sat across the table between Jonathan and Diana. “Like Larry in *VeggieTales* who loves his lips?”

“Lawee!” Keanu and Tara’s one-and-a-half-year-old son, Kai, clapped his messy hands in the high chair beside Keanu.

“I luff my lips!” Elijah broke out in song between Nick and Vicki.

I elbowed my beloved’s ribcage. “Not in front of the children.”

Diana brushed her fingers through Jasmine's dark curls. "You know how Daddy gets home from work but sometimes forgets to find you for your 'hello' hug?"

"Because he's kissing Mummy?" Jasmine glanced between Matt and me.

"That's right." Diana smirked. "Uncle Matt forgets things when he kisses Aunt Bee."

My face flushed.

"Like you and Jonathan." Jasmine narrowed her eyes at Matt. "Do you make Aunt Bee squeal? Like Daddy does Mummy when they play games when I'm in bed?"

Nick coughed, and more snickers echoed around the table.

I glanced at Vicki and her reddening cheeks.

"Always," Matt said.

I elbowed my husband's ribs harder. "How about we say grace and eat."

Diana mumbled something under her breath which sounded like "and I thought I needed therapy."

"Great idea." Nick's voice wavered. He cleared his throat and blessed the meal. "Dig in."

Vicki uncovered a slow cooker filled with honey mustard chicken casserole. "Eat up, there's plenty."

I filled my plate with an assortment of salads, protein, and steamed vegetables, conscious of all the parents fussing over their children's plates. One day I would fuss over my baby.

A shrill cry chimed from the baby monitor on the wooden buffet behind the Evertons.

Tara stilled.

"Lahlee!" Kai clapped and grinned.

Tara slumped in her seat, arranged her knife and fork across her full plate, and straightened. "I'll get her."

Keanu laid a meaty hand on Tara's petite shoulder, pushed his seat backwards, and stood, his broad shoulders knocking Kai's high chair on the way up. "Eat while ya can."

Tara lifted her chin and gazed at her husband through her wispy blonde fringe. "You sure?"

"Shovel it in ya gob, quick." Keanu squeezed her shoulder and stepped toward the archway.

Vicki laughed. "We can always warm food for you later."

"Thanks." Tara heaped her fork with vegetables and crammed them into her mouth.

I lowered my gaze to my plate and halved several green beans. My desperation for motherhood screamed through my veins, heating my blood. I focused on my food and the wonderful company at the table.

Keanu returned with baby Leilani swaddled in his arms. He bounced on his toes and swayed in the corner, serenading his daughter with a goofy smile on his face.

"That'll be us soon," Matt whispered in my ear.

I nodded and blinked back the heat in my eyes, grasping his anchoring hope.

Jonathan shifted across to Jasmine's chair, lifted her onto his lap, and grabbed Diana's hand. His dark eyes zeroed in on his wife's face, and they communicated with their eyes.

What was going on?

Diana brushed her fingers along Jonathan's scarred temple and nodded.

Jonathan clanged a butter knife against a glass of water and glanced around the table.

Conversation dwindled to silence.

"My beautiful wife and I have some news."

Vicki sucked in a sharp breath and clutched her hands together.

"News?" Jasmine asked.

My heartbeat accelerated. Their news could only be work related or … family expansion. I pressed my hands against my thighs.

"Like Di-Di and Tara's paper?" Jasmine twisted around on Jonathan's lap to face her brother-in-law. "They make news."

"Yes, they do." Jonathan chuckled and kissed Jasmine's head. "If you wait a second, I'll tell you."

Matt covered my hand with his.

"Jernawist!" Elijah raised his arms and bopped on his knees in his seat.

"That's right, Di and I are journalists." Tara winked at Elijah, wiped Kai's hands with his soiled bib, and nodded to Jonathan. "What's the news?"

Jonathan beamed at his wife. "We're eight weeks pregnant."

"Yes!" Tara squeaked, raced around the table for her best friend, and wrapped Diana in a big hug.

A baby. Another baby mothered by someone else.

Another baby to love.

Vicki launched from her chair and rounded the table.

My stomach eddied.

Matt squeezed my hand. "Congrats, guys!"

I glanced across the room and collided with Jonathan's intense gaze.

His eyes almost seemed … apologetic? What did he need to apologise for?

I stretched a wide smile to my tight lips. "Congratulations," I whispered.

Nick grasped Jonathan's shoulder and wrapped his son-in-law in a hug.

Jonathan's gaze never left my face. He mouthed "thank you" before embracing Vicki.

I froze, my mind whirring with thoughts. Reasons. Had I let my baby fever get out of control and caused a soon-to-be father to feel guilty for impregnating his wife?

"You okay?" Matt whispered, warm breath brushing my cheek.

My chest ached. I glanced at Jonathan, who now stood with his arms around Diana's flat torso, and swallowed the lump caught in my throat. Who was I to rain on their parade?

"It's okay if you're not okay." Matt thumbed the back of my hand.

I turned and stared at the amazing man I was privileged to call husband. The man who had held me close while I grieved over our joint loss. The man determined to keep a smile on my face, fulfilling any whim or fancy I shared, no matter how insignificant or ridiculous.

"Bee?" Matt's blue eyes glowed despite the furrowed lines marring his forehead.

I smiled and leaned forward. "I'm okay." *Better than okay with you in my life.* I kissed his soft lips. Infertility would no longer dictate my feelings toward the happiness of others, or my future. Not with my adoring, handsome husband by my side. He deserved more. Deserved better than I had given him.

Matt pulled back, a languid smile on his face.

I wanted his smile. Needed it.

"Yeah, you're better than okay," he whispered.

Heat bloomed through my chest and into my limbs. I slipped my hand from under his and covered his smooth knuckles with my palm, sliding his hand higher up my thigh.

Fire burned in his eyes.

My pulse thudded. *I still have it.* I smirked and turned to my excited friends, delighting in the feverish bubbles frothing in my abdomen, and slid Matt's hand higher.

His garbled, incoherent words joined the joyous conversation across the table.

"Are we still on for tomorrow?" Vicki stood in her driveway, stooped, and leaned her forearms on my open passenger window. Her eyes were drowsy yet sparkled after a fun night with friends.

"Why wouldn't we be?" I glanced at Matt in the driver's seat before raising a brow at my friend. "You going to bail? On my birthday?"

She widened her eyes. "No! I just wasn't sure if … you wanted to still do brunch or"—she eyed Matt's hand curled over my leg—"maybe a later lunch? Since it's already after eleven."

Warmth flooded to my cheeks.

"A later lunch sounds perfect." Matt's velvety voice trailed along my skin.

Goosebumps prickled on my exposed arms.

"Great." Vicki avoided my gaze and stepped back. "Safe travels home."

Matt removed his warm hand from my leg and started the engine.

"Thank you." I leaned forward, reached out the window, and touched my friend's elbow. "And thanks for tonight. For arranging my gift."

The Jacobsens, Harrises, and Evertons had pitched in together and blessed me with a gorgeous Kenwood Titanium Chef Patissier stand mixer. Matt had secured my latest kitchen gadget in the back seat minutes ago.

I had dreamed of owning this mixing beast for years, and my friends had cared enough to buy the exact model I wanted. Grateful seemed inadequate a word to describe the emotions bubbling inside my chest. This gift meant the world to me.

Vicki beamed. "It was a group effort. We hope your old KitchenAid doesn't cry too much when it's shoved in the back of your cupboards."

I chuckled and shook my head. "My Artisan is too beautiful to shove into a cupboard. I'll still use her, especially when I batch bake."

"I'm glad." Vicki stepped backward and waved. "See you tomorrow, almost birthday girl."

"Night!" I waved, closed my window, and snuck a peek at the huge box belted onto the back seat behind Matt's chair.

Matt chuckled and shifted the car into reverse. "Ogling your new toy?" He craned his neck and scanned over his left shoulder.

"Maybe." I settled my attention on the road ahead.

He faced forward and laid his hand back on my leg. "I'm a little jealous."

"Why?" I rested my palm over his hand and glanced at him.

"A man likes a little ogling now and then."

I laughed, and the light, airy sound resonated like music in my ears. I had laughed more tonight than I had the previous two years.

"I love when you're happy."

I peered at Matt. "I love when you're needy."

"I'm not needy!" Matt huffed a mock indignant breath.

"You just complained I was ogling my new toy instead of you." I pressed away a smile. "That sounds needy to me."

He turned onto the main road to Tellarine, laughing. "When you put it like that, I sound whiney. Speaking of whiney, how's Alison?"

I snorted a laugh. "Funny you should say, but I received a birthday message from her today."

"Was it wildly inappropriate? Or more 'woe is me'?"

"I'll read it to you and you can decide." I grabbed my phone from my handbag nestled at my feet. "She said happy birthday for tomorrow, Bindy-Boo! Thirty-eight? I—"

"With a question mark?" Matt asked.

"Yes, with a question mark."

"She doesn't remember how old you are?"

"Uh huh." My own sister was uncertain of my age. What a comfort.

He blew out a breath. "Continue."

"I know your anniversary is sometime this month too—"

Matt scoffed.

"So happy whatever year you're up to for you an—"

"Happy whatever year you're up to? Really?" A sharp edge grated in Matt's tone.

"Yep." I glanced at my husband.

Matt's jaw flickered, and his fingers tensed on my leg. "Keep reading."

"H-happy whatever year you're up to for you and the … uh … demi sex god." I inhaled more air, and what I hoped would be more courage. "I hope you g-give it to him good and proper. Still can't believe you bed that bloke on the nightly."

Matt's grip tightened on my leg.

I pressed my hand against his.

He released his grasp. "Sorry, didn't mean to—"

"I know."

"I just …" He blew out a breath, rubbing soft circles along my thigh. "After all you did for her. Protected her. She still has no respect for you."

"Maybe she's jealous." I shrugged. "She's always making comments about how hot you are, like you're way out of my league—"

"Rubbish." Matt growled. "*I'm* the one punching above my weight."

Heat flooded into my ribcage. "No one's above anyone else."

Matt glanced at me with searing flames in his eyes. "Give me half an hour to rectify that."

Images from our kissing session before dinner filled my mind, and warmth spread from my chest along my limbs. I clutched my phone and stared at Alison's message. "What'll I say to her?"

"Do what you usually do … walk in love." He grabbed my empty hand and placed a soft kiss on my knuckles.

I slowly extracted my hand and, with a whispered prayer, pushed past the niggling frustrations nipping in my mind. I typed my reply.

Me: THANKS FOR THE BIRTHDAY/ANNIVERSARY LOVE. HOPE YOU'RE WELL. XX

I read the message to Matt. "Will that do?"

"Perfect."

"Sometimes I wish we could escape these not-so-fun

moments." I leaned against the seat back.

"Like go on holiday?" Matt drove through the outskirts of town toward our house on the other side of Tellarine.

"Wouldn't that be nice." When was the last time we went away?

"It's been almost two years since we visited Perth."

That's right. Perth. Several intimate moments danced in my remembrance, and my skin flushed.

"Great memories." Matt's voice rumbled. *Awesome* memories."

"Yeah," I said, my voice breathy.

"I'd be up for making more." Had Matt just growled?

"S-same." My mouth dried, and I cleared my throat. "You think we could go away in the April school holidays?"

"We have to wait that long?" Matt turned the corner onto our street faster than usual.

My pulse skittered. "Depends on the sort of memories you want to make."

He careered into the driveway and jolted the car to a stop, centimetres from the closed garage door.

I gasped and clutched my seat.

He fumbled with the garage door opener and tapped his hands on the steering wheel.

The ancient garage door groaned wider.

Matt plunged the car into the bricked room, closed the garage door, and snapped off his seat belt.

Darkness filled the garage, and I unbuckled with shaky fingers.

His lips were on mine a heartbeat later, his mouth wet, warm, and slippery, with hints of chocolate and mint. He slid his hands along my bare arms, back and forth, delicious friction zinging through my pores. Spiced cologne and Matt's natural scent overwhelmed my senses.

I gasped for air, desperate for more, and pulled him by his shirt front. When had we turned into a pair of frantic teenagers?

Matt chuckled, and his chest vibrated against my fisted hands.

Time melted away and our fervent kisses heated everything. The air in the cramped car. My perspiring skin and volcanic blood.

Oxygen siphoned from my lungs, replaced by surging fire.

I kissed Matt with all the love I could offer, like a woman sharing final moments with her lover before he deployed into battle. Thank God we lived in an era free from sieging invaders and sword-wielding knights.

He pressed closer, harder, devouring my mouth. Power sizzled through his fingers at the back of my head and lower hip.

My side ached where the seat crushed me, and my focus drifted to the irking discomfort. I pulled my lips away from his. "Matt."

Seemed I was too old for car make out sessions.

"Bee." He nibbled my lower lip with a growl.

"Can we go inside?" I attempted to shift against him but could hardly move. "I'm getting crushed here."

Before I caught my bearings, Matt had slammed his door, keys jangling, and opened my door. "Up."

Up?

He reached for my hands, tugged me from my seat, and sealed his mouth to mine.

I melted against him.

He secured his arms around me and hoisted me along his body until we were eye to eye. "Wrap your legs," he whispered against my lips.

I pulled back. "I'm too heavy."

"Now."

My body reacted to his demanding growl. I coiled my legs around his waist and my arms around his neck without a second thought.

He grunted like the neanderthal he had turned into and slammed my car door.

Served him right if he collapsed from exhaustion carrying me like this.

The car lights winked off, leaving us in total darkness.

"What about my bag?"

Matt rounded the car, toted me to the internal house door, and propped me against it. "I'll get it in the morning." He unlocked the house within seconds.

How on earth had he unbolted the door in pitch darkness, without a struggle?

I squinted against the filtered light in the front entryway and clung tighter. "Do you have your phone?"

"Back pocket." He pulled the door closed and pushed me against the wall, his heart thudding against mine. His gaze dropped to my lips. The blue of his eyes seemed darker.

"And my new toy?" I ran my fingertips along the short hairs at the nape of his neck.

His chest shuddered. "Your old one needs attention first."

I huffed an amused breath and stared at his swollen lips. When was the last time I had this much fun touching my husband? The pressure from the cyclic I-need-a-baby-now thoughts had dissipated, no longer dictating my actions. With the burden lifted, a freedom and ease flowed between us. *Thank You, God, for this emotional breather.*

Matt's chest rumbled, and his fingers twitched at the back of my thighs where he supported my weight.

"What do you suggest I do with my old toy?" I brushed a feathery kiss along his five o'clock shadow.

Something hot and dangerous sparked in his eyes. His gaze dropped, and a predatory smile lifted his lips. "How about I show you?"

My insides ignited and my airway constricted.

Matt strode to our bedroom, eyes gleaming at me with each step, and closed the door behind us.

CHAPTER THREE
Renewed Hope

"Do you need anything from the supermarket?" I leaned against our home office doorframe and eyed my husband's magnificent shorts-covered butt and muscled hamstrings on display, the rest of his upper body tucked under his desk.

He reversed on hands and knees, head ducked until he cleared the glass desktop, and stretched to his full almost-six-foot height. "Do they have electrical tape?"

"Doubt it."

He ruffled his fingers through his hair. "I might head to Bunnings then."

"No problem." I entered the room and pecked his lips. "Message me if you need anything."

He lunged for me and hauled me flush against his body.

My heart clanked.

"You can do better than that," he whispered.

After kissing my husband until our lungs almost packed in, I somehow wobbled to my car and drove to the local IGA.

Three weeks had passed since our car canoodling escapade. We had lay in bed talking, limbs tangled, into the early hours of my birthday. Between kisses and touches, we shared our hearts. My fear of failing to give him a child. His fear of losing me in my grief. We prayed through tears and expressed our love before we succumbed to exhaustion.

I entered the supermarket and grabbed a shopping trolley, lingering images still sweeping my thoughts. My cheeks warmed, and somehow, I traversed the aisles without hitting anything.

"Belinda!"

I raised my gaze from my shopping list app and spotted Cindy holding a shopping basket in the crook of her elbow. "Hi!"

"Need some help." She held up a box of tampons.

I pushed my half-filled trolley toward her. "Not sure I want to help you with them."

She snorted, bumped my elbow, and raised the box. "Have you used this brand before?"

"Nope." I pointed to the brand of organic cotton tampons I used. "These might cost a little more, but they're comfy and don't fall apart. I'm not a fan of sticking chemicals … up there, if I can avoid it."

Cindy levelled me with a borderline wicked grin. "With your husband, I can't imagine you'd nee—"

"Are things getting better for you? With the students?" I decided whatever she had planned to say was inconsequential and pushed for the subject change.

She blinked away her stunned expression and tossed a box of organic tampons in her basket. "Mildly. There was an incident last week, but I held my tongue."

"It can be hard sometimes, but you're doing great."

"I just smile at the kid in question and swear in my head." She eyed the shelf across the aisle. "You should try it sometime. It's therapeutic."

"I'll take your word for it."

Cindy laughed. "I'd better run, I have a date tonight. It was nice seeing you outside school hours."

I met her smile with my own. "You too. All the best with your date."

She wandered down the aisle and extracted shampoo from the

shelf. "Maybe we'll both get lucky tonight!" My colleague waved and turned the corner.

A middle-aged man glanced across the aisle with a severe expression on his lined face.

I spun and faced the wall of menstrual options, my neck and cheeks blooming with warmth. Counting breaths, I slowed my rocketing pulse and glanced at my shopping list. Had I forgotten to add pads, tampons, and liners to my list?

Footsteps tapped behind me.

I peeked over my shoulder where the disapproving older man turned and disappeared. My shoulders drooped. The sooner I left here, the better. I grabbed a box of liners and stilled. When was my last period? I switched from the shopping list to my calendar app and checked dates. What? I stared at the screen and scrunched my brow. How could my period be three days overdue?

An announcement blared over the loud speaker system.

I stared at my phone, pulse climbing.

Was I …?

My hands trembled, and my head spun in an airy, lightheaded way. I glided across the floor, slipped a pregnancy test off the adjacent shelf, and rushed through the rest of my shopping list.

Fifteen minutes later, I reversed into our empty garage and unpacked the car at lightning speed. If I could take this test before Matt arrived home, maybe I would know what to do or how to think. My actions might unlock the part of my brain which had frozen at the supermarket.

I dumped the bags on my clean marble kitchen bench, shoved the frozen foods and cold ingredients into the freezer and fridge, gripped the pregnancy test between my unsteady fingers, and padded along the hallway to my bedroom.

Was I pregnant with our fifth child? Matt's sixth child, if I included the stillborn he and his girlfriend lost when they were sixteen. So many lost children waiting for him in Heaven.

I shut the ensuite door and stared at the small box in my hand.

What would I do if the test came back positive? Or negative? Could I walk this path again and survive?

My phone vibrated in my jeans pocket.

Matty Babe: TOOK LONGER THAN PLANNED. BUMPED INTO NICK AND JON GETTING DIY STUFF. WILL BE HOME IN TEN.

Me: SEE YOU SOON.

I ripped open the pink box and peered at the ordinary-looking white stick. How could something so simple potentially rock our lives? Sucking in a breath, I followed the pregnancy test instructions, washed my hands, and waited.

How were post-peeing-on-a-stick moments always the longest minutes of my life? Each time I had gone through this process, seconds seemed stretched to hours.

I closed my eyes and willed the pressure near my temples and my swashing stomach to ease. *With God, all things are possible.*

Several Scriptures came to my remembrance, and my breaths slowed. I murmured them under my breath, meditating. Reminding myself I had strength to endure because of the Lord's joy. His perfect love threw my fears to the curb. I could trust in Him.

I opened my eyes and scanned my reflection in the mirror. *You can do this.* A soft smile slipped to my lips. I stabilised my breaths and glanced down.

Two lines.

I clutched the edge of the vanity and sagged forward. Sweat beaded along my forehead.

I was pregnant.

Something light fizzed in my chest, stretching my smile. Another chance for us to be parents. My head verged on giddy, and I squeezed the vanity. But the lingering fears crept back into my thoughts. What if we lost this baby at five- or six-weeks' gestation like all the others? Could I endure another disappointment? More grief? My smile slipped away.

Advice from our local GP, Dr. Fallow—to arrange an early ultrasound to check pregnancy viability—echoed in my brain. My stomach swirled. If I spent two hundred dollars on an ultrasound next week and lost the baby the week after—

"You there?" Matt knocked on the ensuite door.

I jolted, rammed the test stick inside its box and hid the evidence at the back of my vanity shelf.

"Bee?"

I plastered a smile on my face and opened the door. "Sorry, had to pee."

"Figured you were desperate if you left half the groceries unpacked." He wrapped his arm around my waist. "Want some help?"

"Yeah." I leaned against him and breathed in his scent.

We ambled along the hallway to the kitchen and unpacked the first bag.

"Nick and Jon are tackling a furniture refurb project. Some of Diana's mum's things." Matt stacked tomato paste and canned tuna on a low shelf. "Was thinking I might give them a hand. That okay?"

Yes, normal conversation. I busied myself sorting packets of dried herb. "You spend lots of time in front of a computer, so I think that's a great idea."

"Was thinking the same." He packed the dry pasta away. "Jon invited us over for lunch in an hour … if you wanted?"

"Wonderful!" Another welcome distraction.

"Great. Vicki and the kids will be there too." Matt poured the four-kilo bag of potatoes into a tub on the pantry shelf.

Cheeky little distractions, just what the doctor ordered. I fiddled with arranging the fruit bowl. Bananas, apples, and pears. "What about Tara and Keanu? Will they be there?"

"Doubt it." Matt turned and appraised me. "Keanu will be needed at Benanu's for the Saturday lunch rush."

"I forgot."

Matt approached me and stilled my hands. "I know it's hard for you, but I was so proud when you asked to hold Leilani at church last week."

Holding the sweet, little girl had been one of the hardest and thrilling things I had done so far in life. Tara had accommodated me with kindness shining in her eyes.

Matt clutched my hands to his chest. "No matter what our future holds, I want you to know how proud I am to be your husband."

My vision blurred.

"Whether we're blessed with children or not, you're the best wife a man could ask for." He leaned down and pressed a soft kiss to my lips. "And I'm not saying this because you're a virtuoso between the sheets."

"Matt!" I whacked his chest with a playful slap.

"You're also a virtuoso in the kitchen, so I'm a sated man." He winked.

I chuckled between kisses and stepped away. "Then you'd better complete this grunt work so my virtuosity can flow."

He saluted and unpacked the final bag of groceries with a wide grin, his happiness fuelling my own.

I watched him stack potato chip packets into the cupboard and knew what I would do. What I *had* to do. My pregnancy would remain a secret to everyone but God until I passed the danger period.

Matt would have to forgive me for withholding this news for a few more weeks.

"You've got the best workspace." Matt peered at the Food Technology microwave oven reheating our lunch.

"What about you, Mr. Head of STEM, living the technological dream?" I pulled a stack of stainless-steel mixing bowls from the storage shelf and placed one at each workstation. My Year Seven class would bake marinated chicken skewers and prepare a simple salad after lunch.

The microwave bleated.

"But you have hot water on tap. And fridges." Matt stirred the reheated leftovers from last night's pasta we had prepared together.

"Don't forget the hidden tub of Häagen-Dazs." I divvied long bamboo skewers, tongs, and large spoons beside the rest of the items on the benchtops.

"Teasing your husband will never pay off."

I snorted a laugh. "There's some grated cheese in the freezer."

"Awesome." Matt searched the freezer and extracted a bag of grated cheese. "Come and eat."

"Gimme a moment." I counted the containers of marinated chicken portions in one fridge, rushed to the other, and counted the bagged salad ingredients my assistant had prepared this morning.

Chair legs scraped in the study nook, followed by the scrape of ceramic against wood.

I joined Matt at one of the desks, prayed over our food, and dug in.

"I think I did pretty good with the pasta sauce."

"I do too." I smiled and swallowed a mouthful.

Many moons ago, Matt was a terrible cook. Horrendously awful. When we first dated, I thought I would keel over the first time he cooked for me. How he had survived the thirty-plus years he had lived up to that point, I had no idea. His kitchen skills were atrocious, and his aunt Crystal still laughed and shared stories about the disgusting food Matt created when he had lived with her and her family.

"Speaking of pretty good, I have some news." He shovelled a forkful of tomatoey penne into his mouth.

I rested a palm over my stomach and mulled over *my* news. Five weeks and two days. Six days had passed since I peed on the stick and tested positive. Six days without bleeding or cramps. I stabbed pasta onto my fork and met Matt's gaze with a smile. "Do tell me your pretty good news."

"We did it." His face shone with a radiant smile.

"Did what?"

"Hit our target."

Target? I furrowed my brow.

"Our share market trading target." He beamed.

"Really?" My heart stilled. I lowered my fork to my bowl, sucked in a breath, and widened my eyes. Was it possible Matt had accrued over two hundred and fifty thousand dollars from our initial fifty-thousand-dollar investment?

"Yes!"

I bounced in my seat and squealed.

Matt laughed, the hearty, carefree sound wrapping me with more joy than his news had sparked.

"I thought you said you'd trade conservatively? That it might take longer? Much longer. Or that it might not happen at all?"

He pushed his empty bowl aside and laid his hand on the table, palm exposed.

I settled my hand against his warm fingers.

"Trading has its risks. But we entered the market at a fortuitous time with blue chip, black gold, and tech capital growth."

"Black gold?"

"Oil." Matt winked.

"It's barely been a year. Are you saying we can be mortgage-free?" I stared at my husband's ecstatic face. My vision clouded.

"That's what I wanted to discuss with you. I thought we could recover eighty percent of our profit and use it to pay the mortgage and open a bullion account."

"As in gold and silver?"

He nodded. "Then leave the other twenty percent for trading where we can funnel future profits into the bullion account."

"Because precious metals hold their value better than cash?"

"Precisely." He squeezed my fingers.

I studied our joined hands, his large fingers caressing mine. "You think this is the right thing to do?"

"Yeah. The sooner we pay off the mortgage, the better."

We had paid the credit cards in full nine months ago, which

had thrilled me, but to pay off our mortgage? What a blessing!

I gazed into Matt's bright eyes and nodded. "Let's do it."

"Great. I'll transfer the money after work, so the funds will be in our account early next week, then I can set up our bullion account."

"Okay." I trusted my husband to look after our financial future. A future which seemed sunnier now that looming debt no longer hung over our heads.

What a perfect time to start a family.

Matt stood and stooped for a kiss.

I raised my face and enjoyed the brush of his lips on mine.

He grabbed our dirty dishes. "Which dishwasher?"

I pointed to the Fisher and Paykel in the corner. "Top shelf."

Matt moseyed to the dishwasher, his stride confident, and stacked our dishes. "Want to celebrate tonight?"

I rounded the corner to my office, grabbed the pile of printed recipes for this afternoon's class, and returned to the workstations. "What were you thinking?"

He leaned against the dishwasher, arms crossed against his yummy chest, and waggled his eyebrows.

I fumbled with the papers in my hands, my cheeks now warmer than when I consumed hot pasta minutes ago.

"I was thinking dinner and a movie." Matt smirked.

"That sounds good." My voice sounded strained, and I clutched the papers to my chest.

He barked a laugh and stepped closer.

I placed the papers on the benchtop behind me with shaky fingers.

Matt stalked toward me until the toe of his shiny black lace-ups were centimetres from my comfortable court shoes, his unreadable blue eyes zoomed into my face.

My heart palpitated.

My husband boxed me in between his arms and rested his hands on the benchtop either side of my hips. "It sounds good, doesn't it?" He leaned closer and brushed the tip of his nose along my jaw.

Shallow breaths escaped my chest.

"You sound good," he whispered, his lips grazing my ear.

I shuddered under his touch.

The fifth period warning bell sounded in the stillness.

"Saved by the bell." Matt pecked my cheek and stepped back. "I'll get out of your hair."

"Bye," I whispered.

His footsteps sounded against the linoleum floor. "Bee?"

I turned toward where he stood in the doorway.

His eyes twinkled. "Kids'll be here in less than three minutes."

The spell my husband had cast on me shattered, and I snapped to attention. "Right. Bye!"

His laughter reverberated down the hallway.

CHAPTER FOUR
An Afternoon Rendezvous

My stomach backflipped and cartwheeled. Its celebrations infected my lungs and shortened my breaths. "Breathe," I whispered to my bright-eyed reflection in the ensuite mirror. With shaking fingers, I applied a final layer of lipstick to my unrelenting grin. *Chill, Bee!* I had to stick to my plan of staying calm and acting natural.

"Ready?" Matt called from somewhere in the house.

"Almost!" I blotted my lips, jiggled my makeup into its zippered case, and shoved the bulky bag into the vanity cupboard.

"You sure you don't want a coffee?" Matt asked from behind me.

I jumped, spun, and palmed my chest. At least my heart now had a reason for its frenzied beat.

Matt grimaced. "Sorry, thought you heard me walk in."

"It's okay." I clamped my hands to my sides. "And, y-yes, I'm sure. I'll live without it today." And for the next seven and a half months.

He narrowed his eyes at me and stared for several long seconds.

I thought my heart might beat right out of my chest. Had someone turned the heater on? I squashed my exuberance and offered a sweet smile.

He "hmmed" and pivoted from the room.

I sagged against the vanity counter behind me.

Hiding the baby had been harder than I had expected. After "not feeling like having a coffee" two mornings this week, triggering Matt's suspicion, I had pretended to drink Matt's morning coffee offering on the way to work—one small sip added enough of a coffee scent to my lips to pass the "goodbye kiss" test—and directed my husband off the scent of his unborn child. Wasteful but worthwhile. Thank God I was an infrequent drinker of alcohol or the game would be up.

And this afternoon, "the game" would officially be up. Today marked the beginning of the seventh week of my pregnancy—the longest I had ever sustained a pregnancy—so I only needed to last a few more hours of this double life, when I spilled the beans to Matt about the baby's existence after church.

I exited the bathroom and gazed out the bedroom window, my post-church plans in the forefront of my mind. The cloudy, darkening sky seemed too dreary for a late-March morning, along with gusts of wind swaying the trees across the road. Autumn had indeed set in. I prayed the weather would ease into pleasant sunshine or lunch would need to be at my backup location.

The coffee machine gurgled and hissed in the kitchen.

I grabbed a cream cardigan from my walk-in-robe, slipped on my low-heeled shoes, shouldered my bag, and collected my phone from beside our bed.

Matt's footsteps tapped along the entryway tiles.

I met him in the bedroom doorway and peeked at his travel mug. "I'll carry that for you, babe."

"Thanks." He grabbed the car keys and escorted me to the garage.

Five minutes later, we rolled into the Tellarine Christian Church car park. Nothing had changed since I started attending the church over a decade ago. Still the same charming orange brick veneered, mission-brown trimmed building with a rust-coloured roof splotched with moss. Gangly eucalyptus trees and dense, untidy native shrubs complemented its seventies mystique.

A place I would cherish the rest of my days.

"We weren't rostered for greeting today, were we?" Matt nodded toward the front door.

The church entry appeared deserted.

What had happened? I switched into team leader mode and unbuckled with haste, gathering my things in my arms. "Chris's on today. I hope everything's okay." Maybe he closed the outer door against the wind until more people arrived? The centre glass door panel was a blessing on days like these.

"Hopefully."

We braced against the strong breeze and trod across the car park, hand in hand.

The heavy door sprang open moments before we reached it.

"Morning, Matt and Belinda." Chris Beaufort, Nick's older half-brother, beckoned us inside.

"Chris, my man, how're you doing?" Matt shook his hand.

"Not bad." Chris offered me a brief one-armed hug and glanced toward the auditorium. "In case Becca pounces, did you receive an invitation in the mail?"

"For your fiftieth?" I asked.

Chris nodded.

"Yes, and I RSVPed to your wifey yesterday." I looked forward to tackling the birthday cake masterpiece Becca had designed, as well as celebrating Chris in a fortnight's time.

He blew out a quick breath. "I'm glad. Becca's nervous because several people said they didn't receive theirs."

"That's Australia Post for you." Matt shook his head.

"Will Anna and Mitch be at the party?" Matt and I had taught the Beaufort children several years ago. Anna was Diana's age, and Mitchell a few years younger.

Chris chocked open the front door, welcomed a family of four, and turned back to us. "Anna said she'll be here, but I'm not sure about Mitch. He's currently in Germany working the European circuit."

I widened my eyes. "DJing?"

"Yeah." Chris scrunched his brow. "He said he's not doing anything stupid, but … please keep him in your prayers."

"Of course." I gave him a soft smile.

More churchgoers arrived, their happy greetings flooding the quiet foyer.

Matt and I waved to Chris and entered the auditorium.

"Do you think Mitch will be okay?" I went clubbing and attended several raves in my late teens and witnessed some eye-opening situations. But the world was a different place now—drenched in darkness—compared to my youth. Clothing was skimpier, dancing more sensual, with an overload of bare skin on display. Pretty girls writhing their bodies to an intoxicating beat could be a heap of temptation for a single country boy in his early twenties. Especially a nice guy like Mitch.

"I hope so. But he is human." Momentary shadows slipped through Matt's serious gaze.

Was he recalling the temptations of his past? I slid my arm around Matt's. "Has he emailed you recently?"

Matt had taken Mitch under his wing and encouraged him in his faith before he travelled around Australia and then abroad. They had kept in contact over the last two years.

"Not in a month or two." Matt touched my hand and escorted me toward the noisier side of the room where Kai and the Jacobsen children played. "I might drop him a line this week and check in."

I pulled on Matt's arm, slowing his footsteps, and leaned up to kiss his cheek. "You're so wonderful."

"I know." He waggled his brows, winked, and stepped toward Nick.

I smiled and nodded to several church folk, many from the welcome team, and stepped closer to my friends.

Tara waved from where she was sandwiched to Keanu's side,

pinned under his bulging bicep. They had been inseparable since they married. No wonder Leilani was a honeymoon baby.

"You're looking lovely, Bee." Vicki touched my arm and grinned while she snuggled said darling honeymoon baby against her shoulder, her gaze darting from me to the playing children.

"You too. Getting some practise, Granny?" I smirked at my dear friend, my pesky backflipping insides delirious at the prospect of sharing my news. What would Vicki do when I told her my baby had stuck around? I foresaw excitable shrieking, potential jumping, and a lot of whooping thanks to God.

Not long until I could divulge this secret.

"I'm forty-three! And pulled out a total of five grey hairs."

I chuckled. "I'm just teasing."

Vicki wrinkled her nose. "If Nicholas were in his fifties, perhaps I would cope with the new status better. But we're still young. Elijah will be an uncle at five and a half!"

A piercing scream sliced the room. Elijah held his chest and howled while Kai lay on his side, wailing. Blood dripped from Kai's mouth onto the beige carpet.

Vicki's eyes widened. "Here." She deposited Leilani into my arms and rushed to the children.

I held the baby close, breathed in her sweet scent, and observed parenting in action.

Keanu scooped a screaming Kai into his arms while Tara checked his bloody mouth, their eyes communicating in an unspoken husband-and-wife language. Nick kneeled beside Vicki—who spoke to Jasmine in a hushed tone—in front of his tearful son, his long arm around Elijah's back, and soothed him with quiet words.

Matt slipped his arm around my back. "You okay with her?"

I glanced up at him and grinned. "Perfectly okay."

Matt smiled. Had his shoulders loosened?

"Did you see what happened?"

"The boys accidentally slammed into each other. Kai bounced

off Elijah's chest and fell backwards, but his face whacked a chair on his tumble to the floor." He winced.

My chest squeezed, and I locked my gaze on Keanu and Tara exiting the auditorium. "The little love."

"Think he split his lip."

I cringed and swayed Leilani. Hopefully she had no idea her mummy and daddy had left the room.

Vicki approached with a sniffling Elijah in her arms, Nick a few steps behind them.

"Everything okay?" I asked.

She nodded and kissed Elijah's cheek. "Just a little sore. Kai has a hard head, doesn't he, sweetheart?"

Elijah shuddered a breath and nodded.

Nick slid his palm over his son's dark hair. "Kai split his lip—"

"No loose teeth, thank God," Vicki whispered.

"So once they get him cleaned up"—Nick nodded toward the bundle in my arms—"they'll be back."

Diana strode through the auditorium entrance, Jonathan in tow, and extended her arms to her little brother. "Tara told me what happened. You okay, Eli?"

Elijah's tears reappeared. He reached for his sister and wrapped his arms around Diana's neck, despite his mother's hold around his waist.

Nick steadied Vicki with a large hand on her shoulder.

"Let me hold his weight for you, beautiful," Jonathan whispered to Diana.

She stilled, her eyes wide. "Oh. Yeah. You're a bit heavy, bud." She smiled at Elijah and nodded to her husband.

Jonathan scooped Elijah from his mother's arms and held him close—the boy's small back against the man's broad chest—and facilitated a pregnancy-appropriate embrace.

I pursed my lips and tightened my hold on the little princess in my arms. Had I lifted anything too heavy this week?

Someone talked on the stage at the front of the auditorium, and we shuffled to our usual seats.

I bounced Leilani in my arms during the praise and worship service, my heart overflowing with joy at her gurgled laughter. A wide smile stretched my face while I sang and swayed, and when I caught Matt's grinning gaze, I wanted to spin on a mountaintop, arms wide, like Maria von Trapp. Now I understood what King David meant when he said "my cup runs over."

Halfway through worship, someone tapped my shoulder from behind. I twisted and met Tara's easy smile.

"You okay?" she mouthed, glancing between my face and the back of her daughter's head.

I grinned and nodded, then glanced at Kai who was snuggled against Keanu's chest. "He okay?" I whispered.

Tara nodded, leaned closer to her husband, and rubbed Kai's back.

I turned and faced the stage.

Leilani fussed during announcements, and I returned her to Tara during the brief "meet and greet" portion of the service.

I leaned against Matt's shoulder and held his hand through Pastor Davidson's sermon, revelling in my husband's closeness, my insides verging on joyful detonation from all the feel-good hormones and wonderful news I hoarded. By the time the meeting ended, my exhilaration pumped through my veins and unsteadied my steps.

"Did you want to come over for lunch?" Vicki glanced between Matt and me.

Matt grabbed my hand. "That would be—"

"A lovely idea, but we'll have to raincheck." I squeezed his fingers, willing him to follow my lead.

"Sorry, Vicki. Seems the wife has plans." Matt turned to me and raised his brow.

I beamed a cheek-aching smile. "I do."

Vicki chuckled. "Have fun. Message me with a date we can all catch up this week."

I embraced my friends and tugged Matt toward the exit.

"We have plans?" Matt smiled at congregants on our trek through the foyer and opened the front door for me.

"All will be revealed, babe." Relief flooded my limbs at the sight of sunshine streaming through the dissipating clouds. "First stop, home."

"All right." Matt shepherded me across the car park and opened the passenger door. He leaned closer and tapped his cheek. "You owe me for whatever shenanigans you pulled in there."

I inclined my face and pressed a soft kiss against his smooth jaw. "You'll be paid back, with interest."

He leaned closer, his blond hair falling forward. "Payment plan?"

I smirked and brushed my lips against his. Once. Twice. Three times, the final kiss lingering. "The first payment of many."

"I like the sound of that." Matt's voice turned husky, and the sexy tone prickled my skin.

Stay focused! I slipped by him and planted myself on the passenger seat.

Matt closed my door and practically ran to the driver's seat.

I hid my smirk behind my hand and held back laughter when we made it home in record time.

Matt unbuckled and leaned toward me, but I was ready for his distraction and escaped his clutches. He chased me into the kitchen.

"Stop!" I raised my hand and heaved with laughter, palm facing forward. "No sex yet."

Matt widened his eyes and pouted like Elijah when Vicki refused his request for lollies. "Why not?" His whiney voice sounded like Elijah's too.

"Food first. Fun later."

Matt grumbled.

I smirked and pointed toward our bedroom. "Into comfy clothes, quick! We're going on a picnic."

"A picnic?" Somehow, his pout deepened.

"Yes, a picnic." I grabbed the covered charcuterie platter I had prepared early this morning, along with a bottle of sparkling apple juice and other refrigerated components of our lunch, and slotted everything into the large insulated bag on the kitchen bench.

"Okay."

Good. I zipped the cooler bag closed, carried the weighty sack to the garage door, and popped it beside another bag which housed nibbles, baked goods—including my double-chocolate brownies, Matt's favourite—and all the other useful things one needed for a picnic.

My plan was unfolding without a hitch. I grinned like a toddler chasing bubbles, turned, and halted. My breath hitched.

Matt's shirt was half unbuttoned, and his chest peeked through the gap. He worked his fingers on another button, and his direct gaze smouldered.

Frozen to the spot, I stared, transfixed by whatever powerful "handsome man" pheromones wafted from my husband.

Stupid pregnancy hormones.

Two buttons to go.

I tugged my bottom lip between my teeth, my breathing shallow.

One button.

Sirens flashed and screamed in my head. *Step away from the eye candy!* My stupid, voracious appetite for Matt Briggs would spoil my well-laid plans.

He slid his shirt off in slow, teasing increments, exposing muscled flesh and those delicious grooves in his taut torso and tanned arms.

I pressed my hands against my sides. *May day! May day!*

Matt's gaze scorched. He pinched his shirt collar between his fingers, flicked this shirt over his shoulder, and smirked. "C'mon, get changed, Bee."

I widened my eyes. Why, that cheater! How dare he siphon my

power when I was dictating terms!

Matt chuckled and turned toward our bedroom, his sculpted back beckoning me closer, and ambled along the hallway.

Ideas filtered through my brain. Naughty, cheeky ideas which might not have been part of my original "how to tell Matt about the baby" plan, but after this stunt? Game on.

I unbuttoned my dress and strutted to my room, thankful I had chosen sexier underwear this morning, each step encouraging myself. Although I was thirty-eight and gravity exerted its force in several wiggly places, I could still get one particular man's engine revving.

Matt squatted on the end of our bed in T-shirt and jeans, lacing his sneakers.

I positioned my body in one of those power stances women tended to do in superhero or girl-power movies, shouldered my dress to the floor, and met his gaze.

His mouth opened and closed, and his darkening gaze roved my red-and-black lace-and-silk covered body.

Score for Belinda the Brilliant.

I lined my face with disappointment. "You're already dressed?"

His Adam's apple bobbed.

"Oh well." I stepped forward and turned, bent low, and scooped my dress from the floor.

An unintelligible, throaty noise sounded behind me.

I straightened, pressed my smile away, and headed to my walk-in-robe, dodging his reaching arm.

Another fun story to exchange with Vicki.

Moments later, I re-emerged fully dressed—after what might have been the fastest dressing session in the history of womankind—and smiled at Matt, still perched on the bed edge with one shoe unlaced. "Hurry up, why don't you? We've gotta go."

He shook his head and tied his shoe.

I scuttled from the bedroom, palm over my mouth stifling my

snorts, and packed the car.

Matt opted to drive to my vague directions, his left hand fidgeting on the steering wheel during our half-hour trip deeper into bushland. Edgy Matt would be difficult to tame, but easy to tease.

More diabolical thoughts swirled in my brain, lifting my lips in a scheming grin.

"Where're we going?"

I pointed toward a gated driveway. "Turn right there."

Matt furrowed his brow. "Whose place is this?"

"A friend's." One of my colleague's parents owned the one-acre property, but said parents were living it up as grey nomads somewhere in Australia.

"A friend?"

I unbuckled my seatbelt. "I'll get out and open the gate."

A minute later, we inched along the dirt driveway and parked in front of a quaint weatherboard. Matt grabbed the bags, and I bundled the picnic blanket under my arm.

"Where to?" Matt surveyed the tree-lined property.

"Behind the house." I followed the bricked path around the house and sucked in a breath.

"Wow." Matt nudged my shoulder, gaze glued to the shimmering, pristine lake and the small wooden jetty parked between shady trees along the bank.

Anita was right, this location was magical.

"You did all right."

I scoffed. "This is better than all right, buddy. A private, romantic, *deserted* location for us to enjoy for the afternoon."

"Deserted?" He glanced at the house.

I batted my lashes in a coquettish way. "Deserted," I whispered.

Matt waggled his brows and headed for the shaded picnic table about four metres from the water.

We set up our picnic on the semi-shaded grass near the dock, our bags stashed on the table away from ants, and dived into our lunch.

Matt brushed his free hand across my knee and chewed on his sixth homemade cracker he had topped with hummus dip, salami, tasty cheese, and gherkin. "So good, Bee."

I nibbled on a hummus-laden carrot stick and stacked the now-empty garden salad and potato salad containers on the edge of the rug.

"Any chance there's dessert?" Matt's eyes pleaded like a puppy dog.

I raised a brow. "Do you even *know* me?"

He laughed, the sound complementing the gentle splash of water against the riverbank and the rustle of leaves above.

I gathered all the empty containers in my arms, awkwardly stood, dumped them in a bag on the table, and grabbed the container of baked goodies. Nerves skittled through my body. "C-can you refill our cups?"

"On it." Matt poured juice into our two plastic tumblers.

I whispered a prayer and returned to the rug. Now was as good a time as any.

Matt's gaze locked on the container in my hand and his grin widened. "What did you bring today?"

I chuckled at his child-like antics.

Matt loved his baked goods.

"How about a toast first?" I placed the container beside me and reached for my cup.

He retrieved his cup and raised it toward mine. "To us?"

I nodded, my throat now in need of a drink, and bumped our cups together. "To us … and our little one."

Matt stared at me, blinking, before he dropped his gaze to my stomach. "Really?"

The smile on my face spread faster than a contagious disease.

"You're pregnant?"

I nodded again.

He laughed and grabbed my cup, placing both cups aside, and

reached around my back, pulling me toward him. "We're having a baby?"

"We're having a baby," I whispered.

Matt squashed me against his chest in an embrace, his laughter trickling between breaths.

I blinked away tears.

He leaned back and captured my gaze. "Have you told Vicki?"

"Of course not! I figured we'd want to wait a little longer before we told others."

His smile slipped, and his serious gaze met mine. "How far along?"

"Seven weeks."

"Seven?" He furrowed his brow.

"Uh huh."

Matt squinted, deepening his creased forehead. "But … how? Did you just find out?"

I bit the inside of my cheek.

"How long have you known?" He tightened his grip on my upper arms.

I dropped my chin and pressed my hands together in my lap. Maybe my decision to keep the baby a secret had been unwise.

"Bee?" He released my arms and lifted my chin with his fingers. His gaze radiated with intensity.

"About two and a half weeks," I whispered.

A flash of something filled his eyes. Hurt?

My chest constricted. "I … didn't want to get your hopes up, so I waited until …" The time we had lost all of our other babies had passed.

"You kept this from me?"

Heat built behind my eyes.

"You carried the burden alone." His pained expression hardened.

Several tears slipped down my cheeks.

Matt's face slackened. He closed his stormy eyes, sucked in a string of breaths, and eyed me. "How could you keep this from me?"

I crushed my hands against each other. Why had I done this to us? To him?

"We promised we'd walk beside each other, no matter what." His voice wavered, and he cleared his throat. "You promised me. Always together."

"I'm sorry." I choked on a sob.

Matt's arms wrapped around me and pressed me against him. "I forgive you. I just wish I'd known and been able to carry the burden with you."

I clutched his T-shirt and sniffled into his neck. What had possessed me to think I should carry this burden all by myself?

"It hurts knowing you were alone in this."

My shuddering breaths eased, and I inhaled his scent.

"But no more." Matt peeled me from his front, cupped my chin, and captured my gaze. "Okay? From now on, we do this together."

"Together," I whispered.

He lowered his hands and fixed them to my hips. The light in his eyes, which I had snuffed out moments ago, returned. "Considering being together is what got us into this situation …"

I huffed a laugh as images of how "together" we had been in recent weeks flooded my mind.

"Are pregnancy hormones the reason you're constantly throwing yourself at me?"

"Not completely."

He pursed his kissable lips. "You been reading more of those kissing books Diana reads? Because Jon swears by them."

I snorted a laugh and shook my head.

"By the way, when did you want to tell Vicki?"

I shrugged. "Week nine?"

"Done. Now back to guessing." He narrowed his eyes. "Am I more addictive than usual?"

"You are." I grinned.

He searched my face, his expression sincere. "But what changed …?"

I interlaced my fingers with his hands on my hips. "I did."

"How so?" He tilted his head.

I sucked in a deep breath. "I decided to give up on my quest for a baby and—"

"Give up?" He froze.

"Let me finish."

"Sorry."

"The pressure to get pregnant got to me." I shuddered a breath. "So, I wanted to switch my focus from what I wanted to what I already had. Appreciate what I had."

"Which was?"

"You." I released his hands and blinked away tears. "I took you for granted, and I'm sorry."

"Hey." Matt tugged me into his lap, my legs across his left thigh, and brushed a tear from my cheek. "None of that. If anyone's to blame, it's me. I should've been better at comforting you during the harder times."

"What?" I widened my eyes.

"I know the miscarriages affected you … differently. In more ways than me." He brushed his lips across my forehead. "I just didn't know how to comfort you."

"You did fine." I sniffed.

"It's not like I could bake you comfort food."

"Please don't." I scrunched my nose.

He chuckled. "And I didn't think my physical advances would've been welcome."

"Comfort comes in many forms." I raised my arms and knitted my fingers behind his neck.

"You don't say?"

I shifted my head so our lips were breaths apart. "And after today's trauma—"

Matt snorted.

"I think I'm in need of a Matt Special."

His hooded gaze roamed my face. "A Matt Special?"

I nodded, and my pulse accelerated.

"And what does that entail?" His warm breath puffed against my lips.

"You'll work it out." I pressed my mouth to his and thanked God for the man lowering me onto my back against the soft picnic rug.

CHAPTER FIVE
Spinout

"Coffee?" I rushed along the hallway in my beige underwear, my unbuttoned pink blouse flapping.

"Yes!" Matt yelled from our bedroom. Desperation seeped in his tone.

I chuckled, flipped on the coffee machine, and buttoned my blouse.

Matt and I had both slept through our alarms. What a way to start a Monday after our indulgence yesterday afternoon.

My husband had changed after I told him about the baby. He had treated me with such tenderness—more so than usual—and seemed determined to look after me. Maybe knowing I had endured the dreaded five-to-six-week miscarriage period alone tipped him over the edge, or the realisation this baby was sticking around. The lake and our delicious picnic might have lulled him into an appreciative state. Whatever the case, he had unleashed his affections late into the night.

I tucked the memories into my mental treasures box, yanked Matt's travel mug from the pantry, and opened the fridge.

Pooh. The milk had expired, and I had forgotten to prepare today's lunches after our lovely time at the lake. Good thing we were satisfied in one particular area of our lives.

I rummaged the pantry for some snacks to keep Matt fed

during the morning, prepared an espresso, and raced to the bedroom.

Matt emerged from the bathroom in his usual Monday attire—a shirt in a variant of blue, tie, and slacks—and raised an eyebrow at me. "Casual Monday?"

"Huh?" I handed him his coffee. "The milk expired, sorry."

He sipped, winced, and stared at my legs.

I glanced down and laughed. Oh yeah, no pants. "Getting to it, Mr. Fast Dresser."

"I don't mind, but the other staff might." He winked.

I tossed his snack at him, and ransacked my wardrobe until I found a clean, unrumpled pair of pants. I shoved them on and slipped into low heels. "Ready!"

Matt grabbed his briefcase at the end of our bed and turned to me. "Hair?"

I stumbled to the bathroom, fixed my hair into a messy ponytail, pinched my cheeks, and applied some lip gloss. "That'll do."

We reversed into the street a minute later, and Matt navigated faster than usual to the full staff car park.

My phone beeped.

"Forgot to tell you." Matt pulled into a parking bay.

"Tell me while we walk." I opened my door.

Matt led me along the footpath and guided me with his hand on my back. "I booked a meeting on Saturday morning with the bank manager to claim the house title deed."

"Oh good! Have you received confirmation about the bullion order you made last week?"

"Yep, got an email on Friday afternoon."

"Good work, my love." What a blessing to be married to a man confident in dealing with financial matters.

Matt opened the staff-only door beside reception. "And we're buying lunch?"

"Yeah." I ransacked my in-tray. "Sorry about forgetting."

He touched my arm.

I gazed at his handsome features.

"Not your fault. We were both a bit … distracted last night." His eyes darkened.

And what a superb distraction. Warmth pooled under my skin. His gaze dropped to my lips.

Did my husband have an Off button? Good thing my pregnancy hormones kept my libido engaged.

The eight fifty-five homeroom warning bell sounded.

Matt widened his eyes and pecked my lips. "Gotta go. See you at lunch."

"Love you." I hurried to the Food Tech room, unlocked my office, and checked my roster. No class first period. *Yes!* I locked up, dashed to the Year Ten class I oversaw each morning, and spent the allotted ten minutes of homeroom marking off attendance and reading reminders.

While students sped along the hallways to their first period classes, I strolled back to my work space with a light heart and beaming smile, and organised the study nook for my second period theory class.

Someone opened the Food Tech door.

"You there, Belinda?" Cindy?

I stepped toward the doorway and met Cindy's gaze. "What's up?"

"Can you watch my class for five minutes? I'm on day two of my period and I've *got to go.*"

"Course. Go." I waved her away, crossed the hallway, and chatted with Cindy's Year Twelve textiles' students, most of them past pupils. I had forgotten what a great bunch of kids they were.

Cindy returned minutes later, her gait less rigid than before, and slipped her phone into her back pocket. "Thanks so much."

"Happy to help." Had my phone beeped earlier? I returned to my office and checked for any text messages.

Alison Davies: WHEN YOU GET A CHANCE, I WAS HOPING WE COULD TALK.

I stared at the screen and waited for my stomach to swirl or my mind to fill with unsavoury words, but my smile never waned. I laughed. My happy life gave me immunity against my sister's antics. I typed a quick reply.

Me: Crazy-busy atm, but will call you later this week. Hope you're well.

Alison's reply popped onto the screen.

Alison Davies: K

"Still the same," I whispered with a laugh.

Thank God everything else in life was changing for the better.

"Did you use the lowest flame setting?" I held back a grimace at the lumpy, scrambled egg-looking mess one of the Year Eight students had created. Custard was a skill of patience.

"Which's low?" Nate stared at the stove top burner knobs.

I pointed to the back left burner and its corresponding Low knob illustrated with a tiny flame.

"Nah. I used the front one."

The hottest burner. Of course.

I blew out a breath, reminded myself one day these boys and girls would outgrow their ignorance, and pointed to the utensils shelf across the room. "Get a sieve, strain the custard, and whisk fast until smooth."

He grunted and dawdled across the room.

I peeked at the clock on the wall. Less than half an hour until lunchtime.

"Mrs. Briggs?"

I turned and approached another student with her left hand raised. "Yes, Mya?"

"Is this okay?" She whisked her thickening custard into a smooth, velvety concoction on the Low stove burner.

"Looks perfect. Well done." I glanced around the nearby

workstations where most students struggled to create a smooth and creamy custard. "If you're unsure what your custard should look like," I said with a loud voice, "come see Mya's."

Several students wandered from their workstations or peered across their workbench and inspected Mya's efforts.

I smiled at the soft pink flush staining her cheeks.

"Mrs. Briggs?"

I glanced toward the opened door where Principal Marsden stood, her expression grave.

Why was she here?

Jonathan stepped through the doorway, decked out in his Victoria Police uniform.

My chest constricted.

Principal Marsden stepped closer. "I need you to come with me."

"What's wrong?" My hands trembled. Had something happened to Matt?

Principal Marsden gazed at the students, tipped her head toward the door, and gestured for me to follow.

My pulse galloped in my neck. I walked on hollow legs and sucked in a breath. *Everything's going to be okay.*

Principal Marsden laid her hand on my elbow and tugged me into the empty hallway.

I stared at Jonathan, now close enough to touch, and examined his unreadable face.

"Matt was injured," my boss said.

"What?" I whispered, my throat tight.

"He's in an ambulance on his way to Emergency." She pursed her lips and eyed me.

An ambulance? How had I not heard the sirens? "Wh-what happened?"

"Senior Constable Harris will escort you to the hospital and explain on the way." She nodded toward my pokey office. "Can you grab your things?"

I nodded and stumbled to my desk. How had this happened? *What* had happened? And why had they sent him off in an ambulance without me?

I heard Principal Marsden address my students, but the words she spoke were muffled by my thudding ears.

"Let me carry that." Jonathan gathered my bag and coat in his arms.

"Thanks," I whispered.

He ushered me from the room, down the hallway, and out toward his Victoria Police Landcruiser.

I settled in the passenger seat and buckled my seatbelt, thoughts invading my mind while my abdomen waged war against itself. What would I do if Matt's condition were serious? I rested my palms on my stomach, desperate to protect our baby from the impending bad news.

Jonathan exited the school grounds and headed in the direction of Robinvale. "Matt's being rushed to Mildura, lights and sirens."

"Mildura?" The potential seriousness of the situation hit me, and my throat and eyes burned.

"He sustained a stab wound—"

"What?" Matt was stabbed? Where? How?

"To the chest which will require surgery."

I gasped a sob and covered my hand over my mouth. Not my beloved Matt. What monster could do such a thing to my sweet husband?

"An investigation is in progress so I can't say much, but we believe an altercation occurred between two male students, and Matt tried to defuse the situation."

Always the hero. My chest ached from the vibrating terror gripping my heart.

Jonathan loosened his grip on the steering wheel. "I'll get you there as soon as possible, but be prepared not to see him right away. Matt may be in surgery when we arrive."

Surgery. How was this happening? And how could a student

stab him? *Why* would they stab him? Because he confiscated their revolting drugs? An awful thought entered my mind. "Were the students high on drugs?"

"I don't know." Jonathan popped open the centre console and handed me a packet of tissues.

I extracted a handful and patted my wet face.

"I sent Diana a quick text so she could let the gang know to pray."

Prayer. Why had prayer not been my instinctive response instead of my fear and growing anger?

"Hope you don't mind."

"Thanks. Not sure I'm up for … keeping people in the loop." I fisted my hands in my lap.

"Understandable."

Heat bubbled in my veins and flooded my limbs. If something happened to Matt, I would rip out the throat of the youth who had stabbed my husband.

And what about forgiveness? Putting away bitterness and wrath?

I pushed aside the Christ-like thoughts slipping into my mind and fenced them behind thick walls. There were times to be the "bigger" person and allow the wrongdoer some grace. But arming oneself at school, producing said weapon during an alleged argument, then stabbing a man? How could anyone expect me to smile and forgive my enemy? Because the moment that boy raised his knife toward my husband, he had become my enemy.

Jonathan clicked on some kind of dashboard technology and spoke a foreign, Victoria Police coded language.

I uttered a string of prayers for Matt in between checking the dashboard clock. Just over halfway in our travels to go. Where was Matt now? Farther down the road? Or had he touched down at the Mildura Base public hospital?

"Do you need anything? Bottled water?"

"No thanks," I said in a strained voice. My throat might be

parched, but the thought of vomiting inside a police vehicle sent shivers down my spine.

"Do you mind if I pray?" Jonathan's voice softened and seemed less assertive than when he had rattled off the hideous details about Matt's injury.

I shrugged and closed my eyes. "It wouldn't hurt."

Jonathan whispered several unintelligible words, cleared his throat, and raised his voice. "Father God, I ask You to comfort Belinda during this difficult time. Envelop her in Your peace. And I ask that You, the God who made the universe, minister Your healing power in Matt's body right now. Bring light and life into the shadows he's passing through. Comfort him and bring about a speedy recovery. I ask in Jesus's Name, amen."

"Amen," I whispered in a croaky voice.

"If you need to rest, go ahead."

I reclined against the seat with my eyes still shut, and listened to the thunderous roar inside my head.

CHAPTER SIX
Shockwaves

"Bee, honey, wake up."

I opened my eyes to Vicki's gentle voice, and blinked against the harsh fluorescent lights of the hospital waiting room.

Vicki rubbed the back of my hand and nodded toward the double doors.

I stretched and turned.

An average-heighted brown-haired male approached. "Mrs. Briggs?"

"Yes?" I sprang to my feet, clasping Vicki's hand in mine, and wobbled.

Vicki stood and pressed close to my side, anchoring me.

"I'm Dr. Gates, one of the surgical team. We completed epigastric surgery on your husband, and he's currently stable."

The suffocating weight on my lungs vanished, and I slumped against my friend. "That's great news."

Vicki wrapped her arm around my back, hooked her hand over my arm, and rubbed soothing circles around my elbow.

Dr. Gates pursed his lips. "He's not out of the woods yet, but the outlook is promising. He's under heavy sedation and will be in ICU for at least another twenty-four hours."

My stomach churned. Heavy sedation and ICU. "When can I see him?"

"Someone will come and get you once he's out of recovery." The doctor glanced at Vicki. "Maximum of two visitors at a time."

"Thank you, Dr. Gates." Vicki's voice sounded tinny.

He nodded, pivoted, and strode from the room.

My best friend led me back to our seats, her murmured prayers comforting me more than her warmth.

I leaned against her shoulder and closed my eyes. Matt was alive and recovering.

Our baby would have a father.

"I'll text Nicholas and Diana. Anything you want me to say or ask them to bring?"

I blinked and stared at my beautiful, selfless friend. Jonathan had given her Matt's car keys, and she had driven Matt's car to the hospital before sitting in a cold room beside me, even with her traumatic history. Could I comfort a friend in a hospital waiting room if it brought back haunting memories? I shook my head. "Just give them an update. I don't need anything. It's enough Jonathan drove me here, let alone yourself."

Vicki's features shifted into a semi-smile. "You're worth the hour fifteen drive. So is Matt. I'll be hard pressed to stop my husband visiting his best mate."

"Their bromance is lovely to see." A smile bloomed on my lips.

She chuckled and hugged me. "It is, isn't it?"

We waited another forty-five minutes before an orderly fetched us. Vicki and I walked arm in arm down the winding hallways—the overwhelming scent of disinfectant and cleaning products clung to my nostrils—until we reached the ICU department.

The orderly pointed to a nearby room. "The lounge area is through there with tea and coffee facilities. Some families use the space to adhere to the two-visitors limit."

Vicki slowed to a stop and blinked.

"And your husband is through there ..." The orderly turned

and furrowed his brow. "Is everything okay?"

"We're fine." I grasped Vicki's cold hand. "Thanks for your help. We're just going to the lounge for a moment."

The orderly narrowed his eyes, nodded, and scurried away.

I guided Vicki onto a seat in the lounge.

"Sorry," she whispered.

"Don't be." Guilt needled my insides. How could I have allowed Vicki to comfort me knowing the severity of Matt's condition? Her son had died in an ICU bed. Mildura hospital differed to other public hospitals in Melbourne, but it shared similarities too.

"Sometimes I dream about Ryan waking from his coma."

I warmed her cold hands between mine.

"But if Ryan had lived, what kind of life would he and I have had with Jude?" She pressed her lips together.

"*If* you chose to go back to him. Who knows, you might've still left your abusive ex and relocated to Tellarine with Ryan."

Vicki slipped her hands from mine and brushed away her tears with her palms. "True. Thank God for Heaven. I have comfort knowing I'll see my children someday soon."

I smiled at my brave friend, encouraged by her tenacity. Life had thrown her punch after punch, but she had shaken off the weights, trusted God, and embraced a new life filled with love.

"I might sit here for a bit." Vicki braced her hands either side of her thighs. "Chat with Nicholas while you grab a private moment with your husband."

"You sure?"

"Go ahead." Colour had returned to her lips and cheeks.

"Message me if you need me, otherwise come in when you're ready."

Vicki opened her bag and extracted her phone. "I will."

I trundled from the lounge and headed to the place the orderly had pointed. Matt's room. *You can do this.* I sucked in a breath and entered the ICU suite.

Matt lay unconscious in a room littered with flashing lights, beeping machines, and colourful cables. An oxygen tube snaked under his nose. His ashen face, neck, and shoulders were on display.

I inched toward the bed with a metallic tang hinting in the air, gripped the cold metal side rail, and scrutinised his blanket-covered chest, rising and falling in steady rhythm. Tears pricked my eyes, and I lowered to the cushioned chair beside the bed, my gaze glued to his chest.

Matt was breathing. Alive.

I pulled the seat closer and slid my hand through the bed rail until I touched his hand.

Warmth radiated through his skin, heating my fingers. Was he overheated?

I glanced at the machine beside his bed and checked his temperature reading. In the normal range. Maybe I was the cold one. I pulled my jacket closer around my chest.

A locked-away memory of a different patient in a different hospital bed resurfaced. A smaller, softer hand. Overwhelming fear battling inside my leaden chest. And my rippling relief when eight-year-old Alison had opened her eyes and smiled.

I should've been there when she fell through the window.

I buried the memory and focused on Matt's sleeping form. What was I meant to do now? Was there anything of use I could do to help my husband?

Pray.

I rubbed my fingers along the meaty part of Matt's hand not covered in medical paraphernalia, near his thumb, and whispered quiet thanks and prayerful requests to God. I needed Matt to wake and walk from this hospital. If not for me, then for my friend who had lost so much in a room like this.

And for our baby.

I switched between praying with my eyes closed and fixing my gaze on Matt's features. At some point during my prayers, an ICU nurse introduced herself and performed diagnostics. Not long after she exited the room, Vicki dropped to the opposite seat with a tired smile, and set to praying with me.

Time in a hospital was a funny thing. Some moments dragged, each long second extending to excruciating lengths, and other moments flitted by without a thought, swallowed by routine and contemplation.

"Want me to get you some dinner?" Vicki shuffled in her seat.

I rotated my neck and checked the time. Six-thirty already? The last hour had disappeared.

"The hospital café closes in half an hour, but I could always get us some takeaway?"

I glanced at my friend. "Shouldn't you be heading home soon?"

"Not before you eat."

"I'm not hungry." I rubbed my face.

"And what will you do if you're suddenly hungry in a few hours?" Vicki raised a brow. "You need to look after yourself."

"I know." I slid my fingertips along Matt's thumb.

"You staying here overnight?"

How could I leave Matt alone? I nodded.

Vicki tapped on her phone screen. "How about I grab the blanket from Matt's car and pop into the supermarket for some snacks? Nicholas has an early start tomorrow, so I should head home soon. If you want me to grab any clothes and toiletries from your place, Nicholas can deliver them tomorrow morning."

"That all sounds great." Not using my mushy brain to think and plan sounded better.

Vicki located my house keys in my handbag and kissed the top of my head. "I'll be back soon. I'll snap a picture of where I park so it's easier for you to find the car. Hopefully a space on Ontario Avenue will open up so it's less walking for you."

"Thank you," I whispered.

She smiled, glanced at Matt, and exited the suite.

♥ ♥ ♥ ♥ ♥ ♥ ♥

I awoke to something warm brushing along my right hand. Caressing rubs, back and forth. Swirling criss-crosses. Comforting strokes.

Where was I?

I shifted my shoulders and groaned. My stiff neck pulsed, and I opened my eyes.

"Hey." Matt smiled despite his croaky voice.

I squinted in the semi-darkened hospital room.

Matt's blue eyes seemed paler than usual, but he was awake and smiling at me.

"Hey." Tears pooled and clouded my vision.

"You okay?"

My husband lay in an ICU bed after being stabbed and he asked how I was?

"You looked … awkward." His scratchy voice sounded stiff. "With your head on your shoulder … and arm on the bed."

"I'll be fine." I brushed my left hand over my damp eyes, straightened, and winced. "How long have you been awake?"

"Ten minutes?" He pursed his chapped lips.

"How're you feeling?" I repositioned, shimmied the cricks from my neck, and settled my left hand over his.

"Been better." He shifted his hips and grimaced.

My heart twisted. "Are the pain meds wearing off?"

"Maybe." His jaw hardened.

"Let's call the nurse." I reached for the Call button.

Moments later, the night nurse bounded into the suite and beamed at Matt. "You're awake!"

"He's in a bit of pain." I clenched my fingers around his.

The nurse grabbed a folder from a nearby shelf. "I'd planned to administer the next dose of pain relief in"—she glanced at her watch—"fifteen minutes. Perfect timing."

I peered at Matt and twisted my lips into a semi-genuine smile.

He needed my strength right now. I could fall apart when I next visited the bathroom.

"How long will I be here?" Matt stared at the nurse.

"In ICU? Or your total time in hospital?" She raised a brow.

"Both."

"At least another day in ICU to confirm there aren't any complications."

Please, God, no complications.

The nurse tweaked several machines, hung two fluid bags onto the metal IV hook, and attached Matt's tubing to the bags. "Once the registrar signs off his approval, you'll be moved to a ward for continued observation."

"Do you think Matt might be home by the end of the week?" I hoped so.

"It's hard to say, but he's recovering well, so it's possible." She checked Matt's blood pressure.

One of the many icicles crowding my stomach melted. We would get through this together.

"You're doing well. Buzz me if you need anything." The nurse smiled and disappeared from the room.

I stood, stretched, and slipped my palm across Matt's unshaven cheek. "You're going to have everyone's hearts palpitating with your sexy stubble."

He chuckled, groaned, and gritted his teeth.

I bit my lower lip.

"Don't make me laugh." A sparkle lit in his eyes.

"Sorry. I forgot how painful laughing must be."

"And moving, laughing …" Matt pulled a face.

"Coughing." I cringed.

He widened his eyes. "This is going to suck."

I gasped a laugh and lowered to the chair. "At least you won't have to do it alone."

He yawned and secured his grip on my fingers. "Thank you for … being here."

"I'm not leaving anytime soon."

Matt locked his glassy gaze on me. "Have I told you lately … that I love you? My beautiful Bee."

"You have now." I leaned forward and kissed the back of his hand. "I love you too. Now get some more sleep."

Matt closed his eyes, his lips curled in a soft smile, and held tight to my hand while he drifted off to sleep.

"Thanks." I smiled wearily and grabbed the tall takeaway cup from the grumpy middle-aged woman at the hospital coffee shop.

She grunted and turned back to the coffee machine.

Nothing like pleasant human interaction while getting my afternoon pick-me-up. I wandered to a nearby café table, flopped on the seat, and removed the lid from my decaf coffee.

Plumes of steam drifted to my nostrils, and I breathed in the delightful scent. The aroma pleased me even without caffeine.

Matt had insisted I take a few moments to myself—after my visit to the toilet—and enjoy a cuppa. Drinking coffee in his presence seemed cruel, and his eyelids had fluttered during our conversation, so I acquiesced.

I sipped the hot, milky brew, and closed my eyes. Sleep had evaded me since Matt woke early this morning. I spent hours tracking his movements and monitors, and his regular breathing and quiet murmurs consoled me during the hushed hours. I had prayed, holding tight to the promise of a new tomorrow, the hope of a future. Our family's future.

Shrieking laughter punctuated the air.

I opened my eyes, shifted my shoulders, and sipped my coffee.

Voices filtered along the hallway from the hospital's main entrance. A couple whispered two tables away, their bodies curved toward each other. A slow-moving elderly man passed by, cane in hand, and a newspaper tucked under his arm.

I retrieved a chocolate from my jacket pocket, unwrapped the treat, and bit off a mouthful. Caramel, chocolate, and coffee. A perfect combination.

While I chewed and sipped, I allowed my mind to mull over the last twenty-six hours. Terror no longer gripped me, but peace seemed far off. A remote destination. Matt had woken twelve-and-a-half hours ago, so we were a long way from "returning to normal," but the hope of his recovery warmed my insides more than my coffee.

I finished my snack and bundled my rubbish into the bin. What to do now? I glanced at my phone—fifteen minutes had passed since I left ICU—and at the nearby signage. To my right was the exit and to my left the Contemplation Room. A walk in the fresh country air or more sitting?

My phone vibrated, and I retrieved it from my pocket.

Vicki Jacobsen: NICHOLAS APPRECIATED HIS TIME WITH MATT THIS MORNING. THANK YOU FOR GIVING THEM A MOMENT TOGETHER. WE'RE STILL PRAYING FOR YOU BOTH. I ALSO HOPE YOU WERE ABLE TO FIND MATT'S CAR. LOVE YOU XX

Matt's car. What better time than now to locate it?

I reread Vicki's directions, scanned the photo she had snapped last night, and exited the building. Cigarette smoke wafted from the patients and visitors congregated not far from the entry, behind the "do not smoke" painted line. I wandered by several empty parking spaces and moseyed along the concrete footpath on Ontario Avenue.

Sparse native trees and shrubs lined the tanbark nature strip. Farther down the road were flat, arid brown paddocks, a clear sign there was little to do in this part of town. At least the air smelled fresh with hints of eucalyptus.

I scanned the cars across the street, a soft breeze caressing my cheeks, until I saw Matt's vehicle. Mid-afternoon sunlight glinted off the windscreen. Now what? I gazed around, checked the time again, and roamed back toward ICU.

Unfamiliar voices echoed through the doorway of Matt's suite.

"And to confirm, you didn't hear their conversation? Just noted their body language," a woman said.

"Yes. They looked ready to fight." Matt?

Who was Matt talking to?

I entered the room, slipped through the drawn curtain, and froze.

Two uniformed Victoria Police officers stood beside Matt's bed, a tall dark-haired man and a shorter, dark-haired woman.

What were they doing here?

"Mrs. Briggs?" The female officer turned and met my gaze.

"Yes?" I dropped to my chair and grabbed Matt's outstretched hand.

"I'm Senior Constable Graham and this is Constable Patel." She glanced at her partner. "We're taking your husband's statement while the … event … is fresh in his memory."

I stiffened. How could they question Matt when he had been conscious for less than a day?

She scrutinised my face. "I understand this might seem an invasion of privacy so soon after surgery, but in order to continue our investigation, we need Mr. Briggs's statement."

"We're almost done, aren't we, officers?" Matt squeezed my hand.

"I believe so." Senior Constable Graham raised a brow at her partner.

"Yep, we should be good for now."

"Excellent." She smiled at us and gestured to a business-sized card lying on a nearby bench. "Don't hesitate to call if you recall anything else."

"Will do," Matt said.

The police officers departed.

"You okay?" Matt slid his fingers across the back of my hand.

"Are you?" My chest vibrated. How could they live with themselves?

"Of course. There's not much to say. I was only part of the

altercation for less than a minute before …"

My eyes watered. "Before you were stabbed," I whispered.

"Hey." Matt's gaze roamed my face. "I'm going to be okay."

"I know." I closed my eyes, sucked in a breath, and met his gaze. "I know."

He smiled, settling the unrest inside of me. "Now, tell me what you got up to while the cops grilled me."

I updated him on my twenty-five minutes of adventure, thankful to have another day sharing my mundane news, and basked in his attention.

CHAPTER SEVEN
Convalescence

I entered the beige hospital ward twin-share room Matt had moved into last night, five minutes after morning visiting hours commenced. Having begged and been denied an overnight stay in the ward, I had somehow driven home, slept, showered, and returned within a ten-hour window.

An elderly woman snored in the bed nearest the doorway.

I slipped through the blue curtain at the end of Matt's bed, dropped my bag and another backpack I had filled with Matt's belongings on the sole chair, and smiled at my husband and the nurse tending to him.

Matt turned toward me and beamed a huge smile, eyes alight.

"I'd like you on your feet today." The nurse handed Matt a small transparent plastic cup containing paracetamol.

I passed him his tumbler of water.

Matt nodded, popped the tablets into his mouth, and swigged some water.

"Nothing too extravagant." She gestured to the closed door several metres from Matt's bed. "To the bathroom and back is a great start. If your bowels open on your trip, bonus."

I returned Matt's water tumbler to the wheeled table at the end of his bed, beside his discarded breakfast tray. "Want to eat any more?"

"Nah." Matt's appetite had shrunk after two days with little food.

The nurse lowered both bed siderails and pointed to the machine administering his IV antibiotics. "Your last dose of antibiotics is this evening. For now, you'll need to wheel it with you."

"Thanks." I smiled at the nurse.

Matt furrowed his brow. "It's Wednesday?"

"Yep." The last two days had been the longest of my life.

He glanced between each side of the bed.

"What're you thinking?" I asked.

"Which way will be easier to swing my legs off the bed." He slid his hand to his right side where a drainage tube protruded from his skin.

"Left," we said together.

Five minutes later, after multiple groans and face contortions, Matt rested upright with his legs dangling over the left side of the bed. His complexion paled, and sweat beaded along his brow. His breaths laboured.

"Want to sit for a bit?" I rubbed his clammy, partially-exposed back. Hospital gowns were not designed with modesty in mind.

He nodded. "Water, please."

I held his cup and helped him sip.

Some colour returned to his features.

"Did the doctor say anything about when you might be able to go home?"

Matt had messaged me brief details after seeing the doctor around seven-thirty this morning.

"She said Friday or Saturday." Matt rested his knuckles on the mattress and dropped his head. "And I have to be able to walk out."

"We'll get you back on your feet in no time."

I spent the day encouraging my discouraged man, cheering him at each milestone. His first wobbly hands-clenched-around-the-

IV-trolley-pole steps and his first trip to the toilet. The mouthfuls of food he ate at lunchtime which he doubled at dinnertime. Although Matt's muscles ached, I could tell he was faster on his feet after dinner than he had been at the start of the day.

"When do visiting hours close?" Matt stretched toward his mobile phone resting on the bedside table and grasped the handset.

"Eight p.m." Less than an hour before I was forced to leave him for the night.

Matt tapped on his phone screen. "Do you still have spare clothes in the car?"

"Yeah. And some snacks." I had forgotten to take everything out of the boot when I had returned home.

"Good. I've sent you an email." Matt grinned and gestured to my handbag.

"What're you up to?" I scrounged in my bag, grabbed my phone, and checked my emails.

Matt had forwarded a booking confirmation for a Motor Inn nine-hundred and fifty metres down the road.

"It's a standard room, nothing fancy, but it'll afford you more time to rest."

"How're you the patient yet you're looking after me?" The backs of my eyes stung. "Thank you, babe."

He reached out for my hand and pulled me closer. "I prayed while you drove last night. I knew you were exhausted and … this is my way of looking after you while I'm not able to be with you."

Tears slithered down my cheeks. "You're so good at looking after me." How had I been so blessed?

"This's okay? It's prepaid until Saturday, so all you need to do is check in and out."

Saturday? "And what happens if you leave here on Friday?"

He smirked and waggled his eyebrows. "Then we get to spend the night in Mildura."

I snorted a laugh and palmed my cheeks dry. "A night of platonic snuggling."

"Or lying side to side." Matt glanced at the drainage tube in his right side. "And celebrating getting this thing out."

I wrinkled my nose at the small plastic bottle dangling by his side collecting blood and bile. "When did they suggest it'll come out?"

"Probably the day I leave."

"Then we'll definitely celebrate." I shuddered and hoped I missed all the drama of the tube removal. "Was there anything you wanted me to set up or help you with before I leave?"

"A final bathroom stop might be in order." Matt peeked through the gap between the curtains.

"And some teeth cleaning therapy?" I removed Matt's toothbrush and toothpaste from the front pocket of his backpack.

"Yes, please."

"Pyjamas?"

"The gown'll do." He nodded toward the backpack. "Any chance you snuck in my laptop?"

I extracted the neoprene laptop sleeve from Matt's bag and placed it on the rollable table.

"And charger?"

"I'm not a novice, you know." I raised my eyebrow and located the charger pouch.

"You're the best wife in the entire world." Matt grinned.

"I know." I stared at the mobile table at the end of Matt's bed. "Maybe you should get ready for bed, then we can set up your computer."

"Good idea."

I assisted Matt to the bathroom, held his gown out of the way while he did his business, and laughed when he dribbled toothpaste down his chin. Clumsy Matt was leagues better than Unconscious Matt.

"Would you complain if I skipped showering at the hospital?" Matt eyed the tiled shower space, with its flimsy waterproof curtain and white plastic chair, like a basket of vipers.

"We've survived five days of showerless camping—"

"But we both lived on deodorant and wet wipes together. This time it'll just be stinky me."

I chuckled and kissed his scruffy cheek. "F.Y.I., you're not stinky, but I packed deodorant and wet wipes just in case."

"I didn't think it possible you could get better, but I was wrong." He popped his toothbrush back into its holder.

"See, you *are* wrong sometimes."

Matt leaned against the minuscule sink, torso shaking. "Stop. Being. Funny."

"I'm sorry. Really, I am." I rubbed his back and hid my smirk. "The sooner you're better, the sooner you can laugh again."

He lifted his head and lanced me with his gaze in the reflection of the mirror. "And do other things."

My cheeks warmed. How was he still able to push my buttons?

Matt smirked, straightened, and grabbed his IV pole.

I unlocked the bathroom and hovered near him while he exerted a moment of independence.

I bounced out of bed at seven thirty-four on Friday morning, and messaged Matt.

Me: Morning, Handsome. Have you seen the doctor yet? Has she confirmed you can go home today?

The doctor had informed Matt yesterday morning he might be discharged from the hospital today. I prayed this was the case.

Matty Babe: Not seen her yet, but the nurse just told me the drain's coming out soon.

Me: That's a good sign!

Matty Babe: Yep.

Matty Babe: I miss you.

Me: I miss you too. Not long until ten o'clock.

Matty Babe: Nurse is back with another nurse. Tube

REMOVAL TIME!

Me: HAVE FUN.

I giggled at the tongue-poking-out emoji Matt sent moments later, set a praise and worship playlist on my phone, and indulged in a long, hot, brain-and-body-numbing shower.

The music paused, and my phone dinged while I towel-dried my hair.

I grabbed my phone and switched to my text messages.

Matty Babe: I'M DRUGGED UP AND TUBE-FREE. DOCTOR CAME BY WHILE I RECOVERED FROM THE ORDEAL AND CONFIRMED I CAN GO HOME THIS MORNING.

Drugged up and recovering from an ordeal? Did I want to know what had happened? Maybe not.

Me: YOU OKAY? BUT FABULOUS NEWS! SHOULD I PARK IN THE 15 MIN PICK-UP PARKING? OR WILL YOU NEED MORE TIME?

Matty Babe: PARK AS CLOSE AS YOU CAN AS I MIGHT NEED MORE TIME. I'M FEELING A BIT OFF AND AM GOING TO HAVE A NAP.

My stomach dropped.

Matty Babe: I'M SORE BUT FINE. WILL EXPLAIN LATER. LOOKING FORWARD TO GETTING OUT OF HERE.

My insides settled, and a soft smile spread across my face. Matt was truly coming home!

Me: SAME. I'LL MESSAGE THE GANG AND LET THEM KNOW.

Matty Babe: K. LOVE YOU.

Me: SLEEP WELL XX

I dressed in jeans and a cupcake-patterned T-shirt, flopped on the end of the Motor Inn bed, and wrote a group chat message to the Jacobsens, Harrises, and Evertons.

Me: HEY, GANG. JUST RECEIVED CONFIRMATION FROM MATT THAT HE'LL BE LEAVING THE HOSPITAL TODAY! WE HAVE ONE MORE NIGHT PAID FOR HERE IN THE MOTEL I'VE BEEN STAYING AT, SO WE'LL SLEEP THE NIGHT AND DRIVE HOME TOMORROW. THANK YOU ALL SO MUCH FOR YOUR PRAYERS AND PRACTICAL SUPPORT. I'M LOOKING FORWARD TO SEEING YOU SOON, ALTHOUGH I DON'T THINK MATT

WILL BE UP FOR CHURCH THIS WEEKEND.

After our hellish week, I wanted to hibernate. Thank God for online access to Sunday's church services.

I combed my hair then searched through the boxes of muesli bars Vicki had bought me. This morning was a chewy apricot muesli bar kind of morning. I slid the bar from the box, opened the wrapper, and bit a chunk of chewy tastiness.

My phone beeped numerous times.

I planted myself on the bed and read my messages.

Tara Everton: WONDERFUL! LET US KNOW IF YOU NEED ANYTHING. KEANU'S GOING TO EMAIL YOU A MENU AND HE'D LIKE YOU TO CHOOSE OPTIONS FOR LUNCH AND DINNER FOR THE NEXT WEEK, STARTING TOMORROW. WE'LL DELIVER THEM TO YOU. XX

Nick Jacobsen: PRAISE GOD. TELL MATT WE'RE ALL UP FOR A LOW-KEY GUYS NIGHT WHENEVER HE'S READY. MESSAGE US IF YOU NEED ANYTHING.

My vision blurred from their overwhelming kindness. I dabbed my eyes with a tissue.

Jon Harris: TOTALLY UP FOR A GUYS NIGHT! AND NICE WORK TEAM EVERTON. I'M JEALOUS I WAS NEVER GIVEN FREE FOOD AFTER I WAS SHOT ON DUTY.

Keanu Everton: YOU DITCHED DI LIKE A MORON. NO FREE FOOD FOR MORONS.

Jon Harris: FAIR ENOUGH.

Diana Harris: THAT'S SO AWESOME, AUNT BEE! PLEASE REACH OUT IF YOU NEED ANYTHING. MY MORNING SICKNESS ISN'T TOO BAD THIS WEEK. AND K-MAN, JONATHAN'S NOT A MORON ANYMORE, SO CAN WE GET A FREE MEAL? ;-)

Keanu Everton: THAT'S DEBATABLE.

Jon Harris: LOW BLOW, MAN. WHAT ABOUT LOVE FOR THE GUY WHO HANDCUFFED AND HAULED AWAY THE DISTURBER OF YOUR PEACE AT BENANU'S LAST MONTH?

Vicki Jacobsen: SO SOON? WOW! WHAT AN ANSWER TO PRAYER! LET ME KNOW WHEN YOU'RE UP FOR VISITORS AND I'LL

COME OVER AND ABDUCT YOUR DIRTY WASHING (NICHOLAS MOWED AND WEEDED YOUR GARDEN YESTERDAY). LOVE YOU, BEE. XX

Vicki Jacobsen: BOYS? KNOCK IT OFF.

Keanu Everton: SORRY MRS. J.

Tara Everton: MY CURMUDGEON OF A HUSBAND WOULD BE HAPPY TO GIVE A HOT COP A FREE MEAL ANYTIME.

Diana Harris: YOU'RE BRAVE, TAR. BUT HE IS HOT.

Keanu Everton: SHE'LL PAY DEARLY FOR THAT COMMENT.

Jon Harris: AS ARE YOU, MRS. HARRIS.

Jon Harris: KEANU, CALL ME IF TARA BEATS YOU UP TOO MUCH.

Keanu Everton: YOU JUST EARNED YOUR FREE MEAL.

Tara Everton: BACK TO WORK, HUSBAND.

I chuckled, finished my muesli bar, and replied to the message string.

Me: THANKS, GANG, FOR YOUR OVERWHELMING KINDNESS AND GENEROUS OFFERS. YOU'RE ALL ACES. WILL REPLY TO YOUR EMAIL THIS AFTERNOON, KEANU. MAY GOD BLESS YOU BOTH FOR YOUR GENEROSITY. NICK, YOU'RE A WONDER. I APPRECIATE YOUR GARDEN HELP! LOVE YOU TOO, VICKI, AND WILL CONTACT YOU ONCE I'M READY. AND DIANA (AND JON)? JUST CHILL AND ENJOY YOUR PREGNANCY. XX

I needed to take my own advice. I had almost forgotten about the baby while Matt was in hospital.

My phone buzzed in my hand.

Diana Harris: I WILL, AUNT BEE!

Vicki Jacobsen: XX

Matty Babe: C'MON, GUYS, STOP BLOWING UP MY PHONE SO EARLY IN THE MORNING. I'M A HOSPITAL INVALID, AFTER ALL. I NEED MY BEAUTY SLEEP.

I snorted a laugh.

Keanu Everton: IT'S AFTER 8, CUPCAKE.

Jon Harris: I JUST FINISHED AN OVERNIGHTER, SO IF ANYONE SHOULD COMPLAIN, IT'S ME.

Diana Harris: YOU DON'T NEED BEAUTY SLEEP, HOT COP.

(AND, SORRY, UNCLE MATT. WE'RE JUST EXCITED YOU'RE COMING HOME!)

Keanu Everton: I'M SURROUNDED BY CUPCAKES.

Tara Everton: STOP TALKING ABOUT CUPCAKES. NOW I'M HUNGRY FOR CAKE.

Keanu Everton: I'LL FEED YOU SOME. MEET ME IN MY OFFICE IN 5.

Diana Harris: UGH, CAN YOU TALK LIKE THAT OFF THE GROUP CHAT? WE DON'T NEED TO KNOW.

Keanu Everton: SAYS THE WOMAN WHO'S KNOCKED-UP.

Diana Harris: IT'S NOT LIKE I FLAUNT MY BELLY ON PURPOSE.

Jon Harris: COME BACK TO BED AND FLAUNT YOUR BELLY, BEAUTIFUL.

Diana Harris: JONATHAN!

Keanu Everton: TWO MEALS ON YOUR TAB, BRO.

Jon Harris: MUCH APPRECIATED.

Vicki Jacobsen: BOYS …

Matty Babe: THANKS FOR CAUSING ME MORE PAIN, GUYS. LAUGHING ISN'T GOOD MEDICINE ATM.

Vicki Jacobsen: DO I NEED TO USE MY TEACHER VOICE?

I covered my mouth with my palm and giggled.

Keanu Everton: SORRY AGAIN, MRS. J.

Jon Harris: SORRY, MUM.

Matty Babe: SCHOOLED BY THE PRO. THANKS VICKI. ;-)

Me: GO CANOODLE WITH YOUR WIVES, GENTLEMEN. HUG YOU LATER, BABE.

I tossed my phone on the bed, rested a hand over my belly, and prayed for our little family and our wonderful—albeit crazy—friends.

CHAPTER EIGHT
Back in Each Other's Arms

"Do you need anything else?" I tucked the blanket across Matt's pyjama-clad chest, and straightened.

"Just you." He glanced at the empty space in our bed beside him.

"I'll be with you soon." I checked the doors, set the dishwasher to wash, and prepared for bed. Ten minutes later, I lifted the bed cover, switched off my bedside lamp, and lay beside my husband.

Matt slid his arm against my side and reached for my hand. He pressed his fingers against mine. Fingers filled with life and vitality.

This moment together might never have occurred if the worst had happened.

My chest heated, and tears pricked my eyes. I had to control myself or our first night together in our own bed would be filled with far too much crying.

"It's nice lying here with you in our bed." Matt shifted his leg and touched mine.

"Yeah." My throat tightened, and I swallowed back tears.

"Being alone in the hospital at night gave me time to think."

Being alone at night had been a battle to keep my mind from dwelling on the details.

"And it reminded me of what's important." He turned his face in my direction. "Who's important."

Don't cry! I gasped a breath, desperate to control my body.

"And what might've happened."

Tears slipped down the sides of my face and nestled in my ears.

"You know I'd want you to be happy, right?"

How could I be happy without him? More tears followed the tracks on my cheeks, dripping onto my pillow.

"Talk to me, Bee." His whispered words carved through the noise in my head.

I heaved a breath.

Matt squeezed my hand. "You're allowed to cry. Just … talk to me."

I wiped my cheeks on my pillow and steadied my breathing. "I-I was so scared. Of losing you."

Memories rushed to my mind. Hearing those horrible words. Waiting for news, chilled to my bones. Shivering in my seat, wondering if he would wake.

I never wanted to experience that pain and fear again.

Matt pressed closer. "This experience has made me realise that we need to plan. I emailed the attorney, and he's emailed me a copy of my will. I want to check it's still in order just in case—"

"Please don't." I choked on a lump in my throat. "I can't have this conversation."

"We must."

"No."

"Turn on your lamp. Please." His voice had sharpened.

I rolled on my side—my back to Matt—and flicked the lamp switch.

"Look at me, Bee."

I lay on my back and turned my face toward his.

"If something happened, I want you to—"

"Please …" Could he read the pain in my eyes?

"If something happened, I'd want you to move past your grief and live again." He slid his palm to my stomach. "It's not just us we need to think about now."

After all of my tears and tantrums over my miscarriages, I needed to put this child in a place of priority. Had to think beyond myself and the painful "what if's" floating through my brain.

"I love you, Belinda. But I need to know if this event had played out differently, you'd know without a shadow of a doubt I'd be thrilled if you found another man to love you"—he raised his eyebrow and smirked—"after the appropriate period of mourning, of course."

"Of course." I snuffled a laugh.

"Just like I'll be chasing skirts a year after you're buried."

"Matt!" I widened my eyes and gaped. "A year? Really?"

His eyes sparkled. "Too long? Six months, then."

I bumped his arm and huffed.

"Okay, what about you pick a woman for me now, and I'll approach her at the funeral."

I bolted upright and aimed my fist at his shoulder.

"Let me recover before you pummel me." He chuckled and gestured for me to come closer. "I might be very tender in many places, but my lips still work."

"Is that so?" I balanced on my elbows against the mattress beside him, my face near his.

"Uh huh."

I licked my lips, leaned forward, and pressed my mouth to his, savouring his minty taste and softness. I could kiss him forever.

Matt sighed against my lips, and I prayed many years of kissing remained.

I scanned the recipe, paused the Kenwood mixer, and scraped chocolate icing from the sides of the bowl. "What about Lily? Or Beatrice?"

"Beatrice Briggs? Really, Bee?" Matt squinted at me from the recliner in the open-plan family room adjacent to our kitchen, mobile phone in hand.

I scrunched my nose. "You're right. It sounded better in my head."

He chuckled and returned to doing whatever he was doing on his phone.

"You need me to get anything while I drop these cupcakes at school?" I scooped the chocolate icing into a piping bag.

"Nope." Matt glanced up. "Just thank everyone for covering for us over the last week and a half."

Principal Marsden had approved my personal leave while Matt recovered from last week's surgery.

"I just received SMS confirmation for the eleven-week ultrasound." Matt's blue eyes glowed along with his bright grin. "You excited?"

"Of course." I beamed at my handsome husband and pressed my palm against the space our baby resided. *Our* baby.

"You more excited for the ultrasound or telling Vicki our news on Sunday?"

"It's a toss-up." My cheeks hurt from my constant smile. Sunday marked nine weeks in my pregnancy. How had nine weeks almost passed?

"When will those bad boys be ready to eat?" Matt nodded toward the island bench covered in cake racks topped with cupcakes. "I'm hungry."

I chuckled and tapped the tops of several mini cakes. "They feel cool now. Which flavour would you prefer? Vanilla with white chocolate and raspberry or double chocolate?"

"Can't I have both?" Matt widened his eyes.

"I don't see why not." I hand beat the white chocolate icing until the texture smoothed, and dolloped it into another piping bag.

Two minutes later, I presented Matt with two cupcakes. "Think I should sprinkle raspberry dust on the white choc one? And grate chocolate on the dark choc?"

He admired the cupcakes before tasting them. "Both are

delicious, as always, but it'll be fancier with the toppings."

"I agree." I returned to the kitchen and set to decorating the seventy remaining mouth-watering treats.

"I've finished my list of potential holiday destinations." Matt stretched his arms above his head.

"Great. Want to read me the list while I work?" Not that creating delicious food was anywhere close to hard work for me.

He cleared his throat. "Okay, in no particular order, we have places closer to home. Hamilton Island, Hayman Island, Perth, Tasmania, New Zealand. Hayman is a child-free island, so it'd be the perfect place to go."

"Hmm." I swirled chocolate icing into a perfect peak. "Keep going."

"Then there's all the places we've talked about like Scotland, Ireland, Spain, Greece, and France."

I lifted my head and met his gaze. "Can we afford to go on a European trip?"

"Are you really asking me that question?" Matt raised a brow.

"I guess not." My face warmed.

He grinned and winked. "We can go wherever you'd like, Bee. I transferred another fifty grand from my share portfolio to our bank account, so we can start booking things."

I squeezed the piping bag too hard and squirted a blob of icing on the cupcake which I had just dressed to perfection. "F-fifty?"

"You know things cost a lot compared to the Aussie dollar. We'll need it and more."

"Maybe we should go to New Zealand. It's cheaper."

Matt chuckled, stretched his long, lithe legs, and stood. "I was thinking we could book two trips."

"Two?" How had our lives gone from rare holidays to planning and booking two vacations?

He crossed the space between us—slower than his regular pace—gingerly wrapped his arms around my waist from behind me, and rested his chin on my shoulder. "We could go somewhere local during the Easter holidays, then travel through Europe at a later date. Maybe the end of next year when Baby is just over a year old? Or we can try for annual leave during the first few weeks of Term Three this year. It'd be in the heat of summer over there, but July's still months away from November, so you shouldn't be as uncomfortable if you were more pregnant …?"

So many great ideas. I turned and kissed his jaw. "Let's get these finished first."

Matt kissed my cheek, grabbed a glass of water, and returned to his recliner.

"Oh, and don't forget to call the bank back and reschedule our meeting." In all the mess of last week, we had both forgotten about the appointment to close down our home loan account and secure our house title deed.

"I'll do that now. Think Saturday week will give me enough time to recover?"

"Yep." I finished decorating the cupcakes, placed each into my special cupcake carry boxes, and packed them into my car.

I towel dried my hair, hung the damp towel over the airer near the ensuite heating vent, and combed my flowing blonde locks. Lightness filled my chest.

An entire week—seven bliss-filled days—had passed since Matt was discharged from the hospital. A week of counting my blessings, holding his hand, and living in the moment.

I grabbed my phone from the ensuite vanity, slid into a pair of shoes at the foot of my bed, and checked for the text message I had heard arrive while I showered.

Alison Davies: I REALLY NEED TO TALK TO YOU.

I stared at my phone screen, cringed, and lowered to the end of our bed. Would my sister forgive me for not calling her back when I had promised?

Me: Sorry for not phoning when I said. Had some serious health stuff going on with Matt. I'll try to call you soon. Love you. xx

I sucked in a sharp breath when Alison responded seconds later.

Alison Davies: He OK?

A genuine question. Not a witty, inappropriate comment in sight. I relaxed my shoulders.

Me: He will be. Thanks for asking.

I noted the time on my bedside clock—half an hour until Matt's wound and dressing check with Dr. Fallow—pocketed my phone, and trudged along the hallway to where Matt rested on the family room couch. "We'll need to leave in fifteen minutes …"

Matt groaned.

I stepped closer, and my heart thumped.

Matt's face was pale, his forehead lined and beaded with sweat. He clutched a hand over his abdomen.

"What's wrong?" I collapsed on my knees beside the couch and touched his warm forehead.

"Stomach hurts," he panted.

"Does your chest hurt too?" My pulse skyrocketed, throbbing an uncomfortable rhythm in my neck.

"A bit." He gritted his teeth.

"I'm calling an ambulance." I unearthed my phone and dialled emergency services. After a brief explanation of Matt's recent surgery—my gaze glued to my husband the entire time—I tried to listen to the operator's calm instructions through the buzzing in my head.

The operator said something about unlocking the door and a MICA ambulance, before they ended the call.

Please let him be okay.

"Someone will be here soon." I pressed a soft kiss to Matt's clammy forehead.

He moaned and closed his eyes.

"I'll be back shortly." I dashed to the entryway and unlocked the front door with shaking fingers. Tears stung my eyes. *Please, God. Please.* I sucked in a breath, wiped my eyes, and returned to the couch.

Matt's face was still creased in a grimace, but his hand over his stomach had relaxed.

"They'll be here soon." I kneeled and stroked his soft blond strands.

Someone knocked at the front of the house—after what seemed like an hour, but my phone reported ten minutes had passed—and opened the door.

I stood on rickety legs and stepped toward two female paramedics wheeling a stretcher through the front doorway. "He's here!"

The ambos footsteps echoed through the house, both women average in height with dirty-blonde hair, one with short-cropped hair and the other sporting a tight bun.

"Are you Belinda?" asked the woman with the bun.

"Yes." I watched the short-haired paramedic extract a dark blue bag from underneath the stretcher before she approached Matt.

"Could you please confirm the patient's name and date of birth?" Tight Bun yanked a pen and pad of yellow sticky notes from her shirt pocket.

I gave her Matt's information, amazed I remembered the details correctly.

The paramedics triaged with efficiency, their voices calm despite their urgent movements, discussing "thoracic trauma" and "peri arrest."

Tight Bun nodded to her partner. "Lights and sirens to Mildura Base." She turned to me. "Our priority is getting your husband to the hospital where they'll prepare for his arrival. We'll monitor him en route."

The paramedics hefted Matt onto the stretcher, strapped him in, and asked him various questions.

A sense of helplessness washed over me.

"Belinda?"

I turned and met the gaze of the short-haired paramedic before she wheeled Matt to the front door.

"Belinda." Tight Bun caught my gaze. "Please gather your husband's phone, charger, and Medicare card."

"Oh, yes." I scurried toward our bedroom, scrounged for a backpack, and gathered a few things for Matt.

"Are you travelling with us?" Tight Bun stood in my bedroom doorway.

"Please." The thought of being separated from him seared my chest.

"Grab your phone, wallet, and keys, and let's go."

I shoved my stuff in the backpack, locked the front door, and raced to the ambulance filling our driveway.

The short-haired paramedic gestured me inside the vehicle before she closed the sliding door. She pointed to a seat near Matt's head. "You can sit over there."

I flopped on the chair, dumped my backpack under my feet, and brushed my fingers through Matt's hair.

The paramedics spoke foreign code to each other. Medical staff were amazing people, remembering all those acronyms.

"Tell me again how long you've experienced abdominal pain," Short Hair asked Matt.

"It was mild, barely there … the last few days, but it's really hurt"—he clenched his teeth—"the past hour or so."

The last few days? When had he been in pain? And why had he not told me?

"Once you roll into Emergency, you'll have an echocardiogram." She checked his blood pressure. "Has anyone checked your sutures yet?"

"We're meant to be at his GP appointment now." An appointment I had failed to cancel! I fumbled with my phone.

"Your GP will receive documentation from the hospital later

today which'll explain your absence." The paramedic smiled and ripped open a bunch of plastic-bagged utensils. "Matt, I'm going to insert a cannula in your hand and see what pain meds I can administer, then inspect your wounds and make sure there's no obvious signs of infection."

"Okay. Bee?" Matt's voice sounded tight.

I leaned closer. "Babe?"

He pressed his lips together before relaxing his face. "Have you messaged Vicki?"

I widened my eyes. How had I forgotten to tell anyone?

"To pray." He croaked.

"I'll do it now." I kissed his stubbled cheek, leaned back in the seat, and opened the group message app.

Me: HEY, EVERYONE. MATT AND I ARE CURRENTLY EN ROUTE TO MILDURA HOSPITAL VIA AMBULANCE. HE'S BEEN EXPERIENCING ABDOMINAL PAINS. PLEASE PRAY. I'LL UPDATE YOU ONCE I KNOW MORE, BUT PROBABLY WON'T RESPOND TO MESSAGES. THANK YOU IN ADVANCE.

I spent the rest of the faster-than-expected trip to Mildura either running my fingers through Matt's soft hair, brushing my fingers along his cheek and chin, or holding his hand. Not a second passed where we did not touch, especially when the paramedic plunged a needle into his chest and extracted fluid.

I lost contact with Matt when the ambos whisked him from the ambulance, and I stepped from the vehicle, bereft.

"Is Matthew your partner?" A sweet-looking brunette in hospital attire stood inside the double doors of the building Matt and a team of people had entered moments ago.

"Husband," I whispered.

She smiled and grabbed the backpack from my hands. "Your husband is off to have an echocardiogram, so come and wait in the lounge."

"How long will it take?"

"About half an hour."

I followed the brunette to the lounge used by ICU, and memories of Vicki's panic filtered to my mind. My hands trembled. I now understood how this place would trigger memories … for both of us.

"Can I make you a coffee? Or a cup of tea?" She laid my backpack on a vacant chair.

"Maybe just some water? Please." I lowered to the adjacent seat.

Thirty seconds later, she returned with a plastic cup of water.

"When can I see him?" I sipped the cool liquid.

"Someone will come find you while the cardiologist reads the results." She nodded toward the doorway. "You'll be okay?"

I nodded, forced a smile, and sipped my drink.

She smiled and exited.

I stared at the now empty doorway for an extended period of time, my heart begging for news. *Please be okay.* My gaze fell to the empty chairs across the room. I avoided glancing in the direction of the few people whispering in the far corner. A room filled with uncertainty. I pressed my palm to my stomach and closed my eyes, thankful for one certainty in my life. My little bean was content.

Sleepiness blanketed my eyelids with heaviness. I opened my eyes and focused on the pink light flashing on my phone in my hands. On, off, on, off. Blinking, warning me I had messages to read. But my heart and my eyes were uninterested in the task.

"Mrs. Briggs?"

I lifted my head and stared at a man standing in the doorway. "Yes?"

"Gather your things and come with me."

I shouldered the backpack and followed the orderly down the hallway which separated ICU and the Emergency Department.

"In here," he pointed to a curtained-off room.

I stepped through the curtain and spotted Matt lying on the bed, his chest exposed with small white pads attached in various places. Two nurses flitted around him.

Matt met my gaze, his eyes shimmering and glassy. "Bee."

I slid to his left side where there was less activity and pressed a kiss to his forehead. "How're you feeling?"

"Still in pain." He gripped my hands and pulled me close. "Kiss me."

I glanced around the small cordoned-off space, noting how the nurses seemed to avoid looking at us, and leaned down. My cheeks warmed, and I pressed my mouth against his.

Matt's lips were soft and pliable, the type of kiss which often ignited my need to peel his clothes from his delicious body, one garment at a time.

My insides swirled with heat. I pulled back and searched Matt's eyes.

"I love you, Bee. With all of my heart." Tears slipped from the corners of his eyes.

"I love you too." I choked on my words, and the backs of my eyes burned in tandem with my cheeks and lungs.

"No matter what happens"—he gurgled a breath—"remember you are loved." His whispered words tore my heart in two.

"What happened? What do you know?" I clung to his hands, my fingers tangled with his.

He pulled our clasped hands to his lips and brushed tearful kisses against our interlocked fingers.

Someone ripped open the curtains behind us.

I twisted around, my hands trapped in Matt's, and stared at a tall, middle-aged man.

"Mr. and Mrs. Briggs, I'm Dustin, one of the hospital cardiologists." He glanced at Matt. "We need to prepare you for immediate surgery."

"What? Why?" I gasped for air.

"The echocardiogram revealed pericardial effusion caused by a nick in your pericardium, possibly from the initial knife wound."

What? How had the hospital missed the nick last week?

"With your poor response to the pericardiocentesis performed by your paramedic, emergency surgery is essential."

Matt's fingers gripped tighter around mine. "Okay."

"I'll see you in there, Mr. Briggs." The cardiologist turned to me. "He'll be wheeled out in the next minute."

A minute. I nodded and faced Matt.

His features had blanched, his eyes and cheeks wet with tears.

I closed my eyes and pressed my lips against his. Once. Twice. Three soft, heartfelt kisses. "You're strong and you'll get through this."

"I love you." He touched my cheek.

"I love you too." I scanned his features, still handsome despite his pallor.

A team of men in blue scrubs surrounded Matt's bed, disconnected cables, and shifted his IV to a metal pole on the bed head.

"Ready, Mr. Briggs?" A young guy asked.

Matt's laser-focused gaze never left my face. "Ready."

"Let's go."

I pasted a damp smile to my lips and held my cries inside as Matt was pulled from the room and out of sight.

CHAPTER NINE
Lost

I jolted, opened my eyes, and stared around the empty ICU lounge. When had I fallen asleep? The ticking clock on the wall mocked me, its chastising hands highlighting my failure to stay awake. Twenty-two minutes. I had missed twenty-two minutes of Matt's surgery. Was this how Jesus's disciples had felt while the Messiah prayed in the Garden of Gethsemane long ago?

Vibrations tickled my fingertips and thighs, and I glanced at my lap. My phone rested along the seam of my thighs, my fingertips touching its case. Must have slipped from my hands while I napped.

I stretched and yawned. More buzzing. I unlocked my phone and blinked. Sixty-two messages? Were Jonathan and Keanu at it again? The ghost of a laugh puffed through my lungs.

"Mrs. Briggs?"

I whipped my attention to the doorway where Dustin the cardiologist and an unfamiliar woman approached.

Matt!

I launched onto my unsteady feet and clutched the back of the chair for support. "How is he?"

The cardiologist closed the lounge door, turned, and met my gaze. Something flickered across his face and disappeared. Sadness?

"Hi, Mrs. Briggs, I'm Greta, one of the on-staff counsellors." The woman stepped close. "Do you have a support person with you?"

"No. I'm alone." *I* was the support person. For Matt. "How's my husband?"

"How about we take a seat."

I lowered to a chair beside Greta. What was happening?

Dustin squatted in front of me, his casual position contrasting with his rank and importance. "I'm sorry to inform you that your husband suffered a cardiac arrest mid-surgery."

Cardiac arrest?

"We weren't able to resuscitate him."

"What?" I scrunched my brow and stared at the cardiologist. "C-can't you try again?"

He shook his head.

I pressed my right hand against my tightening throat.

"Your husband passed away," Greta whispered.

"But … how?" I squeezed my eyes closed and tried to straighten the jumble of letters bashing against my ears. Their words made no sense.

"His heart gave out." Greta clutched my cold left hand.

Not possible. Matt was in his prime. I opened my eyes and searched the cardiologist's face. Nothing made sense.

"I'm very sorry for your loss," Dustin said, his voice tight. "The coroner will perform an autopsy."

An autopsy. How could Matt be gone? I shook my head and tears leaked down my cheeks.

"We have moved his body to a private room down the corridor." Dustin cleared his throat and stood.

Matt was gone? My hearing distorted with pulsing blood. I ducked my chin, lungs leaching air, and avoided the specialist's gaze.

"Once again, I'm sorry for your loss." The cardiologist nodded, opened the door, and exited.

My vision blurred.

"Would you like to see your husband now? Or would you

prefer to call a loved one and ask them to be with you?" Greta handed me several tissues.

I grappled my phone, dabbed away tears, and dialled Vicki.

"Hey, Bee, how is he? Did you see my message?"

"Vicki." I rasped, sucked in a breath, and met Greta's compassion-filled gaze.

"Nicholas and I are about twenty minutes from the hospital."

"He's …"

"You're breaking up, Bee. He's what? How's Matt?"

Tears gushed from my face, and I gasped a breath. My husband, the father of my child, was no longer here on earth.

"Bee? You still there?"

Numbness slithered through my limbs, severing my fingers and toes from all sensation. Somehow, I cradled the phone against my ear. "He's gone."

"What?" Vicki's voice hollowed, an echo of my heart.

Greta squeezed my shoulder.

"Matt died." Numbness. Nothing but never-ending numbness.

A muffled sob echoed through the phone line. Was that Vicki, or the sound of my heart disintegrating?

Greta now held my phone.

I tuned out while she spoke to my best friend about my dead husband. A void now claimed my heart.

"Mrs. Briggs." Greta caught my attention and handed me my phone. "How about I escort you to see your husband and will then arrange for Vicki to join you when she arrives?"

I nodded and stood on unfeeling legs. Dead. Like Matt.

Death had stolen from me once more. My heart would never recover.

I ended up in a small, stark one-bed hospital room, my hand splayed on Matt's unmoving body, my cheek against his. No minty breath to warm me, just the wetness of my tears reminding me I was alive. My agonised breaths beside his still chest. The screams inside my brain blocking out his silence. A picture of Life and Death.

Warm arms wrapped around me. Vicki's perfume wafted to my nostrils, and her soft sobs filled my ears.

"I can't believe he's gone," she whispered.

Me too. Another Briggs in Heaven, another death to live with. More brokenness to wade.

If I wanted to end it all, would anyone care?

My best friend's warmth clung to my shoulders. Voices murmured around me.

I nuzzled Matt's cheek and breathed in his scent, his essence. He still smelled good. So very good. Memories flooded my mind as tears flowed over my cheeks.

He would never again gaze at me with his vibrant blue eyes, intensity and desire flickering in his orbs, like I was the only woman in the world. After the many, *many* women he had slept with in the past, he had looked at me like I was his first.

And now his last.

I snuffled and gritted my teeth. How could I think of sex at a time like this? What was wrong with me?

More voices and movement sounded behind me.

"Why did you leave me?" I whispered in Matt's ear. "Why didn't you fight?" I brushed my lips against his soft earlobe, desperate for him to move. To turn and brush his soft lips against mine. Or smirk and wink. Anything other than stillness and silence.

Anything to feel alive.

I closed my eyes, breathed him in, and forced myself to remember. His scent, his silky skin. Soft hair and hard abs. The tenderness emanating from him despite his mischievous blue eyes. I shuddered with more sobs. Did I have his laugh recorded somewhere? Or his velvety voice? Tears leaked from my closed eyes. Would I always remember his adorable squeak when I pinched his backside or the rumbling growl when his predatory senses kicked in?

Icy darkness chilled me, consuming my heart.

How would I go on without him? Parenting our baby without

his wisdom and knowledge? His innate ability to know what to do and how best to do it?

Warmth circled my back.

How would I do this alone?

"Bee."

I squeezed my eyes tighter and pressed closer to my husband, running my lips against his soft skin. "Don't leave me."

"Bee, sweetheart." Vicki's voice croaked. "I know it's hard to say goodbye. I know. But …"

I shook my head. How could I leave him? How could he leave *me*? My endless supply of tears dampened my face.

A deep, garbled groan echoed on the other side of Matt.

I lifted my head.

Nick stood on the other side of the bed, left hand gripping his forehead and somewhat covering his dark eyes, his right hand touching Matt's shoulder. Tears dripped from his stubbled chin onto his shirt front.

Shattered.

"It's been over an hour." Vicki rubbed my back, her voice broken. "I know it's hard, but you need to say goodbye."

I gripped the sheet covering Matt's chest, pain pinching my fingertips, and fought the screams clawing for escape. My skin prickled with goosebumps, and ice crystals spread through my body like hoar frost, invading my extremities.

"He loved you." Nick's throat bobbed.

I replayed our final moment together. Matt's kiss and declaration of his love. Had he known something was wrong?

I glanced at Nick.

"He'd have stayed if he could." Matt's best friend was teary-eyed and distraught. He understood the pain of losing a spouse. Now he understood the loss of a close mate.

Vicki squeezed my shoulder.

It was time.

I stood, palmed my eyes, and leaned over Matt. One final

glance at my beautiful husband. I lowered my face, my lips close to his, and kissed his cold mouth. "Goodbye, love."

Several sniffles echoed in the small space.

I straightened. A memory resurfaced, and I huffed a wry laugh. "You didn't pick anyone for me." Not that I would approach a potential date at my husband's funeral.

"He didn't do what?" Vicki rested her hand on my shoulder and leaned closer.

"Nothing. Just … nothing." I slid my fingers across Matt's lips, sighed, and stepped back.

Vicki wrapped her arm around my shoulder.

"Let's go," I whispered, and walked from the room.

"I think blue and white would be best, don't you agree, Bee?" Vicki leaned forward in her seat and pointed to a large book on the funeral director's desk filled with casket colour accents. "Matt's favourite colour was blue."

"Yeah. Sure." Sometimes it sucked my best friend had once dated my husband … before he was my husband. But it sucked more my husband was dead.

"And the casket itself? We can meet any budgetary requirements," the funeral director said in his nasally voice.

"Whatever you like, Bee." Nick touched my shoulder from where he stood behind Vicki's seat. "Money's not a problem."

"Poplar? Or would you prefer the darker cherry wood?" Vicki hummed.

What I preferred would never eventuate. I stared at the page and pointed to the darker one. Done.

Matt had left me three days ago. Three days of wishing he would walk through the door and shout "Surprise!" or send me a cheeky text message. Three days since I slept for longer than two hours.

I leaned against the semi-comfortable chairback and indulged in a moment of what I now called "Matt time." Pulling up memories which dulled the ache in my chest. His smile, the way he tilted his head to the left when he focused on his computer monitor. Those exposed, muscled calves I drooled over when he wore running shorts.

Last night I sacrificed sleep and scrolled through old text messages. How had I not realised how hilarious my husband was until now? Witty and, at times, salacious, but in the nice-naughty kind of way a husband messages his wife to get her juices flowing.

Now the Sahara resided in that particular part of my life.

"Brian and Crystal said they'll pay for catering, and Pip's husband has some florist connections, so I think we're all set." Vicki's tone was far too cheery for a place like this. A place revolving around death.

Aunt Crystal had wailed over speakerphone when Vicki called Matt's uncle and aunt. I understood the sentiment. Uncle Brian and Aunt Crystal were more like parents to Matt, and their daughter Pip was closer than a cousin. Even Pip's husband, Troy, treated us like siblings.

Now we were one family member short.

"Thanks for all of your help." Vicki tugged on my hand.

I stood, my vision glazed, nodded toward where I presumed the funeral director stood, and leaned against my friend on our journey to the car.

Nick and Vicki discussed who-knew-what—everything blurred in my head—on our way back to their house. Vicki had insisted I stay over when we returned to Tellarine on Friday night. Going home seemed a challenge too big for my grief-addled brain. Three days later, I wondered if I would ever have the courage to walk through my front door.

My stomach tightened, and I clutched my belly. Another mountain to climb. Alone. Yesterday marked nine weeks. Matt and I had planned how we would tell our friends. Now the task was left for me to complete by myself, and I had no desire to share the only piece of Matt I had left with anyone else. Maybe one day when I could no longer hide my news.

"Did you hear me, Bee?" Vicki asked.

"Huh?" I wiped my hand over my aching eyes.

"Jonathan messaged and said he'll need to talk to you once we're back."

"About what?" Was it about the boy who had destroyed my life?

"He didn't say, but I'm guessing it might be about … everything that's happened." Vicki grabbed Nick's hand, which rested on the gearstick of his ute. "He's driving over now."

Good. I woke this morning from my microsleep with thoughts tumbling inside my head, igniting my anger. If the cardiologist was correct the nick in Matt's heart was from the stabbing, would it mean the youth at school would be held accountable for my husband's death? And what about the hospital staff who had treated him to begin with? Were they negligent? I wanted the coroner's report, yesterday.

Ten minutes later, Nick parked in his garage and escorted me to their lounge room. Not long after, Vicki handed me a cup of tea with a store-bought biscuit.

I sipped, chewed, and stewed on my thoughts.

"Belinda." Jonathan perched on the ottoman at my feet.

When had he arrived? I lowered my tea and saucer to the nearby side table.

He removed his navy-blue Victoria Police cap, ran his fingers through his dark hair, and grabbed a piece of paper from his front pocket. "I've been asked to give you the Coroner Support Service Registrar's details. You'll need to liaise with them going forward."

"What?" I held the paper between shaking fingers. "I can't speak to you about it?"

"No." Jonathan sighed. "I don't have jurisdiction now that … Matt's gone."

I furrowed my brow. "Why?"

"We anticipate the coroner's report will indicate the initial trauma led to his death." He rubbed a finger along the scar on his right temple. "Detectives will handle the investigation."

"But you think the drug-addicted youth will be charged with murder?"

"Manslaughter, but, yes, if the coroner's report says what we anticipate, he'll be charged."

"Good." I fisted my hands. Just desserts would be served to the punk kid I wished had never been born. "And the hospital's negligence?"

Jonathan creased his brow. "I can't speculate what the coroner will report."

"But they *are* at fault." I flexed my jaw. "They missed the nick in his heart!"

Jonathan stared at me. "None of us are perfec—"

"Don't."

Jonathan's back stiffened.

"We live in a world filled with technology. How could they miss it?" How was it possible in this day and age?

"I'm not a doctor, but even the latest technology can miss microscopic things."

I glanced at the paper and tucked it inside my pocket. "Thanks."

He nodded, donned his cap, and stood. 'If there's anything you need—"

"Except for information I *want* to know." I grumbled.

"Anything other than that. Please … reach out." His dark gaze settled on me. "Diana and I want to do whatever we can to help."

My throat clogged, and I nodded.

Jonathan scanned my face, pressed his lips together, and padded from the room.

I wrapped a blanket around my shoulders and hid from the world.

♥ ♥ ♥ ♥ ♥ ♥ ♥

Don't cry. Don't cry. Don't cry.

"I take comfort in …" Nick clutched the church podium, arms taut, and dipped his head. He sucked in several shaky breaths and faced the crowded auditorium packed with friends and family, colleagues and townsfolk, even old school buddies of Matt's from Melbourne. "Sorry."

Vicki and Aunt Crystal sniffled on either side of me.

Don't. Cry.

Nick thumbed his eyes, streaking wetness over his temples. "I take comfort in knowing … one day soon, the dead in Christ will rise and"—his voice cracked—"I'll see Matt again."

I gritted my teeth and crunched hard in an effort against the heat building in my eyes and throat.

He stared up at the enlarged snapshot of my handsome husband on the widescreen monitor beside the casket. "Love you, mate."

Vicki wrapped her arms around me, pressed her forehead against my shoulder, and sobbed.

I closed my eyes, my final defence against the impending water works.

"Thank you, Nicholas." Pastor Davidson's voice echoed through the room. "And thank you to Matt's family for their wonderful words. Belinda has asked me to thank you all for coming. Although we've been brought together through this tragedy, I wanted to share something Paul told the saints at Corinth."

I blinked away tears and glanced around the room. Shining eyes and distraught faces all around, carrying the same ache for the same person. Why did this happen? How would we survive?

Nick lowered to the seat on Vicki's left, peeled his wife from my body, and pulled her against his chest.

"'Who comforts us in *all* our affiliation, that we may be able to comfort those who are in *any* affliction, through the comfort with which we ourselves *are* comforted by God,' emphasis mine."

Comforted by God? Where was my supposed comfort? A week had passed since Matt's death and not a moment passed where I did not experience heartache, grief or anger. No comfort in sight.

People whimpered, sniffed, and sobbed all around me. Someone blew their nose to my left.

Where is my comfort, God? The dam burst, and I covered my mouth with my hands, pressing my palms hard to silence my cries. I wept, my lungs airless, trembling. Warmth encompassed me, and I was secured in someone's arms. Was this the comfort God had promised? I clutched tight to the possibility, but the image of the boy—I had searched the school intranet for his photo and had glared at it for half a day—Jason Kyneton, Matt's murderer, filled the cracks in my parched, dusty, hardening heart. Everyone in the room had suffered because of him. That selfish, terrible monster. He deserved all that came to him.

I cried on the church pew, nurturing my hatred, and comforted myself.

CHAPTER TEN
Shattered

Buzzing. Insistent buzzing, like a mosquito beside my pillow on a hot summer's night, vibrated in my head. I groaned, pulled my arms from underneath the warmth of my—no longer our—bed covers, and batted my hands near my ears.

The buzzing ceased.

I rolled to my side and sniffed Matt's pillow, breathing in his familiar, comforting scent. I might have fought against Nick's suggestion to go home after the funeral, but walking around our space, feeling closer to Matt in our home, had settled something inside of me.

It had broken something inside too.

The landline phone screeched.

I jolted, blinked bleary eyes at Matt's bedside table, and crawled across the bed far enough to reach the handset. "Hullo?"

"Hi, this is Leif Salverson from Bendigo Bank. Is Matt Briggs at home?" A smooth-sounding male voice echoed through my tired brain. "He booked an appointment with me for eleven …?"

I squinted at Matt's bedside clock. Eleven twenty-two.

"I tried his mobile but it went straight to voicemail."

Matt's mobile number. Another job to add to the pile of things to do. I blustered a breath. "What's this about?"

"Sorry, who am I speaking with?"

"Belinda Briggs."

Keyboard-tapping filled the silence. "Right. Matt's wife."

Was I still his wife after death?

"Matt wanted to wind up your home loan and discuss title deed storage."

Today was the Saturday of the bank appointment? It seemed a year had passed since Matt booked it.

More keyboard and mouse clicking. "You're in Tellarine, right?"

"Yeah," I whispered. Tears wet my eyes. Always tears.

"I'll be in the area on Thursday. Can you let him know—"

"He's dead."

"Beg your pardon?"

I wiped away ever-present tears, snuggled against Matt's pillow, and balanced the handset over my cheek. "Matt died last week. We buried him yesterday."

"I… I'm so sorry, Belinda." His whispered words nipped at my tender heart.

"So am I."

He cleared his throat. "Do you mind if I call you next week to discuss what needs to be done going forward?"

I closed my eyes and loosened my grip on the phone. "Sure, whatever."

After confirming my mobile number, Leif whispered, "My sincere condolences on your loss," and disconnected our call.

I dropped the handset on Matt's bedside table, wrapped my arms around my belly, and howled into his pillow.

I stood in the kitchen dunking my tea bag and stared at Matt's empty recliner in the lounge. Ten days. How had I survived ten days without him?

My phone buzzed on the couch. More text messages from

well-meaning people I wished would leave me be.

I sighed, dumped the used tea bag in the rubbish bin, and carried my mug back to the couch. Who wanted my attention now? I lowered my mug to the coffee table and peered at my latest text.

Alison Davies: ARE YOU IGNORING ME? OR JUST FORGETTING TO CALL ME BACK? I'M STARTING TO WONDER IF YOU ACTUALLY CARE ABOUT ME.

My breaths sharpened. How did she have such skill arousing my guilt? And she had no idea about Matt. I dropped my phone and covered my mouth with my hand. How was I meant to tell her about him?

My phone shrilled. Vicki.

"Hey."

"Did I wake you?" Vicki's voice sounded pained.

"No."

"Oh, good." She blustered a breath. "I've had several people from the College contact me—"

"Who?"

"Cindy, Anita, and Sandra. Anita dropped over some freezer meals for you this morning, and Cindy said she had something she wanted to pass onto you but didn't know your address."

"And Sandra?" I had disregarded all of Sandra Fishbourne's phone calls and texts, but knew I needed to contact her soon. No one ignored Principal Marsden's assistant for long.

"She needs to know what you want to do."

I would like to know what I wanted to do too.

"You have six weeks of accrued personal leave remaining. Did you want to use all of it? She needs to cover your classes, Bee."

"I know," I whispered. Not answering Sandra's messages inconvenienced staff and students. But my life was one huge inconvenience, and I struggled to summon a care for their woes.

"She also wanted to know if you intended to take a longer break by using your long service leave." Something clacked on Vicki's end of the call. "Or are you thinking of returning to work?"

A chill shot down my spine, and I pressed against the softness of the couch, wrapping Matt's windcheater closer to my body.

"Bee?"

"I'm not thinking anything, to be honest."

"I understand. I really do." She blew out a breath. "Why don't I tell Sandra you want to take another month of personal leave, then you can decide in the next few weeks what you want to do?"

"Okay." Another month made no difference to the decimation of my heart.

"Done."

I grabbed my mug and sipped my tea.

"Would you like to come over for dinner tonight? Or tomorrow night? Nicholas is happy to pick you up on his way home from work."

Dinner without Matt. Sitting at his best friend's table without him. No thanks. Staying with Vicki last week had been different. Like a grief-filled nightmare bubble. Returning to "do dinner" without Matt would be difficult now the bubble had burst and reality needled its way into everyday life.

"You're welcome to come over on Friday night too if you wanted."

Friday night was Family Night at the Jacobsens. Would Matt and I have started our own Family Night once our baby was older? I rested my palm on my stomach.

"We just want to make sure you're okay," Vicki whispered, her voice hitching.

"I know. I… just don't want to go out." My gaze drifted to Matt's recliner. How could this be my life?

"Could I drop by on Thursday morning? I can pop Anita's meals in your freezer."

"Sure." Saying no would make no difference with Vicki. She had a house key and would use it.

"Great. Message me if you need anything, okay?"

"Okay."

"Love you, Bee."

"Bye." I disconnected the call, popped my phone on the coffee table, and nuzzled my face in the soft neckline of Matt's windcheater. His faint scent, mixed with my unwashed body, drifted up my nostrils. Thank God I had forgotten to do the laundry in Matt's final week, but how long would his scent remain on his clothes?

Tears stung the backs of my eyes. Would I recognise the gravity of the moment I sniffed my final whiff of Matt, whenever that happened? And what of our baby? Would he or she never benefit from being enveloped in the comfort of Matt's scent? Once I lost his smell and forgot the sound of his voice, the sole reminder of Matt's existence would be our child.

I needed to tell Vicki about the baby. And somehow tell my sister that my husband was dead.

"Morning!" Vicki elbowed my front door open, arms laden with shopping bags and mail, and kicked the door closed behind her. "Your letterbox was overflowing."

"Thanks." I peeled myself off the couch and grabbed the pile of mail from her outstretched hands.

"Sorry I'm here later than last night's guestimate. Nicholas was called to an emergency and needed me to return home for a delivery after the school and kindergarten drop offs." Vicki dumped the shopping bags on the kitchen bench and unloaded food into my freezer, fridge, and pantry.

"No need to apologise." I filled the kettle with water, flipped it on, and settled on a bar stool.

Vicki flattened and smoothed her cloth grocery bags, piled them on the benchtop, and eyed me. "You look…"

I glanced at my shirt—Matt's work shirt—and leggings ensemble. "What?"

"Like a grieving wife." Vicki's green-blue eyes softened

despite her piercing gaze. "Everyone's concerned for you."

"Pretty sure that's normal. I've been a widow for thirteen days."

Vicki scrunched her brow. "A widow who's lost a lot of weight. Have you been eating?"

"When I feel like it." I shrugged. My relationship with food was strained. Too many memories of meals and snacks I had joyfully created for Matt.

"You need to eat."

My little one also needed nutrients to survive. If Vicki knew about the baby, she would force-feed me. How could I tell her now?

"What is it?" Vicki walked around the bench, lowered to an adjacent stool, and touched my shoulder.

Tell her.

"I can see by your face something is wrong."

"You read me too well." Matt had the same superpower. How could I go on without him?

Vicki squeezed my shoulder.

I sucked in a deep breath and straightened. "I'm pregnant."

Vicki stared, face slack, before a huge grin split her features. "Truly?"

I nodded and slumped. "Ten weeks and four days. Roughly."

She wrapped her arms around me, pressed me close, and held me tight. "Did Matt know?"

"Yes," I croaked through my thickening throat. "We planned to tell you at nine weeks but …"

Her arms gripped tighter. "I know now."

I grasped onto her emotional support and sucked in her warmth, thankful Vicki had responded well. No finger pointing or "why didn't you tell me sooner" remarks. How had I doubted my friend?

The kettle whistled.

Vicki pulled away. "Get comfy on the couch. I'll be there soon."

I wiped my wet cheeks with my fingers and settled on the couch cushion which had shaped to my body after days of constant use.

Vicki handed me a cup of tea and a shortbread before settling beside me.

"I have an ultrasound next week." I nibbled the dry cookie.

My friend stilled. "Want me to come with you?"

I nodded and blew on my tea. Who else could I stand to share this moment with now Matt had abandoned me? Abandoned us.

"Send me the details."

"I'll text you later."

"Diana had her eighteen-week ultrasound." Vicki sipped her tea.

I forced my face and tone into a pleasant smile. "How'd it go?"

"The sonographer was happy with the baby's measurements and growth. They also found out the gender." She beamed.

Play the game, Belinda. You can do it. "Girl or boy?"

"A girl!" Vicki's voice trembled with a squeal. "Jonathan is going to be besotted."

"As is Nick. He's going to be the most protective grandfather in history."

Vicki chuckled. "I think he's still getting over his baby being married, let alone pregnant."

A comfortable silence permeated the room, and I finished drinking my tea. My gaze drifted to Matt's recliner, and a ball of heat simmered in my chest. That boy had destroyed my marriage and added a strenuous burden to this pregnancy. To my future. *Our* future. I gritted my teeth and controlled my breaths.

I hoped that druggie boy's future burned into ashes.

"Come to church with me on Sunday."

Church? My heartbeat accelerated. Church was the last place I wanted to be. Memories of Matt's funeral pummelled my brain, stripping my mind of any pleasant thoughts once associated with the place.

"I think it'd be good for you." Vicki extracted the empty mug from my hand, stood, and tidied the kitchen. "See some friendly faces and let people love on you."

"I don't know."

She retrieved a wheel of brie from the fridge, sliced several pieces, and layered them on a side plate with some crackers. "Will you think about it?"

"Okay."

Vicki poured a glass of sparking apple juice, handed me the plate of cheese and crackers, and deposited the juice on a coffee table coaster.

"I'm not hungr—"

"Just try. For me. Nibble and nap. Please?" Her eyes shimmered with tears.

I placed a slice of crumbly cheddar on a cheesy cracker and bit into the tiny morsel. My tastebuds danced.

"Is there anything else I can do for you? Elijah's kindergarten session ends in twenty minutes." Vicki reached for the pile of mail and pushed it closer to me.

My sister's face swam into my vision, and I groaned.

"What is it?" Vicki furrowed her brow. "Want me to see if Diana can get him?"

"No, no." I foraged for my mobile phone, found Alison's message, and showed Vicki the screen. "Here."

Her eyes widened. "Wow. Can't she understand you're grieving?"

"She doesn't know."

"What?" Vicki squinted and shook her head.

"I guess I forgot to tell her." My voice quavered. I was the worst sister.

"You haven't told her about Matt?" She dropped to the couch beside me.

"No." Tears stung my eyes. "I … just … how do I tell her? I don't know if I can deal with her drama right now."

Vicki reached out and squeezed my shoulder. "I could call her if you like?"

"Would you?" Yep, definitely the worst big sister in the history of sisterhood.

"Anything for you, Bee." She whipped her phone from her pocket and copied Alison's contact details.

I flopped back against the couch, a weight lifting from my shoulders. "Thank you," I whispered.

"Message me if you need anything." Vicki kissed my temple and stood.

"Will do." I smiled at my friend and watched her go. After a few more bites of the nicest snack I had eaten in a while, I thumbed through the mail. A gas bill. Several condolence cards. Two "To the household" unsolicited letters, and an express post letter from a Melbourne GPO address with a sticker on the back which read "This envelope contains sensitive information. You may prefer to be in the company of a loved one when reading its content."

I furrowed my brow, ripped open the envelope, and extracted the paper.

Matt's death certificate.

My vision blurred, and I placed the letter beside me with shaky fingers.

Even the government accepted his death. When would I?

I drooped against the couch and closed my eyes, determined to dream of my husband one more time.

CHAPTER ELEVEN
In Search of Solitude

I startled awake on Saturday morning with sandy eyes and a gummy mouth, my heart pacing in time with my ringing mobile phone. "Hullo?"

"I woke you again, didn't I?"

"Who is this?" I rasped and squinted at my bedside clock. Ten past ten.

"Leif Salverson from Bendigo Bank."

"Oh." Him again.

"I apologise for waking you."

"Haven't you got something better to do on a Saturday?" I stretched and yawned.

"I'm the Branch Manager, so I live to serve the community. Even on days the bank is officially closed."

Officially closed? "Then how did Matt score a Saturday appointment?"

"He had friends in high places, and I have no life. I usually work on paperwork most Saturdays."

"That's pretty sad." I scrubbed my palm down my face, sat up, and threw the bed covers off. Not that my life was any better.

"It is what it is." He cleared his throat. "Is now a good time to chat? I'll be brief."

"Go ahead." I meandered to my walk-in-robe and slipped into

my dressing gown and moccies.

"Great. The next interest payment is almost due on your home loan and—"

"I thought Matt said it was paid out?"

"The funds are in the account, but because the account hasn't been wound down, the interest is negligible."

"Right." I padded along the hallway, desperate to ignore the slight churning in my stomach, and opened the kitchen blinds. This was why Matt handled our finances. He knew what he was doing.

"Has Matt's death certificate arrived yet? I need you to sign some transfer papers to avoid paying interest."

"It arrived a few days ago." I checked the water level in the kettle, switched it on, and pulled a mug from the cupboard.

"I can drop by on my way home later today."

"Today?" My chest tightened, and my stomach somersaulted.

"Would next week be better?" Leif's voice dropped.

No week was better to make serious decisions. "I just … I …"

"I'll do all the work for you, Belinda, and explain everything to you when I visit. Or if you feel more comfortable, you can come to my office here in Swan Hill?"

Driving—or asking someone to drive me—sounded worse.

"Whatever is best for you."

Matt living was best for me. I wrapped my arms around my waist and leaned against the kitchen cupboards. I had to deal with this matter. Why not get it over and done with? "Today will be fine."

"I'll finish here around three-thirty, four o'clock at the latest, so I'll get to you sometime after five."

"Okay."

"I can give you my number in case—"

"That won't be necessary. Bye."

"Good bye, Belinda."

I ended the call, brewed tea—which I wished were coffee—and invested my day sharpening my couch potato skills.

Someone tapped against the front door halfway through an

episode of *The Dropout*.

I pressed Pause, hoping they would go away.

Another knock echoed into the lounge room.

I stood, tightened my dressing gown waist ties, and opened the wooden door.

A familiar-looking guy in a suit, with a pleasant smile and coppery, slightly tousled hair, stood behind the security screen door holding a briefcase and a large brown paper bag. "Leif Salverson at your service."

Oh, shoot. The bank guy. How I had forgotten about him? I glanced down at my tea-stained dressing gown.

"Is that you, Belinda?" His smile faltered, and he glanced over his shoulder. "Or have I gone to the wrong address?"

"No, you're all good." I unlocked and opened the door.

His eyes widened before a kind smile graced his lips, and he stepped inside. "Thanks for letting me drop by."

Seemed I had little choice. I closed the door and pointed toward the kitchen. "That way."

His gaze travelled around the living areas before settling on my face. "You have a beautiful home. Your kitchen looks impressive from here."

"Thanks. Matt blessed me with a kitchen upgrade a few years ago." An amazing, generous upgrade which complied to FSANZ food standards code, not that I could stomach baking anymore.

"You enjoy cooking?"

I did. But now? I gripped the back of a dining chair. "I've catered for several local events over the years."

Leif lowered his briefcase to the dining table, rummaged in the brown paper bag, and removed several takeaway containers. "Hope you don't mind, but I brought along some food. I've hardly eaten today."

I shrugged. "Help yourself."

He narrowed his eyes, tilted his head, and stared at me. "Maybe we've met at a function. You look familiar."

"Maybe."

"You catered for any of Nick Jacobsen's parties?" He placed several napkins and plastic cutlery in the centre of the table.

Did everyone on earth know Nick? "Yeah, I helped cater his fortieth birthday, his wedding, and a bunch of other things for him and Vicki."

"Small world." Leif removed his suit jacket and lay it over the back of Matt's dining chair. "Did you make those delicious double-choc brownies I often dream about?"

"Yeah." Matt's favourite. Would I be able to stomach a brownie ever again?

His eyes and grin widened. "You're talented."

"Thanks," I whispered and dropped my gaze.

He cleared his throat. "I bought enough food to share."

"Not that hungry." I slid onto the nearest seat and willed him to sit in any seat other than Matt's designated chair.

Leif pulled out another seat and settled on the chair.

Thank You, God.

He cuffed his shirt sleeves and piled food onto a paper plate. "I have paperwork for all of Matt's accounts and your joint home loan account."

I eyed the cardboard box of fat potato wedges. "Benanu's?"

He grinned. "I'm not in Tellarine often, but when I am, I like eating there. Great atmosphere and fabulous food."

Matt loved Benanu's too. *Everyone* loved Benanu's.

Leif pushed the food containers closer to me. "Mind if I pray?"

"Go ahead."

He prayed and dug into his dinner with gusto.

I nibbled on potato wedges and crumbed chicken tenders, my biggest meal in weeks.

After I had nibbled a few more crumbs and Leif sated his appetite, the bank manager extracted a bunch of paperwork from his briefcase, and discussed each account. He quoted large figures, pointed out fine print, and marked each place I needed to sign.

His explanations blew through my ears and slipped out of my brain.

All I could see was a man doing Matt's job. Telling me things Matt should be telling me, sitting at Matt's dining table. How could I have thought sitting here with a strange man would be a good thing? Alone, in my home, with a man I hardly knew?

"All right? I also suggest paying the nominal storage fee and Bendigo can keep your title deed secure."

What? I pressed my fingers against my thighs. I had to get him out of my house. "You're the expert, so let's do that."

"Wonderful." He leaned closer, pointed to a blank line, and handed me his pen. "Sign here."

I leaned away from him and scribbled my signature—or something that might resemble my signature—on all the pages he pointed to until my hand ached. What had I gotten myself into?

"Great." He tapped the papers into alignment against the table and offered a wide grin.

Stop smiling and go away.

He stood and gathered all of his things. "Would you like to keep the leftovers?"

"You have them." I rose and pretended to look like I cared.

Leif gathered everything into the brown paper bag, including the rubbish. "I'll pencil in a follow-up for twelve to eighteen months' time, but feel free to contact me before then."

"Okay." So many words he spoke which meant nothing to my buzzing ears.

"Thanks for giving me a moment of your time." Leif walked to the front door. "I'll post hard copies to you next week."

"Thanks." Go already!

"Goodnight, Belinda." He tipped his head, opened the wooden and security doors, and stepped outside.

"Bye." I locked the doors with shaky fingers, fisted my hands, and flopped back on the couch, ready for another evening of mind-numbing television.

♥ ♥ ♥ ♥ ♥ ♥ ♥

Vicki Jacobsen: I MISSED YOU ON SUNDAY. LOOKING FORWARD TO TOMORROW! LOVE YOU, BEE. XX

I had woken on Sunday morning still shaken from my meeting with the banker, so had skipped church—not that I had felt like going before Saturday evening—and spent most of Sunday and Monday on the couch. Today, dressed in leggings and one of Matt's jumpers, I ventured into the backyard to read a book on the bench seat.

My stomach gurgled, and I checked the time on my phone. Lunchtime. I replied to Vicki's text with a peppy "LOOKING FORWARD TO THE ULTRASOUND TOO!" and moseyed indoors for some sustenance.

Halfway through my vegemite toast, someone banged on the front door.

I sighed, stuffed a few more bites into my face, and pulled myself from the couch.

Another bang.

Talk about impatient. I padded toward the door.

More banging.

"I'm coming!" *Sheesh, hold your horses.*

Voices sounded on my front verandah.

I unlocked and opened the wooden door.

"Surprise!" Alison grinned on my front step, her strawberry-blonde hair chopped short around her ears like a pixie. She stood beside a lanky guy with dirty brown dreadlocks and piercings all over his face.

"What're you doing here?" My heart pounded. The last time I had seen my sister was at my wedding.

"Rob and I came to see how you're doing." She yanked on a wheeled suitcase which lay at her feet. "Aren't you going to let us in?"

"Oh. Sure." I unlocked and opened the security door, and stepped backwards before Alison's suitcase rolled over my bare toes.

"Nice place." Alison abandoned her suitcase in the middle of the walkway and wandered into the living room.

"Thanks for having us." Rob shouldered a backpack and pulled Alison's suitcase toward the kitchen.

Thanks for having us? What the heck was going on? I locked the doors and scurried to where my "guests" now lounged on my couch.

"This place is a palace compared to your last one." My sister scrolled through Netflix movies on my TV.

I wrenched the controller from her hand. "Why're you here, Ali? You've had no interest visiting when I've invited you for Christmas each year, and you're never been enthusiastic when I suggested we visit you."

Alison raised her eyebrow. "Well, I'm here now."

"And I'd like to know why you think it's a good time to visit now." I narrowed my eyes and stared at my sister.

She smirked at her boyfriend. "Figured you'd lie to me if I called and asked how you were."

I collapsed on the end of the couch, sighed, and ran my fingers through my knotted hair. "There's such a thing as video calls, you know. Would've been cheaper too." And less stressful for me.

"But far less fun." My sister leaned against Rob—who appeared to be a decade younger than her—and snatched the controller from my loose fingers. She clicked on a movie and grinned at me.

Whatever. I gritted my teeth and stood. "I'm going to have a nap. Don't break anything."

♥ ♥ ♥ ♥ ♥ ♥

I woke hours later to the smell of … something burning? I jolted in bed, gasping, and wildly kicked my legs from the tangled sheets before I launched from my bedroom in the direction of the kitchen.

"There she is. Have a good nap?" Alison stood at the island bench holding a tray of what I imagined were once cookies before they were baked to death.

I rubbed my eyes, flipped the range hood exhaust fan to maximum, and swung the back door wide open. "What're you doing?"

"Baking." My sister hummed and removed each cinder cookie from the tray to the cooling rack.

"That's debatable." I stormed to the front of the house, opened the heavy wooden door, and returned to the smoky kitchen.

"Not everyone is good at baking like you." Alison hmphed and deposited the empty tray into a sink of soapy water.

Then maybe you should leave it to the bakers to bake. I opened the wide kitchen windows and prayed the smell would leave.

The laundry door creaked and slammed shut.

I exhaled, opened the door, and slid an empty laundry basket in front.

"I'm sorry, Bindy-Boo."

I stilled. Had my sister just … apologised?

"I wanted to do something nice for you."

Nice for me? I turned and eyed her. Was she sick?

"I know we barrelled in earlier without an invitation, but after your friend called and said the demi sex god was de—"

"Don't call him that."

"And you were pregnant with his baby, I just had to do something."

But visit? Any normal sister would have phoned or at least texted. Not shown up on her grieving sister's doorstep two days after hearing the news.

"I figured something must've been up. Well, Rob thought something might've been wrong when I was telling him what a crap sister you turned out to be, for you to outright ignore me."

"Not everything is about you, Ali." I clenched my fingers and slowed my breathing.

"A shame too." She grinned and scrubbed the baking tray. "So that's why I'm here. To support my sister in her time of need. I thought it would be nice to help you for a change."

Alison acknowledged the many times I had protected her? Bailed her out? And I thought she was oblivious to everything related to me and our whacked relationship.

"Don't look so shocked. You're not the only adult in the family."

You could've fooled me. I checked the kettle water level and switched it on. "It's nice you want to help, but you could've called first."

"Rob said the same thing." Alison shrugged and popped the tray on the drying rack.

I glanced around the kitchen and lounge room areas. "Where is he?"

"He went on a nature walk. Had to get his zen back after your rude welcome."

My rude welcome?

"You could stand to be a bit nicer to him. He's the one that reminds me of your birthday after all. And bought your Christmas gift last year. The least you can do is be grateful."

My chest tightened, and my lungs burned. My gratitude would explode with thankfulness the moment they left me alone.

Alison dried her hands and plated several ghastly cookies. "Mum says 'Hi' if you happen to care."

Adrenaline poured through my veins. I grabbed two mugs with shaky hands.

"When's the last time you spoke with her or Dad?"

Not long enough ago. Matt and I were cliché with our parent issues.

Alison drained the dirty dishwater. "She's out of prison and rehab, and selling Tupperware, can you believe?"

Conning buyers, no doubt. I dropped tea bags into the mugs and covered them with hot water.

"Dad's still living the layabout life and asks for money anytime we chat."

I huffed a breath. The last time Daddy dearest and I "chatted" about money, he had trapped me in a headlock, crushing my windpipe, telling me to return the twenty bucks I had supposedly stolen from his wallet, only to realise he drank it away at the pub the night before.

"It's a shame Matt's gone. He'd have been a heck of a lot better at parenting than our—"

"Here's your tea." I shoved her mug across the benchtop, grabbed mine, and exited the kitchen in search of my comfy couch seat.

"Thanks." Alison blew across the surface of her drink and sipped. "Mmm, you remembered. Just the way I like it."

How could I forget the hundreds of things I did as a teenager and young adult to keep my little sister alive? My survival instincts—what I later came to see as God's guidance—were smarter and stronger than our parents' abilities combined. What twelve-year-old would leave her six-year-old sister to fend for herself?

"You have your ultrasound tomorrow?" Alison lowered to the seat beside me and offered me a crispy, charred cookie.

"No thanks." A soft smile played on my lips. I lay my palm over my belly and glanced at the blank television screen. My official introduction with our baby would occur tomorrow.

"I'd like to come."

I whipped my head to the right and blinked at my sister. Why would I want her there? Was she for real?

"Since Matt's not here, you need family there."

I leaned toward the couch arm. "I will have family there. Vicki."

She snorted. "She's not family, Bindy-Boo. *I* am. What time is your appointment?"

I suspected my sister had a warped view of what family was meant to be. Vicki was more family to me than my sister had been in a long time. I sipped my tea and mulled over my words. Matt would remind me to walk in love.

"Because I currently don't have my licence—"

"Alison."

"But Rob can drive us."

"Alison." I counted my breaths.

"He might be young and fabulous in the sack, but he know—
"

"Alison!"

She stared at me. "What?"

"You're not going."

"Where?"

"To the ultrasound."

"Why not?"

"Because I can only have one person with me, and I've asked Vicki to be that person."

Alison pouted. "So un-ask her. She'll understand I'm your sister and more imp—"

"No." I stood. "I want Vicki there. End of discussion."

She rolled her eyes and shook her head. "You're even more stubborn when pregnant."

"It's my choice. Deal with it." I stormed back to my bedroom, annoyed at my sister and myself.

CHAPTER TWELVE
Obliteration

"It won't be much longer." Vicki patted my vibrating hands, which rested on my lap in the ultrasound clinic waiting room. "Thirty minutes is a standard wait time."

"Not sure why they make us take appointment times if they never stick with them."

"One of the mysteries of the medical industry." She smiled at me.

"Mrs. Briggs?" A short, rotund woman in her sixties stood beside the hallway leading to the ultrasound suites.

I stood and smiled at her.

"This way." She disappeared around the corner.

Vicki and I followed her down the rabbit warren of hallways to a private room at the rear.

"The sonographer will be with you shortly." The woman pointed to an examination table beside a complicated-looking computer. "Please lie here, unbutton your pants, and leave them open for the sonographer to tuck in a towel."

"Sure." I loosened the top of my jeans, and Vicki assisted me into position.

Minutes later, the sonographer strode into the room with a folder in her arm. "Mrs. Briggs, it's lovely to meet you. I'm Morrigan, and I'll be performing your eleven-week ultrasound."

"Wonderful." I glanced at Vicki and smiled, despite the nervous energy bouncing inside my stomach.

"Just give me a few moments to set up and we'll be on our way."

The next fifteen minutes were spent lying on my back, bladder pressed with the cold, gel-covered instrument Morrigan wielded. I stared at the monitor displaying images of my insides, trying to decipher whatever it was on the screen. A limb? I glanced at the sonographer, but her face gave nothing away. Her light conversation had stalled five minutes earlier.

Vicki squeezed my hand.

I turned to my friend and noted lines had formed in her brow. What was going on?

"Okay." Morrigan pushed out a long breath and wiped the gel from my belly. "You'll need to book an appointment with your GP as soon as you can. The results will be sent over within the next two hours."

"I don't understand." That was it? I furrowed my brow. No fancy snapshot keepsakes? What of the excitement about showing body parts? Or 3D printing?

Morrigan searched my gaze. "I'm sorry, I can't say much more. Please see your GP ASAP."

"Thank you." Vicki slid my T-shirt into place and helped me upright. "We appreciate your time."

What had happened? I stood, clutching my best friend's arm, and followed her back to reception.

"Just sit here for a moment." Vicki stepped toward the front desk, whispered to the receptionist, and handed over her credit card.

Another payment? I thought we had paid for the ultrasound when we checked in?

Vicki extracted her phone, dialled a number, and spoke with someone.

I leaned my head against the wall and closed my eyes. Was something not right with the baby and now I had to have a doctor check? I slid my palm along my belly and prayed everything would be okay.

"Good to see you, Victoria." Dr. Fallow closed his consultation room door and lowered to the oversized leather chair on wheels behind his wooden desk. "How're you doing, Belinda?"

"I'm okay." Would be better if I knew why I needed to be here.

He glanced at his computer screen before directing his piercing green-hazel gaze in my direction. "This morning's ultrasound didn't … go as I had anticipated."

I agreed with his sentiment one hundred percent.

He ran his fingers through his short-cropped salt-and-pepper hair and sighed. "I'm sorry to inform you you're not pregnant."

What?

Vicki grasped my shoulder.

"The ultrasound revealed an anembryonic pregnancy with suspected Placenta Percreta."

I scrunched my face. "So I *am* pregnant?"

"No. It's what some call a blighted ovum, where a fertilised egg implants, and an embryonic sac forms and grows, but the embryo fails to develop."

No baby. There was no baby inside of me. Just a sac?

"I'm sorry, Belinda." Dr. Fallow pursed his lips together before returning his attention to his computer. "We will need to book you in for a routine dilatation and curettage."

"She needs a D and C?" Vicki's voice wavered.

Dr. Fallow nodded. "We need to remove the unnecessary tissue promptly. I'm also concerned about the placenta implantation. The scan revealed shadows near your bladder which shouldn't be there. Removing everything now instead of waiting for a spontaneous miscarriage is vital for your health."

Having Matt's baby was vital for my health. But once again,

what I wanted failed to happen.

Dr. Fallow phoned a local day hospital and booked in my procedure for early next week.

I stared at my hands balled in my lap. Why had I not booked in an earlier ultrasound like Dr. Fallow had suggested long ago? Matt could have been there with me, and we would have mourned together, but at least we would have shared this pain. Now I had nothing. My final connection to Matt … severed. My vision blurred. At least my useless body knew how to produce more tears.

Dr. Fallow wrote on a card and offered it to me.

Vicki grabbed the appointment card from him. "Is there anything else we need to do?"

He said something, but I missed the words. His mouth moved, again and again.

I turned toward the foggy light of the window, my face wet, and settled into my latest loss.

My mobile phone shrieked with an incoming call, brightening the darkness of my closed-up bedroom. Two days until surgery.

"Hello?"

"Hi, Mrs. Briggs, this is Niles Stanton. I'm a Coroner Support Service Registrar and wanted to inform you of the findings relating to your late husband's death."

I shuffled upright and leaned against the bed head. "Go ahead." Please have good news. I needed good news.

"The coroner has ruled the initial stab wound was the contributing cause of death, and the youth in question has been charged with delinquent manslaughter."

Good! "And the hospital?"

"Has been cleared of negligence."

"H-how can that be? They missed a freaking nick in Matt's heart!"

The registrar cleared his throat. "The nick was microscopic and difficult for any machine to detect. The hospital is not at fault."

I huffed a breath. How had they evaded justice?

"I've written to Larry Stockton, the lawyer in … Robinvale you specified in your paperwork, and his office will liaise with you regarding future court proceedings. All the best, Mrs. Briggs, and my condolences on your loss."

I tossed my phone toward the end of my bed and slid under the covers. Tiny shards of afternoon sunlight dotted through the top of the closed curtain. The hospital might be officially cleared of all wrongdoing, but I knew the truth. The hospital was at fault and should be paying penance for their failings.

Just like I paid penance for everyone else's choices and mistakes. Every single day.

CHAPTER THIRTEEN
The Last Straw

Sweat pooled under my armpits, slipped down my spine, and puddled underneath my knees. I clutched the sides of my assigned plastic hospital seat in all its uncomfortable glory and glanced at my two companions.

Vicki offered me one of her maternal, consoling smiles, and glanced at the wall clock. Again.

Alison chewed gum and scrolled on her phone.

"I'm sure it won't be too long," Vicki said after another glance at the clock.

Alison lifted her head and gazed at the wall. "When they removed my breast lump, I waited two hours in my surgery gown, sweating bullets."

I widened my eyes. "You had a lump removed?"

She shrugged and tilted her head in my direction. "A few years ago. Benign."

What else had happened in my sister's world that I had no idea about?

You didn't tell her about Matt. Or the baby.

I pushed the niggling thought into the ether of my frantic mind. Most of today's thoughts slipped through my brain like grains of sand.

"You'll be fine. It's a routine procedure." Alison caught my gaze for a split second and returned to scrolling on her phone.

I supposed this was more sympathy than I usually received from my sister.

Vicki stretched in her seat. "Did you want me to—"

"You're up, Mrs. Briggs!" The pert nurse who had deposited me in this smaller waiting room almost an hour ago bounded into the room with a grin.

"Can we wait here?" Vicki asked.

"You'll need to wait downstairs, I'm afraid." The nurse pointed to a tall man pushing a gurney. "Pop on, love, and we'll take you to theatre."

My heartbeat pummelled in my chest and between my ears.

Vicki hugged me. "I'll be praying," she whispered in my ear before releasing me.

I sat on the gurney and allowed the staff to position me into place.

"See you afterwards." Alison stood beside Vicki and waved.

The hospital staff escorted me to theatre, each step and wheel squeak echoing in the quiet hallway like a death knell to my future.

Fear reigned as king in my heart.

I was wheeled into position, where a team of people moved about the room, talking amongst themselves.

A middle-aged man, trussed up in his medical uniform with a swarthy forehead and dark eyes, stood beside me. "I'll be overseeing your procedure this afternoon." His voice muffled behind his face mask. "First up, we'll put this oxygen mask over your nose and mouth"—he lifted the breathing apparatus—"and I ask you to breathe deeply. This will render you unconscious so we can start. Okay?"

My throat tightened, and I nodded. *Please, God, help me.*

He lowered the oxygen mask over my face.

Was this thing meant to be such a firm fit? My pulse skyrocketed, and I sucked in a panicky breath, my eyelids fluttering closed in the surrounding darkness.

♥ ♥ ♥ ♥ ♥ ♥ ♥

I awoke from a deep sleep and sucked in a painful breath.

Good grief, was my entire body meant to throb like I had been dragged across a southern Spanish bullring, trampled by a seven-hundred kilo bull, and tossed onto an adjacent cobbled street? I groaned, desperate to lift my heavy eyelids and admit some light.

Machinery beeped nearby. Perhaps I was still in the recovery room? I had never been under an anaesthetic before, so had no idea how I would respond. So far, everything seemed sluggish. My movements, my thoughts. Slower than sluggish. Slothish.

I cracked my eyelids open, amazed how exhausting the simple movement had been. Anaesthetic was not my friend.

"Bee?" Vicki's soft voice trampled my sensitive eardrums.

I grimaced and inched my eyelids up.

The room seemed less like what I imagined a recovery room to resemble and more like a hospital room at Mildura Base Hospital. Tubes sprung from my body into the machines near my bed.

This was a simple procedure?

Something dinged near my head.

"How're you feeling?" Vicki's warm hand enveloped my cold digits.

"Been better." My throat ached. I blinked and gazed up at my friend. Were her eyes red?

Alison stepped close. "You almost died."

"What?" My voice scratched, and I scrunched my forehead.

"Some rare blood clotting disord—"

"Thanks for pressing the buzzer," a brunette in a Mildura Hospital uniform stepped into my room.

A thin man followed in her wake. "Mrs. Briggs, I'm Dr. Stanbill, one of the ICU registrars."

ICU? I shifted my head ever-so-slightly, moaned, and surveyed the space.

"Unfortunately, you suffered from serious complications during your dilatation and curettage, so the Robinvale clinic sent you here for further surgery. The growth connecting your placenta and bladder was disconnected, but your blood failed to clot, and we performed an emergency, life-saving hysterectomy."

Emergency … no. *Please, God, no.*

Vicki sniffled beside me.

"I'm sorry it came to this, but it was imperative for your health we performed the surgery."

Voices and machinery sounds faded into the background as my heart hollowed. No uterus meant no children. At all.

My chest squeezed, and my breaths shortened. Pointless. Everything was pointless.

Blood whooshed between my ears, blocking out the dismal apologies and heartfelt condolences.

"Thank the Lord you're alive," Vicki whispered, tears glossing her eyes.

Thank the Lord? I crushed the rough waffle-textured hospital blanket between my fists. Thank the Lord? Blood boiled through my veins, scorching my skin. My airways thickened, and the edges of my vision blurred.

What good was God to me? My children were dead, my husband was dead, and now my reproductive system had died.

Where was God when I needed Him? He chose not to lift His hand for me.

He allowed the dream killer to annihilate my soul.

Fire proliferated through my limbs and radiated to my vital organs. My fisted hands burned, and I squeezed the bed linen between my aching fingers. External pain was easier to process than my internal agony.

What else was left to lose? My thoughts hitched from the stability of their usual secure space in my mind and free-fell into a black abyss. To a place where I cursed God and wished to die.

How could He abandon me like this? God knew my dream to

have children. A child. Was it too much to ask for one freaking kid? But, no, my uterus was thrown into the hospital scrap heap along with my dreams.

I laughed bitterly. Here I had thought my life was already at the point of no return. But I had been wrong.

Life *could* get worse.

I closed my eyes against the bright ICU lights and sympathy-filled eyes. If this was how God cared for me, He could get stuffed.

I was done with church. With pretending. With this life He had "blessed me with." God could take a flying leap off a tall cliff into a shallow lake.

I was done.

CHAPTER FOURTEEN
Hiatus

One week. An entire seven days had passed since my dream for children died.

I punched the couch cushion beside me. Not that I had a *husband* to have a baby with. Because that would be too much for *me* to have. All I could be trusted with was a crappy job, which had harboured a murderer, and a bunch of ungrateful snots-for-students who would be better off tossed in the too hard basket than educated.

Thanks, world.

And how could I forget the bunch of nosy colleagues who ogled my dead husband and still blasted my phone with platitudes and commiserations.

Did they message Kyneton the Killer's parents and wish them all the best? Or tell them to drop dead?

I would tell them straight to their faces and not even flinch.

"You plotting someone's murder, Bindy-Boo?"

I jolted upright at Alison's question and met her gaze. When had she flopped on the couch?

She smirked.

"This's my normal face." I relaxed the muscles around my eyes and forehead.

"Sure."

"Why're you still here? Invading my personal space. In my home. Don't you have a house to go to?" Could my sister ever take a hint?

She snorted. "You've really turned your snark to 'High' since your surgery."

"And you're still a huge pain in the butt."

She choked on a laugh.

Did she think I was being funny?

"I used to love it when you got cheesed off like this. You'd say the funniest things while looking like you wanted to punch someone in the face. Was great entertainment during my teen years."

"Glad to know my protecting you entertained you." I glanced at the ceiling. "Would you mind leaving the lounge room? I want to stare at the wall in peace."

"Not happening, sisterino. Your friend messaged me today, said you were ignoring her."

"Which friend?" Did I have or want a friend at the moment?

"Vicki. She's coming over in"—Alison checked her fancy step-counting watch—"fifteen minutes, so be on your best behaviour."

I gritted my teeth. My sister was not only a pain in the rear end, she cared little about my desire to be alone. Because it was so selfish of me to want to crawl into a hole and never come out.

Maybe I could stuff her in the hole and get my house back.

"You really are a mess, but we'll have you fixed in no time."

Fixed. Fixed? I shot to my feet, leaned toward my sister, and pointed at her smug face. "You can't fix your own pathetic existence, so how're you going to fix mine? You're in your thirties, for crying out loud, and you still called me to borrow money like an ungrateful teenager."

Alison narrowed her eyes.

"You haven't even said how sorry you were that he died. Do you even care? Or are you crushed because now your sex fantasies with my husband are dead like him? Do you care anything about how I feel? Or do you and our worthless parents laugh about me? That I'm too gullible and living in a dreamworld?" I straightened and thrust my arms into the space around me. "'Cause this is certainly the world I dreamed of! Of dead babies, a dead husband, and the death of all I wanted in life. But what would you care? It's always been about you and will always be about you."

I stormed to my bedroom and locked the door, my cavernous, black heart rigid from rigor mortis.

Someone knocked on my bedroom door.

I glanced at Matt's bedside clock and closed the pages of the time travel novel I had barely read since marching into my room forty-five minutes earlier.

"Bee? You awake?" Vicki's sweet voice permeated the empty space between us.

I slowed my breaths and lay still. Matt had thought the creakiness of the bed base was hilarious, but any movement would give me away. I cared about my friend—possibly more than I cared for myself at this point—but I needed time to regroup. And I knew her first suggestion would be to reach out to the church community Matt and I had been an integral part of for many years.

No, thank you.

"Bee?"

Church folk had an annoying habit of seeing the best in any situation. They would find something positive in my current— pointless—life, and I could not deal with them right now.

Maybe never.

Matt would chide me for throwing out the baby with the bathwater, but since he left me a month ago to fend for myself, he no longer had a say.

Footsteps shuffled away from my bedroom door until silence filled its place.

Silence filled all the holes inside and out.

I waited another thirty minutes before sneaking from my bedroom into the kitchen. My appetite had shrunk again, so I filled a glass with water and drank every drop.

"Vicki just left." Alison padded from the front of the house and dropped onto a bar stool. "We've decided you need to see Dr. Fallow."

I crossed my arms and leaned against the sink benchtop. "We've decided. Right."

Her eyes burned with an unfamiliar fire. "You might not care about yourself right this minute, but we do. You're spiralling and throwing your best punches to get rid of us, but it won't work."

I stared at her, my eyes hard. Flinty.

"You have an appointment tomorrow afternoon at two p.m., whether you like it or not."

Whatever.

"And I'll break your bedroom door down if you pull another 'hide and lock yourself in your room' stunt."

"Yes, Mum." I spat the spiteful name from my lips, turned, and marched back to the silence of my bedroom.

I stared across my backyard and inhaled a long breath of cool mid-May air. Since seeing Dr. Fallow last week and taking the prescribed antidepressants, my life seemed … less bleak.

A robin trotted across the top of Matt's covered barbeque, wiggled its tail, and glided to the fruit trees Matt had lovingly cared for. Matt's success with the garden had surprised me since his brain worked best when staring at a screen or creating something more technical than dirt and seedlings.

I missed him so much. Would I ever get used to him being gone?

I shifted on the bench seat and sucked in several more lungfuls of fresh air. Everywhere I turned, I recognised God's fingertips or footprints dotting my space. He sure knew how to create wonders in the world. Too bad He had no time to keep my world afloat.

I stood, stretched and opened the back door.

A strange smell whacked me across the face.

What on earth? I closed and locked the door, slid through the crowded laundry, and halted in my tracks.

Alison leaned toward the oven—my oven—with oven mitts and an odd look on her face.

"What're you doing now?" I slumped onto a bar stool and rested my weary head in my palms.

"Baking brownies."

Please, no. Not those disgusting vegan rubbish brownies which taste nothing like chocolate or butter … or anything remotely appealing.

Alison dropped the Pyrex dish onto the cooling rack, turned off the oven, and beamed at me. "No nasty butter or oil, and it's filled with fabulous things like black beans, flaxseeds, banana, and walnuts."

Oh, what joy those words stirred inside my bakers' heart. I refrained from gagging at the thought of her brownie monstrosity touching my lips.

"Smells good, baby." Rob sauntered into the kitchen, dreadlocks swinging behind him.

Had his sense of smell died along with his tastebuds?

"Thanks, hun." Alison pulled the oven mitts from her hands and wrapped her arms around Rob's neck. "We should get an oven like this one. I could fit the dish in longways or sideways. In fact, I could bake a quadruple batch and fit both glass containers on one shelf."

My poor, abused oven.

"That'd be awesome! Have you looked up the oven model online? My man Colm might be able to get it for a better price."

"A great idea." Alison grinned and leaned in for a kiss.

"Then we can invite him over for vegan buffalo chicken wings and brownies."

"What?" Vegan buffalo chicken wings. Vegan. Chicken

wings? I shook my head, desperate to understand the gibberish these two constantly talked.

"What?" Alison leaned against Rob's chest.

I scrunched my brow. "How can you have vegan chicken wings?" Who were these people?

She chuckled. "It's cauliflower."

"Then why don't you say baked cauliflower with buffalo sauce?"

Rob shrugged. "Sounds cooler."

I squinted the pain from my brain. "I thought vegans thought meat's evil? Why call faux-meat 'vegan sausages' and 'vegan chicken wings'? Just call it what it is. Soy-something or tofu or vegetables with a dipping sauce?"

"It is what it is," Rob said with a casual hand gesture.

"Exactly." I grumbled. "At least when I bake chicken wings or chocolate brownies, you know what you're getting."

Alison released her boyfriend and turned to me, hands on hips. "Yes. We know how *glorious* you are in the kitchen with your saturated fats and your heart-destroying"—she bent her fingers into air quotes–"flavour."

I bristled at her tone. "You're happy to mock me after you use my kitchen. At least I enjoy what I eat and don't need to ride a high horse when I do it!"

Alison slow clapped. "Feel better now?"

"No. I want you and your toy boy out of here. You've leeched off me for two weeks now. That's plenty long enough, don't you think?"

"I've hardly leeched off you. I've been contributing with baking and … and vacuuming."

I snorted. "You sound like a teenager. What about all the food you've eaten and destroyed with your so-called baking? You going to reimburse me for that?"

"Some of your ingredients were near their Best Before. I did you a favour baking real food for you." Her scoffing laughter grated against my last nerve.

"Real food? We just talked about how fake your food it! Calling it one thing to hide another." I had nothing against the vegan lifestyle. I just disliked how some would vilify me for my personal choices.

"At least my food won't give you a heart attack!"

"Ali." Rob shook his head and smiled apologetically at me.

"No, it'll bore my heart to death with its tasteless, fibrous wonders." I pulled my phone from my pocket and checked the calendar app. "I go back to work next week. I want you both gone on Sunday night."

"But you shouldn't be alone," Alison whispered.

Tell that to God who decided I could cope fine without anyone significant in my life.

I sighed, rubbed my eyes, and levelled a stare at my sister. "I'll be back at work. Surrounded by people. I have a freezer full of meals. I don't need squatters in my house. Or babysitters."

Alison glared at me.

Why was she struggling to revert back to her flaky self and go away?

"Fine. I'll book flights for this weekend."

"Great." Excellent. Freedom was in sight.

"Can you drive us to the airport?" She fluttered her lashes at me.

Nice try. "No. But I can drive you to the bus stop where you can take a bus to Melbourne to catch your Brisbane flight. Unless you want to catch a bus to Canberra and grab a flight there."

Alison grumbled something under her breath.

"Excellent." I eased from the island bench stool and directed my gaze between my sister and her lover. "Please make sure to leave my house as neat as it was before you set off bombs in my kitchen, laundry, and spare room."

"Neat freak," Alison whispered.

"Pain in the butt." I wandered toward the lounge room and

reclaimed my seat, a place I would soon no longer have to share with anyone.

CHAPTER FIFTEEN
Closing Another Chapter

I readjusted my handbag across my fatigued shoulder and closed my office door. Day four done and dusted. After a quick glance around the neat school kitchen, I padded to the main entry and exited my workspace.

"You're leaving early today." Cindy leaned against the Textiles room doorframe, eyed several straggling students walking by, and crossed the hallway. "You happy with how they ran your kitchen while you were away?"

When I turned up to work on Monday morning, I had spent more time avoiding memories of happier times than doing work. I was still to perform a thorough inspection of the pantry and storage cupboards. Something inside me had died with Matt. The part of me which cared about my job and doing it to the best of my ability.

I nodded. "Seems to have been handled fine in my absence."

Cindy smiled. Not her usual soft smile, but something tinged with sympathy.

I hated sympathetic smiles.

"It wasn't the same without you across the hall." She clasped her dainty hands together.

"Guess life's not the same for any of us." *C'mon, Bee, chin up. Make the effort.*

"You must miss him terribly," she whispered.

I nodded. The permanent ache in my chest comforted me.

"I really am sorry what happened."

Two senior students trundled by, their gazes flicking between me and each other, whispers on their lips.

Would students ever stop whispering when I entered a room? Or my colleagues, for that matter.

Our Monday morning staff meeting was riddled with awkward moments, hushed comments, and sympathetic looks. Just as I had feared. I hoped sometime between now and next week's meeting, someone sent out a memo telling staff to lay off their concerned gazes, or I could not guarantee my response.

I shrugged at my colleague. "Can't be helped. It's not like I can bring my dead husband back to life."

"No." She glanced down the hallway as though deep in thought.

Would the residue of my memories of Matt in these hallways ever stop calling to me?

"You're looking well, despite the circumstances." Cindy appraised my neat outfit.

"Thanks." Too bad my insides were dead and putrefying.

"Is your sister still staying with you?"

How did people know so much about my personal affairs? Seemed good news travelled fast. "No. She and her boyfriend returned to Brisbane over the weekend." Arriving home to a quiet, empty house each evening this week had been beyond wonderful.

"That's a shame. I wish my sister visited more often."

I hitched my bag against my shoulder blade.

Cindy stepped back. "I'll let you go. See you tomorrow."

"Have a great night." See, I could say something nice. Not all the lovely parts of me died with my husband and my uterus.

I strode along the hallway, my focus on my destination and not the shadows of past conversations with Matt. Past laughter. His ghost around every corner and bend. I had yet to go anywhere near the IT end of the campus. Had they removed the bloody stain from the flooring near his office? Was it too much to hope the stain was drilled into the mind of Matt's murderer so he would never be free of the shame and guilt?

What a fitting possibility.

I bounded through the exit toward the staff car park, shunted the overwhelming memories haunting the pathway, and fisted my keys in my hands. Clutching the driver's door, I threw my bag into the passenger seat and slid behind the wheel.

Matt and I had lingered in this car park many times, particularly when we were dating. We would huddle in my car and talk for ages. And kiss. Boy, that man had perfect lips attached to his perfect face.

Five weeks without his mouth on mine. Five weeks without his exhilarating touch.

Tears dripped into my lap, and I sniffed mucous back into my nostrils. I palmed my eyes and inspected the scenery. A school riddled with too many memories. A classroom with students I cared little for now. A career I could live without.

Why had I returned to school? Maybe I should quit and move on completely.

I mulled on the idea, the flavour of freedom strengthening with each thought. Annual leave and long service leave would be paid out the day I quit, so I would still have funds for the interim. Matt's life insurance would be paid out at some point. And the savings he had transferred for vacation expenses. Not to mention the hundreds of thousands still tied up in his share trading account which the accountant and lawyer said would be dealt with in line with Matt's final will and testament.

Why on earth was I working a job I hated with a bunch of people who had no idea how to talk to me anymore?

I grabbed my handbag, exited my car, and walked the path toward Principal Marsden's office.

♥ ♥ ♥ ♥ ♥ ♥ ♥

"Please, Bee, reconsider your decision." Vicki grasped my elbow, stared at me with pleading eyes, and leaned her hip against my kitchen island.

"I did. I spoke with Principal Marsden three weeks ago, to which she said to give myself some more time to contemplate. And I have. I've spent every single day thinking about what to do, and I've decided. I don't have a heart for the students anymore." I shifted on the barstool, loosening but not freeing Vicki's grip from my arm, and glanced across the kitchen.

I had no heart for anything anymore.

"Once the antidepressants kick in, you'll see things differently. I don't want you to do something you might regret."

How long did the blasted antidepressants need to "kick in"? I had been on them for an entire month—half of May and half of June—but my work enjoyment had tanked, not improved.

I stared at my well-meaning friend and shook my head. "Do you think it'd be fair of me to teach students I have no vested interest in helping?"

"No. But if you took more time off to think—"

"My decision is final. I don't need to think more about this. I don't want to be a teacher. I don't have to work at the moment, so why put myself under extra stress just to keep all you people happy?" How had everyone forgotten my happiness in the scheme of things? Many had fears for my sanity, but my happiness had fallen to the wayside.

Vicki sighed, released my elbow, and met my gaze. "Okay, you've decided. Now what?"

A great question. What would I spend my hours doing? Not volunteering at church, that was for certain. Two months had passed since Matt died, so most of the paperwork changes and account updates were completed.

"What about speaking with someone at church and volunteering in one of the ministries? Meals on Wheels?"

"No." Steel tightened along my spine. "Do you know if Pastor Davidson still works in the office on Tuesdays?"

"Yes. He's there this afternoon too. Why?" Vicki sipped her cool tea.

"Just have to speak to him about something." What better way to spend a Saturday afternoon than letting the good folk of Tellarine Christian Church know I no longer cared to volunteer for them.

Vicki looked at the clock on the wall and gulped the final dregs of her tea. "I've got to go. Nicholas needs to work this afternoon, so I'm taking the children over to Diana's and we're going to have a movie afternoon."

"Have fun." I stood, hugged my friend, and escorted her to the door.

Vicki met my gaze. "Will we see you at church on Sunday?"

Not likely. "We'll see. Have a great afternoon."

"You too."

I closed the door, retrieved my mobile phone from my pocket, and opened my text messages. I had little interest in physically hauling myself to church to tender my resignation, and speaking on the phone would be difficult to do without my voice becoming emotional or sounding wrong, so a text message would have to suffice.

Something hard and cold coiled inside my chest. Volunteering was the last tether keeping me bound to church and God. Once I cut the line, I would be free from the hurt. Because it hurt too much to be in a place which was close to Matt's heart.

It was once close to your heart too.

I clicked on Pastor Davidson's contact details and drafted a message.

Me: Hi, Pastor Davidson, it's Belinda Briggs. I just wanted to let you know I have decided to step down from my leadership role in the Greeting Team and any future volunteering opportunities. Please thank your wife for looking after my duties since Matt's death. Have a great

WEEKEND.

I read and reread the message. Succinct and to the point. Maybe on the heartless side of the scale, but what did they expect me to do? Throw myself into helping at church while I was miserable? Who wanted a greeter without their smile or sparkling personality?

Such was my life. They could deal with it.

I pressed Send, shut off my phone, and switched on an action movie which would numb my emotions, one explosion at a time.

My phone rang in its car phone holder on my way to work on Monday morning. An unfamiliar number filled the screen. Suspected spam or someone I needed to hear from?

The ringtone blared through the car speakers.

I scrambled and pressed Answer. "Hello. Belinda speaking."

"Mrs. Briggs, this is Paige from Larry Stockton's office. Is this a good time?"

The lawyer's office? What news did they have for me? "Sure is."

"Great." Paige tapped on a computer keyboard. "The committal hearing for the Kyneton file is set for next Tuesday morning at ten o'clock."

The committal hearing. A trepidatious yet borderline delicious something slammed within my gut, a war of clashing worlds fighting for my attention.

"I will email you a link to the hearing in case you'd like to attend online. Your presence would be anonymous."

"Th-ank you." I squeezed my hands on the steering wheel and swung into the school car park.

"If you have any questions or concerns, please reply to my email, and I'll do my best to assist you."

"Okay." I pulled to a stop and switched off the engine.

"Thanks."

"You're welcome. All the best." Paige disconnected the call.

I stared through the windscreen, my internal conflict notching toward vomit levels. I sucked in a deep breath and slowed my pulse. That drugged-up youth was not worth the work involved to clean my vehicle from the stench of spew. He had taken my husband, my peace, and my future. He would not take any more time than necessary to wish the worst on his heartless soul.

Could I curse him to a life of unending suffering and dismay? Probably not, but my mounting hatred was ready to throw every dagger I could find at the mental voodoo doll I had formed of his pretty face.

I wrenched my hands from their death grip on the steering wheel, massaged my temples, and gathered my things. Two weeks left until I escaped this hell hole of crushing memories.

After a quick pop-in with Sandra Fishbourne informing her I required next Tuesday off work, I wandered the school hallways toward my office and contemplated the idea of using annual leave for next week and not returning to work. Why suffer when I could avoid it? They had a suitable emergency teacher to handle the kitchen, why not give them the work they enjoyed?

My desk phone rang. Sandra's extension.

I dropped my bag, grabbed the handset, and slid onto my desk chair. "Hi, Sandra."

"Is it just Tuesday? Or did you need more time off?"

Why not? "Actually, I was thinking … maybe I should just take all of next week off. Because I don't know how the hearing would go and don't want to jeopardise the learning outcomes for my students if I'm not … in the best headspace." Yes, focus on the students' education, not my unwillingness to dodge the ghosts in the halls.

"Oh. But that would mean Friday is—"

"My last day. Yes." Anything to bring the date forward.

"I see." She shuffled some paperwork. "The team will be

disappointed not to be able to celebrate with you when we had planned."

What a shame. I extended an olive branch I had hoped to withhold. "We could go to Benanu's on Friday night? Just for a round of drinks …" Or something less time consuming.

"That's a great idea!" Sandra's voice brightened. "I'll arrange for our usual area near the bar and email invites."

Yippee. Only five more days of work and a mini party to survive, before I could curl up into a ball and hide.

CHAPTER SIXTEEN
The First of Many

"You sound chirpy today. What've you been up to?" Vicki's voice echoed from my phone handset.

I lounged in my pyjamas on the couch. I had been a lady of leisure for four whole days and liked my time away from other people. Well, not *liked*. Endured. With little eating because my appetite was shot. But after this morning's hearing, I had hope for the future.

"Bee? You still there?"

"Yeah. Sorry." I smiled at the paused Netflix movie on my television. "The committal hearing was today."

Vicki gasped. "It completely slipped my mind! I'm so sorry. Did you watch it?"

"Yeah." No one needed to know it took me a full eight minutes to click the live link.

"How did you go?"

"I was fine. The actual proceeding was quick, almost like a whirlwind once you decipher what everyone is saying."

"And?"

I grinned. "It's moving to the County Court!" Talk about progress and justice served.

"I'm glad it's moving through the system as it should, but,

Bee?" Vicki's voice softened. "You sound … full of glee. But a life hangs in the balance."

"So?" I huffed a breath. "He took my husband's life. It sounds like just desserts to me."

"You know you'll need to forgive him … at some point. Otherwise, bitterness will take root and poison your heart."

Why could Vicki not understand the freedom—the lack of restraint—unforgiveness gifted me? Church people were so quick to judge and warn against unforgiveness, but could they not understand the strength it gave me? I was no longer under the power of that youth, but I stood above him. I could freely point my finger in his face and smile. It was almost … pathetic how quick Christians were to forgive and open themselves up for more abuse.

Not me. That boy could not reach my heart with a ten-foot pole.

Vicki sighed. "I know you're hurting. We're all hurting after Matt's death, but I just want to protect you. Protect your heart from further injury."

"And you think the key to my happiness is to forgive the boy who killed my future?" How could she think such a thing?

"I …" Vicki sighed again. "I'll be praying for you."

Awesome. I quelled an eyeroll and cleared my throat. "I'd better let you go and get back to it."

"Yes. I've got to collect Elijah from kindergarten soon."

"Have fun. Thanks for calling."

"Look after yourself. Love you, Bee."

"Bye." I ended the phone call and stared at my phone. Was it too hard for my friend to be happy for me? But, no, she had to mother me and find fault. Like I was incapable of surviving without her righteous wisdom. How ridiculous to limit oneself from feeling the full spectrum of emotions *her* God had created. If I wanted to spend my time hating that punk-faced murderer, so be it.

Exhaustion enveloped me, and I glanced at the plate of barely-nibbled crackers resting on the coffee table. With no appetite and energy, it was a wonder I scrounged the 'get up and go' to hold unforgiveness.

I yawned, closed my eyes, and drifted off into the darkness of dreamless sleep.

I spent the next two months in a similar position on the couch, wishing death on that boy, hardly eating, and napping my days away. And no matter what I ate, I gained weight. Lots of weight.

"I have so many rolls, Matt, I could open a bakery." I stared at my puffy reflection in my ensuite mirror, stepped onto the nearby scales, and grimaced.

Ninety-one kilos. I was twenty kilograms heavier than the day Matt died. How could a handful of crackers, cookies, and dried fruit every few days cause my weight to blow up and off the charts?

I pressed my palms against my flabby jaw and blinked away the burn behind my eyes, at the back of my nose, and lingering in my throat. "Happy birthday, babe. Maybe it's best you're not here to see this."

Today was Matt's forty-sixth birthday. Last year we had spent the day at work, followed by a quiet evening of snuggling on the couch. My emotions had been all over the place because of another miscarriage.

If only I had seen a year in advance, I might have snapped out of my mini depression and given him his favourite birthday present.

Me.

I eyed my frumpy figure in the mirror. How do overweight women bear to expose their bodies to their partners? The thought of making love with the man I had tumbled in the sheets many times— but with the figure I now sported—sent a shiver down my spine. Would Matt have wanted me if I had stacked on the weight when he was alive? Would he have craved me like he once did? Or would the extra padding have turned him off?

"Not that it matters anymore," I whispered. Month four without my husband was turning out to be the worst month yet. The ache in my chest had dulled a fraction while my loneliness had tripled.

Self-imposed loneliness. That was what Alison had spat down the phone line the last time she called me. Whenever that was. Like I cared to hear her philosophise about life when she behaved like a teen and had her live-in lover cleaning up her messes. If she saw how much weight I had gained, she would point her finger, laugh, and tell me I would never get fat eating a vegan diet.

Other than the cheese, I was close to vegan these days. Because who wanted to go to the shops and buy nutritious food? Matt cooked the steak in our family and I baked the goods. Well, I used to bake. Now I sat and stored up fat for the figurative winter my life had ushered in.

I sighed and leaned against the bathroom vanity. August seventeenth. Winter would be over soon. Would this winter in my life ease up too? I opened Matt's vanity cupboard door, extracted his favourite cologne—or was CK One my favourite of his collection?—and untwisted the metal lid.

A delightful, citrusy mix of aromatic freshness, summertime, and sadness leached from the frosted bottle. I breathed in the scent of kisses, laughter, and sunshine, and allowed my mind to wander into an extended session of "Matt time."

My phone vibrated in my back pocket and jiggled my backside. Once. Twice.

I shut off the distraction, closed my eyes, and ventured back into the recesses of my mind. Shirtless Matt with his trademark smirk, oozing virility, and spinning my head with naughty thoughts.

My phone buzzed again.

I groaned, yanked my phone from the stretched pocket, stomped into my bedroom, and flopped on my bed.

Vicki Jacobsen: NICHOLAS AND I WERE HOPING YOU MIGHT BE HOME THIS AFTERNOON? IT'S BEEN WEEKS SINCE WE SAW YOU, AND WE WANTED TO SEE YOU. YOU SHOULDN'T BE ALONE TODAY, BEE. XX

"Say it's his birthday, Vicki. Don't beat around the bush like everyone else." When had mentioning Matt's name become taboo?

Did people think I would break down every time I heard his name? I typed out several responses, most of them harsh and snarky, but decided to keep it civil and simple.

Me: Thanks for your message, but I'm busy today. Catch you another time.

I furrowed my brow at the Google icons at the top of my screen. Two of my Google alerts had been triggered. That explained the earlier buzzing.

I clicked on the icons and waited for the page to load. Two news articles relating to my little murderer and the proceedings. I scanned the headline and frowned.

My phone vibrated in my hand with a call from my lawyer's office.

I had finally been smart and saved the number in my contacts. I swiped the call. "Hello?"

"Hi, Mrs. Briggs, it's Paige from Larry Stockton's office."

"Hi, Paige."

"Mr. Stockton wanted me to let you know the proceedings have been adjourned for two months."

"Adjourned? Why?" Was our legal system so clogged it could hold off serving swift justice?

"This is standard procedure. It can take up to two years for a case to reach a verdict."

"What?" Two years?

"We progressed quickly from the committal hearing in Magistrates Court, but it will take time. We just wanted to let you know."

"Right. Okay." I blew out a breath. "Thanks for the update."

"Until next time." Paige farewelled and disconnected the call.

Sometime later—I had failed to check the time of Paige's call—I roused from my stupor on the bed to the sound of faint tapping at my front door. Or was it a bird pecking the window? Whoever or whatever was trying to visit could try another day. Today was my day to miss Matt, sniff his cologne, and reminisce. If someone wanted to think about him, they could do so at their own house.

Five minutes passed without any further knocking. I peeled myself from the comforting bedspread, padded into Matt's office, and opened the walk-in-robe cupboard. A white archive box with handwritten block letters stared at me from the middle shelf. My treasures. I carried the box to my bedroom and lowered to the bed.

"I'm sorry I failed you, Matt." I lifted the cardboard lid and breathed in the sweet scent of fabric softener.

Four tiny Bonds press-studded coveralls—one blue, one pink, one white, and one grey—with the name "Briggs" handstitched near the logo lay atop a white crocheted baby blanket and a Bright Bots rainbow-coloured cot doona cover and sheet set.

I lifted the blue baby romper suit and pressed the soft fabric against my cheek. Matt and I had held these outfits many times before, declaring health and fertility over our bodies, buoying our hope. Now every ounce of hope was gone. Just like Matt and all of our children.

A chest-heaving, painful sob wrenched its way up my throat and out of my mouth.

I groaned and sobbed, my tears dripping onto the baby romper or slipping into my lap. There was no point keeping any of these things because there would never be a Briggs baby. But contemplating tossing these items away ripped another tear in the dead tissue of my heart.

I caressed the blanket Aunt Crystal had given us years ago, my tears flowing with each stroke. Would this get any easier? The missing him, and missing what we had, part of life?

And what of the people I pushed away? Would they eventually give up? I sniffled and wiped my fingers under my damp eyes. I had given up a long time ago, so I could hardly blame Vicki and Diana from doing the same. When they did.

Maybe there was nothing left to live for. Maybe my life had reached its natural end.

I re-boxed the baby items, burrowed under my bedspread, and fell into a dreamless, hiccupping sleep.

♥ ♥ ♥ ♥ ♥ ♥ ♥

Two weeks after Matt's birthday, my heart still pumped blood, and my lungs insisted on processing oxygen.

Somehow, I lived, although my existence was … insignificant. Purposeless. My days were filled with empty activities. The sole thing I had improved in, skills wise, was avoiding other humans. And wearing the same knickers five days in a row. Without a liner.

Living on the edge.

Matt's T-shirts were too tight to wear. His business shirts fit when left unbuttoned. Even his oversized hoodies and jumpers were snug on me.

And my body kept on living, with no reason other than I could not be bothered to off myself.

How lazy I had become. Life had fled months ago when death came on the scene. When God had abandoned me to this hellish existence.

I shuffled into the kitchen, poured a glass of water, and swallowed the fat-storing pills. Antidepressants, my foot. More like "caused you to store fat and fluid which depressed you more" pills. But from the websites I had found, this was typical. Like a practical joke the pharmaceutical companies created to brighten up their days.

Let's help women fight depression by giving them something else to think about!

Great plan.

My landline phone rang. I ignored it and flopped onto the couch.

While I scrolled through Netflix—another task which had become more difficult because scrolling when apathetic was not a recipe for making choices—my mobile phone rang.

Alison.

I returned my gaze to the television and tried to choose something.

Alison phoned again. And again.

I switched to Amazon Prime and my sister called. I flicked to the Disney+ app on her sixth dial.

Phone call number ten chimed when I opened the Paramount+ app.

"What does she want?" I scowled at my phone.

My phone rang again.

I stabbed the Answer button, enabled the speakerphone, and gritted my teeth. "What?"

"Wow, you're a happy camper today." Alison chuckled at her own joke.

"I figured you weren't going to give up." Where had my irresponsible sister gone?

"Good guess. Rob bet eight calls, but I guessed it'd take at least twelve. You cracked sooner than I expected."

"What do you want?" Why had I answered her call?

"Just want to see how you're doing."

"I'm fine."

"Yeah, you sound great." Alison chuckled again. "Your friends say you're avoiding them."

Sometimes I wished I had never given Vicki my sister's number.

"Are you avoiding them?"

"No," I grumbled.

She laughed, loud. "Puh-leeze. I wrote the book on avoidance."

Wish she would use that book right now, the little brat.

"Look, Bindy-Boo, I was talking to Rob about the little pickle you find yourself in and—"

"Here we go," I whispered.

"I think you should see a therapist."

It was my turn to laugh. I huffed several amused breaths. "And you're qualified to suggest this to me … how?"

"I'm concerned for you. You're in a real bad funk, and I want to help you get out of it."

The irony. My sister, the serial avoider and irresponsible party of our growing-up duo, now wanted to flex her maturity muscles and be responsible to help me.

"It's really not a good look on you, sis."

"Why do you care?" The question had finally tumbled from my lips.

"Because you're my sister. And I want you living life … the saner way."

I shook my head. "You never cared before."

"Yes, I did. Hello? I visited, remember?"

"Not before he died, though. Not once did you say anything which hinted at caring when I struggled with infertility."

"It's not like I know it was a huge struggle. You didn't say much."

"I shouldn't have to spell it out! I distinctly recall telling you of two of my miscarriages … and all I received was the sound of crickets over the telephone line."

"I felt awkward." Alison huffed a breath. "What was I meant to say?"

"I dunno!" I fisted my hands. "That you're sorry? That you wish the babies had lived? That you cared?"

"Of course, I cared!" Alison's voice boomed down the phone line.

"Well, you could've fooled me!"

Silence filled the space between us. A silence dotted with a few huffing breaths, most on my end of the call.

"I'm sorry," Alison whispered. "You've always been there for me. When Dad and Mum went AWOL or left me to fend for myself, you were always there, picking up the pieces. I guess … I guess you were always so strong and capable that I never figured you … weren't."

"Well now you know." I rubbed my damp eyes and glanced back at the phone lying on the couch cushion. "I've gotta go—"

"Please talk to someone."

"Bye, Ali." I ended the call and switched off my phone.

For the next month and a half, I ignored Alison's weekly calls. Her record peaked at twenty-six calls in a row. I had shoved a piece of popcorn into my mouth with each phone vibration. Vicki, Diana, and even Tara, continued to send me text messages, with updates about their families and their ever-present concerns for me. They passed on messages from church congregants who apparently missed me too.

Not that anyone would miss me if I walked through the church doors. My weight had plateaued at ninety-three kilograms, so I was bigger than I had ever been.

Being larger than life was overrated.

I unlocked the front door and trundled down the footpath for my daily dose of exercise. The late-September afternoon sunshine warmed my exposed arms. Springtime was my favourite season of the year, infused with hope and the bright colours of nature. Matt and I had often gone on Saturday day trips and enjoyed the beautiful weather and fresh country air.

Now my life seemed more in tune with winter.

I plodded along the weedy footpath, my upper arms and thighs vibrating, and bent low to inspect the contents of the letterbox. My back twinged. I sucked in a sharp breath, extracted several envelopes, and straightened with a groan. After numerous slow breaths, I surveyed the yard and grimaced. Matt would be disappointed with the number of weeds in his garden. But what could I do? I rubbed my lower back and glared at the letterbox. My back ached from bending. How could I sit on my knees and yank weeds from the garden? Perhaps it would be worthwhile employing a gardener, not just the bloke who mowed the front and back yards for fifty bucks each fortnight.

Movement caught my eye in my periphery. Mr. Yates stood

from kneeling over his garden bed.

The last thing I wanted was to be stuck in polite conversation about his dog's worms or the terrible state of the economy. I returned to the house at the fastest pace I could keep without tripping, my letters clutched tight in my hand.

I locked the door, tossed the envelopes on the kitchen island bench, and poured myself a glass of water. The liquid cooled my throat, and my harried pulse slowed. I creaked onto a barstool, flicked through the envelopes, and opened a one-page nondescript letter from Matt's life insurance company.

A cheque for eight hundred and fifty thousand dollars nestled between my fingers. Another matter finalised.

I furrowed my brow and tried to recall the day Vicki had visited and helped me complete pages of paperwork. Had it been the same day we filled out the ownership transfer paperwork for his vehicle to me and cancelled his driver's licence? I closed my eyes and urged my memory from its cubby hole.

Vicki and I had gathered all of Matt's and my utility, banking, and telecommunications bills and jotted a list of people I needed to call or websites to visit and print off documentation. VicRoads had been the easiest to deal with once Vicki replaced the ink in Matt's printer.

Several tears dripped into my lap. What should I do with this payout apart from depositing the cheque into my bank account when I felt up to leaving the house? I wished I had an inkling of confidence when it came to financial matters. Why had Matt left me without forearming me with his financial understanding? I missed his quiet, confident wisdom and his long-contemplated thoughts. Yes, I was far from destitute, but what good was money if I was clueless how to utilise it?

Ask Vicki.

Heat billowed in my chest and stained my cheeks. Vicki had been good to me, and what had I done to repay her kindness? Ignored her messages.

My mobile phone screeched from where it lay face down on the couch. Who was trying to call me?

"Probably Alison." I sighed and stepped toward the couch, but by the time I reached my phone, the ringing ceased. I flipped my phone over and checked the missed calls list.

Vicki.

Why had she called instead of sending a text message like she had the last few months? And what were the odds of her calling at the exact moment I had been thinking about her?

My phone toned with a message.

She left a voicemail message?

I clicked Play.

"Hi, Bee, I hope you're well, it's been a while since I saw your beautiful face." Vicki sighed. "Sorry to miss you, but would you please call me when you receive this message? I have some news I want to share, but it would be better over the phone or in person, rather than through text messages. Please call me at your earliest convenience. Love you, Bee."

I stared at the black phone screen. Was Vicki trying to manipulate me into seeing her or talking to her? The heat in my chest chilled at the possibility. My sister was never beyond manipulative tactics, but Vicki? Had she spent too much time talking to my sister and learned a few tips in dealing with me?

I fingered the insurance letter and bent the cheque at the bottom along the perforated line. If Vicki was amping up her efforts to get me to communicate, then I would knuckle down in my efforts to ignore her. How dare she use tactics like this to force my hand? She had lost children and once mourned a broken marriage, and I had been kind to her and never pushed for information. I had given her time to grieve and gather her strength. Why could she not grant me the same curtesy? Alison had something to do with instructing my so-called friend.

I crafted two strong, no-nonsense responses in my brain—one for my sister and one for my "friend"—but decided against issuing any replies.

My silence would speak for me.

CHAPTER SEVENTEEN
The Determination of a Friend

Insistent knocking echoed from my front door.

"Open up, Bee!" Vicki's voice trailed down the hallway to the lounge room.

I shifted on the couch, paused, and muted the television.

Sturdy, rhythmic thumps reverberated against the glass panel.

A muffled, "Please open the door," glided into the house.

Why was she hounding me today, of all days? Did she know the significance of today's date? October tenth. The six-month anniversary of Matt's death.

Tap-tap. Bang.

Probably.

"I'm not leaving. Please, Bee."

After Vicki's voicemail message two weeks earlier, her subsequent text messages had reduced in frequency and volume, and I had hoped it had been a sign she was giving up.

Bang. Bang-bang.

It seemed not.

"Belinda!"

Ugh! I flung the lightweight cotton blanket from my lap and stormed to the front door.

Tappity-tap-tap. Bang-bang.

I pried the wooden door open, relieved to remain hidden

behind the privacy screen door. "What!"

Vicki stilled her fisted hand mid-air, wide-eyed. "Bee."

I squeezed my eyes closed and clutched the door handle.

"Can I come in, please?"

The urge to slam the door and stomp to the couch slivered through my veins. I tamped down the vibrations tightening my shoulder blades.

"Please." Vicki's voice cracked.

I opened my eyes and stared.

Her forehead was etched with lines, and the bags under her eyes seemed darker than usual.

The fight in me shrivelled, and I unlocked the door. I shuffled along the hallway to the lounge room—Vicki's footsteps echoed behind me—and dropped on the couch.

Vicki settled on the arm chair adjacent to my seat.

I flitted my gaze to hers for a brief moment. Was she staring at me? The last time I saw her, I had only added about five kilograms. Would she comment on my bloated features? Was I a fright to behold?

"You look tired." Vicki clasped her hands in her lap.

I lifted my chin and eyed her. "So do you."

"I …" Vicki rubbed her nose. "I've been spending time during the night praying for my friend."

Was that friend me? I hated the thought she lost sleep because of me.

"How are you?" Her voice softened.

I shrugged. "How do I look?"

"Exhausted with carrying life on your shoulders."

I stuffed my hands into my hoodie pockets. I had caved last week and bought some larger sized Bonds tracksuits online.

"Is there …" Vicki sighed. "Are you distancing yourself from us because I did something wrong? Or are you simply determined to hide away from the world?"

My throat tightened, and I pressed my lips together.

"Because if I did something wrong, I ask you to please forgive me." Her voice wavered. "And if not, then I'd like to help you from your burrow."

An image of a smiling Vicki snuggled in Nick's arms wrestled to the surface of my memories, followed by Jasmine and Elijah laughing and hugging their mother.

"It's been six long months since Matt died." Vicki met my gaze, her eyes sincere, almost misty.

I clenched my jaw.

"I want to help you, Bee—"

"You're so happy with your stud muffin husband and gorgeous children." The words fled from my lips, unbidden.

Vicki's mouth drooped, and she scrunched her forehead.

"I can't be around you. Or Diana and Tara, for that matter. Your bliss-filled happiness is …" I squeezed my eyes closed, and a sob screamed in my throat.

The couch dipped a moment before Vicki's arms wrapped around me. "I understand. Really, I do. I couldn't stand to be around my sister after the children died because Christine was happy. Patrick loved her, unlike my abusive ex, and she could still love on her boys while my children were six-feet-under."

Tears spilled over my cheeks and dripped from my chin.

"I know what it's like to live under the shadow of death. To have hopelessness swallow you whole and hold you captive." Vicki rubbed my arm. "To feel the burden of grief and wallow in the pain, day after long, agonising day."

I inhaled measured breaths in the hopes of slowing my fast-flowing tears.

"I've lived with loss"—Vicki huffed a mirthless laugh—"Who am I kidding? I still live with it and miss my babies so much."

If I still carried the loss of my first miscarriage years after we lost the baby, then of course Vicki lived each day missing her children. How had I failed to see my situation was not unique?

"I barely survived." Vicki sucked in a steadying breath. "But I clung to my faith, some days by the skin of my teeth, but I hung tight nonetheless. Jesus was my anchor in the roughest storm I had ever endured, and I thank Him every day I wasn't swept away in the current of my sorrow."

Jesus was her anchor.

Something sharp twisted against my ribcage. I counted my breaths and focused on easing my heartrate.

Jesus wants to be my anchor.

But did He? I allowed the past years of struggle, pain, heartache, and despair to wash over me. The many losses I had sustained. The death of my unborn babies and husband. My extinguished dreams.

Jesus wanted to be my anchor? Unlikely.

Was God even interested in me? In my mental health and wellbeing? Or my happiness and contentment? My experiences proved otherwise, and I shut down the voices whispering in my heart. I would reconnect with Vicki after our chat today, but God? The benefits for me were zilch. Nada.

"I love you, Bee, and relate to the pain you must be experiencing." Vicki's voice lowered. "Please let me help you."

"Okay. But give me time. To think." I could commit to reopening my heart to friendship, but nothing more today.

"Absolutely. There's no rush. Just … let me walk this journey with you."

I leaned away from my friend's embrace and offered a small smile.

"I missed you."

"I did too." The truth of those three words chorused inside my heart.

Vicki hugged me again, and we smiled at each other through our tears.

"I'd offer you some lunch but there's not much in my pantry." Perhaps it was time to reevaluate more than my friendships. Soon.

Vicki glanced around my unkempt lounge room and kitchen.

"That's okay. I was thinking a nice meal at Benanu's would hit the spot."

I stared at my thick thighs. Benanu's? Did I have the courage to go out in public right now?

"Do you mind if I call in a takeaway order and bring it back here?"

I slouched against the couch, and the coils in my stomach unfurled. "That would be great."

Vicki grabbed her phone, and we scrolled through their online menu. Once we decided on what to eat, she called in our order, and left the house.

I spent the ten minutes she was away tidying the lounge room and neatening the kitchen benchtop while thoughts swirled and ideas hummed.

A new beginning was on my horizon. All I needed to do was reach out and hold tight.

I pushed a rickety supermarket trolley along the frigid freezer aisle at Ritchies IGA in Robinvale—bumping into people I knew at the Tellarine IGA set concrete in my gut—and scrutinised the range of frozen vegetables. I grabbed a packet of Australian-grown peas and a bag of mixed veggies, and popped them on top of the free-range chicken thighs riding in my trolley. My gaze caught the specials tag on beer-battered chips and wedges. I pursed my lips, shrugged, and tossed a bag of each onto my frozen peas.

Matt would be proud of my efforts to restock the pantry, fridge, and freezer. Vicki might be too. Since her visit almost two weeks ago, we had messaged daily, and not once had she pressured me to change. If I survived my outing, I would tell my friend, and hope she celebrated with me instead of scolding me for not sharing my shopping plans.

On my way past the ice cream freezer, I yanked out a one-litre tub of half-price Hershey's chocolate ripple ice cream, and aimed my wobbly cart toward the checkout registers.

"Afternoon." A redheaded checkout chick offered me a kind smile.

"Hi." I forced a smile and removed the frozen food from my trolley, followed by meat and fresh fruit, bottled and canned goods, boxed foodstuffs, a large bag of flour, sanitary liners, a carton of free-range eggs, and a loaf of bread.

Matt had always laughed at the order I stacked the conveyor belt, but it made sense to me. This method ensured my cold items would be packed together, and my eggs and bread would be safe from the inevitable crush of a poorly planned packing system.

No one liked squished bread.

The redhead scanned my items, her time focused more on my food than on me.

I appreciated a less chatty server today. Once I paid for my groceries and emptied the trolley load into my car, I collapsed in the driver's seat.

One task scratched off my long list.

My phone rang inside my handbag.

I scratched through my bag, found my phone, and checked the caller.

My lawyer?

"Hello?" Had I swiped in time?

"Hi, is this Mrs. Briggs?" An unfamiliar woman's voice greeted me. Where was Paige?

"Speaking."

"My name is Carrie and I'm calling from Larry Stockton's office. I'm covering Paige's role this week while she's on leave."

So, it was a new girl. "Hi, Carrie. How can I help you?"

"I've been asked to let you know the case has been adjourned another three months."

Adjourned again? I ground my back molars against each other. When would we move out of this limbo toward an equitable outcome?

"The accused is remanded at a youth justice centre, and we believe this arrangement will remain unchanged for the foreseeable future."

"Okay." I released a long breath. Why had I never bothered to ask where that boy resided? At least the little murderer was locked away from society. But what a cushy way to live, with three square meals a day and access to counsellors and television while Matt decomposed in his casket.

"If you need anything else, please give us a call."

"Thanks, Carrie." My voice cracked.

Matt was dead because of him.

"Good bye, Mrs. Briggs."

"Bye," I whispered.

Silence filled the car, and my phone screen darkened.

I stared out the windscreen, my heartbeat thundering like a wild horse crossing the Nullarbor. *Matt was dead.* My hands tremored, and I pressed my palms flat against my thighs.

A mother, laden with grocery bags and a jumping toddler, crossed the car park, her hand wrapped around her son's.

I dug my fingers into my squishy legs and expelled rapid breaths. My eyesight blurred around the edges, and a cold, creeping sensation settled along my skin, dancing down my back. My intellection tumbled into nothingness, my brain unable to grasp the smoke-like thoughts wisping through my head.

Had my mind finally cracked? Was this my breaking point? The fog between my ears multiplied, and I squinted at the shapes and colours passing before my eyes. My breaths sharpened, tight and airless. Pain jolted through my taut fingers and along my legs. My uncontrollable pulse ached inside my neck.

Incoherent and crazed. Unhinged.

Light dissolved in a sea of gasps, and I woke to the sound of heavy rain beating my vehicle, my head lolling against my right shoulder.

What had happened? I twisted my neck from side to side, groaning, and rotated my shoulders. Had I blacked out after a … panic attack? I had never experienced one before, but had coached Vicki through two attacks.

Maybe Alison had the right idea when she had suggested I talk to a therapist. Not that I would say anything which could inflate her ego bigger than it already was. But who could I trust to help me? Attending a counselling session facilitated by Tellarine Christian Church was out of the question.

Tara's face appeared in my mind like an apparition. She had spent time with a therapist she trusted. Could her therapist help me too?

I flexed my fingers, glad the shakiness had departed, and sighed when the rain ceased, and sounds of the supermarket car park filtered through the closed window. Blood no longer roared between my ears, so I buckled my seatbelt, started the engine, and travelled home.

My phone buzzed halfway through depositing the frozen food in my freezer.

I shoved the rest of the shopping into their new homes, drank a glass of water—unpacking groceries was thirsty work—and glanced at my phone.

Vicki Jacobsen: Would you be up for a visit in the next few weeks? Nicholas and I would love to catch up with you. Will happily bring Benanu's for dinner.

I glanced at the calendar app. October twenty-sixth. I could pull myself together for visitors. I surveyed the mess at the kitchen sink, the dirty clothes escaping from the laundry, and the mess dotted around the lounge room. If I tackled each space one task at a time, I might be back in a routine of cleanliness by mid-November.

Me: Give me a few weeks to pull myself together? Send through your available dates around or after Nov 15.

A handful of seconds passed before my phone buzzed.

Vicki Jacobsen: Sounds great. I'll talk with Nicholas

AND SEND THROUGH SOME POTENTIAL DATES THIS EVENING. XX

Me: NO WORRIES. PS I WENT GROCERY SHOPPING TODAY!

Vicki Jacobsen: THAT'S WONDERFUL, BEE! I'M SO PROUD OF YOU. DID YOU FEEL MORE CONFIDENT?

I snorted a laugh. Confident was not the word I would use to describe the disaster of my outing.

Me: NOT REALLY, BUT I DID IT AND SURVIVED TO TELL THE TALE.

Vicki Jacobsen: GOOD WORK, TAKING ONE STEP AT A TIME. WELL DONE! XX

I smiled and reread our messages. Opening myself to our friendship was the best decision I had made since Matt died.

CHAPTER EIGHTEEN
Companions in Grief

Three faultless table place settings? Check. Drinks in the fridge and snacks in the pantry? Check. Tissues? Double check.

A familiar rhythmic knock tapped against the front door.

I surveyed my home one final time before I bounded to the front entryway, sucked in a deep breath, and swung the door wide. "Hey, guys."

The Jacobsens stood on my doorstep. Nick's left hand rested on Vicki's back while his right fist overflowed with Benanu's brown paper takeaway bags.

Vicki smiled and wrapped her petite arms around me. "You're looking great, Bee."

"Thanks." I glanced up at Nick and met his gaze. Was he shocked by my weight gain? Or had Vicki warned him not to react?

"We appreciate you opening your home to us." He tipped his head in my direction, his soulful dark eyes focused on my face.

I smiled, stepped away from Vicki's embrace, and gestured inside. "Come in."

Once Nick deposited the bags of food onto the dining table, the three of us emptied the bags, filled our plates, and enjoyed a dinner of delicious food and polite, unintrusive conversation.

Vicki cleared the table, Nick gathered some clean glassware, and I filled the tall tumblers with sparkling apple juice.

Nick dipped his chin at the drinks I had poured and motioned toward the lounge room. "I'll bring these over."

"Thank you." I plonked onto my favourite couch cushion and waited for my friends to settle on the nearby chairs.

Vicki grabbed the tissue box from the kitchen island benchtop, deposited it on the coffee table within arm's reach, and settled on the couch beside me.

Nick handed Vicki and me a glass of sparkling juice, retrieved his own, and lowered to the armchair he often used beside Matt's chair.

Old habits were hard to break.

I stared at Matt's chair, and the realisation he would never fill the seat tightened my throat. When would it finally compute in my brain? Matt had been gone seven months now, yet there were moments each week, sometimes every day, when I had to remind myself he was gone.

"He's never going to sit here and yak with me again, is he?" Nick's quiet words shot an arrow into my heart.

"No." I blinked the wetness from my eyes and stared at Matt's best friend. How had I been so blind to his pain? In avoiding my friends, I had denied this opportunity to share in their grief and their comfort.

Vicki slid her arm around my shoulders.

"I really do miss him." Nick rubbed his salt-and-pepper studded jaw with his palm, the rasping, scratching sound filling the silence.

"He was the life of the party, after all." I missed his cheeky grin and mischievous eyes.

A slight smile slipped to Nick's lips, and he huffed a breathy laugh. "Filled with amusing observations."

Vicki sighed. "I'm glad you two were so close. It didn't look possible once upon a time."

I snorted a laugh as a flood of memories washed over me.

Jealous Nick keeping his cool when Matt had his girl.

Nick's eyes flashed. "Don't know what I would've done if you'd dated him any longer than you did."

Vicki's cheeks flushed. She glanced between me and her husband, bit her lower lip, and stared at the tumbler in her hand.

Some days I wished we had discussed the whole "Matt and Vicki dated for eight agonising months" saga. But when best friends dated the same guy before and after each other, it tended to become awkward.

Vicki turned to me. "I never apologised."

Apologised?

"For dating Matt."

What?

Vicki aimed her tortured eyes at Matt's chair, locked her gaze with Nick's equally intense expression, and faced me. "I'm sorry I dated Matt. Deep down I knew it would affect you, no matter what you said to the contrary."

The years peeled away like onion layers, and I stepped back into the shoes of sixteen-year-old Belinda Davies, ever the responsible youth with the irresponsible parents. I had been invited to youth group by a school friend in Year Eight, and by age sixteen I was determined to help my school crush see God in a good light. But I had failed Dale, and he had walked away from youth group and all things Christianity. Years swam before my eyes to the overwhelm of responsibility when Matt became a Christian, a mirror of my high school heartache. I broke up with him only to have the man I still loved—even if I hid it as best as I could—date my best friend. He had chosen her after my rejection.

"Call it a moment of weakness on my part, seeking affection from someone who cared. When you two broke up, I knew you were both hurting, but I …" She shrugged. "I was still processing my marriage breakdown, the aftermath of losing the children, then losing Nick's confidence and … Matt was hurting too. We offered each other comfort."

And I had climbed into bed each night imaging the comfort they shared with each other, whether Matt kissed Vicki with the same soft-lipped intensity he had kissed me. If he brushed his fingers across her palm and spoke of love like he once had with me.

What a tortured soul I had been. If my pre-marriage self could see me now.

"Since Matt and I kissed once and never slept together, I thought my dating him would become a non-issue." Vicki's eyes widened. "But our emotional entanglement was intimate, so I should've addressed this issue years ago instead of packing away the events, unforgotten by us all. I'm sorry we never talked about it."

I glanced at Nick and sucked in a breath.

His face shone like a child after receiving an unexpected treat. Was he … pleased with his wife and her confession? How many times had they discussed this matter over the years? Matt and I had spoken about it a number of times, and he knew how I wished this particular elephant would leave my friendship with Vicki. Maybe today was the day its lumbering feet plodded from our lives forever.

"I'm sorry too," I whispered and pressed closer to my friend. I had chosen to withhold the truth of my feelings about their relationship and had paid a price for my decision.

"Matt would be pleased to see this thorn in your friendship fall away." Nick's deep timbre echoed across the room.

"I have to agree." Vicki pulled back and chuckled. "He'd then tease us all for being silly and encourage us to move on."

I smiled.

"I do miss him." Vicki grabbed a tissue and dabbed her eyes. "It all still feels surreal."

"You're telling me. My life imploded, then burned up on re-entry." And somehow, I was expected to keep living life with all this pain? Would it get any easier?

"I wish I could do more for you, Bee." Vicki's voice broke. She sniffled into a tissue and rested her petite hand on my knee.

"Whatever it is you want to do, I'll be here cheering you on. If you need a shoulder to lean on, I'm here."

"Thank you," I whispered.

"We're all here to help," Nick said.

My throat clogged. Even after all I had done to push them aside, my friends still volunteered to assist me. A lightness I had not experienced in a long time surged inside my chest. How had our shared grief somehow lightened my burden? And why had I not connected with them sooner?

A thought crossed my mind, and the words plunged from my mouth. "Do you think Tara would be willing to share her therapist's information? I-I've been thinking it might be a good idea to … talk to someone."

Vicki's eyes widened before a soft smile lifted her cheeks. "I think she'd think it's a wonderful idea. Want me to ask?"

I nodded, afraid to speak while my insides trembled.

Vicki grabbed her mobile handset, tapped out a message, and rested her phone on the couch armrest. "Done."

I sipped the rest of my drink, my parched tongue thankful for moisture.

Vicki's phone vibrated, and she snatched it from the couch edge. "Tara says she'll message you Dr. Braithwaite's information. You know she's based in Melbourne, right?"

"Yeah."

"And you'll probably need to get a referral from your GP."

"I figured as much." I had a long way to go, but this was a start.

Nick topped up our drinks.

"Oh!" Vicki beamed and scrolled through her phone. "I haven't shown you photos of our grandbaby."

How had I completely forgotten about the Harris baby? My stomach plummeted. When had Diana had her baby? Had that been the news Vicki had phoned me about last month? And I had shunned her because of her call. Heat stung my face.

Vicki squinted at the screen. "She's six weeks old and growing so fast."

Six weeks. My insides swirled. What a horrible person I was.

Nick chuckled. "She's a darling and has her father's hand wrapped around her little finger."

Vicki leaned closer and held her phone between us. "Here she is. Chelsea Mae. She looks like Diana as a baby with Jonathan's darker complexion."

I stared at the screen and watched the photos slide by with each swipe of Vicki's finger. Squishy, puffy newborn shots at the hospital, followed by several of Jonathan holding his daughter in his arms. A pang volleyed in my chest. Change-table photos, "tummy time" photos with baby Chelsea lying on the floor, black hair rising from her scalp in long, fluffy spikes. "She's beautiful. How's Diana coping?"

"Really well." Vicki handed me her phone. "I knew she'd be brilliant at motherhood after the way she mothered Jasmine and Elijah. So capable and confident."

"Unlike my son-in-law." Nick chuckled again. "He almost fell apart when Chelsea arrived."

"Diana did experience a difficult birth, so it's understandable."

"But amusing." Nick's grin stretched wider. "It's strange to think he's a proficient police officer."

Vicki tsked. "You were a tad … overwhelmed… when Elijah arrived, so leave the boy alone. Jonathan's growing into his father role each week."

I listened to my friends' banter while I scrolled through the remaining photos, my heart torn between their happiness and my loss. If Matt and I had just one of our children survive, I would have photos like these to cherish.

And a child to raise alone.

I sobered at the thought. How could I have looked after a child these past seven months when I had barely looked after myself? No matter the scenarios I imagined, life would be difficult.

The sooner I shook myself from the darkness penning me in, the better.

CHAPTER NINETEEN
Therapy for One

I stared at the phone number on my mobile screen—heart clanging and feet locked in place on my kitchen tiles—and pressed the Call button.

"Doctor Braithwaite's office, Carolyn speaking."

My pulse thwacked inside my neck. "H-hi. My name's Belinda Briggs."

"Hello, Belinda."

"My friend Tara Everton gave me your number."

"I trust Tara's well?" Carolyn's kind voice hinted with a mix of … concern?

"She's doing great." Well, I assumed she was great. She had been months ago, when I last saw her.

"I'm glad. So, how can I help you today?"

I swallowed the lump clogging my throat. "I was hoping Dr. Braithwaite might be able to take on another patient."

"With a GP referral, we should be able to arrange a time to visit."

Visit. How could I travel all the way to Melbourne in my current state?

"Do you live in Melbourne?"

"No." I racked my brain for who I could see locally. Was there anyone I could trust? "I-I live in the same country town as Tara."

"Oh." Computer keyboard clicks sounded down the phone line. "Dr. Braithwaite prefers to see all new clients in person."

"Please." My voice rasped. "Can we do a telehealth video call instead? The thought of travelling all the way to Melbourne is …" My throat closed.

A silent moment—maybe a handful of seconds which seemed longer than an hour—passed by, and time stilled along with my thoughts, hopes, and plans.

"Could I put you on hold for a moment, please, Belinda?"

"Sure." Soothing instrumental music sang into my ear. I lowered myself onto my kitchen barstool and squeezed my eyes closed.

How had the possibility never occurred to me that Dr. Braithwaite might suggest I see another therapist? And why had I pinned so much hope on seeing her? I had never met the woman, but when Tara restarted her therapy sessions, they brought about a remarkable change in her. Dr. Braithwaite was an enormous factor in Tara's transformation and had to be the key.

God was a greater factor in Tara's transformation.

I pushed the thought aside and steadied my breaths. Dr. Fallow might know someone trustworthy in our area. He had to know *someone* to refer his patients to when they required extra help. But was his contact in the field as capable, knowledgeable, and compassionate as I was led to believe Dr. Braithwaite was with her patients? Maybe I should hang up and forget the idea ever crossed my—

"Belinda?" Carolyn's voice snapped me from my thoughts.

"Yes?"

"Dr. Braithwaite is willing to meet with you remotely on Friday afternoon."

Thank Go-oodness.

"Could I have your email address so I can send you a New Patient form? Please fill it out and email it back to us before Friday."

"No problem." I rattled off my personal email address.

"Great." Carolyn typed on her keyboard. "We'll still need a GP referral. If your GP can't email it directly to us, please scan the document and also send it to me before Friday."

"Okay."

"I'll email you a link to your telehealth appointment on Thursday afternoon."

"Thank you, Carolyn." *Thank you, thank you!* "I appreciate you accommodating me." What would I have done if I had been refused?

"You're welcome. I've just emailed the forms to you."

"Appreciate it."

"Enjoy the rest of your Monday, Belinda."

"You too." I disconnected the call, raced to my laptop, and printed off a copy of the paperwork.

An hour later I had returned the completed form to Carolyn and booked an appointment with Dr. Fallow for tomorrow morning. My hands trembled, and something fluttered in my stomach. I burst through the back door, breathed in the warm November afternoon, and settled on the verandah bench seat.

Me: I HAVE A VIDEO APPOINTMENT BOOKED WITH DR. BRAITHWAITE ON FRIDAY! GETTING MY REFERRAL LETTER FROM DR. FALLOW TOMORROW MORNING.

I stared at my phone and waited for Vicki's reply.

Vicki Jacobsen: FABULOUS! WHAT TIME IS YOUR DOCTOR APPOINTMENT TOMORROW MORNING?

Me: 9:40

Vicki Jacobsen: I'M DROPPING ELIJAH AT KINDERGARTEN AT 9:00 AND HE'S STAYING UNTIL AFTER LUNCH. I COULD DRIVE YOU AND WE COULD HANG OUT FOR LUNCH?

Me: THAT SOUNDS GREAT. THANK YOU.

Me: PS WHY'S ELI AT KINDY LONGER THAN NORMAL?

Vicki Jacobsen: GREAT! I'LL SEE YOU NOT LONG AFTER I DROP HIM OFF. AS FOR HIS LONGER DAY, THE KINDERGARTEN EXTEND THEIR SESSIONS IN NOVEMBER AND DECEMBER TO PREPARE THE

CHILDREN FOR PRIMARY SCHOOL. I THINK IT'S A GREAT INITIATIVE.

Me: WHAT A SMART IDEA. SEE YOU TOMORROW.

Vicki Jacobsen: XX

I glanced at the yard and bit my lower lip. Weeds sprouted at the base of Matt's fruit trees, in his garden beds, and in between the pavers underneath his barbeque. I needed to prioritise getting someone to tend to the plants. With ample funds in my bank account, what better way to spend Matt's life insurance than investing in someone who would bring life and vibrancy back into my husband's garden.

♥ ♥ ♥ ♥ ♥ ♥ ♥

"Hello, Belinda, I'm Dr. Braithwaite. It's nice to meet you." A woman in her mid- to late-fifties with greyish-blonde shoulder-length hair, dark-framed glasses, and a friendly disposition smiled from my laptop screen.

"Hi." I wiggled in Matt's computer chair, annoyed at myself for not setting myself up on the couch where it was much more comfortable. How had Matt used this chair, day in and day out?

She tilted her head. "Before we get started, I wanted to check you're comfortable where you're seated now? It'll be a long session, possibly more than an hour, and I want you to be at ease while we go through this process."

Had she read my mind?

"If you'd like to snuggle up in bed or on your sofa, please feel free. You can switch your camera off while you get settled."

"Thank you." I relaxed my shoulders. "I might take you up on your offer."

Dr. Braithwaite smiled. "Please do. I've kicked my shoes off here."

I switched off the camera, grabbed the laptop and its charger, and padded to the lounge room. After plugging the charger into the socket near the couch, I balanced the laptop on the couch arm and sunk onto the cushioned seat. My back popped, and I gushed a garbled half-sigh, half-moan.

A soft chuckle filtered through my laptop speakers. "Don't get too comfortable. I'd hate to have to wake you from a nap."

I grabbed my computer, rested it on my lap, and turned on the camera. "Sorry about that."

Dr. Braithwaite waved her hand in front of her chest. "No need to apologise. Your comfort is essential."

If my comfort was essential, why was I subjecting myself to a therapist's scrutiny and potential embarrassment?

"I've read the notes you included on the New Patient form." She locked her gaze on her camera so she appeared to look directly at me. "I'm sorry about your husband and your miscarriages. What a difficult time you've had to navigate."

My throat muscles jammed, and moisture gathered in my eyes.

"Do you have a support network? Or are you doing this alone?" Her reassuring voice comforted me.

"I have a few friends here in Tellarine who've been supportive." Everyone had been helpful and caring before I shunned them all.

"Any family?"

I shook my head. Not family I could rely on.

"That's okay. I'm just building a picture." She glanced away and shuffled some papers. "You're on medication for depression. Anything else you think I should know?"

I pursed my lips and thought about what I had written on the form earlier in the week. Dead husband, dead babies, dead wom— wait. "Did I mention I had a hysterectomy roughly six months ago?"

Dr. Braithwaite shuffled the papers and tapped on a keyboard. "No. Was this elective surgery?"

"Emergency. In early May." How had six months already passed? It seemed like the surgery only happened last week.

"I'm sorry, Belinda. You lost your husband and your ability to have children within a month?"

"And a baby." Several tears slipped down my cheeks. "Well … not a baby. Matt and I thought I was pregnant but …"

"I see. Trauma upon trauma."

I nodded.

"It was very brave of you to reach out to me. I'm glad you did."

Warmth pooled in my chest, and I wiped the tears from my face. Somehow, I was glad too.

We spent the better half of an hour talking through my history, my family, my work situation, my support network, and my feelings.

So many feelings.

"Going forward, I'd like to book in weekly appointments." Dr. Braithwaite stared at her computer camera and met my gaze. "But if you struggle or need to talk, never hesitate to call my office, okay?"

"Thank you."

"I'll have Carolyn email you your goals list we compiled, and between now and next Friday, I would like you to tackle the first goal on the list."

Getting out of the house. We both figured it was something I could cope with, a small step in the right direction.

"You can so this, Belinda. You've endured a world of pain, more than most, but you're more than a survivor. You can turn your life around. And you know how I know this?"

I furrowed my brow. "How?"

"You went grocery shopping. You opened the door again to friendship, and you contacted me." Her lips curved in a kind smile. "You've already started. Getting out of the house on a consistent basis is the first step of many, setting you on a path destined for success."

I was more than a survivor.

"I understand how overwhelming sessions like these can be, particularly the first, so I jotted down your ideas for places to visit. Carolyn will send these as part of your goals list. You'll have them at your fingertips and won't need to remember all the details."

"Thanks."

"Take care, and I'll see you next week." After a wave and exchanged farewells, Dr. Braithwaite ended the telehealth call.

I closed my laptop and my eyes. Even, regular-paced heartbeat. An absence of rushing blood between my ears. Dry palms and steady breaths.

Maybe she was right and I could do this.

CHAPTER TWENTY
Incremental Progress

Outing ideas:
Window shopping in Robinvale
Order a coffee at a café (not Benanu's)
Buy fresh produce at the green grocer
Go supermarket shopping again
Walk along the local bike track (but avoid the play equipment area)
Browse in a plus-sized clothing store
Drive or walk past Tellarine Secondary College

I reread my list, happy I had crossed off several items over the past three weeks. Dr. Braithwaite had been pleased with my report each week, adding extra tasks—the thought provoking, emotional kind—to my weekly routine.

Today's plan was to work on two goals at once. When I had window shopped in Robinvale last week, I spotted a café in the quieter part of town, so I hoped to cross off "order a coffee" and start on my "write down a vision of my future" homework. Sitting at the café appeared the easier assignment of the two.

Dr. Braithwaite believed I could accomplish these tasks, so I had to trust myself and try. I slid my lightweight cardigan over my T-shirt, tied my hair into a ponytail, and threaded my hair through the back of one of Matt's sports caps. Seizing my courage, I gathered my bag, phone, and keys, and drove to Robinvale.

I crossed the threshold of the quaint café, Jestaminet, and surveyed the room. Twelve rustic wooden tables paired with matching chairs filled the small room, its stark white walls and tiled floors clashing with the deep timber wainscotting and bushland landscapes framed along the walls. A charming coffee bar and payment area filled the far-right corner, and an elegant glass cake display cabinet nestled in the left. More than half of the tables were empty.

"Good morning." A lithe, pretty brunette with an olive complexion approached, her eyes alight.

I pressed my hands to my ample thighs and smoothed my tracksuit pants. Why had I come here again?

"Would you like a table?" She tilted her head, bouncing her ponytail.

I nodded and forced a smile. "Please."

"Will anyone be joining you today?" The server stepped toward a timber stand beside the entrance.

"No," I whispered.

She smiled at me, grabbed a menu, and gestured at a table away from the window. "This way."

I settled onto the surprisingly sturdy chair, tucked near the wall.

The waitress poured water into my glass. "I'll give you a few minutes."

"Thanks." My stomach pinched, and I glanced at the time on my phone. Eleven forty. An early lunch, followed by a hopefully-not-disappointing coffee, would do me good.

After drooling over the French-inspired menu, I ordered what I hoped to be the cheesiest and tastiest croque monsieur toasted sandwich I had ever eaten, with a tomato salad, and a tall glass of sparking orange drink.

I retrieved the notebook and pen from my bag, flipped to a

blank page, and scrawled "Vision for my future" along the top line. Now what? I leaned against the firm seat back and twiddled the pen between my fingers. A vision for my future. I scrunched my brow and stilled my fidgeting fingers. My future? What was there to look forward to anymore?

A familiar Scripture in Jeremiah whispered to me, hinting of hope for my future.

I pushed it aside and stared at the page. Matt was gone. My desperate desire to birth a child was now impossible. And the thought of teaching secondary students sent unpleasant shivers down my spine.

A pleasant smell from the café kitchen wafted to my nose. I closed my eyes and breathed in the flavours. Frying butter. Tarragon. And something sweet. Caramelised sugar?

I opened my eyes and pursed my lips. I enjoyed the idea of creating food. Baking treats and testing recipes. Dr. Braithwaite had even suggested I might like to reacquaint myself with my kitchen. Maybe not this week, but soon.

"Sorry for the delay." The lithe brunette placed my drink on the table. "Your food will be ready in the next few minutes."

"Thanks." I smiled and sipped the bubbly beverage. My lunch arrived two minutes later, and I bit into the delicious toasted sandwich.

This time last year, I never would have imagined sitting at a café, alone, eating a ham-and-cheese toastie, and contemplating my future. Belinda of yesteryear had everything worked out according to her masterplan, and bore the strain of frustration and heartache when baby after baby refused to stick to the roadmap. Now my husband had ditched our plans, followed closely by my uterus.

Dr. Braithwaite was right. I needed to regroup, reassess, and reinvigorate my future. My husbandless, baby-less future.

"Are you enjoying your meal?"

I glanced at the waitress, covered my mouth with my hand, and nodded. I hoped my face was greaseless and cheese-free.

"I'm glad." She grinned and jetted off to another occupied table.

I crunched another mouthful and studied the space around me.

An elderly couple dined across the room. A suited man with his laptop tapped away near the window. Two young women, possibly in their early twenties, snuck furtive, raised-eyebrow looks over their shoulders in my direction.

I chewed, my jaw slowing with each sneaky glance. Was there something wrong with me? I grabbed the napkin from my lap and wiped my face.

A loud snort crossed the room from the women's table.

My cheeks heated. Were they talking about me?

Several snickers echoed, followed by what sounded like "she should lay off fatty food."

My insides recoiled. I dropped the final quarter of sandwich on my plate, brushed crumbs from my fingers, and drained my drinking glass. Why had I thought a meal was a good idea? Dr. Braithwaite had written down coffee. Now my stomach swirled too much for coffee.

I gathered my things, all thoughts about my future fleeing, and paid for my meal.

"Please visit us some other time." The brunette waitress handed me a payment receipt with a beaming smile.

I nodded and turned toward the door.

The twenty-something women stood behind me, chatting, both with hands resting on rounded bellies.

Pregnant. Why was the world so unfair?

I gritted my teeth, dropped my gaze, and scuttled from the café, my legs stiff and eyes stinging. *Get a grip, Belinda.*

"Tabby!"

Something small slammed into my legs.

Gravity pulled, and I flapped my arms, stopping its force. My pulse hastened, and I set my wide-eyed gaze on the unkempt hair of a child gripping my legs.

"I'm so sorry! Are you okay?" A woman with dark rings under her eyes and a three-wheeler pram grabbed at the child and hoisted the creature onto her hip.

I spotted a tiny bald baby sleeping in the pram, and my heart cramped.

"That was not nice, Tabby. You apologise to this nice lady for running into her on purpose."

On purpose? This woman had her hands full.

The dark-eyed child raised her head and stared at me. "But she looks like the bouncy toy we run into at kindy."

Bouncy toy?

"She looks squishy like the bouncy toy."

The woman's eyes widened further and her cheeks reddened.

My face burned.

"I-I'm sorry, miss, for my unruly and"—the mother glared at her daughter—"rude child. I hope you're okay?"

"I'm fine." Other than random children seeing me as the local Goodyear blimp.

"I'm really sorry." The poor woman looked redder than the tomato salad I never tasted.

"It's fine." I twisted my lips into what I hoped was a friendly, and not murderous, expression, withdrew my traitorous gaze from the sleeping babe, and escaped to my car.

I scrunched my nose at the disgusting-looking brown-and-green furry substance growing inside a small glass container in my fridge. Did I dare open it? How could I justify throwing away a perfectly good Pyrex dish? I placed the container on the kitchen island, opened the lid with my gloved hands, and dry retched from the putrid smell.

I could buy more Pyrex.

Snapping the lid closed, I dumped the container into the

rubbish bin and extracted four other containers from their cold home. Why had I waited this long to clean out the questionable containers at the back of the fridge? Buying fresh produce was great progress, but maintaining the cleanliness of my kitchen had turned into a priority.

My phone buzzed against the counter where it lay beside my tepid cup of tea.

What I would give for a break from this horrible job. I glanced in the direction of my mobile, gritted my teeth, and opened another jar with questionable contents. Dr. Braitwaite had stressed the importance of completing a task, and considering my fridge had been ignored since Vicki cleaned it out a month or two after Matt died, I needed to stick with it.

Five minutes and four putrefying tubs of dip later, my phone buzzed again.

No distractions. Vicki would be glad to wait if she knew I tackled kitchen toxicants.

I discarded green-and-white fuzzy cheeses—had I known Matt had placed them on the wrong shelf, I would have eaten them months ago—liquified cucumbers, a rotten, watery mound of what I hoped had been lettuce, a bag of unidentified somethings, and a sealed packet of slimy, green bacon.

I grimaced at the mishmash of festering items in the bin, and vowed to never again allow my fridge to become a cesspool of contamination.

The *Jaws* theme trilled from my phone.

I stilled. Alison. What did she want? I waited for the looped sinister composition to complete its cycle, followed by the soft beep of a received voicemail.

Another text message tone chirped thirty seconds later.

Nuh-uh. Today was the day for dealing with my fridge and pantry, not my sister. I could talk with her another day.

Maybe.

After surveying the Best Before dates on everything else in my fridge, I opened the pantry door, and set my sights on clearing away stale foodstuffs. What a shame it was harder to clear out the stale relationships in one's life.

I checked dates on boxes of cereal and muesli bars, discarding thoughts of Alison and why she had called, but the pesky theories invaded my headspace. Had she guessed I now lived a "life of luxury," thanks to Matt's life insurance, and needed money to pay for the next gadget or vacation she wanted? I huffed a breath. She had better not have called to invite me to Queensland for Christmas, which was less than two weeks away. The last thing I needed was my first Christmas without Matt hanging with my sister and her toy boy.

A vision of my cramped childhood lounge and dining room flickered across my mind. Mum snored on the threadbare couch, her stick-thin arm dangling, hand on the floor near where Alison squatted on the aged carpet playing with an ancient second-hand Barbie. Dad sprawled on the broken, stained La-Z-Boy recliner, flicking channels on the too-loud television. And I tried to study for my Year Twelve exams.

I squeezed my eyes and fisted my hands. Maybe Alison had good news to share. Had she decided to cut off all ties to our parents? I sucked in a sharp breath. Or one of them had finally overdosed or crossed the wrong person.

Was it bad that the thought of my parents expiring lifted my lips in a sardonic smile?

I shook away the notions and doubled my focus on each pantry shelf. Squishy, wrinkly potatoes with eyes growing out of the potato box, gone. Weightless garlic blackened with mould joined the refuse pile. And a bag of roasted cashews I had lost behind my boxes of tea three years ago.

I tied the rubbish bag and disposed of the heavy sack in the green outdoor wheelie bin, my chest loosening. Today's kitchen cleanse was another step toward getting my life together.

I replaced the bin bag, washed my hands, and checked my

phone.

Every message I had received was from Alison.

My breath hitched, and a familiar heaviness burdened my shoulders. I might have embarked on this slow, painful journey coming to terms with my "new" life, but adding my sister into the mix seemed … counterproductive.

Alison would have to wait.

CHAPTER TWENTY-ONE
Resurrected Memories

Despite ignoring last week's text messages and voicemail from my sister, Alison stayed in my mind each day. When I hung the washing in the hot summer sun, I imagined her childish giggles echoing as she ran through a water sprinkler. Fluffing couch cushions and folding sheets reminded me of the blanket forts I created for her in our tiny bedroom, hiding her from our parents' junkie friends, or the inappropriate activities they participated in with other people in their bedroom. Or the lounge room.

I sipped a latte, comfortably reposed on my couch, and thumbed through my favourite vintage recipe book. A preloved copy of the 1987 *Australian Women's Weekly Cakes and Slices* cookbook I found at the local Salvos when I was fifteen. I had babysat for the lady across the street—Mrs. Wilson?—the afternoon before. She had kind eyes and insisted Alison play with her twin boys while I watched all three. She gifted me a generous ten dollars, and I had handed the grey-haired charity shop volunteer three precious dollars for the book, my other seven dollars going towards a pair of scuffed but intact shoes for Alison, and a pair of jeans for myself. I had kept my cookbook treasure secured in my school bag until I left home three days after my high school graduation.

Apple cake. Black forest cake. Moist treacle gingerbread. I snickered. Matt had enjoyed the tangy lemon icing more than the cake. What a sweet tooth my husband had … but he would never taste my baking again.

Life was unfair.

My phone vibrated on the arm of the couch.

Ali's Toy Boy: GOOD MORNING, BELINDA, IT'S ROB COOPER, ALISON'S PARTNER. I HOPE YOU'RE WELL. I'M REACHING OUT IN THE HOPES YOU'LL GIVE ALI A CHANCE TO TALK WITH YOU. PLEASE HEAR HER OUT. SHE LOVES YOU AND JUST WANTS THE BEST FOR YOU.

Tension radiated in my chest. I dropped my gaze to my knees and grimaced. Had I behaved irrationally? Should I show her some grace and … what? I furrowed my brow. Maybe I should ask Dr. Braithwaite how to deal with the situation.

I returned to the cookbook and relaxed my shoulders. Zucchini walnut loaf. Lemon fruit twist. Moist coconut cake with pink coconut ice frosting. I stared at the page but relived another memory.

Flour and coconut scattered across a roughened kitchen countertop. My echoed footsteps, pacing back and forth in front of the oven, my insides twisting with anticipation for my almost-baked cake and dread Dad would come home and throw it against the wall like the banana loaf I had baked the month before. The squeak of the rickety chair with each swing of Alison's legs. I had bought all the ingredients, borrowed a cat-shaped cake pan from the old lady next door, and baked the coconut cake for Alison's tenth birthday.

I launched from the couch, cookbook in hand, and surveyed my pantry staples and refrigerated dairy items. Everything. I had every single ingredient, even the sour cream, on hand. Why not? Kneeling to peek into one of my kitchen cupboards, I grabbed a twenty-two-centimetre round cake pan, buttered and lined it with baking paper, and gathered all the ingredients.

Alison and I had endured many horrible things over the years, events I had tried to forget or my brain had mercifully suppressed. Living in a home where you knew your parents cared less about you than their next hit had a way of burrowing deep into your soul. Their apathy and neglect shaped me, but also fuelled me in my efforts to protect my little sister. Playing hide and seek in our wardrobe when the longhaired man with scary eyes stared at my sister longer than I liked. Or the guy my mum slept with on and off, who sometimes stumbled into our bedroom at three in the morning, and I would redirect him down the hallway while he copped a feel through my thin pyjamas.

I gritted my teeth, turned the dial higher on my Kenwood stand mixer, and stared at the gyrating cake batter. My parents' behaviour was unconscionable. How could Alison choose to allow them into her life? Had I protected her to the point of innocence?

No. She experienced her fair share of grief after I was "forced from the nest."

The day my parents kicked me out of home was the best and worst day of my life. Dad said their "responsibility" ended the day I graduated, and he had given me a three-day grace period. I was relieved to escape the hellhole of my upbringing, but broken-hearted because Alison had to stay behind.

The recipe blurred, and I wiped my eyes. I had begged my parents to allow me to look after Alison, but they refused. And when I tried to visit her, they slammed the door in my face. I had stormed down the concrete steps, certain my presence would have been welcomed if I carried a bag of white powder for them.

I visited with my sister after school most afternoons, unless I was working or at university. When I saved enough money to rent my own small apartment a year later—not a shared dorm room or shared apartment—Alison stayed with me most weekends, and moved in permanently after Dad blackened her eye.

She was fourteen.

Once I attained my teaching degree, I scoured Brisbane for teaching positions, but demand for Textiles and Food Studies teachers was low, so I widened my search.

I found the position in Tellarine during the summer holidays when I was almost twenty-four. The opportunity was fabulous, and starting life afresh in a small town appealed to me. But not to Alison.

I submitted my job application online. We fought during the two-week wait. Alison, determined to stay, declared I was no better than our parents by deserting her. Me, desperate to trade in my waitressing and retail jobs for a teaching role.

Sandra contacted me for a phone interview, and Principal Marsden offered me the role after ten minutes of conversation. My heart knew this was the place for me.

I switched off the mixer and poured the batter into the prepared cake tin. Alison was manipulative, but what could I expect after the upbringing she had?

But you chose a different path.

I slid the pan into the oven and set the timer for forty-five minutes. I had chosen to break free from my parents before I left home, when I went to youth group with my school friend. Claire had been one of the few people I shared stories from my home life, and youth had been a lifeline for me.

I pressed my hands against my legs, shook my head, and gathered the ingredients for the icing. I whipped up the coconut ice frosting—unsettled by the many reminders of my past—and popped the bowl into the fridge.

My tummy roiled despite the delicious coconutty scent permeating the kitchen. What to do with this cake? Vicki might like it, but driving to her home seemed daunting. Diana or Tara might like a slice, but an entire cake?

The oven alarm beeped, and I placed the cake onto a cooling rack.

I rested on the couch and mulled over what to do. Dropping into the church was a hard "no," and while the staff at Tellarine Secondary College would enjoy the treat, I would not enjoy the third degree from my old colleagues. I pressed my hand to my lips. What about Tellarine Retirement Village? Old people liked cake and coconut.

When the cake cooled, I rewhipped the icing, slathered it across the top, and boxed the cake into my travel container. What an easy experience. I foresaw more baking in my future.

♥ ♥ ♥ ♥ ♥ ♥ ♥

"I have a question." I repositioned my legs on the couch and returned my gaze to the laptop.

Dr. Braithwaite smiled and nodded on the screen. "Go ahead."

I shared what had happened with my sister.

"This all happened last week?"

I nodded.

"And her boyfriend messaged you this week."

"Correct." I rubbed my hands along my thighs. "I know we only talked about Ali briefly when I shared my history with you, and I'm taking small steps every week, but …"

Dr. Braithwaite raised a brow.

"I don't know if things will get better or worse should I reach out to her." Alison equalled risk.

"How did you feel after your last conversation"—she looked away from the camera and pursed her lips—"in late August?"

Wow, the woman was the queen of note-taking.

"You mentioned in our first session that you hated the way your sister made you feel. Can you expand on that thought?"

I cleared my clogged throat. "I guess … I spent my childhood raising myself and my sister, so I've always struggled with why she's involved with our parents. It became a bit of a joke between Matt and me how she'd only contact me when she wanted something. I'm used to that type of relationship—"

"The parent-child relationship? You being the parent and her the child?"

"Maybe?" I furrowed my brow. Was that how I saw us?

Dr. Braitwaite smiled. "But your relationship is changing. Maturing. And the unknown can be daunting."

"Not sure about maturing." I blew out a breath. "But I take your point. I'm not used to her caring about me. She can be frustrating, but she can be genuine too. And the therapy idea was a seed planted for me."

"Where do you see your relationship heading?"

"I'm sceptical her days of asking for money are over." I rubbed my cheek.

"Do you think that's why she called last week?"

"I did at first, but I'm not sure now. Not after Rob's message. It didn't sound like she wants to connect for a bank transfer but … because she cares?"

"Rob seems like a stabilising force in your sister's life."

I thought back to their visit. Dr. Braithwaite could be right.

"If she has his support, Alison might be trying to connect with you simply because you're her sister. No strings attached."

There were always strings attached with my sister. I stared at the screen.

"I suggest, if you feel comfortable doing so, reply to your sister, and let her know you're open for communication." Dr. Braithwaite steepled her fingers, elbows resting on the arms of her chair. "It doesn't need to be a long text, and it doesn't have to be this week. Your focus is to still paint a picture of your future, where you might like to be in the coming months and years. But if you want to reach out? Do so."

Dr. Braithwaite shared healthy coping mechanisms I could use when anxiety or fear hit, and we brainstormed additional tasks I could accomplish outside my house. The session ended quicker than I expected, and soon I huddled on the couch, hopeful for tomorrow.

"I'm so glad you were here." Vicki walked beside me along Diana's driveway toward my vehicle parked on the street in the shade of a huge eucalyptus tree.

Summer had cranked the heat to sweltering.

My belly was full after a lovely Christmas lunch at the Harrises with all the gang. But two hours with everyone—including a little hug with three-month-old Chelsea—was enough for today. Tears had pricked when Diana served Matt's favourite Christmas dessert. Chocolate date pudding with butterscotch sauce and vanilla ice cream.

Diana had made the delicious pudding four or five Christmases ago, and Matt had declared it his favourite. The man had roughly fifty-two favourite desserts, but his comment had elicited a beaming smile from its creator, so I knew his compliment hit the mark.

But eating the pudding today? My mouth dried, and my insides curdled with the first taste.

Matt would be disappointed.

When I stepped through the Harrises front door, I had breathed through the initial nerves jittering my body, but soon settled into the familiarity of loud conversation, fun banter, and tasty food.

"You did really well." Vicki embraced me.

"Thanks." A bead of perspiration dribbled from my forehead to my ear.

"Enjoy a quieter afternoon." She stepped backwards into the shade.

"I will." I opened the driver's door, plonked onto my seat, and travelled the few minutes home.

During my most recent session with Dr. Braithwaite, I had shared about the growing restlessness I experienced. Fidgety limbs, impatience when I stopped for longer than a bathroom break. Less thoughts of Matt's murderer and more questions about my future. Dr. Braithwaite suggested these were signs I was mentally preparing to reinvent myself.

She might be right.

I grabbed my laptop, notebook, and a pen, perched on a kitchen stool, and scribbled my thoughts. Teaching was still a big "no" I suspected would never change, but my reignited passion for cooking could not be ignored. Was there another pathway available for my kitchen skills? Matt's death and my surgery had clouded my judgement, so I was thankful my head was clearer, and I could contemplate a baking career. But what, exactly?

Pulling my laptop closer, I skimmed several forums of people asking similar questions. A Food Studies teacher in New South Wales wanted to enter the restaurant industry. An ex-baker—the yeasty, bread kind—contemplated opening his own patisserie. Several people with little kitchen experience asked how to break into the cooking world or the best steps to gain experience.

"The best experience is practice." I chortled, glanced at my spotless kitchen, and checked the time. Not yet three p.m. An itch to bake something twitched through my skin. Dr. Braithwaite had given me a phrase to repeat for moments like these.

What would bring me joy today?

I closed my eyes and slowed my breaths. Vanilla cupcakes. No. Vanilla butterfly cupcakes with fresh cream, sprinkled with icing sugar.

I set the oven temperature and measured out ingredients. Muscle memory kicked in, allowing an opportunity for contemplation. What career direction would bring me joy? Cooking … where? When? As an employee? Or could I run a small business of my own? I dropped softened butter, sugar, eggs, vanilla extract, milk, and sifted flour into the stainless-steel mixer bowl. A local cupcake shop? A patisserie filled with sweet treats and baked goods?

The Kenwood whirred to life. Would locking myself into baking, frosting, and decorating cupcakes, day in and day out, offer me satisfaction? I scrounged in the kitchen cupboard, extracted two cupcake trays, and inserted paper cases into the twenty-four spaces. I liked cupcakes, but not to bake every single day. At least a patisserie bakery offered a general range of sweet goods, providing variety in my work kitchen.

I ladled cake batter into paper cases, slid the trays into the oven, and washed the dishes. Although my friends often asked me to bake, I enjoyed creating savoury dishes. I had catered for many parties and gatherings in the past, and from the feedback I had received, I was quite a decent cook. Would something along the lines of catering be a better fit? I had imagined, once or twice, what working a catering role fulltime would be like. A varied job would fulfil me.

But without Matt by my side? Running an enterprise without his all-round wisdom or input on the financial and accounting arm of the business seemed … daunting. Could I jump the considerable hurdles, regardless of who helped me?

I was a cook, a baker. A creative. My pragmatic thinking switch seemed to be broken. That was Matt's job. Or had been.

The oven timer beeped.

I removed the trays from the oven, allowed the cupcakes to cool for five minutes, and transferred the golden gems onto the cooling rack. While the fluffy treats cooled, I draped myself over a vacant section of the kitchen island nearer the air-conditioning vent. Chilled marble cooled my face and refrigerated air dried the wet patch across my back. Something logical slammed inside my head, and I jolted upright, my head spinning at the sudden movement. I groaned, blinked, and stared at the cooling cupcakes. What was I meant to do with them?

Keanu and Tara's conversation at the lunch table sprang to mind, and I grabbed my mobile phone.

Me: Hey, Tara, was lovely seeing you. What time did you say Benanu's was catering the community Christmas dinner tonight? 6? I've baked 24 vanilla butterfly cupcakes, but they'll need to be eaten sooner rather than later because of the fresh cream. Would they be a welcome addition to your menu?

I set to whipping the cream while I waited for Tara's response.

My phone buzzed when the cream reached soft peaks.

Tara Everton: Are you serious? We experienced an issue in the kitchen and were just brainstorming another quick dessert option to complement the other treats. What a blessing and answer to prayer! Yes, please! Want me to pop

OVER IN ABOUT AN HOUR TO GET THEM? OR WOULD YOU BE OKAY TO DROP THEM AT THE COMMUNITY CENTRE BY 6:30PM?

I widened my eyes. My cupcakes were an answer to Tara's prayer? No, purely a happy coincidence.

Me: WONDERFUL. I'M NOT SURE I'LL BE READY IN AN HOUR (CAKES ARE STILL COOLING) BUT CAN DROP THEM AT THE CENTRE. WHICH ROOM WILL YOU BE IN?

Tara: THE LARGE MULTI-PURPOSE ROOM. WALK PAST THE ART AND WEIRDO SCULPTURES. WE'LL HAVE SIGNAGE UP. THANK YOU SO MUCH FOR THIS GIFT TO THE COMMUNITY AND AMAZING REMINDER GOD ALWAYS HAS A WAY.

I pressed my palms against my upper thighs. Maybe God had a way for people like Tara and Keanu, both novices in their faith, desperate to please God. But He appeared to forget forging a path for veterans like me.

Like I *used to* be.

God never forgets. Maybe you forgot yourself.

"Nope, not going there," I whispered. Inhaling a breath, I replied to Tara with a "GREAT, SEE YOU LATER," covered and refrigerated the cream, and located my shallow cupcake travel boxes.

This afternoon would be spent focused on preparing the best cupcakes I could share with my community, not the mounting whispers from a part of me determined to derail my life again.

CHAPTER TWENTY-TWO
To Dream the Possible Dream

Luminous colour shimmered around me, a kaleidoscope of texture and light. I drifted along a walkway, my body weightless and unencumbered, and floated into a large room. Stainless-steel benchtops gleamed, dotted with oversized white dinner plates. A gargantuan stovetop housed an eclectic collection of pots beside a wall of glass-fronted ovens. My extremities glowed, and my vision captured an out-of-this-world workspace with food processors, stand mixers, hand mixers, blenders, juicers, and microwaves. Light splashed across my path, and something soft and airy bloomed from my body into the atmosphere.

Happiness.

Movement resumed in the room, like a movie switched from Pause to Play. Faceless workers bustled at each workspace, a symphony of light with every motion. Stirring, whisking, beating. Chopping, plating, kneading. Clockwork precision.

"What's next, boss?" a voice asked.

Boss? I slipped from the kitchen, accelerated through a doorway, and halted. A billboard—Belinda's Catering Service—glimmered above a shopfront, its pink-and-green signage vibrant and welcoming. The blooming inside my body intensified, and wisps of curling colour and light painted my vision.

I inhaled a breath and opened my eyes to the hazy early-morning light trickling under the sides of my closed bedroom curtains. My heartbeat sprinted, its thudding beat echoing in all of my pulse points.

A catering company. I lay unmoving, my gaze focused on the light creeping into my room. Did I have the chops to run a catering business? Would employees want a wreck-of-a-boss like me?

YOU ARE STILL MY MASTERPIECE.

Warmth dispersed through my chest and heated my cheeks. I threw off my summer sheet and the sweet voice inside my head, and focused my thoughts on the promise of tomorrow. I showered and imagined, dressed and thought. Dwelled on the possibilities until a pool of heat bubbled in my gut and my face could no longer hold in a smile.

This excitable sensation of promise felt a thousand times better than grief's weight. By the time I had consumed my breakfast, my fingers itched to call Dr. Braithwaite.

"Doctor Braithwaite's office, Carolyn speaking."

"Carolyn! It's Belinda Briggs."

"Good morning, Belinda. You're sounding chirpy today. How can I help you?"

"Is she available for a quick chat?" I grinned. Grinned! What had the dream unlocked inside of me?

"You've called at the perfect time. Her first appointment called in sick, so let me put you through."

I bounced on my toes beside the kitchen island.

"Belinda. How're you this morning?" Dr. Braithwaite's comforting voice oozed down the line.

"I had a dream I owned a catering company."

Dr. Braithwaite chuckled. "You sound happy at the prospect. Does the idea excite you?"

"It does." How had a simple dream boosted the light in my life?

"That's wonderful, and great progress toward you discovering what you would like to do with your life."

I shimmied on the spot.

"Have you told anyone else about your dream?"

I stilled. "You're the first." Would Vicki support me if I launched out in this direction?

"I think it would be a wise idea to share your progress with your closest friends. Being vulnerable with your loved ones would help knit your relationships and give them confidence that you're trusting them again."

I furrowed my brow. "If I share this idea with Vicki, it would be more than me sharing a dream?"

"Everything we do either builds relationships or pulls them apart. You're not the only one growing your confidence and trust in your friends."

Wow. How had I not thought from someone else's perspective?

"What do you think?"

"I reckon I could tell Vicki." Even knowing, at the back of my mind, my friend would be praying for me.

"I think that would be a wonderful idea." Something rustled on Dr. Braithwaite's end of the call. "Let me know how your conversation went when we meet on Friday."

"Thank you for taking my call."

"Anytime, Belinda. Keep working on your homework, and enjoy your day."

"Yes, boss." I disconnected the call, severing myself from the woman who instilled confidence in me, and stared at my phone. How could I call Vicki and tell her about a dream I had, out of the blue? I rarely recalled my dreams, so discussing my imaginings was uncommon conversation between us. Would she think I had cracked again?

I distracted myself with vacuuming the hallway and bedrooms, each minute cooling my zeal and heightening my anxiety. Sweat traced my spine, dampening the back of my T-shirt, and I huffed several laboured breaths. What was I afraid of? Embarrassing myself? Sounding like someone missing a few marbles? Or was it my old foe, rejection? Heaviness settled in my stomach.

The vacuum whirred loud, reverberating in my head. I pushed the Off button, leaned the handle against my bedroom wall, and lowered to my bed. Fumbling my phone with shaky fingers, I unlocked the screen and drafted several versions of the same, odd-sounding message.

No. A message would never do. I sighed and dialled my friend's number.

"Hello, lovely lady. How're you doing this morning?" Vicki's joyful tone chipped away a layer of my icy panic.

"Well." I drew in a loud breath. "Puffed from vacuuming."

My friend laughed. "You've been productive. I've managed the school run and a cup of tea."

"I was going to message you, but …" I pursed my lips.

"What?"

"I had a dream last night and wrote a few drafts, but explaining over a text wasn't working for me."

"Must've been some dream." Vicki cleared her throat. "Was it … anything like the ones I had years ago?"

What dreams?

"Because I completely understand if you're experiencing something … similar. You must miss Matt and the intimacy you shared."

A memory involving Vicki's ex invaded my muddled brain, and I snorted aloud. "No, no. I'm not having sex dreams like you did."

"Belinda!" Vicki emitted a choked chuckle. "They weren't 'sex dreams.'"

"Really. I recall you saying you and Jude were naked in them." How had we diverged on this path?

"Fine." She blustered a breath. "But they were more like tormenting memories."

"Well, mine wasn't like that." Not sure I wanted to dream about a naked Matt anytime soon. His perfect muscle tone and body shape would remind me how he would never change and my body would. Already had.

"So, tell me about this intriguing dream of yours."

I smiled. "I didn't say it was intriguing."

"But purer than my past dreams."

"Totally." I chuckled and stretched out against the bed. "I dreamed I owned a catering company, with lots of swanky appliances, and plenty of kitchen staff."

"That's a wonderful dream to have. How did you feel when you woke up?"

I stared at the tall, swaying trees through the opened curtains. "Like I actually could do it."

"Because you can, Bee. You could run a successful catering business. You already have plenty of local clients you could approach, and past clients from the parties you've catered, to ask for official feedback and leads to more work."

"You honestly think so?"

"Of course! You're great with people, so your staff would love working with you, and you're precise about details and planning. If you believe this is the right thing for you to do, you'd excel."

The last layer of apprehension melted, warming my insides. "I'd need a lot of help getting things off the ground, and possibly more money as this investment might be more than I'm comfortable paying upfront."

"It's early days, but after you work on your due diligence and have someone crunch the numbers, you'll have more confidence in your decision."

My confidence had grown while Vicki spoke.

"I'll be praying for you."

I pressed my lips together and counted to three. "Thanks for chatting, I've appreciated it."

"Anytime. I'm here for you."

I had no doubt about Vicki's support. But the Jesus part of her life … I could do without.

Why had I driven here?

Chilled refrigerated air blasted my left cheek and right hand, the car air-conditioning vents whistling from the force of the loud, gusty temperature setting. I flexed my fingers clutching the steering wheel and stared through my side window.

A gated driveway filled my view, the private dirt road disappearing around the bend, obscured by bushes and trees.

What had possessed me to drive thirty minutes on a Sunday afternoon to stare at a dusty driveway and closed gate?

Memories of our time on Anita's parents' property steamrolled my mind. Sharing a picnic in the idyllic spot with Matt, water rippling from the light breeze. Divulging my pregnancy. Making love to my husband for the very last time. Tears blurred my vision, and I rubbed the wetness away with my partially-frozen right hand.

I missed him so much. Over nine months had passed and the ache in my heart reminded me every day of my loss. When would this pain ease? Would my life ever become easier?

I studied the rustic scene outside and wished I could have one more day with Matt. One more picnic. One more shared laugh. One more moment, skin to skin.

My phone buzzed on the passenger seat.

Vicki Jacobsen: ANY CHANCE YOU'RE HOME? NICHOLAS AND I WANTED TO POP IN FOR A MOMENT, IF THAT'S OKAY?

I sniffled, lowered the air-conditioner temperature, and glanced across the road. Sitting in the sweltering January sun was unproductive. Maybe I should visit Vicki for a change.

Me: I'M ABOUT TWENTY MINUTES FROM YOUR PLACE. I COULD POP IN?

Vicki Jacobsen: SORRY, WE'RE AT DIANA'S TODAY. WHEN DO YOU THINK YOU MIGHT BE HOME? SOON?

Me: IT'LL TAKE ABOUT 30 MINS TO GET HOME. I'LL LEAVE HERE

SHORTLY, SO GIVE ME A FEW MOMENTS TO CHANGE MY SWEATY CLOTHES, THEN COME ON BY.

Vicki Jacobsen: EXCELLENT. WE'LL SEE YOU IN ABOUT AN HOUR. XX

I replied with a thumbs up emoji and locked my gaze on the gate one final time. "I wish I could rest my head on your shoulder and bask in your love. I miss you, Matt."

Moments later, I nudged my car in the direction of home, and by the time I parked in my garage, my back and buttocks were drenched with sweat. I peeled myself from the driver's seat, shed my clothes onto my bedroom floor, and luxuriated in a refreshing shower.

My hair was semi-dry when a knock reverberated on the front door.

"Bee." Vicki beamed and pulled me into a firm hug. "You smell delicious."

"You can thank whatever bodywash and shampoo I've got stashed in the shower."

"Afternoon." Nick smiled and escorted his wife inside.

I padded toward the kitchen, filled the kettle, and eyed my friends now perched on kitchen barstools. "Hot or cold drink?"

"I'm fine," Vicki said.

"Do you have peppermint tea?" Nick rubbed the back of his neck.

"Sure do." I grabbed a mug and a tea bag. "No kids today?"

Vicki chuckled. "Jasmine's quite obsessed with her little niece, so they're both spending time with Chelsea."

"She is a lovely little thing." I poured hot water into Nick's mug, dunked the tea bag, and nodded toward the lounge room. "Here or in there?"

The married couple glanced at each other with unreadable expressions.

What was that about?

"Let's sit in the lounge." Vicki shooed me away from the kettle and looped her elbow with mine. "Come sit with me. Nicholas can finish up."

After I was guided to my spot on the couch, I settled beside my friend, and waited for Nick to occupy his usual seat. "What's up?"

Nick sipped his tea. "Victoria tells me you're researching what's required for starting a catering company."

"That's right." I wrinkled my nose. If research included jotting down business name ideas and an hour of trawling through online forums.

"I think it's a great idea." He rested his mug on a coffee table coaster. "She also mentioned you might need some capital to fund your venture."

"It's a possibility. I don't like the idea of sinking all of Matt's money into a business—"

"It's your money, Bee." Vicki squeezed my hand.

I shrugged. "I won't know until I go through the numbers."

Nick leaned forward, rested his elbows on his knees, and cupped his hands, fingers intertwined. "Well, should you decide you need more capital, we'd like to be investors."

"What?" I whipped my gaze between my friends. "Why would you do that?"

"We believe in you." Vicki grinned. "And we want to support you in any way we can."

I blinked, my cheeks heating, and studied Matt's empty recliner. "I appreciate the offer, but—"

"There's no pressure … or strings attached. We just want you to know the offer's available should you need it." Nick focused on my face. "Okay?"

I nodded.

"Good." He consumed the rest of his tea and stood. "We should probably rescue my big princess from her zealous sister."

"You're probably right." Vicki stretched her arms and rose from the couch.

I shuttled my friends to the door—my head in a daze—farewelled them both, and returned to the lounge room. Had I imagined our brief conversation or had my friends actually offered to put their hard-earned money into my business? I lowered to the couch and rubbed my chin. Heaven knew I appreciated their offer. A generous, unexpected offer. But was it wise to mix business with pleasure? What if my business tanked after a few months and we all lost money?

An image of the Jacobsens greeting people at church sprang to my mind. With their money came their faith and prayers. I slid my palms down my face. Jesus no longer directed my world, but He was still important to them. Entangling myself financially with my friends might not be wise.

CHAPTER TWENTY-THREE
Seeking Silver Linings

"How are you this morning, Belinda?" Dr. Braithwaite's kind eyes focused on the screen.

I aimed a smile at my laptop camera. "I'm feeling … up. Like I might actually walk this new life path and even succeed."

"I'm pleased you're starting to believe in yourself because you *can* do this."

A peaceful sensation enveloped me.

"Share with me one positive moment from this week."

I pursed my lips and furrowed my brow. "I had some friends pop over on Sunday and offer to invest in my catering business, should I decide to start a business and need money."

"How did this offer make you feel?" Dr. Braithwaite tilted her head.

I seesawed my shoulders. "It's very generous of them, and certainly a confidence booster, but …"

She raised an eyebrow.

"I can't keep thinking it would be unwise to tangle ourselves financially. Many friendships and relationships have failed when something like this doesn't go to plan."

"And you think it might not go to plan?"

I shrugged. "Nothing in life is guaranteed." I had learned this lesson the hard way.

Dr. Braithwaite jotted something into her notebook. "Tell me one low moment you experienced this week."

"Apart from the doubt this offer gave me?"

She nodded.

I flipped through the events of the past week. Grocery shopping. A slow walk in the park. Refuelling my car at the petrol station with the skinny youth who kept staring at my oversized body. My Sunday drive.

I released a slow breath. "I somehow found myself outside the property where Matt and I had last picnicked … where I told him about the baby."

Dr. Braithwaite lowered her pen. "You hadn't planned to go there?"

"No. I … went for a drive and ended up parked outside the gate."

"How did you feel?"

"Heartbroken." I swallowed the lump in my throat. "That intense sense of missing him washed over me again. I recalled some of the memories from that wonderful afternoon and cried. But then Vicki messaged me, which snapped me out of the heaviness, and I drove home."

Dr. Braithwaite's gaze met mine. She had an amazing knack for looking at me although she was hours away in Melbourne. "You will experience more moments like these, but you're now equipped with the tools to process them and make it to the other side."

"I don't feel as helpless as I did a few months ago." I wiped away a stray tear.

"Which means I'm doing my job."

I chuckled. Another memory popped into my brain, and my smile wavered. "My lawyer called on Wednesday."

Dr. Braithwaite retrieved her pen. "And how did you feel after you received the call?"

I thought back on my brief conversation with Paige. "Okay. I mean, it's frustrating the case has been adjourned again, but … I'm honestly okay."

"Did you dwell on the case or the perpetrator?" She scratched something into her notebook.

I shook my head. "I was in the middle of sorting through my baking supplies, so I took the call, accepted the situation, and returned to my kitchen."

Dr. Braithwaite smiled. "That's remarkable progress, Belinda. You should be proud of yourself."

Heat singed my cheeks, and I shifted in my seat. Was it a big deal I no longer plotted the murder of Matt's killer? I scarcely thought about that boy anymore, and months had passed since I dreamed of him receiving his just desserts. Knowing he was tucked away from harming anyone else comforted me.

"I was reviewing your file last night and noted you've been taking antidepressants for eight months." Dr. Braithwaite tapped on her keyboard. "You've shown great progress the last two months, and I believe you're ready to start being weaned from your medication."

Huh?

"Would you feel comfortable speaking with Dr. Fallow and setting a plan in motion?"

"Is that an option?" I peeked at my reflection on the bottom right corner of my screen. A soft, peaceful-looking expression glowed on my face.

"This is the goal, to help you reach the point where you no longer need medication or weekly therapy to function and be happy."

I *had* achieved a lot of great things during the last eight weeks. And I had accomplished it all without God.

"So, what do you say?" Dr. Braithwaite smiled at me through the computer. "It will be a slow road, but I believe you're ready."

A giddy warmth spread through my chest and limbs. "Yes. I can do this."

"You can. And I'll be here, walking with you the entire time."

My therapy session concluded twenty minutes later, and I booked in a doctor's appointment for four o'clock.

I trudged along the footpath and weaved through the doctor's full car park. Sweat beaded my brow and dampness tickled my armpits. I squeezed my arms against my sides and hoped any dreaded sweat patches would choose not to form today.

A young mother with a toddler exited the building. She nodded and stepped to the side.

"Thank you," I whispered, and entered the foyer with a minute to spare.

Blessed cool air swept across my face and exposed skin. I exhaled a breath and approached the reception desk.

A twenty-something woman in a red high-backed chair smiled at me.

"Hi. I have an appointment with Dr. Fallow? Belinda Briggs."

She studied her computer screen and nodded. "Great. Please have a"—she looked past me and wrinkled her brow—"seat."

I turned around, glanced across the waiting room, and swallowed a moan. Every single seat was taken.

Great.

"Someone should vacate a seat soon." The receptionist spoke with far too much hope in her tone.

I pivoted and faced the desk. "One of those days today?"

She sighed. "We have all three GPs in today, but also several emergencies."

"I understa—"

"Excuse me, are you done?"

I jolted and twisted around.

A petite brunette with a slim figure and impeccable makeup bored her gaze into my makeup-free face. "Because you're clogging the queue."

"Sorry." I stepped aside, my face and skin fiery.

"I have a three-fifty appointment with Dr. Yeoh."

She was ten minutes late and had the audacity to be so rude?

The receptionist offered me an apologetic smile and addressed the intruder. "Your name?"

"Bella Vaughn." She glanced at the waiting room and crinkled her nose. "How many people are before me?"

The receptionist plastered on a bright smile and consulted her computer. "Three."

The ever-pleasant Miss Vaughn executed a theatrical eyeroll and straightened. "Call me when you're ready. I'll wait in the car."

I widened my eyes as she strutted to the exit.

"Hey, tubby, there's a seat here for you," a gruff male voice called.

Tubby? I glanced around the room.

An elderly man held a wooden cane across the seat beside him with his left hand and pointed at me with his right. "Chubby. Come sit next to me."

My fiery skin prickled, and my gut swirled.

"Mr. Lake!" The receptionist's voice sounded strangled.

This was not happening.

"What?" The old man shrugged. "I'm doing my civic duty helping fat, pretty ladies have a rest."

The air in my lungs vaporised, and I dropped my gaze to the grey carpeted floor. I could feel eyes staring at me, itching my skin.

"You can't speak to people like that." The receptionist sighed.

"Give it a break, Dennis, and shut your trap," an elderly woman's voice echoed nearby.

I lifted my chin and spotted a sprightly-looking elderly woman with sky-blue eyes sporting a blue rinse in her short-cropped waves. She seemed familiar. Had she attended an event I catered?

"So sensitive." Mr. Lake grumbled and thumped his cane on the hard seat. "Well, sit down already."

The woman in her eighties grabbed her oversized handbag, stood, and offered me her chair. "Sit here, love, and I'll sit over there."

"Stop interfering, Dawn." Mr. Lake's grumpy voice grated

against my nerves.

"Knock it off, you old coot." She waved her hand in his direction and smiled at me.

I shook my head. "That's okay. I'll—"

"He'll talk your ear off whinging about his aged dog being in difficulty or the history of his bunions."

Gross.

"I will not!" Mr. Lake whacked his cane against the hard, vacant chair.

The delightful elderly woman stepped closer and patted my arm. "I've put up with his nonsense since Form Four. I'll survive."

"Thank you, Mrs. …"

"Inglebar. Dawn Inglebar."

"Thank you, Mrs. Inglebar." I offered her a thankful smile and lowered to the warm chair, my pulse hammering in my neck.

"You're welcome, love." She crossed the room and brushed the wooden cane aside, filled the seat beside Mr. Lake, and winked in my direction.

"Why'd you spoil my fun? You know I like meat on my women."

Mrs. Inglebar widened her eyes at her neighbour. "You think that lovely young lady would stoop so low to spend more time with you?"

"Heavier women are often more desperate for attention." He twiddled his cane against the carpet. "I'm quite the stallion, if you catch my drift."

"May the Almighty spare me."

Heat blasted under my skin. My face had to be redder than a beetroot. I balled my hands in my lap, stared at my bundled fingers, and waited for my name to be called.

♥ ♥ ♥ ♥ ♥ ♥ ♥

"Any questions?" Dr. Fallow handed me a sheet of paper

containing the new gameplan for my medication.

"I need to keep track of my mood swings?"

"If you have any, yes. Or days when tasks which didn't overwhelm you while on a higher dosage are suddenly difficult."

"And whether my sleep is affected." I skimmed the page. "Or my health."

"The next fortnight is crucial. Be self-aware in everything you do because it's better to nip an issue in the bud than deal with complications."

"Will do."

Dr. Fallow leaned forward in his chair. "Having someone alongside you, helping to monitor potential symptoms, is another successful strategy. Usually, a spouse or adult child helps facilitate this, but you could ask a close friend to pop in more often than usual."

Maybe Vicki would agree to a few morning coffees at my place?

"Call if you experience any symptoms."

"Thanks, Dr. Fallow." I smiled, stood, and exited the consulting room.

After huffing through the late-afternoon heat to my parked car, I drove home and messaged Vicki while I prepared a light dinner.

Me: HAD A PRODUCTIVE SESSION WITH DR. B AND SAW DR. FALLOW TO REDUCE MY ANTI-D DOSAGE. DR. F SUGGESTS I HAVE SOMEONE AWARE OF THE WEANING PROCESS ABLE TO KEEP AN EXTRA EYE ON ME OVER THE NEXT 2 WEEKS. YOU UP FOR SOME POST-SCHOOL DROP OFF COFFEES NEXT WEEK?

I threw chopped vegetables into a sizzling pan and tossed them along the scorching surface. The pan hissed, spitting water and oil, and steam billowed. I dropped strips of seasoned beef, which I had cooked moments ago, back into the veggie mix, and knocked the stir-fry around until the broccoli had softened.

My phone chirped beside my place setting at the island bench.

I flicked off the stove, poured the food into my bowl, and

squatted on the barstool.

Vicki Jacobsen: WOW! WHAT A TREMENDOUS DAY YOU'VE HAD! COUNT ME IN FOR COFFEE. AND IF YOU FEEL UP FOR IT, I COULD TAKE YOU OUT FOR LUNCH ONE DAY NEXT WEEK? CALL IT A TRIAL RUN FOR YOUR BIRTHDAY WHICH IS AROUND THE CORNER.

My birthday. Good heavens, I would turn thirty-nine in three weeks. I glanced at my healthy dinner and stared down at my chunky, larger-than-life thighs. Maybe I should start an exercise routine. Take my health more seriously so I could enjoy a lunch out with my friend without feeling self-conscious.

Me: THANK YOU. AND LUNCH MIGHT BE DOABLE. XX

I had many things to tackle and work on ... why not add another problem or two to my schedule?

CHAPTER TWENTY-FOUR
Trip and Tumble

"Just checking up on you." Vicki's bright voice greeted me while I walked along the concrete bike track through the Tellarine parklands.

"I'm well." I passed the noisy play equipment teeming with toddlers and clutched my phone closer to my ear.

"You out so early on a Saturday morning?"

"Fresh air's vital for women living the final year of their thirties."

Vicki laughed. "It's great for women in their forties, too."

I increased my pace, satisfied with my speed when the slight burning sensation grabbed at my thighs, calves, and lungs.

"Any plans for this weekend? I can't believe February is almost over."

I followed the path toward its natural end on a local street. "I'm baking some leaf-shaped vanilla cookies for a childcare centre to use this week. The kids will decorate them as a way to celebrate autumn."

"That sounds fun."

I had imagined the idea during one of my afternoon walks. I had perfected a cookie recipe and wanted to see how it translated for batch cooking, so bought baking supplies along with store-bought icing and decorations for the children to use, and contacted the childcare centre several streets away. After checking allergy concerns, my idea was approved.

I looked forward to getting into the kitchen tomorrow morning.

"Any chance you want to attend the church picnic this afternoon?"

A flood of memories impacted my thoughts. Many happy moments, and others … not so happy. I faltered and steadied myself.

"I should've asked you last week, but it slipped my mind," Vicki said.

I stood under the shade of a tree beside the footpath, heart clip-clopping. "I don't think so."

"That's okay." Something crackled on Vicki's side of the phone line. "We should arrange another time to catch up. Message me the mornings you'll be home this week."

"Sure."

"I'll leave you to enjoy the sunshine."

"Thanks. See you later."

"Bye." Vicki ended the call.

I glanced around the quiet street and trekked along the path toward home. So much had happened at church picnics over the years. Mentoring of youth, playing games with the children. But the hardest picnic had been the one I had broken up with Matt—a month or two before—and I had to watch him flirt with my best friend. Nick also endured their flirting, the poor guy. Matt and Vicki started dating four months later … until the next picnic.

A familiar chill cooled my insides. I had tried not to interact with Matt too much that afternoon, but the pull was strong, and Vicki had been distracted. I knew he was dating my friend, and we never crossed any lines, but lounging on a picnic rug beside him and talking about anything and everything, with an ease I had missed, reignited something inside me. I had wanted to be with him more than I had when we dated.

And then Vicki appeared. I had been so engrossed in Matt, I

failed to see her approaching.

Betrayal and guilt shared a similar awful taste.

"It's in the past," I whispered and glanced ahead.

A man jogged across the road wearing Matt's running gear.

Matt? I sucked in a startled breath, tripped, and tumbled to the concrete path.

Pounding footsteps approached.

I whimpered. My knees and palms stung, and a sharp pain stabbed my arm.

"You okay?" A deep male voice spoke above me.

Not Matt.

I missed his voice.

Warm, firm hands guided me into a seated position beside the road.

I moaned with each gentle movement, my hip throbbing with the rest of my injuries. Tears dampened my cheeks, and I covered my face with my hands.

"Did I hurt you?"

I stilled. Why did this man's voice sound familiar? I wiped my face and glanced up.

Leif Salverson, banker extraordinaire, squatted in front of me, forehead glistening with sweat, and blue eyes focused on me. A small V punctuated between his eyebrows. "Belinda?" His gaze flitted around my face.

He recognised me. Great. "Yep. I'm fine," I croaked, and my face heated. Another thing to add to my pile of embarrassing moments for the day.

He reached for my hands and inspected my palms.

Warmth seeped into my cold, clammy skin. I stared at his face. Had he always resembled Dr. Owen Hunt from *Grey's Anatomy*?

"These'll be sore for a few days." He turned my hands over, his fingers gentle.

I slipped my hands from his. "I'll be fine."

"But your arm mightn't be." He winced.

I peered at my right arm where a slow-bleeding gash dripped a trail of blood to my elbow. No wonder my arm hurt.

Leif yanked his navy T-shirt over his head.

I gurgled at the lean contours of his pecs and gentle abdominal definition. My brain malfunctioned, and I dropped my gaze. To his groin. *Look at his face!* I squeaked and lifted my head.

He wrapped the warm fabric around my injured arm.

I gritted my teeth and stared at his face.

When had he become so handsome? *Stop it, Belinda! You shouldn't be noticing handsome men.*

Leif stood, planted his feet, and leaned down with his arm outstretched. "Need some help up?"

I nodded, grasped his warm fingers, and ignored how much weight he currently supported. Once upright and stable, I pressed my left hand against my wound.

"Let me clean this for you. I live around the corner."

The handsome hero lived locally?

"Moved here last month."

I shook my head and grimaced. "I can handle it."

"Please. Let me help." His blue eyes lacked Matt's mischievous glint but held an ocean of kindness.

"Okay." I gingerly stepped forward. "Which way?"

He tucked his arm around my back and pointed farther down the road.

I ignored the heat from his shirtless torso pressing my side and followed his directions. Each step juddered my frame, my jellified legs losing traction.

Leif tucked me closer to him.

I fought against the mishmash of sensations coursing through my body. *Focus on the pain, not the pleasure of human contact. This isn't your husband. You're not attracted to this man, and he'd never be attracted to you.*

"You're looking great." Leif directed me across another street.

What? I had to be at least fifteen kilograms heavier than when he saw me last year. Might even be twenty.

"Apart from the ripped-up palms and bloody arm." He opened a small gate leading down a path to a lovely whitewashed weatherboard home.

"And my sore knees, hip, and rear end." I widened my eyes. Had I mentioned my backside to a near stranger?

"You took a hard tumble. It might be an idea to see a doctor, just in case." He extracted a set of keys from his pocket and unlocked the door.

"Once you patch me up, I'm sure I'll be fine." How many times had I uttered the word "fine" in the last ten minutes?

"My place isn't as fancy as yours, but it's home." Leif led me to his neat, modest kitchen and pulled out a wooden chair at his kitchen table.

I sank to the seat, groaning.

"I'm planning to renovate it over the next year or two and rent it out." He padded to a kitchen cupboard and grabbed a first aid box. His bare shoulders shifted and stretched with every motion.

Was he going to put on a shirt?

I peered around the room. "It's a lovely place."

"Thanks."

"But how will you find the time to renovate?" I furrowed my brow. "I thought you worked all the time, and now with the extra commute from Tellarine, you'll have even less free time."

"A lovely widow once told me my life was pretty sad because I dedicated my service to the community and had no life of my own." He raised a brow.

I sucked in a breath.

He chuckled, dug through the box of medical paraphernalia, and carried several items to the table.

Had I said such things? To a stranger?

"I needed to reevaluate my life, and your words helped me do just that." Leif unwrapped his bloodied T-shirt from my arm.

"That was very rude of me. I'm sorry … but I can't be held

accountable for anything I said in the early weeks of my grief."

"I'm not asking you to apologise. I'm thanking you." He dabbed antiseptic against my arm.

"Ow!" Stinging pain pierced my arm.

"Sorry." He scrunched his nose.

I wiggled my toes, blinked back tears, and closed my eyes. "Go on, get it over with."

"I'll try to be careful." He cleaned the wound, each swipe shooting agony through my arm.

Nausea bubbled inside my stomach and bit at my throat. I pressed against the seat back.

"Almost there. You're doing great." He dressed my arm and clipped a bandage into place.

"You done torturing me?" I opened my eyes, and my gaze collided with his bare chest.

Nope, the torture continued.

"I just want to dab some antiseptic on your palms. Anywhere else you think you might be grazed?"

"I'm sure I'm—"

"Fine. Yeah, I gathered that. You said your knees hurt?" He grasped my left hand and wiped it with a damp cotton ball.

I sucked in air between my teeth. Pain and comforting strokes.

"Can I check your knees?" He cleansed my right palm.

"Might as well." If my knees were scraped, I'd have to clean it up once I was home, so what did I have to lose?

Leif kneeled on the tiled floor in front of my chair, leaned forward, and gradually raised my left pants leg with both of his hands, inspecting my skin with each exposed centimetre.

Cool air connected with my shin … and my leg hairs. Far out! More heat gushed to my cheeks and upper body.

"I can't see any scratches on your leg." He tucked the bunched material nearer my lower thigh and slid his forefinger across my exposed knee.

I squeezed the sides of the chair between my fingers, sore

palms forgotten.

"There doesn't seem to be broken skin on your knee either."

"The other one's probably fine too." My voice choked.

"I'll check to make sure." He lowered my left pants leg and repeated the process with my right. "This one's more battered and bruised. You must've landed hard on your right side."

"Probably." I gritted my teeth.

He narrowed his eyes and inspected my skin. His soft fingers brushed my kneecap, and he leaned away.

I blew out a long breath. *Cheater. Stop being conscious of another man.*

Leif dabbed antiseptic on my right knee, fixed my pants leg into place, and packed away the first aid kit. "Would you like a drink? Cup of tea?"

A quick getaway? I leaned forward, readying to stand, and hissed. My head spun.

"You 'right?" He bounded toward me.

My gaze collided with his bare chest. Again. I closed my eyes. "Maybe a cuppa is in order. Do you have coffee?"

He rummaged through a kitchen cupboard and groaned. "Sorry, I'm out. Tea okay?"

"Herbal?"

"I can do that." He prepared a cup of tea, placed the elegant white mug on the kitchen table, and settled into a chair opposite me.

"Thanks." I sipped the warm beverage. "Any chance you can put on a shirt now?"

Leif widened his eyes and glanced at his torso. "I forgot about that." A deep shade of scarlet spread over his face, ears, and neck, and dotted the top half of his torso.

I pressed away a smile.

"I apologise." He stood, disappeared through a doorway, and returned a minute later wearing a charcoal T-shirt. "I'm sorry if I made you feel uncomfortable. It wasn't my intention."

"Don't worry about it." *Because you enjoyed it. Admit it, then get it together and forget the handsome man!* I wrinkled my brow, sipped my tea, and racked my brain for a conversation starter.

"So, what're you up to these days?"

Business ideas! Yes. "I'm in the throes of working out what I'd like to do over the next few years."

"And what're your possible plans?" Leif rested his elbows against the table and leaned forward.

"I've been researching what's involved in running my own catering company."

He raised his eyebrows. "That's impressive. Will you need any capital for your business venture?"

I tapped my fingers against the porcelain mug. "It's possible."

"I might know a guy who could help." The corner of his mouth lifted.

I laughed. "Really."

He grinned. "Have you got my business card?"

"Um …"

He stretched back, yanked a card from his running shorts, and slid it across the table.

"You have business cards on you when you're out running?" I pocketed his card.

"You'd be amazed how often the opportunity arises."

I huffed a laugh, consumed the final drop of tea in my mug, and slowly stood. "I'd better head off."

Leif shot to his feet. "Let me drive you home."

"Thanks, but I think a brief walk might help loosen some of the stiffness."

"You sure?" His gaze skittered from my head to my shoes.

"Certain." I would rather limp home than get in a car with him.

Leif escorted me to the front door.

"Thanks for patching me up."

"Anytime."

I wrinkled my nose. "I certainly hope I don't embarrass myself again with a public fall and need you to patch me up."

"My offer was more of a"—he waved his hands in front of his chest—"general offer to help. Banking, mending. Whatever you required."

I stepped through the front door and turned. "I appreciate your help."

"Look after yourself, Belinda." His voice oozed with sincerity.

"Happy renovating." I wandered down the street and hoped to forget the entire morning.

CHAPTER TWENTY-FIVE
Stop and Check

Numbers and letters jumped around the spreadsheet and swam in my vision. I dropped the financial printouts onto the island bench, rubbed my eyes, and slouched on the barstool.

Writing a financial strategy for my business plan sucked.

I had spent most of March thinking, imagining how and where I wanted to run my business, and jotted notes and questions into my phone. By the first of April, I was neck-deep in research, mainly online or over the phone. I emailed Keanu and Tara for any insight, and they forwarded several fruitful contacts. I also visited a catering company in Robinvale and picked their brains.

Some of the equipment I needed was easy to choose, but kitchen fit outs were more complex. Falling down that rabbit hole accounted for several sleepless nights, but I now had more of an idea of potential expenditures. And despite hating this financial stuff, I needed the distraction today.

I glanced at my phone and reread Vicki's message.

Vicki Jacobsen: THINKING OF YOU AND PRAYING FOR YOU. I'LL COME OVER IF YOU WANT THE COMPANY. PLEASE LET ME KNOW. I DON'T WANT TO CROWD YOU, BUT I DON'T WANT YOU TO BE ALONE. LOVE YOU XX

Year one, gone.

Heat accumulated behind my aching eyes. I leaned my elbows

on the benchtop and rested my face against my palms.

How had an entire year passed without Matt?

I missed him. More than I thought possible. He enjoyed spreadsheets and budgets, and would have dived gleefully into helping me with this plan. The man had garnered money from all the scary recesses of the internet, trading stocks and bonds. Doing … long things and shorting … short things? Stuff I cared little to understand.

If only I had gleaned some of his wisdom before he died.

Fire built in my chest, and my breaths shallowed. I was alone and financially uneducated. The thought of walking this path by myself … I gulped for air. How could I do this? Where was my anchor in this fiscal storm?

I wiped my face and glanced across the room to the microwave. Leif's business card lay on top of the stainless-steel appliance. He lived and breathed finance. Maybe I should call him for help.

My desperate thoughts wandered from the economics of business toward the hope I once experienced in prayer.

I stretched my aching neck. *No.* I might be inept when it came to financial forecasts, but I did possess some skills.

I shuffled my laptop and papers to the end of the bench and grabbed the recipe card I created for a sultana and choc chip banana cake I had played with last weekend. The local football club were playing their first home match for the season later this afternoon, and the town had been littered with flyers for people to celebrate at the Tellarine Secondary oval.

Matt had enjoyed playing and watching local sports games. What better way to celebrate his life and love for footy on a sunny autumn Saturday than with banana cake?

I located ten medium-sized non-stick loaf tins from the storage cupboard, greased and lined each container, and gathered all of my ingredients. Today called for my Kenwood and my pretty KitchenAid mixers. The three of us would make an incredible team.

While the stand mixers beat the cake batter, I wiped flour from the bench.

Leif's business card beckoned to me again. I brushed the mess into the sink and contemplated my options. Nick and Vicki were genuine in their offer, but borrowing money could muddy our friendship. What if my business went belly-up? How could I sign legally-binding contracts which had the potential to destroy my friendships?

If I borrowed money from the bank, there would be no collateral damage if I lost everything. No business partner inspecting the books or asking about their investment. Just a compassionless system expecting regular payments. And with my mortgage-free home and large savings nest egg, the bank would deem me low-risk. Leif might even suggest a personal loan or equity home mortgage—I had once heard Matt talk about options like this—if it meant the interest rate would be lower.

Something settled inside of me, and I blew out a slow, calming breath. I would go with a bank loan. But not yet. I had time to commit to a plan.

I scraped the sides of the mixing bowls and set them to beat for five more minutes. My heartbeat steadied with each dissolved second.

After pouring the cake batter into loaf pans, I smoothed their tops and slid the tins into the oven. A smile traced my lips, and I dumped the empty mixing bowls into sudsy sink water.

I would get through this money stuff. But before I signed my life away on the dotted line, I needed to talk to a particular someone.

I clutched my tote bag to my chest and followed a narrow, cracked path through Tellarine Cemetery, past the grassy area I once walked with Vicki when she visited Diana's mother's grave, to a place I had avoided for twelve months.

Matt's plot lay between the children's section and a group of weathered, two-hundred-year-old timeworn gravestones. The space had cost a fortune, but the funeral director declared it a wise investment for when I died.

A comforting thought.

I skimmed my fingers along the double-sized granite headstone—large enough to engrave my details when I left this earth—and traced the letters of his name.

A soft breeze tickled my neck and exposed forearms.

"Sorry I've not come to visit until now." I kissed my fingertips, pressed my fingers against his name, and sighed. "I'm sure you can guess it's been horrible since you left, and I bet you'd be disappointed in how I've dealt with life since."

Matt would never condone the anger I had allowed to rule my days, or the hatred for the boy who ended his life, but he would have been sympathetic to my pain. And devastated for our baby loss. Yet he often spotted the silver lining in tough situations.

Would he see any upside to my loss?

"I'm sorry to tell you I'm not a sleep-deprived single mother. Our baby didn't make it. My pregnancy ended, then I had an emergency hysterectomy, so I'll never have a baby."

Never have a baby. Never wake to Matt's face.

Too many "never" moments.

"I left church months ago. If my brain had been screwed on right, I should've insisted your funeral be somewhere else. But none of this can be undone." A dull ache dug into my lower back, and I shifted my weight. "Your killer still awaits trial, which is frustrating, but I feel less inclined to run him over with my car these days. Maybe time can heal some wounds."

An elderly couple passed by in the direction of the children's section.

"Your sister-in-law's still a problem for me. Some things were said, which won't surprise you, but I've been too chicken to contact her. Any suggestions?" Matt always had a wise word or piece of advice for the Alison issue.

"Jonathan and Diana have a little girl. She's six months old. I don't mind holding her for brief moments." Brief enough not to stir any dreams, but each short encounter set me on edge quicker than the last. "She smells like a lost dream," I whispered.

So many parts of me needed fixing. Would I forever be a work in progress?

"I'm trying hard to turn my life around. I'm seeing a therapist and planning a Matt-less future. What do you think about a catering business? Your bestie offered to back me financially, but I think I'll go with a bank loan instead. Do you think that's a wiser choice for me? Mixing business with pleasure seems unnecessarily complicated."

Several noisy cockatoos flew overhead.

"There's a nice guy at Bendigo Bank who's offered to help me. Leif Salverson." I winced. It seemed … wrong to talk to Matt about Leif.

A memory resurfaced. *I'll be chasing skirts a year after you're buried.*

I clutched the top of the headstone and steadied my feet. I knew Matt had spoken in jest, but the seriousness of our conversation gripped my lungs and shook my insides.

Why had Matt insisted on having that conversation? Had he known there was a chance he might not make it? Or was it a way for him to have peace of mind?

He had been adamant I moved forward if something happened to him.

I glanced around the quiet cemetery. Was I living the embodiment of moving forward? I pursued career plans and some of my friendships. Leif flashed to my mind, and I bit my lower lip. Physical attraction had reawakened, but chasing a relationship? No thanks. How could I hold another man's hand? Or breathe in the scent of another man's skin?

I brushed my fingers along the headstone in a similar way I

used to run my fingers through Matt's hair. A distant, far-in-the-future relationship might be possible once enough time passed—or my loneliness intensified—but for now I was content to stay single.

"I'm not sure what to do with your stuff. It feels strange to enter your office without you there, and I feel like I'm snooping. You don't mind if I sort through your things, do you? They've remained untouched and … I think I'm ready to spend some time sorting."

The wind picked up and caressed my skin.

"The guys at the footy club cheered when I dropped off some baking an hour ago. Their team started the season well and won all their games. Oh!" I pulled a small Ziplock bag from my tote and deposited a plump profiterole on the headstone. "Made these cream puffs yesterday and thought of you while I baked. Probably not crunchy enough, but the custard filling was perfect."

I threw the empty Ziplock into my tote and glanced at the nearby gardens, eyes misted. "I miss you so much, Matt. My chest still hurts when I think of you, but …" I wiped my nose with the back of my hand. "I think I'm going to be okay."

Two crows squawked from a nearby eucalyptus tree.

"I love you." I blinked away tears, smiled, and blew another kiss. "You better eat that before the birds do. And thanks for listening. I'm feeling much better after our chat. We should do this more often."

Time to go. I stepped away from Matt's resting place and I meandered the path to my car.

CHAPTER TWENTY-SIX
Decluttering

"More thermal paste, Matt?" I sighed, closed another box of random computer bits and bobs, and stacked it atop the other boxes in the corner of his office.

How had I not known he was a tech hoarder? I had unwrapped and rewrapped small metal boards with tiny, fragile pieces attached, keyboards and mice, teeny-tiny metal screws, and heavy, boxed-in fans. A large container of memory sticks, external drives, and hard disk drives had almost punched me in the face when I pulled them from a high cupboard shelf. Oh, and tiny cables. Good grief, so many different cables with different labels. SATA, VGA, HDMI, Ethernet. Even something called CAT5.

Who needed all this stuff?

At least Matt had labelled most things. Not that I could tell the difference between an SSD or HDD thingamabob. But I did know what a USB stick looked like.

Matt would be proud.

I rubbed my forehead with the back of my hand and dragged the final box from the shelf.

More SATA data and power cables. Surprise, surprise. What would I do with all this stuff? Nick was more hands-on than technical like Matt. And from what Tara said, Keanu and technology were on a need-to-know basis.

Would Jonathan use any of this stuff? I collapsed onto Matt's black leather swivel desk chair, fetched my phone from the glass desktop, and typed a message to Diana.

Me: WOULD YOUR HUSBAND BE INTERESTED IN CHECKING OUT SOME OF MATT'S RANDOM TECH STUFF? I'VE FOUND BOXES OF COMPUTER-BUILDING PARTS.

What if Jonathan only grabbed a handful of items?

Me: OR IF YOU KNOW OF ANYONE INTERESTED IN THESE TYPES OF THINGS, THE MORE THE MERRIER. I DON'T NEED ANY OF THIS STUFF.

I opened the top drawer of the white mini filing cabinet beside Matt's desk. Post-it notes, highlighters, and Sharpie markers lay in perfect order beside a pair of scissors, a few rulers, and paperclips. The second drawer housed a hole punch, stapler, labeller, and a battery-operated sharpener.

Memories of Matt and our sharpener purchase dropped into my mind, and I relived a trip to Melbourne where we spent far too much at Costco. Matt had spotted the sharpener in the stationery section, moments before his cousin Pip dragged him toward the bakery and Matt added two trays of oversized Costco muffins to our trolley.

Another thought hit me in sudden succession: I would never create another memory with Matt.

Pain knifed my chest and diffused through my torso. I gasped and pressed my palm over my heart. Was this how Matt felt when that boy—no. I shook the awful thought away and swiped at unbidden tears slipping along my cheeks.

Matt was gone for good. Why was this truth so difficult to comprehend?

My phone trilled, vibrating the glass desk, and shaking the metal mesh penholder beside Matt's keyboard and trackball.

I jolted, picked up the handset without checking the screen, and assumed a friendly tone for Diana. "Hi."

"Hey, Belinda, it's Leif Salverson."

Leif? Almost two months had passed since my run-in with him. Fall in … fall over?

"Have I called at a bad time?" His deep voice dipped.

"Uh." I cleared my throat and pressed against the chair back. "No. No, it's fine."

"You certain? I don't want to intrude."

I closed my eyes and relaxed. "How can I help you?"

"I was thinking of you this morning and wanted to check you're okay."

I froze to the chair. He was thinking of me?

"And as it happens, a follow-up reminder on my calendar alerted me to call you this afternoon."

A reminder?

"It's been twelve months since you signed all of your banking paperwork. I thought you might've had a chance to think about whether you'd like Bendigo Bank to continue holding your title deed?"

"Um." Since signing the papers, I had spent zero seconds thinking about this matter. "I …"

"It's not crossed your mind?" His voice sounded lighter, bordering on a chuckle.

"Not once."

He huffed a deep laugh. "That answers my question. Would you like to think about it or are you happy leaving things as-is?"

I stared at the black computer monitor. "Leave it for now."

"Not a problem." Leif tapped at a computer keyboard. "And it's safe to assume you're still working on your business plan?"

"Yeah." Sorting Matt's office had become more of a priority this past week.

"Would you like to partner with Bendigo and work on a plan? Or are you happy to go with private investors?"

"That's a question I can answer."

"Oh, good." He chuckled.

"I'd like to get a loan through the bank, but I'm dealing with some more personal things at the moment and—"

"I'm not calling to pressure you into anything."

"I never said you were."

Leif had never behaved in a way where I felt pressured or uncomfortable … apart from his overwhelming performance as The Shirtless Wonder.

An image of Leif's bare torso jumped to the forefront of my mind.

I sucked in a breath, cleared my mind, and shifted in the chair. "I just wanted to give you the courtesy to know why I'm dragging my feet."

"I appreciate your candour." Seconds ticked by before he spoke again, his voice lower and deeper. "And I want to offer my services again. I'm happy to help in any way you need, business or otherwise."

"Thank you, Leif," I whispered.

"I mean it."

I believed him.

"Well, I'll let you get back to whatever you're doing."

I opened my mouth and "How old are you?" tumbled from my lips.

"Ah … forty-one."

I cringed, and heat built in my face. What was wrong with me? Why had I asked his age?

A flood of thoughts pummelled my brain.

He looked good for forty-one.

Why was he unmarried?

Had he ever been married?

What would he look like with a day's worth of scruff?

Could he even grow a beard or was he one of "those" guys?

Enough! I squeezed my eyelids closed.

Leif chuckled again. "I won't ask you because it'd be impolite … and I already have your birthdate in the system."

Great.

He cleared his throat. "Look after yourself, okay? And call me anytime if you need anything."

"I will, thanks." I ended the call and collapsed against the chair. Was I doomed to be the awkward, overweight, childless widow forevermore?

A light flashed on my phone.

I opened the message app and checked Diana's reply.

Diana Harris: JONATHAN'S EXCITED BY THE IDEA AND OFF WORK TOMORROW. YOU HOME TOMORROW MORNING AROUND 11? WE COULD ALL COME OVER? SAM MIGHT POP AROUND TOO, IF THAT'S OKAY?

Sam Kono was an IT specialist and Jonathan's womanising best friend. Matt and I had spent time with him, mainly at a Jacobsen or Harris gathering, where Sam and Matt chatted about computer things. Like most women with a pulse, I found him pleasing to the eyes. But a philanderer was still a philanderer in my book, even if he looked like a younger, cuter version of Adam Noshimuri from *Hawaii Five-O*.

Me: THAT'LL BE FINE. AND GREAT IDEA INVITING SAM. SEE YOU TOMORROW.

Diana Harris: WONDERFUL! WE'RE LOOKING FORWARD TO SEEING YOU.

Was I excited about seeing them? I loved the Harrises, but the broken parts of me struggled with their joy. Could I last an extended period of time in the presence of two doting parents and their perfect little princess? I hoped so.

I pushed the desk chair backwards and stood. If my guests were looking through Matt's things tomorrow, I had better shift these boxes into a larger space today. I stretched my arms in the air, flexing my stiffening muscles for another workout.

How had this happened? I swallowed, my tongue thick and

throat constricted, and clutched pudgy Chelsea on the edge of my knee where Diana had plonked her several minutes before. My locked elbows tingled with discomfort from my rigid extended arms.

I must look ridiculous holding this baby stiff-armed.

Chelsea drooled and grinned between babbled sounds, her wide, dark eyes unblinking and focused on my face.

Sweat pooled under my arms, and I shifted on my couch.

"All okay over there?" Diana stood beside Jonathan at my kitchen bench, her arm draped around her husband's waist, and her face turned toward us.

"Great." My voice croaked, and I wrinkled my nose.

Chelsea squealed with laughter.

"Someone's having fun with Auntie Bee, aren't you, darling?" Diana chuckled and turned back toward the benchtop covered with boxes of computer components.

"There's some great stuff in here, Belinda." Sam looked around Jonathan's shoulder from the opposite side of the bench and set his sparkling gaze on me. He furrowed his brow. "You sure you don't want us to pay?"

"I'm certain." Free tech seemed like a fair trade for the kindness everyone had bestowed on me over the past year.

Sam flashed a cheeky grin, winked, and glanced at his buddy. "I messaged Andy, and he sent me a list of things to tuck away for himself and Tom."

"I thought Andrew was still training overseas?" Diana asked.

Sam shook his head. "He finished up in Washington late March and moved to Adelaide a few weeks ago."

"Who finished training?" Did I know Andy-Andrew fella or this Tom guy?

Diana faced me. "You remember Andrew Daley? He was in my year level and had his heart set on aerospace engineering."

I wrinkled my brow. "The blond boy who pined for you most of secondary school?"

Sam snorted.

Diana's face reddened. "He's working for ASA."

"ASA?"

Jonathan pulled Diana against his side with his left arm, his back still to me, and examined a gadget in his right hand. "The Australian Space Agency."

"And Tom?" I raised a brow and glanced at Sam.

Diana pressed her lips together.

Sam's gaze skittered between his friend's face and the back of Diana's head. "He's Andy's cousin."

A memory resurfaced of the time Jonathan and Diana had broken up and she dated another guy. "Didn't you date a Tom for a while?"

"Yeah," Diana whispered.

Oh. "Do you all stay in contact with each other?"

"Andy and I catch up when we can." Sam smiled in my direction before rummaging through a box. "Matt saved some decent components."

Jonathan kissed Diana on her forehead, dropped his arm, and swivelled to face me. "We do appreciate this. I needed a few HDMI cables for our new media setup—"

"No freaking way!" Sam's high-pitched tone squeaked across the benchtop.

"What?" Jonathan spun and faced his friend.

"A ROG Strix!"

A what?

"Are you kidding me?" Sam's voice pitched higher.

"What did you find?" Jonathan rounded the bench and peered at the box Sam cupped in his hands like Professor Henry Jones admiring the Holy Grail.

Sam whooped.

Chelsea startled on my lap.

"An Asus ROG Strix GTX ten-eighty graphics card. This is gold." Sam widened his eyes and stared at me. "Why the heck was this boxed away?"

"Since I've no idea what you're talking about, I doubt I can answer that question." I smiled at Chelsea and relaxed my arms

She wriggled, giggled, and plunged her fisted hand into her wet, dribbly mouth.

I stared, transfixed, my chest aching. Why had this joy been taken from me? My long-lost friend, Grief, slid a weighty tentacle around my chest, and the conversation around me dulled. I studied the little person I held upright with a firm grip, and indulged in tasting the bitterness of my loss.

Even after more than a year of processing, and now armed with everything I had learned from Dr. Braithwaite, I remained alone in the world. No husband. No children. Nothing.

I counted my breaths and blinked away tears. Why was life still hard for me?

Chelsea whined.

Could the little girl sense how much pain she inflicted on my brittle heart? How her existence reminded me of the little ones no longer alive, highlighting all the good I no longer possessed?

"You okay?" Diana loosened Chelsea from my grip.

"Yep." I glanced around the room.

All three adults stared at me.

"Just need to use the bathroom." I stood on unsteady feet, lumbered through the house, stared at my sad reflection in the ensuite mirror, and cried.

CHAPTER TWENTY-SEVEN
Setbacks and Shortcomings

I stared at the Netflix show playing on my television. Since the Harrises visited two days prior, I bordered on exhausted most of the time. Baking seemed an unappealing effort, as was tidying or completing my business plan. My body cried for rest, and I indulged in hours of idleness.

This morning, when Vicki called in for coffee, she asked far too many times if I were okay. Did she think I was a newbie to the world of pain? That I was unequipped for dips in my productivity, or down moments? Dr. Braithwaite had armed me with enough tools to survive the Apocalypse.

How could Vicki doubt my ability to pick myself up? I could—and would—do this … when I felt more inclined. Which would be soon. My energy had to increase in the next day or two.

This was just a blip on the radar.

I flicked through watching options for another hour, disappointed nothing captured my interest. What happened to great TV viewing, with captivating plotlines, excellent acting, and cinematography worthy of the screen? When had streaming services minored on decent shows and majored on paying the bills of D-list actors who were best suited to game shows and reality television?

My home phone chirped on the side table at the other end of the couch.

To answer or not to answer? That was the question.

I glanced at the subpar TV viewing, dragged myself to the other end of the couch, and picked up the handset. "Hello?"

"Belinda, sweetheart."

My throat clogged at the gentle lilting feminine voice. "Aunt Crystal?"

"It's me."

I pressed my lips together and imaged her kind hazel eyes and warm, welcoming hug. My eyes misted.

"I'm sorry for not calling you sooner," she whispered. "It's unforgivable of me not to have reached out after Matthew's funeral."

Aunt Crystal had loved Matt like a son, and had probably grieved him like a mother.

A caring mother, not like the waste-of-space thing I had been gifted with to parent me.

"I get it." I had drowned in my grief too, with no thought for anyone but myself.

"Phillipa sends her regards too, and is sorry she didn't reach out more often."

Matt's cousin, Pip, had messaged me a few times, but after I ignored her for months, it was no wonder she no longer inquired about me.

"It's really unnecessary to apologise. I've ignored more messages than read them in the past year. After I lost the baby, I—"

"You were pregnant?" Her voice sounded strained.

"Matt and I thought I was, but after a scan not long after his funeral, I was told there wasn't a baby. I had a blighted ovum."

"Oh, Belinda." Aunt Crystal sniffed.

"And then during the clean-out procedure, I almost bled out, and they removed my uterus."

Sobs filtered over the phone line.

I sniffled and brushed away tears from my cheeks.

"I wish I'd dealt better with my grief and been there for you." Her staccato breaths echoed.

We all wished for the improbable.

I closed my eyes, placed my shaking hands on my thighs, and rested my head against the couch back. "You've called now, so that's what counts."

Aunt Crystal coughed. "Pardon me, I've been a little unwell."

"Are you okay?" I was not in the mindset for a funeral this week.

"Getting better each day." A ruffling sound shuffled over the phone line. "I called not only to check on you, but also for a specific reason."

"Oh?"

"Brian found a box of Matt's belongings in the garage."

I smiled. Matt had mentioned a box stashed in his uncle and aunt's garage, but never divulged what it contained or whether he wanted it.

"I wondered if you might like it? Or perhaps some of the things?"

"What sort of things?" I scrunched my nose and stopped myself from slapping my own face. What did it matter when they were things which Matt had once treasured?

"There are a few medals and other sports memorabilia from his high school days, plus a few other items." A smile returned to her tone. "Interested?"

"Please." Anything to have more of Matt.

"I'll post it up to you in the next few days."

"I appreciate it."

"I wish we could visit, but having been unwell has put me behind in all of my Melbourne commitments."

"It's fine. Really." Having Matt's family stay might go as successfully as when my family stayed. I huffed a quiet breath. Matt's family were sane, so the likelihood of a falling-out was unlikely.

"Is there anything Brian and I can do for you, sweetheart?" She sighed. "Entice you to move to Melbourne and be closer to us?"

"I'm happy in Tellarine." Maybe not happy, but close enough for now.

"I'm glad. It was worth a try." Her soft, melodic laughter filled the airwaves. "Do stay in touch, sweetheart. Just because Matt isn't here doesn't mean we stopped caring."

"Okay." My hands trembled, and I crouched against the couch.

"We love you. Talk soon." Aunt Crystal disconnected the call.

I stared at the darkened phone screen and envisioned past times with Matt's family. His aunt and uncle were intentional with their love toward us both, and often shared their joy in knowing we both walked life together with God by our sides.

An icy heaviness settled in my stomach.

Matt had loved Jesus with his whole heart, and I had witnessed the positive changes in him.

But now? I had abandoned the life Matt loved, and the niggling sensation permeating my chest seemed too similar to guilt.

"How can I help you?" Dr. Braithwaite's voice slid through the phone handset.

"I've been … struggling." Waiting another day for our usual appointment was not an option.

"Tell me how your week's been."

"I've been sorting through Matt's office and some of his wardrobe."

"And how have you felt doing these tasks?"

"Fine." I shuddered a breath. "Well, I had been fine until some friends visited to go through stuff."

"Did something happen between you and your friends?" Her tone changed. Was she concerned?

"Not exactly. I …" I sighed. "I was lumped with holding their baby, and it brought up all the old feelings."

She hummed.

"And then Matt's aunt called and …"

"Sounds like a tough few days for you."

I huffed a harsh laugh. "I need some new coping techniques and tips."

"You've followed your list and performed all of my suggested methods?"

"Yes."

"Counted your breathing?"

"Lots of times."

"Meditated on the good in your life?"

What good? "Yes."

"Written in your gratefulness journal?"

"Ah huh." A lot of good that one did.

Dr. Braithwaite rattled off several more suggestions which I had tried, but they had failed to help.

"I've done them all and still feel awful." I gripped the phone closer to my ear. "Could it be my medication?"

"The pathway your GP set is conservative, and having not experienced these symptoms in the first month after the reduced dosages, I doubt they could be contributing to your situational and emotional responses."

A jittery heat billowed in my chest.

"I suggest you call your GP, share your concerns, and see whether your medication plan needs an alteration."

"I can do that. Do you have anything else I can try?" She had to have something else up her sleeve?

"Calming breaths, perhaps find a cosy place to read a book with a nice drink."

That was her advice?

"And we can go over strategies in your appointment tomorrow morning."

"Great." There had better be new strategies introduced.

"See you tomorrow."

I ended our frustrating conversation, dialled the GP's office, and waited on the line to speak with Dr. Fallow.

"Belinda. What can I do for you?"

"I need my antidepressant reduction schedule altered."

"Why do you think it needs an adjustment?" Dr. Fallow asked.

"I'm not feeling too great. Struggling emotionally."

"We could increase your dosage slight—"

"No, I want to get off the meds, not increase them." Were the medical experts in my world having a dumb day?

"That wouldn't be wise. Your health could be impacted detrimentally with any sudden changes like—"

"But it wouldn't be sudden! I've been weaning off these things for close to three months already, and I've read online it usually only takes about eight weeks for someone who was on the meds for eight months like me."

"We decided to follow this slower path for several reasons. There are no shortcuts when it comes to antidepressants, I'm afraid."

What a load of garbage! I mumbled my thanks, ended the call, and hustled to the kitchen to tackle my sink of dirty dishes.

I scrubbed a shallow pot and splashed water onto my white T-shirt. How could these so-called "professionals" not help me? What about their duty of care? With the amount of money dropped into their bank accounts after each consultation, I expected more.

Someone firmly knocked on the front door.

"Coming!" I removed my washing gloves and strode to the front of the house.

A grey-haired man with whiskers and hard eyes stood at my door balancing a large box in his arms. "Belinda Briggs?"

"That's me."

He shoved the box at me and walked toward his van.

"Hey!" I sucked in a breath and grasped the heavy load, somehow maintaining my balance, no thanks to him. "Rudeness!"

With his back still to me, the delivery guy thrust his arm out, stuck his middle finger up, and opened the van door.

"Go jump off a cliff!" I gritted my teeth, reversed inside my house, and locked the door.

What a horrible man!

I trudged to the kitchen, slipped the box onto the bench, and rummaged the drawers for Matt's retractable utility knife. Where was it?

Ten minutes of searching five different rooms ended with an awkward box opening ceremony with scissors. I wiped my brow and delved into the box.

Layers of brown paper and bubble wrap covered the contents of the box. I peeled away the layers and removed items from their protected space. Basketball and football trophies, medallions, and ribbons.

I flipped the box side flap and noticed Aunt Crystal's neat handwriting. Matt's things! I dug into the treasures and extracted several sports jerseys, three unframed team photos, and a soft, black Melbourne High School jacket.

Matt would have looked cute wearing it.

I opened a Melbourne High haversack and unleashed a musty smell reminiscent of a boys' locker-room. "Nice one, Matt," Wrinkling my nose, I tipped the bag upside-down. A pair of tracksuit pants, some football socks, a school scarf, and a pair of maroon bathers fell onto the bench.

Matt wore Speedos at school? I smirked and imagined what he might have looked like as a teenaged boy wearing tiny swimming trunks.

At the bottom of the box was a worn hoodie and an aged envelope. What was this?

I pulled a card from the envelope and turned it over.

A drawing of a baby girl in a pink bassinet with the words "Congratulations! It's a girl!" covered the card front.

I drew in a slow breath and opened the card.

M,

You would've been a great dad.

C

The words blurred on the paper. A storm brewed inside my head, spinning through my chest, and vibrating my hands and legs. I dropped the card and clutched the benchtop.

Matt had lived with the pain of loss his entire life. Not one of his children lived long enough to breathe oxygen.

I inhaled a raspy breath.

"C" must have been his pregnant girlfriend. Matt's parents would never have acknowledged him or the illegitimate stillborn like this—not when they practically disowned him after they found out about the baby—and the handwriting was nothing like Aunt Crystal's.

What would I have done if I knew Matt back then? Would I have acknowledged his pain or shunned him like many others in his life had done?

Tears dripped down my cheeks. More blasted tears.

I moaned and stumbled toward the couch. A vice tightened around my lungs, and I gasped for air. Darkness invaded my thoughts, weighing my limbs. The weight of hopelessness froze any ability to see logic.

I fell to the couch, dropped my face against the soft cushions, and screamed until my throat ached. I hated these sensations! Everything had been going well and I had been moving on.

What had happened? Neither my GP or therapist could help me now.

I was utterly alone.

CHAPTER TWENTY-EIGHT
In the Shadow of Injustice

I peered out my bedroom window into the dreary mid-May chill, balancing books in my arms, and pressed the paperbacks to my chest.

My bedroom carpet was littered with piles of papers I had sorted from the deep bottom drawer of Matt's bedside cabinetry, and I had gathered an armload of books from a leaning pile resting near his bedside clock. An eclectic collection of books about computers and technology, Biblical teachings and know-how, and several thrillers.

I deposited the books on the empty bookshelf in Matt's—no, my—office, returned to the bedroom, and sorted the papers on the floor. The "recycling" pile hit the paper rubbish bin with a satisfying thwonk. I filed the "keep" pile in the office and slid the "don't know what to do with it yet" pile back into the bottom bedside drawer.

I opened the middle drawer and tossed random keys, keychains, nail files, and hand lotion on the bed. An old Nokia phone handset with earbuds rested in its original box, alongside an empty Samsung Galaxy box, a digital camera with a broken battery cover, and several notebooks with various scribblings and sketches.

More proof Matt was a hoarder.

I cleared the middle drawer and, with a small shove and some elbow grease, opened the tight top drawer.

Matt's well-worn Bible nestled inside.

A sharp sting prickled my chest. I lifted the book—the chilled soft leather familiar against my fingers—and lay it atop Matt's drawers.

Memories of reading the Bible with Matt filled my mind. Moments we had discussed Scripture or shared our thoughts, bouncing ideas off each other.

No denying Matt's love for God and His Word.

But what about my experience? God had abandoned me in my darkest time. The church had not stopped me from stepping back and choosing a life apart from them. Even on the rare occasions I bumped into churchgoers, they seemed awkward and unable to carry a decent conversation. Did they feel sorry for me? Or were they happy I had left the church?

"Argh!" Enough of this merry-go-round torture! No more thinking about church or Bibles or God.

I stepped away from the bed, my back to Matt's favourite book, shook away the arguments and taunting words my mind threw at itself, and skedaddled along the hallway to the sound of ringing.

I thundered into the kitchen and answered the phone call on my mobile. "Hello?"

"Mrs. Briggs, it's Paige from Larry Stockton's office. Glad I caught you."

I exhaled a rushed breath. "Sorry, was in another room and hadn't realised my phone rang. How can I help you?"

"We tried to call earlier in the week but never got through."

I grimaced. Had I known I had missed an important call, I might have answered my phone.

"The hearing has been adjourned for another six months."

"What!" Balls of fire burst inside my chest and behind my eyelids.

"Mr. Stockton also said you should be made aware of the change in … sympathy toward the accused. Due to circumstances I cannot divulge, the final decision may lean toward a more lenient outcome."

"I can't believe it!" Blood rang between my ears, and I strained to hear Paige's voice.

"I'm sorry, Mrs. Briggs, but we wanted you to be prepared."

Prepared for the failure of our justice system? What happened to swift judgement, or justice at all? My skin itched, and I fisted my hands. Where were those breathing exercises when I needed them?

"We also received a phone call from the youth justice centre. The accused would like to speak with you."

My pulse and heartbeat clipped at an unhealthy rate. I clenched my jaw, counted to ten, and slowed my breaths. "The people over there must be insane if they think I'll speak to him."

"We were obligated to inform you." Paige's voice sounded strained.

"Anything else?" I cringed at my biting tone.

"That's all for now."

Plenty of damage for one brief conversation.

"Take care of yourself, Mrs. Briggs."

I grunted and ended the call. My breaths quickened, and my raging thoughts swarmed.

Jason Kyneton deserved his head on a pike, not a conversation with the widow of his victim.

I gripped my phone in my hand, screamed, and threw the handset across the room.

My phone landed safely on Matt's recliner.

I screamed again, blood pumping fast and hard. I searched around the kitchen, eyes wide, my gaze frantic. My fingers itched to hurt someone. Break something.

There. I rampaged through my pantry, tossing jars and containers on the floor. Glass shattered. Plastic bins thudded on the tiles. My fingers and arms vibrated, desperate to release the energy coiled inside my gut.

More. I needed more. I stepped over glass shards and slammed an open kitchen cupboard door, again and again, revelling in the reverberating vibrations along the benchtop.

Not enough. My frenetic movements failed to dull the pain behind my eyes and inside my chest. Sweat gathered on my brow, and I ripped off my cardigan.

"I hate you!" I screamed and pulled my box of expensive food colouring bottles from a high shelf, throwing them one by one onto the floor. "I"—smash—"hate"—smash—"you!"

Liquid colour splashed the floor tiles, kickboards, and kitchen cupboard doors.

"I hate you," I whispered and stumbled toward my bedroom.

Wetness trailed down my cheeks and dripped onto the floor.

My shoulder impacted the hallway wall, and I cried out.

Leniency. How was this justice? If God was so good, why had He allowed my husband's killer the chance at a future while Matt's future was stolen from him? From us?

My throat screamed with pain. I tripped through my bedroom to my ensuite, and stared at the mirror.

Dots of colour spotted my face and my T-shirt.

"Why?" The blood which had pumped violently through my body now slowed, opening the door to a limb-heavying, eyelid-closing exhaustion.

Dr. Braithwaite had failed me. Dr. Fallow had failed me.

I dropped my gaze and spotted my antidepressant medication below the vanity mirror.

Everyone had failed me. I had no one but myself to help me.

Swiping the box, I popped half a dozen little tablets onto the vanity with trembling fingers and filled a glass with water. I downed the lot and collapsed onto my bed, my mind sluggish.

My pulse and breaths accelerated, and I squinted, unable to see through my blurred vision. Sweat pooled under my arms and behind my neck.

I had no one but myself.

My shoulder, arm, and leg muscles twitched. I tried to move my arms, but the signal between my brain and limbs had short-circuited, and I lay on the soft doona cover, dazed.

No one but me.

Dark shadows crept into my vision, and my eyelids shuttered, pulling me into blackness.

I opened my eyes and glanced into the darkened room, blinking at the crustiness crinkled around my eyelids.

Where was I?

Soft, damp material pressed against my cheek. I slid my hand across the cool fabric and bumped into a firm surface.

A bedside table? Was I on my bed?

I inched my hands in the direction I hoped the wall would meet my fingertips, toward the head of the bed, and flicked the light switch.

Light beamed from the overhead downlight.

I stared at the spine of a large black book resting on the bedside table.

Matt's Bible.

Murky memories unlocked with each passing second. A six-month adjournment. Throat-damaging screams. Faces of the professionals trying to help me. And too many pills scattered on the bathroom vanity.

What had I done?

I covered my mouth with my palm and stared at Matt's Bible. Fresh tears brewed, and I gasped for air between sobs. Whatever I had done to myself, I had survived. My mind was clear, free from cloying sluggishness, and my limbs moved with ease.

Death had visited, and I had shoved it away.

My chest bloomed with delicious, comforting warmth.

I was alive.

My gaze returned to Matt's Bible, and a sharp longing nestled in my chest. If I wanted to continue living, I needed to change *how*

I lived.

Bright, sunshiny memories swiped through my mind, image after image. Times with Matt and our simple, everyday life routines. Work, home, church. Dinner table conversation with friends. Laughter and tears, shared within the safety of the church community.

My heart panged. I missed Matt and our relationship. The day-to-day discussions about weekend plans, troubles with work, and where to holiday next. And if I were honest, I missed our physical closeness. But Matt was gone, and I would never share another moment with him on this earth.

I AM HERE.

I set my gaze back on Matt's Bible. More memories, filled with hope, love, and laughter, dripped into my consciousness. The good times—so many to recall—revolved around my church friends, our friendships, and the satisfaction of growing and serving together. How had I forgotten all the good times? Years of living life with a bunch of understanding individuals could never dissolve under a single memory.

The funeral.

No matter where I lived, I would always remember Matt's sendoff. Did it matter where we hosted his funeral? The church was a group of people walking life together, not a physical building. They were the people Matt loved most. People I had loved.

Still loved.

How had I been blinded to this truth?

I had sucked at life the past thirteen months. Even before Matt died, my trajectory had been aimed toward my pain and suffering. Self-absorbed. Had my inward focus blocked out all the good in my life? The supportive friends and positive relationships. Weekends sowing my time and energy into helping the less fortunate, or volunteering my time as a gift to God Himself.

Another thought struck my spine like a bolt of lightning, and I straightened on the bed, heart roaring.

Had God abandoned me? Or had I abandoned Him?

I slipped my fingers across Matt's Bible, afraid to contemplate my disturbing questions. But I had to face facts. My life sucked, and the longer I steered toward selfishness and destruction, the suckier my existence became.

My gaze anchored back on the book under my fingertips.

Matt might be gone, but his Bible was here for me.

I edged from the bed, yawned, and glanced at the clock. Almost quarter past eleven. My mouth felt dry and fuzzy. Maybe a cup of peppermint tea would soothe me before I returned to bed. I padded down the hallway and switched on the kitchen lights.

My kitchen resembled a colourful demolition site after a rainbow grenade detonated a glass object.

My heart dropped, and I ran my fingers through my messy hair. Hundreds of dollars of speciality food dyes, gone. What stupid—no, imbecilic—selfish behaviour. Matt would have roasted me over this drama.

No more. I had hurt myself in my anger, and now had to clean my own mess. Even if midnight was less than an hour away. Where to start? I glanced at the floor, then at my bare feet. Hmm. I returned to my bedroom for a pair of thick-soled shoes, tiptoed through the debris to the kitchen sink for my rubber gloves and an empty plastic bag, and set to work.

My thoughts tumbled while I gathered glass shards, wiped away traces of food dye, and scoured the floor. Faces of friends and family zipped through my mind's eye, more relationships in need of repair than not. My brain processed, working overtime, and my lungs laboured from my physical exertion.

Tackle one relationship at a time.

"I know it's late and it's been a while since we last talked, God." I slowed my movements, my arms and lower back aching with each scrubbed stroke along the grout, between the tiles. "But I figure it's best to bite the bullet and get through this awkward part."

I stood, and a loud groan escaped my throat. I surveyed the

semi-clean room. "I've failed doing everything in my own strength, and I'm sorry I told you to take a flying leap off a tall cliff into a shallow lake."

Had I said those terrible words to Him or thought them? No matter, the sentiment was nasty.

"Forgive me. Please." I rubbed my gloved palms together. "I don't know how You'll get me through this mess, but ... I want to put my trust in You."

I tied closed the garbage bag filled with the collected mess, switched on the front verandah light, and carried the tinkling bag to the outside green rubbish bin. The moon peeked from behind a cloud, and I basked in its gentle glow.

Trudging indoors, I guzzled a glass of cool water, and completed the kitchen cleanup. Twelve forty-three flashed on the oven clock. I stretched my aching back and neck, and dragged myself to bed.

Matt's Bible called to me.

I deposited the heavy book onto the empty bed space beside me. If I wanted to change, I needed to make different choices.

Gathering the covers around me, I closed my eyes. "Okay, God, I'll go to church on Sunday," I whispered.

I might have imagined it, but a moment later, it seemed like someone dropped a soft kiss onto my cheek.

CHAPTER TWENTY-NINE
Complete in Him

I gripped the steering wheel tighter than necessary. My palms ached, and my fingers tingled from the pressure.

The Tellarine Christian Church car park overflowed into street parking, a common occurrence most Sundays, but it had been years since I searched for a parking spot after the service had started. A late entrance into church had been almost unheard of for me.

Not today. I parked a street away and walked along the footpath, conscious each step either moved me closer to Shalom or a nervous breakdown.

The heavy front doors were closed and absent of the usual greeters.

I slipped through the entrance with slow steps, and peace enveloped me.

Home.

I breathed in the familiar scent of lavender and eucalyptus, and pulled the door shut behind me. All street noise disappeared, and I closed my eyes and listened. Muffled talking echoed from the auditorium ahead. Squeals of kids in the children's church rooms filtered down the hallway. Soft clatters and conversation resonated in the nearby kitchen … volunteers cleaning up after Communion?

I opened my eyes, stepped toward the main service, and slipped into the back row.

The congregation laughed, and Pastor Davidson chuckled.

I missed Matt, but I also missed this atmosphere. A family of likeminded people gathering to learn about God and His ways. His never-ending love for us.

For me.

"You found Colossians two ten yet?" Pastor Davidson's eyes twinkled.

People murmured their assent.

I had always liked our senior pastor.

"'In Him you are made full.' Several translations word this as 'complete in Him' or 'complete in Christ', that we're complete because of our union *with* Christ. We share in this fullness with Jesus, a completion God has granted us through his Son."

I was complete because of Christ?

"Our lives are filled to fullness because of Jesus's sacrifice and has nothing to do with our hard work or amassed wealth." Pastor Davidson glanced around the room. "I have a beautiful wife"—he looked at the front row and winked—"and three awesome sons, but who I am in Christ has nothing to do with my family. I could be unemployed and single, yet be complete in Him because my identity is found in the Father and His love for me."

Tears clouded my vision. My identity was found in the Father's love.

"My purpose is God-designed and unique, not contingent on knowing what my future holds or the way I behave."

I wiped my eyes and pressed my hands against my thighs. The moment I crossed the church's threshold, peace had clung to me. Tormenting memories of Matt's funeral had not bombarded me like I expected. And the few people sitting nearby, where I had accidently caught their gaze, reflected soft, friendly eyes. Not an iota of disgust or disappointment.

Had my problems all been in my head? If my relationship with God and the church could turn around, maybe other parts in my life would turn around too.

Pastor Davidson closed his Bible.

I stood and exited the auditorium doors, my head lowered, and my heart high.

"Belinda?"

I lifted my chin.

Leif stepped from the church kitchen.

Why on earth was he here?

"I thought it was you." His kind gaze searched my features. "You visiting?"

Visiting? I pressed away a smile. "How long have you attended?"

"Since I moved to Tellarine. Nick's always talked about his church, but I wasn't committed to driving over an hour each Sunday … when I wasn't working."

"But now?" I tilted my head.

"I don't work Sundays and I live within walking distance." A sweet grin spread across his face, and he shrugged. "Ran out of excuses."

I smiled.

"I should've shifted churches years ago, but better late than never, right?"

Better late than never. I pointed toward the front door. "I've gotta run …"

"Yeah, sure." He shifted on his feet. "Have a great week."

"You too." I walked toward the foyer exit.

"And Belinda?"

I stopped and turned.

"Let me know if you need anything." His blue eyes shone with sincerity.

I nodded, turned, and exited the building.

I unearthed my business plan from beneath a pile of Matt's

books I had dumped on the computer desk, and settled onto the swivel chair.

The past five days since attending church had been promising. This morning's appointment with Dr. Braithwaite ran longer than usual. I had shared my unpleasant kitchen-throwing and overdosing-on-medication moment, and her controlled, often unreadable expression became a transparent mirror to her worries for me.

I still wondered how I had smashed so hard against the rock bottom of my existence and survived. But I had survived, and my perspective was brighter than it had been in a long time.

I'm not a religious person, but even I can see the merits of faith, and the possibility of Someone looking out for you.

Dr. Braithwaite's comment echoed through my mind. God had protected me from myself.

I stretched my neck and focused on my business plan. My future was bright, and this business would add another layer of colour to my rejuvenating world.

Three hours later, I rubbed my eyes and smiled at the completed digital document on my laptop. I reached for Leif's business card and drafted a message.

Me: Hi, Leif, it's Belinda Briggs. I was hoping I could book a time to meet with you at your office and discuss my business plan.

I narrowed my eyes and reread my message. Polite and professional. Our last two interactions had been unscripted and unexpected. Too … personal. Meeting him in his office would draw a line in the sand. A boundary I required for my peace of mind.

I pressed Send and returned to my paperwork.

My phone beeped at two past five later in the afternoon.

Leif Salverson: Great to hear from you, Belinda. Happy to save you the trip to Swan Hill and could swing by your place on my way home?

I scrunched up my nose.

Me: A kind offer, but I know your time is precious. I'd

PREFER TO BOOK AN APPOINTMENT DURING OFFICE HOURS.

Leif Salverson: NOT A PROBLEM. WOULD MONDAY AT 1:30 P.M. WORK FOR YOU?

My breaths slowed, and I mulled over how to reply. Would a stranger wish someone a good day via text? Would he think I was fishing for conversation if I mentioned the weekend? I rocked side to side in my computer seat. Polite but professional.

Me: PERFECT. THANK YOU.

Leif Salverson: HAVE A GREAT WEEKEND.

No leading question or discussion about him seeing me at church on Sunday. Maybe mentioning the weekend was safe.

Me: YOU TOO.

I drove to Swan Hill on Monday morning and parked on Campbell Street at one o'clock, not far from Bendigo Bank. Tara had once raved to Matt about a nearby bakery, so what better time to dine and snoop.

One steak and mushroom pie, a mouthful of cherry cheesecake—just a taste, not the uncomfortable sensation from overindulging—and a latte later, I exited the bakery, pleased with the ideas their sweet and savoury selections had inspired. The notebook app in my phone had a thorough workout during my lunchbreak.

I strolled along Campbell Street, pleased the early June sunshine warmed the wintry breeze, and unlocked my car. A small plastic container rested in the passenger footwell beside my business plan, a gift for Leif I had baked this morning in-between rolling, forming, and proofing my spelt croissant dough. I had second-guessed myself while I baked, but baked goods seemed appropriate to give a banker who would soon partner with a food business. Proof of my future successful endeavours.

And who would reject a double-chocolate brownie? Baking Matt's favourite had comforted me this morning, as though he was somehow with me while I prepared for my big meeting.

I popped the container and my business plan into my tote bag and headed toward Bendigo Bank.

"Can I help you?" A young, attractive woman with light-brown hair and a pretty smile greeted me at the front desk.

"I have an appointment with Mr. Salverson."

She typed on her computer keyboard. "Your name?"

Right. My name would help. "Belinda Briggs."

She pointed to a nearby chair. "Have a seat and he'll be with you shortly."

I clutched my tote against my chest and lowered to the seat.

Leif called my name eight minutes later. "Sorry for the wait. Got stuck in a Zoom management meeting."

"No need to apologise." I stood and followed him into a medium-sized office.

"Would you mind if I closed the door?"

I glanced around the room with several glass-panelled walls looking out to the reception area. "I don't mind."

He closed the door and rounded his desk. "Some female clients requested my door remained open when I first started here, even if a passerby could hear their private details, so I've fallen into the habit of asking."

I perched on the chair in front of his desk. "I trust you won't molest me."

He widened his eyes, and a soft pink glow touched his cheeks.

Had I actually uttered the word "molest" aloud?

"No, I'm not one to molest women."

Please stop saying that word. My face and neck warmed.

Leif blinked, and his eyes bulged. "Or anyone else, for that matter."

I ignored the heat of my skin, and tried to disregard the redness of his face. Time to steer this awkward and unprofessional conversation from the killer iceberg it approached. "So, I brought my business plan—"

"Excellent. What do you have in mind?"

I retrieved my thin folder of papers and handed it to Leif's outstretched hand. "It's a conservative five-year plan with ten-year goals, designed to be realistic, yet a challenge for when I'm ready to spread my wings."

He flipped through the pages and hummed.

"Finances aren't my strong suit. Matt was the financial guru and understood these matters better than me, so I apologise if it's not comprehensive or too simplistic. I used online templates and—"

"You've done a fabulous job." He smiled and scrutinised each page. "I particularly appreciate the picture you've painted of the where, why, and how of your business. Your goal-setting is clear and realistic, yet thorough, and expresses the heart of your business. Well done."

"Thanks." Was the room hotter than when I walked in?

Leif spent the next half-hour asking me questions and fine-tuning my plan. His expertise shone with each intelligent question, as did his kind encouragement.

Matt and I had once spoken about financial matters in a similar way.

I missed our conversations.

"Bendigo Bank would be pleased to partner with you in your new business venture."

"Pardon?" Had I missed part of the conversation?

"You seem surprised and I'm not sure why." He chuckled. "You've crafted an excellent plan. Any bank would take your business onboard."

Any bank? Not possible.

"I'll have Tamara draft up a contract and email it through to you."

"Great." Now what? How could I turn my plan into a reality?

"I would also like to offer any assistance I can give," Leif said. "Starting a business from scratch is no small feat. I could help you outside office hours."

"But you're already busy with your house." Although his offer was just what I needed, spending extra time with him might not be in my best interests.

"I'd rather take another six months renovating and helping you than get the house fixed faster but do nothing to help you establish your business. After all, Galatians six verse ten encourages us when we have opportunity, do what's good toward everyone, especially those who are of the household of the faith."

I pressed my lips together. Nominal Christians never quoted Scripture. Leif's faith in Jesus was real and established. Why did this thought comfort me?

"So, would you allow me the honour of using my experience to further your business?"

How could I refuse? "Of course. Thank you, Leif."

He slipped his fingers through his coppery hair, tousling his mane, and stood. "I appreciate you coming all this way, Belinda."

I stood, reached for my tote, and spotted the disposable container. "Oh! I forgot to give you this."

"What?" Leif stepped closer.

I focused on removing the container from my bag, not his spiced aftershave wafting up my nose, and passed my gift to him. "I baked these this morning."

"Were these meant to bribe me?" He raised a brow and smirked.

"More like a statement of my faith ... baking in celebration of a successful outcome."

He peeled off the lid and breathed in sharply. "Are these your double-choc brownies?"

I grinned. The guy knew his desserts.

"You remembered." His eyes zeroed in on mine, and his gaze intensified.

Remembered? I scrunched my brow. Had we once talked about brownies?

"Thank you." He lifted the container closer to his nose, sniffed, and grinned. "And thank you for not wielding this weapon until after

I'd offered you a loan."

"You're more than welcome."

"Once you read the loan documents, reach out if you have any questions about the term and conditions … or any other questions."

"Will do." I turned the door handle and glanced at him. "See you later."

"Drive safely."

I strode from the bank, thankful for the successful outcome, and excited to share my news with Vicki. When was the last time we had spoken? Before my overdose? I unlocked my car and buckled my seatbelt. How many times could a friendship navigate serious issues like this? Would she want to hear about my struggles again? Or news about a bank loan after she and Nick had offered to invest in my business?

I drove home, my confidence drooping with each kilometre. Should I put a spin on the bank loan? Beef up the advantages and incorporate the bonus of Leif's expertise?

No. Vicki would see through any excuses I offered for what they were. Excuses. Best to be honest and open about everything as soon as possible.

I reversed into my garage at a quarter to four, dumped my bag on my bed, and shuffled to the kitchen where my chocolate spelt croissants proofed for the final time.

Me: I KNOW IT'S KINDA LATE NOTICE, BUT IS THERE ANY CHANCE YOU'RE HOME THIS EVENING? AFTER DINNER?

I switched on the oven and stared at my phone, waiting for Vicki's response. The last time I had set foot in her home was the day of Matt's funeral.

Maybe it was time to process some more memories.

Vicki Jacobsen: I'LL BE HOME WITH THE CHILDREN. NICHOLAS WILL BE OUT WITH HIS BROTHER. YOU'RE WELCOME TO COME FOR DINNER?

I smiled and relaxed my tight shoulders. Now I knew why I had a sudden need to prepare chocolate spelt croissants yesterday afternoon. For my best friend.

Me: THAT'D BE GREAT. WHAT TIME? I'LL BRING DESSERT.

Vicki Jacobsen: YES, PLEASE! IT'S BEEN ONE OF THOSE DAYS, AND I WANT TO EAT CLOSER TO 6 P.M. SO I CAN GET THE CHILDREN INTO BED EARLIER.

Me: I'LL SEE YOU BEFORE SIX!

I whisked the cream-and-egg wash and hummed while I brushed the mix across the tops of the pillowy dough. Bubbles fizzed in my stomach. What were the odds of me creating one of Vicki's favourite desserts—a complicated pastry which required more than a day of preparation—the day before she needed some baking therapy?

Almost impossible. But with God, all things were possible. Even the simple dream of comfort food.

I popped the trays into the oven and whispered my thanks to God for His guidance, even in the small things.

CHAPTER THIRTY
Dessert for Dinner

"Come in." Vicki sighed and hugged me with less enthusiasm than usual.

"You look tired."

"I am." She closed her front door and wandered down the hallway beside me.

"Good thing I baked today." I grinned, lifted a bag housing a large container of chocolate croissants, and a smaller box filled with double-chocolate brownies.

"Yes." She slumped her shoulders and widened her eyes. "Thank you."

"I've got you." I wrapped an arm around her shoulders and directed her to a kitchen stool.

The Jacobsen house appeared unchanged since I last visited, and the expected pangs of grief over memories of Matt never assaulted me.

Vicki yawned. "Jasmine and Elijah just finished their dinner—I couldn't wait any longer—and they're having some quiet time in their rooms before bed."

I glanced at the microwave clock—five forty-two—and filled the kettle. "Jazzy's eight now, right?"

She nodded. "And Elijah turns six next week."

"And they're okay with having moments of quiet time like

that?" I scrunched my brow.

"Yeah." She blew out a long breath. "It's a blessing for busy days like today."

I pulled two mugs from her kitchen cupboard. "Cuppa?"

"Please." She pointed toward the stove. "There's pasta in the big pot, meat sauce in the smaller one, and grated cheese in the fridge. Help yourself."

"You eaten?"

She shook her head. "Not sure I'm hungry yet."

"We can eat later. Or we can eat chocolate spelt croissants for dinner."

Vicki moaned. "You made them yourself?"

"From scratch, just for you." I grabbed the herbal tea box from the pantry and slid the collection in front of my friend.

"Maybe we can eat them for dinner." She chuckled and pointed at the peppermint tea bags.

"I won't tell if you don't." I swiped two bags, dumped them into our mugs, and covered them with boiled water.

She peeked around the room. "Might be safer once they're in bed."

Vicki would find herself in trouble if Jasmine spotted her eating anything chocolatey without sharing.

I placed a mug on the bench near Vicki, leaned my hip against the other side of the benchtop, and sipped my tea. Matt and I had perched in similar positions over the years, he and I on the stools, Vicki and Nick draped over each other in the kitchen.

Warmth puddled in my chest. Matt might be gone, but his sweet memories remained.

"So, was this an impromptu visit, or did you have something specific you wanted to share?"

How well Vicki knew me.

"Not that I don't appreciate last minute visits." She nodded toward the food containers. "Or your baking. You could drop by anytime with your delicious treats."

"Did you tell Nick I'm visiting? With dessert?" I smiled at my friend.

Vicki pressed back a smile and shook her head. "If there's anything left, he can eat it."

"I'll try not to eat it all."

"Me too." Her smile erupted.

I blew over the top of my tea and sipped. "I've been approved for a bank loan for my new business."

"That's wonderful news!" Vicki beamed and sipped her drink.

"You don't mind I went with the bank?" I ran my finger over the rim of my mug.

"Why would I mind?" She met my gaze. "We're enthusiastic about your plans and want to be part of it, whether that's as investors or taste testers."

"You sure?" I hated the idea of disappointing my friends.

"One hundred percent! Now that Matt isn't here to taste for you, I believe Nicholas, Jonathan, and Keanu would put their hands up to help." She smiled into her mug.

I chuckled and drank my tea.

"Mah-mee!" Elijah's cry echoed down the stairs. "I need you, Mah-mee!"

Vicki rubbed her hands over her face and smiled. "Don't think I'll ever get used to him calling me that."

"Why?"

"It's what Ryan called me. Elijah's voice and his inflections are similar to Ryan's too." Her blue-green eyes softened.

What were the odds both of her sons had spoken similarly?

"I miss the children, but little reminders of them bring joy to my day." She stretched, stood, and met my gaze. "I pray reminders of Matt will do the same for you."

"Mah-mee!"

"Coming!" Vicki plodded from the kitchen and returned minutes later, Jasmine and Elijah leading the way.

"Auntie Bee!" Jasmine wrapped her small arms around my

waist and peered up at me, her hazel eyes bright.

Elijah pressed against Vicki's side.

"How're you, Jazzy?" I glided my hand over the top of her dark curls. Had twelve months truly passed since I saw the children?

"Good! Did you bring me a treat?"

"Jasmine," Vicki admonished.

I smiled at my friend then her daughter. "If Mum says it's fine, there might be a brownie waiting for your morning tea tomorrow."

"Yes!" Jasmine fist pumped her arms above her head.

"Uncle Matt liked brownies," Elijah whispered.

I stared into his large brown eyes and fought against the lump in my throat. "He did. And he'd want you to enjoy them."

Matt would want me to enjoy life too.

"We're very thankful for the treats, aren't we, children?" Vicki raised a brow and tilted her head toward her daughter.

Jasmine smiled up at me, bright and cheery. "Thank you for the treats."

"Thank you," Elijah echoed.

Vicki brushed her fingers through Elijah's hair. "And now it's time to brush your teeth and get into your pyjamas."

Elijah squirmed from Vicki's touch and exited the kitchen.

"Can I stay up a little longer and read?" Jasmine sandwiched her palms together like someone praying. "Please?"

Vicki nodded. "I want your lamp off by seven."

"Yes, Mum!" Jasmine bounded from the room.

I studied the doorway the children had exited through. "They're growing fast."

"They are." She sipped her tea. "Does seeing them still … bother you?"

Bother me? I furrowed my eyebrows.

"I know you struggled when they were babies."

Had I been transparent in my pain and grief back then?

"I could tell, but"—she sighed—"I wasn't sure if I should've said anything."

I had struggled with everyone in my friendship circle having babies, but now? The ache seemed to have dissolved.

Another miracle from above.

"Are you okay?"

I nodded and smiled. "I know I struggled with everyone but me having babies, and I'm sorry you carried that weight, but … seeing your kids doesn't sting."

"Even when Elijah mentioned Matt?" Vicki bit her bottom lip.

"Even then." I drank the last half of my tea. "Yes, I'm sad, but coming here today has reminded me of the sweet moments. Being here with Matt, sharing life with you."

"They were great times." Vicki's eyes seemed distant, like she had stepped back in time.

"They were." I gazed at my friend and opened my heart all the way. "But recent times have been hard, and I apologise for the heartache I've caused you during the past fourteen months."

She slipped from her seat and wrapped her arms around me. "I love you."

"I love you too." My vision blurred.

"And I know you don't like hearing it, but I pray for you every day." She smiled at me with glassy eyes. "We all do."

"And I appreciate it."

She widened her eyes. "You do?"

"I went to church." A tear spilled over my cheek.

"You did?" Vicki's mouth slackened.

"Yeah. I …" Uncomfortable weight pushed against my shoulders.

Vicki grasped my hand.

"We're ready for prayers, Mah-mee!"

My friend's shoulders slumped. "I'm sorry. I'll be back in ten minutes or less and promise, no more interruptions."

"Meet you in the lounge." I grabbed the containers of food, popped their lids, and settled on the couch, whispering several prayers while I waited for Vicki's return.

Sometime later, Vicki ambled into the lounge and collapsed on the couch beside me, eyes closed. "Give me a moment to catch my breath and focus on you."

I smiled at my gorgeous friend and waited in the peaceful quiet.

Vicki covered a yawn with her hand, opened her eyes, and grinned at me. "Continue."

I chuckled and repositioned myself to face her.

"You went to church?" A controlled smile lifted her cheeks.

"I snuck into church the weekend Pastor Davidson preached about completeness in God."

"And?"

"And I remembered the good times I had at church."

Vicki's smile broke out into a wide grin.

"And I want to … somehow … navigate my way back." Why were my words so difficult to speak?

She leaned closer and slid her arm behind my back. "And I'll be here the entire time, by your side, helping in any way I can."

"I appreciate it. But …" How could I tell her about my overdose?

"But what?"

"I …"

She murmured under her breath.

Was she praying? For me?

"Did something happen? Which caused you to go to church?" She wrinkled her forehead.

The band of pressure around my torso tightened.

"You don't have to tell me if you—"

"I overdosed on antidepressants."

Vicki gasped, and tears gathered in her eyes.

"Things had become painful again, and I was in a bad place."

She pressed closer.

"I … I couldn't shake it. The dark feelings." I squeezed my eyes shut.

"And you decided to take extra medication? To numb your pain?" Her voice was soft, without a hint of accusation.

Something broke inside my chest, and my lungs breathed easier. "It wasn't a conscious choice. It was more that I didn't trust my therapist and GP, and decided to increase my dose to help me feel better."

"But your plan backfired."

I grunted a cheerless laugh. "The whole episode frightened me, but it also highlighted I wasn't doing particularly well leading my own life."

"Something inside called to you."

I nodded.

"And you opened the door to God again."

"Yeah. Something like that."

Vicki rested her head against my shoulder. "I'm sorry you went through this, and felt so alone, but I'm glad you've opened your heart to God again."

So was I.

"Nicholas and I are here for you, day or night." She lifted her head and met my gaze. "I mean it. For whatever reason, at any time."

Tears blurred my vision, and I nodded.

"Diana mentioned their visit the other week."

The pleasant sentiments inside my chest fizzled away, and I clenched my jaw. Had Diana told Vicki how long I had hidden in my bathroom, crying? And my abrupt behaviour after I returned to the kitchen?

"Did you end up sorting out all of Matt's things, or would you like some help?"

Matt's things. I relaxed my face. "Between Jonathan and Sam, and Andrew and his cousin, apparently, most of the tech components were taken away."

"Andrew and Tom were there?" Vicki's eyes widened, and she stilled.

"No, no. Sam had spoken to Andrew who had given him a list

of things to look out for."

"Oh." She melted against my side.

"Jonathan and Sam did a great job finding everything all four guys wanted."

"Really?" Was Vicki's tone laced with … scepticism?

"Of course. Why would there be a problem?" I raised an eyebrow.

"I know it's been years since Diana dated Tom, but I often wonder if Tom's a reminder of the difficulties Jonathan and Diana faced." She pursed her lips.

"Diana asked about the guys, and Jonathan seemed happy to help Sam in his search."

"Good." She chuckled. "Family dynamics can be an issue sometimes."

Alison's image flashed in my mind, and anxious tendrils burrowed inside my gut. Had I behaved in an unfair manner toward my sister? Could I somehow repair the fracture in our relationship? Or would we end up at war once more?

Another face flared into my brain, the image of the school boy who had upturned my world. Why had he asked to speak with me? What did he want to say?

"So, would you like help?" Vicki's voice pulled me from my entrenched thoughts.

Right. Sorting Matt's things. "If you have any free time, yes, I'd like to take you up on your offer." Maybe she would find something I could give to Nick. A memento of his wonderful friendship with my beloved.

"Say the day and I'll be there!" She clasped her hands together like a giddy child. "Can we eat croissants now?"

I leaned toward the coffee table, hoisted both containers into our laps, and grinned. "Help yourself."

CHAPTER THIRTY-ONE
Ties that Bind

I unlocked my internal garage door, stepped inside the house, and dumped my bag on the couch. My feet ached. I rolled my neck from side to side.

What a long but enjoyable Saturday. The Jacobsens had celebrated Elijah's birthday this afternoon with the usual suspects—the Harrises and Evertons—and I had walked into their home more excited than not. Seeing my friends chatting and laughing with each other, their children playing and mingling with the adults, had reminded me of the times Alison and I had enjoyed each other's company as kids. Our parents often invited "friends" over, but their parties were nothing like the wholesome, family-friendly events my Tellarine family hosted. Despite the filth and fear, Alison and I had carved out moments of joy.

I plodded to my walk-in-robe and kicked off my shoes. A moan escaped my throat. I extracted my phone from my pocket, slipped into my dressing gown, and plunked on my bed.

Me: THANKS AGAIN FOR INVITING ME TO CELEBRATE WITH YOU. HOPE ELI HAD FUN. XX

Vicki Jacobsen: IT WAS WONDERFUL HAVING YOU HERE. WE ALL HAD A GREAT TIME, BUT ESPECIALLY THE BIRTHDAY BOY. THANK YOU FOR BUYING HIM THE TRESTLE TRACKS TOY. HE AND NICHOLAS HAVE BEEN HUNCHED OVER THE TABLE STACKING CUBES AND

TRACKS, AND ROLLING MARBLES SINCE YOU LEFT!

I grinned. Matt and I had walked past a toy store, roughly two years ago. He had spotted the kits in the window and wondered if it might be something Elijah would enjoy when he was a little older. The box recommended the game for children Jasmine's age and older, but Elijah was an inquisitive six-year-old, and when I saw the sets yesterday afternoon, I thought of Matt and had to buy Elijah the engineering game.

I tugged the navy-blue woollen blanket from the foot of my bed, reposed against my pillows, and snuggled into the warmth. Ensconced in fluffiness warding off the cold winter evening, I scrolled through my texts.

Alison's thread popped into view. I hovered my finger over the screen, pressed my shoulder blades closer to the bed, and reread the texts between me and my sister. Would she reply if I messaged her?

Snippets of our last conversation jarred my thoughts, and my heart stung. A text would never do.

I exhaled a loud breath and glanced at the time. Seven past eight. If she answered, great. If not … what else could I do? I stared at my phone screen, gathered my thoughts, and dialled her number.

Five long, time-slowing rings echoed.

"Hello." Alison's voice lacked its usual spark.

She had every right to be wary of me.

"Hey, Ali," I whispered.

A hush permeated the distance between us. Physical and emotional.

"I wasn't sure you'd pick up." How could I blame her otherwise?

"I'm not you." Her biting tone stung.

"I'm sorry. I really am." My lungs stalled, and I gasped for oxygen. "I've ignored your messages and it was wrong of me."

"Yeah, it was."

My sister was never one to take it easy on me.

"What did you want?"

I gripped the phone tighter. "To apologise and ..."

"And?"

"To let you know I'll do better."

"Good. That all?"

I grimaced. "My therapist suggested I reach out a while back, but I've had so much to deal with ... I put this conversation off for as long as I could."

"Your therapist?" Her breaths puffed.

"Yeah." The ghost of a smile crested my lips. "I took your advice."

"About time." Was there less prickliness in her voice?

"Yeah." Why was this so hard?

"Do you see the therapist often?"

"Every Friday morning." Yesterday's session had been encouraging. Dr. Braithwaite would be pleased to hear about this conversation next week.

"That's great."

I twisted the corner of the blanket around my finger. "I'm sorry for pushing you away, Ali. Sometimes things get so ... big in my head, and overwhelm sets in. I had a big setback last week an—"

"What setback?"

I paused my movements. "I, ah, took a few too many pills."

"Pills?" Alison's voice squeaked.

"I overdosed on my antidepressants." Heat flooded my face and neck.

Her sharp intake of air reached my ears.

"But I came to my senses, regretted the whole thing, and am making positive steps forward."

"I'm glad," she whispered. "Glad you called, too."

I closed my eyes and smiled. "Do you think we can start again and be friends?"

"I couldn't do that."

A fissure formed in my heart.

"Starting again means forgetting everything that's happened to us and between us … and I never want to forget the ways you rescued me."

Tears spilled over my cheeks and dripped onto the blanket.

"I love you, Bindy-Boo, and I'm sorry for the times I've been difficult to deal with."

"So am I," I whispered.

"Rob's also helped me understand a few things in your silence."

Rob? Maybe I misjudged him.

"I think I finally get why you go cray-cray at me for spending time with our parents. It's just that …"

"What is it?" I pressed the phone closer to my ear.

"If I give up on them, it'll mean my terrible childhood would be for nothing."

My heart hurt for my sister. "It wasn't always terrible."

"The parts with you were good." She chuckled. "But our parents were the worst."

"Worse than the worst." Forgiving my parents was a journey I could take another day. I already had plenty of monuments along my path of recovery.

"I know it's only mid-June, but …" Alison cleared her throat. "Do you think Rob and I could visit you for Christmas?"

I widened my eyes. "Um." I had not expected her question.

"Maybe have a think about it."

"Yeah, of course. But … will you and Rob still be together in six months?" I rubbed my lips with my index finger.

"I hope so." She chuckled. "He's a wonderful companion, and he has an incredibly talented mouth."

"Don't want to hear about the goings on in your bedroom." I wrinkled my nose.

"But fornication is fun. You should try it sometime."

"Alison!"

Her cackling tugged a smile to my lips. "But seriously, are you open to, you know, a future relationship?" Seriousness bled into her voice.

"Matt said he'd want me to be happy if something happened to him."

"That's good, yeah?"

"I guess." This conversation twisted my gut in strange ways.

"I don't want to pry, but from what I saw, Matt treated you well. He was your first, yeah?"

"You mean my first consensual partner?" I would never forget the men who touched me as a teenager without permission.

"Yeah," she whispered.

"He was."

She sighed. "I hate our parents."

"The feeling's mutual." *But I would work on it, God. With your help.*

"Do you think you could sleep with another man?" Alison's voice sounded cautious.

A particularly handsome bank manager's face filled my vision. I pushed the thought away, but not before my skin prickled with heat.

"I don't mean to pry."

"Maybe." I pushed back the stifling blanket. "One day. But that could be years away." And not until I overcame my body image issues.

"I know the drill. Good Christian girls and boys don't have sex before they tie the knot."

Glad to know my sister had listened to me over the years.

"It's good to hear you say it, though."

"Say what?" I squinted.

"That you could remarry. It seems to me you contemplating the small likelihood of romance means your heart is piecing itself back together."

Or God was piecing me back together, spirit, soul, and body.

"Well, I'd better go. Rob wants to Netflix and chill." She snickered.

"No more oversharing!"

"Look after yourself, sis." Alison's tone softened.

"You too." I ended the call and stared at my phone. A text message popped up on my phone.

Alison Davies: LOVE YOU.

Three kiss emojis soon followed.

I replied with three smoochy emojis of my own. When was the last time my sister and I exchanged kind sentiments via text?

Laughter bubbled in my chest. How had the important things in my life experienced a sudden turnaround? Reopening my heart to Jesus had paved the way to greater peace and happiness.

My mind boggled at the wonder of His goodness to me.

I scrolled through the latest email from the local real estate agent I had nominated to find the perfect location for my fledgling business.

Nothing appealed to me despite Jan's efforts. I blew out a frustrated breath. July twelfth and still no progress on a property. I picked up my phone and sent Leif a message.

Me: IS IT NORMAL FOR THE PROPERTY SEARCHING PART OF STARTING A BUSINESS TO TAKE THIS LONG?

We began texting each other a few weeks ago, mainly about business-related matters. But the occasional personal factoid slipped into our conversations, along with a few emojis. And several amusing memes.

Leif was a sweet guy, and the more we interacted, the more I wanted to communicate with him.

I hated myself for it.

Leif Salverson: IT CAN SOMETIMES TAKE MONTHS TO FIND AN APPROPRIATE LOCATION. DON'T LOSE HEART, GOD WILL PROVIDE THE PERFECT PLACE.

His unwavering faith spurred my own, but the accompanying

feelings which bubbled when we conversed unsettled me.

Leif Salverson: NO JOY TODAY?

Me: NO. IT'S FRUSTRATING AND I'M NOT SURE WHAT TO DO WITH MY NERVOUS ENERGY.

My list of appliances and white goods to purchase had been completed weeks ago, along with a bulk baking staples checklist. I had spent hours each week testing recipes and feeding everyone in Tellarine.

Leif Salverson: HAVE YOU THOUGHT ABOUT CREATING SAMPLES AND USING THEM TO TALK WITH LOCAL CAFÉ OWNERS? SEE IF YOU CAN DRUM UP LOCAL BUSINESS? THE SWEET AND SAVOURY GOODS I'VE TESTED HAVE BEEN TASTY, WORTHY OF ANY DECENT ESTABLISHMENT. WHY LIMIT YOURSELF TO CATERING WHEN YOU COULD ALSO SELL YOUR GOODS WHOLESALE? HAVE TWO ARMS IN YOUR BUSINESS. JUST A THOUGHT.

Catering and café clientele? What a brilliant idea! I grinned at the phone.

Me: YOU REALLY THINK THAT'S POSSIBLE?

Leif Salverson: YES. YOUR FOOD IS DELICIOUS. SPEAKING OF WHICH, DO YOU HAVE ANY SNEAKY SAMPLES I COULD TRY?

My skin warmed. When Leif offered me a compliment during face-to-face conversation, his sincere expression and kind words seemed genuine. Like the way Matt had complimented me about my food in the past.

I lowered my phone to the desk and stood. Should I be messaging a single man like this? Would he think I was flirting if I asked him to drop by after work? I cringed. Leif would never think of me as a potential life partner, but I feared my heart would do something stupid, like fall for the guy.

There was no denying Leif was a wonderful man with high moral standards and an attractive face. But the lines between personal and professional had blurred. How could I insert some distance between us without offending him? Yet still be friendly, in a professional sort of way? As horrible as it seemed, I enjoyed his attention.

I needed to *not* enjoy his attention, pronto.

I snatched my phone and reread his messages. Would Keanu and Tara be open to the idea of selling my food? I pondered the thought and dropped Tara a line.

Me: Would Benanu's be interested in selling baked goods my company produced?

Tara's response was immediate.

Tara Everton: YES! Yes, yes, yes. Benanu's would eat it up (pun intended).

My phone rang, and Tara's face popped up on the screen.

"Hey, Tara."

"Did I say yes?"

"You did." I chuckled at her enthusiasm. "But isn't this something you need to run by Keanu?"

"Doing it now." A door squeaked, and scratching, muffled sounds filled the ear piece, followed by garbled chatter.

"Belinda." Keanu's voice rumbled over the line. "Y'planning to sell wholesale to cafes and restaurants?"

I opened and closed my mouth, swallowed, and straightened my sagging spine. "It was a thought Leif had."

"Smart man. Wanna swing by in about an hour to discuss it? It'll be quieter then."

Was he serious? "Ah, yeah. I could do that."

"Makes sense to show what our customers tend to order. Could help with yer planning."

"It would help a great deal." Was this conversation actually happening?

"Great. Benanu's'd be onboard with that plan."

"Really?" I whispered.

"If the option is on the table, we'd jump at your business."

"Thank you, Keanu."

"Anything to have my wife straddle my lap like she just did."

"Keenie!" Tara's high-pitched squeal echoed through the

phone.

Keanu cleared his throat. "Any chance ya got choc chip cookies?"

"I could in an hour?" I had prepped and refrigerated cookie dough this morning to bake with Vicki's children after school tomorrow.

He growled and cleared his throat again. "It's Tara's kryptonite."

I ignored the heat in my face. "Yep, sure. Okay. I'll, ah, leave you to it and see you in an hour."

Tara whispered "Shut up and kiss me" a millisecond before the phone connection severed.

I snorted a laugh. Marriage was a fun beast.

Several heated memories—baking-related and otherwise— entered my thoughts, and I lowered to the office chair, fingers gripped around the metal arms. Now seemed the perfect moment to enjoy some "Matt time" and pull my thoughts into order. He might be dead, but deep inside my heart, Matt was still my husband.

I would love him for the rest of my life.

After savouring several delicious moments of my marriage, I walked to the kitchen, phone in hand, and switched on the oven. I retrieved the cookie dough from the fridge and returned to Leif's text, my attraction toward him somewhat cooled. *Thanks, Matt.*

Samples. Several tasty treats were stacked in the pantry from the last two days of baking, and since Leif was a church friend, I would treat him like any other.

Me: I DO HAVE A FEW THINGS. I'M HEADED OUT SOON BUT CAN LEAVE THEM ON YOUR FRONT STEP IN A WATERPROOF CONTAINER. PREFERENCES?

Today was freezing. Leif's baked goods would happily survive outdoors.

Leif Salverson: ANYTHING YOU COOK IS GREAT. THANK YOU, BELINDA. I'LL RETURN YOUR CONTAINER WHEN I SEE YOU NEXT.

An invasion of tiny buzzing, fizzing bubbles tickled my

stomach. Why had the thought of seeing him again sparked such a reaction? I dumped my phone on the benchtop and snatched a baking tray from the cupboard. How could my body betray me? Matt had been in the ground a mere fifteen months.

I added another uncomfortable thought to ignore onto my lengthening list of things to avoid.

CHAPTER THIRTY-TWO
An Uncomfortable Truth

"You seem ... pensive this morning." Dr. Braithwaite levelled her probing gaze on me through her computer camera.

"I've had a lot on my mind."

"I'm listening."

I closed my eyes and channelled my brain power to organise the buzz of commotion inside my head. "Where to start ..."

"How're your business plans progressing?"

I pressed my hands together. "It's the end of July and I still haven't found a suitable location."

Dr. Braithwaite hummed.

"I've garnered potential clients for the catering and bakery arms of my business."

"That's great progress." She furrowed her eyebrows. "Isn't your home kitchen equipped for commercial cooking?"

I nodded. "But I wanted to avoid having to set up at home."

"Why?"

"The workflow differs from the kitchen fit out I've planned, and lugging equipment and bulk items more times than necessary seems like a needless step in this process."

"But without clients of any kind, you're paying bank interest with personal funds?"

"Yes." Maybe Leif was correct last week when he suggested I

use the space I had and start small.

"What're you thinking about? Your face changed." Dr. Braithwaite narrowed her eyes.

My cheeks heated. Blasted Leif setting off my therapist's radar.

"Belinda?" She tucked strands of greyish-blonde hair behind her ear. "Are you thinking about Matt?"

My face burned hotter.

Dr. Brathwaite's eyes widened ever-so-slightly before returning to normal size. "What's his name?"

I sucked in a breath. How did she know?

"It's okay to experience feelings. Attraction is normal."

"But he's not Matt," I whispered.

"You're not betraying Matt by feeling something for another man."

"How can I feel like this? I love Matt. I'll always love him." Tears pricked the backs of my eyes.

"Of course. Love knows no bounds." She flipped through her notebook, wrinkling her forehead. "I recall us speaking months ago. Matt made it clear to you before his death he wanted you to be happy? Marriage was what he hinted at. Am I correct?"

"Yeah," I sighed.

"You're allowed to love Matt and cherish what you shared with him. But you're also allowed to love him and move forward with someone else." She scribbled something into her notebook. "What's his name?"

"Leif," I whispered, and cleared my throat. "He's the man handling my business bank loan."

"What attracted you to him?"

"Many things." Where to start? "His gentle eyes and generous heart. He treated me with kindness and utmost respect just after Matt passed, and he helped me sort out Matt's financial stuff. He's since moved a few streets away and attends the church I attend."

"Would you like my advice?" She tilted her head.

I stared at my laptop screen. Some guidance would never go astray, and I trusted Dr. Braithwaite. "Please."

"Be open to the prospect of friendship with other men. Single men. You spend time with your friend's husbands, which is a safe zone for you"—she focused on the camera and widened her eyes—"unless you're attracted to any of your married friends?"

"No!" I scrunched up my face.

She smiled. "But single men, like Leif … I assume he's single?"

I nodded.

"Single men are different. Because the potential for more hovers in the back of your thoughts, even before you get to know them."

Was this why I feared crossing the line from professional to personal? "But he's attractive and—" I glanced down at myself and back up to the screen—"I'm not in great shape."

"That's why we're working on your body image and self-esteem. However, you can't assume you're unattractive to *any* man." Her sharp gaze penetrated into my soul. "Has Leif told you you're unattractive?"

My eyes widened. "Not at all."

"Has he showed signs he's interested in you?"

My cheeks warmed. "He stared at my mouth a few times while we spoke on Sunday." After our conversation ended, I had rushed to the church bathroom to check nothing was between my teeth.

"What about eye contact?"

"It's constant, but he's like that with everyone he speaks with." Why I noticed was beyond me.

"Do you recall if his pupils dilate when he speaks to you?"

"Uh." I lifted my eyebrows and shrugged. "Maybe? His eyes seem to brighten when we talk."

"Body language? Does he lean closer when you speak? Or reach out and touch you?"

"We walked from the car park into church, and he touched my

lower back when we entered the building." The heat in my face intensified.

"Have you noticed him step closer when others join your conversations?"

"Not that I can think of." Although I had accidentally brushed his side when one of the single women at church entered our circle of chatter a few weeks ago, then berated myself for my strange behaviour. Leif had twisted slightly so his shoulder rested behind mine.

Weird.

"Does he make you laugh?"

"Often. He's financially savvy, like Matt was, which I also appreciate. And always courteous." The perfect gentleman. I rubbed the side of my face and slid my forefinger across my lips.

"What is it?" Dr. Braithwaite watched my movement.

"Matt was … assertive." I dropped my gaze to my keyboard.

"In the bedroom?"

"And in everyday life. He was often cocky, always confident, and drew attention. But Leif's such a … gentleman."

"And you think he mightn't satisfy you?"

I cringed. Did she have to be so blunt? "Not exactly. It's more I'm used to how Matt … operated. How he responded to things. But then I think, 'Does it really matter?' because if I ever remarried, things would be different since my new husband wouldn't be Matt. We'd just make things work, right?"

"You would adapt, and communication is vital for things to work. However, you can't pigeonhole someone into how you think they might respond to a situation. A thoughtful 'nice guy' like Leif might become aggressive when it comes to protecting his loved ones, or the type to unleash himself in the safety of his bedroom and break bed frames."

"I get the picture." Now to purge the picture from my brain.

"Regardless of how the men in your life respond, only you can decide to open up to the possibility of more." Dr. Braithwaite smiled.

Jason Kyneton's image entered my mind. "My lawyer also told me the boy in custody for Matt's death asked to speak with me."

She wrinkled her forehead. "How did you feel when you were told this?"

"Angry, initially. But … I can't seem to shake it." I glanced at her face on the screen. "Why would he want to speak to me?"

"There could be many reasons, but in most cases, the police suggest avoiding contact with an offender."

"They do?"

"But it's possible something has occurred—like new information or something brought to light—which would allow the accused to reach out to your lawyer." She jotted something on her notepad and glanced at the screen. "Do you believe speaking with the accused would help you? Perhaps bring you closure?"

Did I want to know why he stabbed my husband?

"I suggest you think some more. You're religious, so pray about it."

"Thanks for your help today."

She smiled. "Okay, now we've dealt with this, let's get into what I hoped to discuss in today's session."

Someone knocked on my front door.

I stabbed the slim stainless-steel skewer into several muffins. Good, cooked through. I switched off the oven, removed the muffin trays, and rested them on the cooling racks covering the island bench.

More knocking sounded.

"Coming!" I rushed to the door and grinned through the security screen. "Leif, I didn't expect you."

Leif smiled and ran his fingers through his hair. "I apologise for dropping by unannounced, but … wow, are you baking? Something smells great."

"Just removed some blueberry muffins from the oven." Should I ask if he wanted one?

"Thought so." He straightened his tie. "While I drove home, a business associate called and informed me of some potential properties to be on the market soon."

"Really?" An explosion fizzed in my chest. I unlocked the screen door and opened it wide. "Come in."

"I don't want to intrude." His gaze dropped to my comfortable closed-toe shoes and back to my face.

"Please intrude." I offered my brightest smile, nodded behind me, and stepped toward the kitchen. "Just snib the security door lock."

I busied myself popping muffins from trays and focused on being hospitable. "Would you like a cuppa?"

"That would be great."

I lifted my focus from the muffins.

"You look radiant today." Leif smiled, removed his suit jacket, and lay the jacket on top of his overcoat which rested over the back of my couch. He uncuffed his shirt sleeves.

"Thank you." My gaze locked onto the set of appealing forearms he exposed with each twist of fabric. *Sweet Lord above, save me from myself.* I spun toward the kettle. "Tea or coffee?"

"Bit late for coffee for me. Do you have earl grey?"

"Sure do." I prepared two cups of tea and placed several of the warm muffins onto a small plate.

"Are you baking for an event?" Leif propped himself on a stool.

"The primary school has a fundraiser fete this evening." I delivered the plate of muffins to the island bench. "Once they cool, I'll drop them off."

"Are you staying for the festivities?" He selected a muffin and peeled away the paper case.

"No." I grabbed our mugs and deposited them near my guest, but remained on the other side of the bench. "I'm happy to donate my time baking, but not interested in staying."

Leif chuckled then bit into his muffin. His eyes shuttered, and a gravelly sound rumbled in his throat.

My lungs faltered. I stared at his lips, his square jawline.

He chewed with a pleasant expression on his face.

I could watch him consume muffins for hours.

He opened his eyes and met my gaze, open and forthright. The blue rims of his eyes shrank.

"Good?" My throat dried. I dipped my head and grabbed my mug.

"Very." He leaned forward.

"So, ah, what was this about a property?" I sipped my tea.

"Right." He blinked and straightened. "I believe the florist on Oakland Street isn't renewing their lease next month, and another tenant is cancelling their lease on a similar-sized lot in Robinvale."

The florist on Oakland Street? Matt and I had bought flowers from the local store many times. I squinted and tried to recall the dimensions of the shopfront.

"My contact said he'd email me the dimensions of the shops, and will include potential costs and inclusions on a rental agreement."

"Why'd he call you?" I picked at a muffin.

"I mentioned to him in June I was on the lookout for a certain space for a friend." He dropped his gaze to his hot drink.

I leaned forward and touched his wrist. "Thank you, Leif."

His gaze dropped to my hand on his warm skin.

I withdrew my arm.

His throat bobbed. He lifted his chin and surveyed my face. "I said I wanted to help and I meant it."

I smiled at him and replayed the many moments we had shared over the months since we met. Leif was deep-rooted in God, and wisdom flowed through him and into everything he touched. His quiet strength called to me, even in his contrasts to Matt.

Was Leif attracted to me? Did he feel anything like I did for him? I locked away the dangerous questions. Dr. Braithwaite had said to contemplate the idea of friendship with a single man, but asking him if he reciprocated feelings for me pushed the safe platonic boundary.

"I'll forward the information onto you when I receive it."

"I appreciate it." Another thought snuck through my barriers, and a gentle peace settled over me. I could trust Leif. "Do you know the circumstances surrounding Matt's death?"

"I am, and I'm sorry you had to endure such a terrible tragedy." His voice lowered.

"The boy in question reached out to me." I peered at his kind eyes.

Leif inhaled a loud, quick breath, and straightened. Something glinted in his gaze. "Is he allowed to do that?"

"He did so through proper channels." When Vicki asked a similar question, we had spoken with Jonathan, who confirmed, due to the youth's confinement, this request was legal.

"Good." His posture eased.

I sipped the last of my tea and stared at my empty mug. "I think I might speak with him," I whispered.

Leif emitted several rapid breaths.

Did he think I was crazy? Would he talk me out of it? I had spent the last week, on and off, in prayer, and had informed Dr. Braithwaite of my decision at this morning's scheduled appointment.

"That's very brave." His voice held a hint of something strange.

I glanced at his face.

Warmth exuded from his features, and a soft smile lifted his cheeks. "You're quite an amazing woman."

My stomach fluttered.

"What happens next?" He lifted his mug to his lips.

I turned to the baked goods and checked for warmth. Cool enough to box. "I'll call my lawyer on Monday and give them possible dates and times I'll be available for the phone call. I believe they'll then arrange a time with the youth detention centre for the call to take place. Vicki will be with me when I receive the call."

"That's a wise plan."

I smiled and boxed the muffins. "I'm praying nothing will happen to tip me over the edge and set me back."

"I'll pray your experience is positive, gives you closure, and brings you closer to the One who loves us all."

"Thank you." Heat prickled at the back of my eyes and throat, and I glanced at my friend.

"You love God, Belinda, so all things will work together for good. Even in this tragedy, His grace and love will shine through the darkness."

"You always know what to say to encourage me." Tears dampened my face, and I swiped my palms along my cheeks.

"I'm glad." He wielded a pleasant smile, stood, and boxed the remaining muffins. "Would you like me to drop these off for you?"

"I appreciate the offer, but I could do with some fresh air." I sealed the box.

He gathered his things and turned toward the front of the house. "I'll see myself out. Look after your precious cargo."

"See you on Sunday." I waved goodbye, grabbed my keys, and gathered the large box of muffins. After depositing the box on the front seat of my car, I locked the house, and set off to keep the locals fed.

CHAPTER THIRTY-THREE
But God

"You're certain you want to do this?" Vicki's concerned eyes zeroed in on my fidgeting fingers. "We forgive people who hurt us because God forgave us. But it's possible to forgive someone without having to speak with them."

"Have you spoken to Jude since …?" I stilled my hands in my lap and straightened on my couch.

"Not had any contact with him since the police escorted him from the Benanu's car park."

"Don't you wonder what became of him after he got out of prison?" I would want to know where a dangerous ex like him resided.

Vicki pursed her lips. "I don't have to wonder because I know."

"What?" How had she never told me?

She clasped her hands in her lap. "Christine spilled the beans a few Christmases ago."

"What happened?" I knew Vicki's sister wanted to throttle her ex-brother-in-law, but what had she done after Jude's release? Or had her husband, Patrick, pulled some strings?

"You remember my cousin Steve?"

"The police sergeant? Diana lived with him and Stacy in Melbourne for a while, didn't she?"

Vicki nodded. "Steve and Patrick cooked up a scheme. They

wanted to be the first faces Jude saw the moment he stepped back into civilization."

I widened my eyes. "You're kidding."

"Not a word of a lie."

"Wow." Steve and Patrick were great guys, but they could intimidate someone if they wanted.

"Being the good Christian boys they are, they didn't touch him. In fact, they offered him the chance at a new start."

"Huh?" I tilted my head.

"Jude's been making an honest living in Western Australia since his release, and from the little I've been told, might even be happy." Her eyes shone with tears.

"That's … some story. And you're happy for him?"

"I am." She wiped away tears. "He was once a wonderful husband, and Nicholas and my prayers have always been for Jude's restoration, especially with his Creator."

Had I heard her correctly? "Nick prays for your abusive ex-husband?"

"He does."

I stared at my friend and shook my head. "Here I thought you two were an amazing couple. But this is … wow."

"It's the manifestation of God's grace in our lives. And the peace we have because of forgiveness." She levelled her gaze at me. "Now, I'll ask again. Are you sure you want to do this?"

"Certain."

"And you have peace in your heart?"

I nodded.

"Okay." She squeezed my hand and relaxed against the couch.

My phone rang minutes later with an unknown number.

I passed the handset to Vicki as we had planned.

"Hello, Victoria speaking … yes, Belinda is here with me. Ah huh … correct." She turned to me. "Do you consent to this conversation being recorded?"

"Yes." My voice shook.

"Consent is granted." Vicki smiled at me and narrowed her eyes, listening. "Okay, that won't be a problem … right … yes."

I counted my breaths and stared at my battle-ready friend.

"We are ready … hello. Hold, please." She handed me the phone. "He's on the line."

I grasped the handset with shaky fingers and gripped it close to my ear. "Hello."

"Mrs. Briggs?" A soft pubescent male voice spoke.

"Speaking." My throat tightened, and I swallowed.

Vicki rested her palm on my knee and offered me a kind smile.

"Thanks for … this." His voice wavered. Nerves?

I wiggled my toes and focused on my breathing.

"I …" His voice cracked. A loud puff reverberated, and he sniffed.

My eyes stung. *God, help me get through this.*

"I'm … sorry." Soft sobs echoed along our connection.

Heat built in my eyes, nasal passages, and throat. I pinched the bridge of my nose.

Vicki wrapped her arm around my back. Her lips moved in murmured prayer.

"I didn't mean f-for M-Mr. Briggs to …" More sobbing filled the phone line.

Tears trailed my cheeks.

Ask the question.

I sniffled and exhaled an extended breath. "Why did you do it?"

His breathing quieted. Time seemed to pass at a glacial pace.

I had spent over a year embracing silence, what was another few minutes? I leaned into Vicki's side and waited.

He cleared his throat. "Alan threatened to hurt my sister."

Alan? "Who?"

"The guy I had aimed for but …"

Matt had stepped in the way. *Oh, Matt.*

"Alan raped a girl in the school toilets."

What! "When?"

"Last year. He said he'd do the same to Melissa. I … I had to protect her, b-but Mr. Briggs stepped in to separate us and … it was too late." His voice wavered, and another soft sob drifted to my ears.

"Were you high at the time?"

"No, ma'am. B-but Alan might've been."

My heart twisted. The poor kid.

"I'm sorry, Mrs. Briggs," he whispered.

Vicki shoved a handful of tissues into my lap.

"Truly sorry."

I fisted several tissues, dabbed at my wet face, and stared at my friend.

Her eyes seemed to communicate one word.

Forgive.

More tears spilled from my tired eyes. "I forgive you, Jason," I whispered.

He whimpered.

Vicki pressed closer.

"And I'll pray for you."

Jason's inconsolable cry pierced the air.

Something broke free inside my chest, and I smiled through my tears.

Muffled voices and scraping filled the earpiece.

"This conversation has concluded," a gruff, male voice said. "Thank you for your time."

"Ah, y-yes. O—"

"Good bye." The phone call disconnected.

I stared at my dark phone screen.

"You did really well, Bee." Vicki squeezed me tighter.

"Thanks," I whispered.

"Matt would be so proud of you." She kissed my damp cheek.

"He would be, wouldn't he?" I blotted my remaining tears and sucked in a breath.

"He would." She released me from her embrace and stretched

her arms. "Want to go out and celebrate? Diana invited us over after your phone call. Tara's bringing snacks and all the passwords to Keanu's streaming service accounts."

I peered around my neat lounge room and spotless kitchen. Nothing here needed my immediate attention, and I had earned some time out after this phone call. "Why not?"

"Let's go." Vicki assisted me from the couch, linked her elbow with mine, and escorted me from the house.

I occupied the last available chair in Dr. Fallow's waiting room and retrieved my phone.

Leif Salverson: SEVEN WEEKS UNTIL YOU TAKE POSSESSION OF YOUR NEW PREMISES. YOU EXCITED?

I grinned at his message and imagined the agent handing me the keys to the lovely building on Oakland Street. September thirtieth could not come soon enough.

Me: VERY!

Leif Salverson: I'VE EMAILED YOU THE DETAILS FOR THE KITCHEN FIT OUT CONTRACTOR. HE'S RECOMMENDED SEVERAL INSTALLERS.

Me: THANKS. WILL LOOK AT IT WHEN I GET HOME. AT THE DOCTORS, SO MIGHT NOT REPLY IF I'M CALLED IN.

Leif Salverson: EVERYTHING OKAY?

"Belinda." Dr. Fallow nodded toward me, turned, and disappeared along the medical complex hallway.

I stood from my chair in the crowded waiting room, followed him into his consultation room, and settled on an empty seat.

He smiled and lowered to the chair behind his desk. "What can I do for you today?"

"I'd like some advice to do with my physical health."

During a moment of prayer and time with God, the Scripture about my body being a temple of the Holy Spirit had pierced my heart. Dr. Braithwaite helped me deal with emotional and mental issues related to my bigger body shape, but by scientific standards, I was heavier than was healthy. And although I was learning to love me for who I was—barrenness and all—I knew the uncomfortable sluggishness would dissipate when I lost several kilograms.

I had shared these thoughts with Dr. Braithwaite last week, and she suggested talking to my GP. My therapist could help my emotions, but Dr. Fallow was better equipped to deal with my body.

"What would you like to know?" He aimed his green-hazel gaze at me.

"As you're aware, I'm no longer on any medication." I clasped my hands in my lap. "It's been almost two months and I've been unable to budge any of the extra weight I added when I started the antidepressants."

He leaned against his backrest and crossed his arms. "Are you eating regularly?"

"No. I often forget to eat." Since the beginning of August, I worked in my kitchen most days, fulfilling delivery orders and breathing in delicious aromas, so my appetite was sated.

He hummed. "What about portion sizes?"

I furrowed my brow and recalled my recent meals. Did a handful of cashews or a banana qualify as a meal? "Small."

"How small?" He raised an eyebrow.

"Very."

He hummed again. "And exercise?"

"Who has time for that?" I pouted.

His lips formed a grim smile. "Are you working again?"

"I have a few clients, and I'm baking most days."

"So, you're on your feet all day?"

"Pretty much."

He narrowed his eyes and scrutinised me.

I straightened in my chair.

"You need to eat more." He uncrossed his arms and leaned forward. "Focus on regular, healthy meals. Lots of fresh produce, less baked or fried foods.”

“And exercise? How much is too much?”

“Start off slow and easy. Walking each day and building up to a jog. Extend the time and distance when your body allows.” He captured my gaze. “And reduce the stress. Have someone help you with your orders.”

Reduce stress. My mind tumbled with the many things calling for my attention, and the big-ticket stressor had nothing to do with my work.

Matt’s forty-seventh birthday was next week, and with Vicki, Diana, and Tara’s help, we were arranging a large gathering next Saturday evening. A final celebration of his life. I had few recollections of Matt’s funeral, and wanted to remember this night and the wonderful people coming to celebrate my beloved husband.

I cleared my throat. “I’ll be moving into a work premises at the end of next month, so my routine will change, along with help from the added staff.”

“Good.” He smiled and relaxed in his chair. “Anything else?”

“Not today, thank you.” I stood, farewelled Dr. Fallow, and exited the building with an extra spring in my step.

My phone beeped while I drove home.

I bustled through the internal garage door, switched on the kettle, and noticed several text messages from Leif.

Leif Salverson: WOULD YOU TELL ME IF SOMETHING WAS WRONG?

Leif Salverson: I’M HOPING YOUR SILENCE MEANS YOU’RE IN YOUR APPOINTMENT.

Leif Salverson: PLEASE MESSAGE ME AND LET ME KNOW YOU’RE OKAY.

Warmth flushed under my skin, and I bit my lower lip. Dr. Braithwaite’s advice lingered in my mind.

Open up to the possibility of more.

Almost sixteen months had passed, but I knew many women—some older and some younger—who had waited years before remarrying. Why was my heart egging me on prematurely to risk my friendship with Leif?

Children.

I inhaled a harsh breath.

All the women I knew had children and invested their time, energy, and focus on their little ones. If any of our babies had survived, would I feel anything for Leif so soon?

I reread Leif's messages and checked the time. Mid-afternoon. Would he answer if I called? Might be better to call and leave a message to unburden his mind.

The phone rang once.

"Belinda? Is everything all right?" Leif's voice sounded higher than normal.

"Yes, I'm fine." I smiled and inserted as much cheer into my tone as possible.

He expelled a long breath. "I was concerned, but I'm glad you're okay."

"Sorry to stress you." I held my phone in my left hand and filled a mug with hot water using my right.

"It was silly to jump to conclusions." He cleared his throat. "So, you're all right?"

"Asked for some advice about my body." I choked on a breath. "As in my health. Getting healthy and shaking some of the weight … off me."

"Oh."

My face burned. Why was I so awkward?

"What did your doctor suggest?"

"Common sense stuff. Eating regular, healthy meals. More fresh produce, less fried or processed stuff."

"A good plan so far."

"And"—I groaned—"exercise."

Leif chuckled. "Did your doctor give any suggested activities?"

"Walking. He said to start small and build from there."

Several seconds passed. "Would you like a walking buddy?"

"Maybe?" Was he offering?

"I run early most mornings."

"Early morning exercise sounds horrible. Matt often ran before work or at some insane time on a Saturday morning."

"You don't seem like the early morning type." Humour tinged his voice.

"The only time I woke early was to insistent kisses." I widened my eyes. Had I said that aloud?

"Can't say I've had that experience."

"You're missing out." Shut up, shut up!

"I'll take your word for it." He cleared his throat again. "Regarding your new exercise routine, I'd be happy to accompany you if you wanted to go on a late afternoon walk, once I'm home from work?"

Leif still wanted to walk with me after I had flaunted my past early-morning bedroom activities?

"Um, yeah. That sounds great. Well, as great as the prospect of exercise can be."

His laughter vibrated through the phone line.

"Leif?" I tilted my head.

"Belinda?"

"Have you ever been married?"

His steady breaths hummed over the line.

A weight grew in my stomach. Whoever coined the term "Silence is golden" had never waited for an answer in uncomfortable silence.

"No."

"But why?" I wrinkled my brow. "You're such a nice guy."

His even breaths whispered into my ear. "Nice guys don't often get the girl."

If I had met Leif ten years ago, would I have chosen him over Matt? I blew on my hot drink and sipped. Probably not.

"For twenty years I've watched friends settle down and start families.”

“Does that make you sad?” I whispered.

“Sometimes. But the few women I dated weren’t right for me in the long run, and I take comfort knowing I made the right choices.” A rustling noise filled the silence. “I know many men in loveless marriages.”

“My parents are like that.” My tone dripped with disgust.

“You don’t get along with them?”

“They don’t deserve the title of ‘parent’ after the terrible things they did and allowed to happen to their daughters.”

“I’m sorry, Belinda.”

“Me too.” I gulped another mouthful of tea. “I’d better let you get back to work.”

“Want to go for a walk tonight?” Was that hope in his voice?

“Come by when you’re ready.”

“You doing okay?” Leif glanced at me with narrowed eyes.

“Yes,” I rasped. My face and lungs burned with every step, as did my calves and thighs, and I wheezed.

Leif had knocked on my door at five forty-five dressed in a T-shirt, tracksuit pants, and runners. We set out for what Leif deemed “a leisurely walk” minutes later.

“How long … has it b-been?” Surely an hour of this torture had passed.

“Seventeen minutes.”

“Wh-at?” He had to be kidding.

He glanced at his wristwatch. “Almost eighteen.”

I moaned, huffed hot air, and rested my hands on my hips while I walked. The gradient of the concrete path sloped steeper, and my feet faltered.

Leif grabbed my elbow and steadied me.

“I … think I”—my lungs squeezed—“might die.”

“I hope you’ll live.” Leif laughed.

“Why?” I fought for more oxygen. *Breathe, you blasted lungs!* “So you can … kill me a-another day?”

Leif's laughter rumbled along my heated skin. "This too shall pass."

I bumped his side with my elbow—which he may or may not have felt, but I sure did—and growled. "Stop … waxing … poetic."

"Would you like to stop? My house is a street away."

I turned my head too fast and lost my balance.

Leif caught me around the waist and pulled me upright. "You all right?"

"Yeah." I stared into his blue eyes, the colour difficult to see with the waning light, and puffed rapid breaths.

He released me and stepped backward. "My place?"

"Yes." I tugged my T-shirt hem over my backside and snuck a furtive peek at Leif.

He seemed focused on the path ahead.

"Thank you … for your support." I spluttered a breath.

"Anytime." He glanced at me and smiled.

We walked into his house a few minutes later.

I dropped to the carpeted hallway, crawled to the lounge room on shaky hands and knees, and rested my sweaty head on Leif's couch.

"Water?"

"Please."

Moments later, he touched my shoulder.

I lifted my head and sipped from the glass Leif held between his steady fingers. "Thank you."

"You did well today." He lowered to the floor and crossed his legs.

I chuckled a humourless laugh. "I almost died from an activity my elderly neighbours excel at."

"Once you're feeding your body nutritious food and you're more active, it'll get easier." He offered me another sip of water.

Sweat slicked my brow, and I tucked several wet blonde strands behind my ear. "Is my face red?"

"Like a beetroot."

I glimpsed my T-shirt where bands of sweat dampened the fabric. "Do I smell?"

"Not in a bad way."

"But I do smell." I lifted my quivering arms, grabbed the glass from his hand, and swigged.

"Some sweat smells good." He retrieved the empty glass from my hands.

A joke Matt used to say popped into my mind, and I wheezed a chuckle.

He furrowed his brows.

"Just thought of an inappropriate marriage joke about sweat Matt used to say."

He widened his eyes. "Right."

"You're not fazed by me, are you?" I studied his features.

"What do you mean?"

I twisted and leaned against the couch. "That I'm sweating like a pig, completely out of shape. The total opposite of you."

"So what?" Leif stretched his legs and leaned back on his hands.

"Many men would care." I pursed my lips.

"I care for your wellbeing, but I see you." He tapped his forefinger against his chest. "The person inside."

"You do?"

His gaze locked onto mine. "I like her most of all."

My mouth dried.

"In answer to your question, no, I'm not fazed by you."

I dropped my gaze and steadied my breaths. Would he feel otherwise once I asked him to come to Matt's party?

"What is it?" Leif's voice lowered.

I shuddered a breath. "Next Saturday I'm helping to host a get-together at Vicki's place."

He raised his eyebrows.

"And I was hoping you might like to come, but …"

"What?" His eyes searched mine.

"You might recall I wasn't 'with it' soon after Matt died."

"I picked up on that possibility." A smile tugged at his lips.

"I don't remember the funeral much, and wanted to spend a final time reminiscing with those who knew Matt and loved him."

Leif's smile disappeared. "I'm not sure I'd be the best person to attend. I only knew Matt in a professional capacity."

"It's his birthday next week."

"How old would he be?"

"Forty-seven."

Leif ran his fingers through his hair. "I'm not sure I—"

"Please."

"It'll be awkward." He scrunched his brow.

"Only in your brain."

"He was your husband."

"He was. And he'll always live in my heart." My fingers itched to touch Leif's face. "But you're important to me too."

He levelled his potent gaze on me.

Sweet Lord above, I could drown in his eyes. "I can't promise anything but friendship right now."

"I'm not asking for or expecting more," he whispered.

Would this sweet man ever run out of patience?

"But whenever you're ready for more?"

Were we on the same page? *Please, God, let us be on the same page.*

His throat bobbed. "I'll be here."

Shivers danced along my spine, and I relaxed my shoulders. "Okay. But I'm asking you to think about the gathering. Please?"

He blew out a breath. "Yeah, I'll think about it."

CHAPTER THIRTY-FOUR
Thanksgiving

"Where are the dip refills?" Tara poked her head inside Vicki's humungous fridge stored in the butler's pantry adjacent to the kitchen.

"Third shelf on the left." Diana arranged sliced fresh fruit on a platter at the large island bench. "We running low on anything else?"

Tara bumped the fridge door closed, arms laden with dip containers. "Keanu ate the last of the curry puffs and rice balls. When's the sweet stuff coming?"

"Soon." I piped the last of the icing onto the trayful of chocolate cupcakes. "Once you finish with the dips, can you slice up the brownies?"

"On it." Tara scurried from the kitchen.

"I can do that," Diana said.

I dropped the almost empty piping bag and levelled my gaze at Diana. "Are the mini tarts closer to room temp?" Tarts always tasted best off the chill.

"I'll check in a sec." Diana washed and dried her hands.

Tara re-entered the spacious kitchen. "Anything else?"

"Refill these. I'll cut up the brownies." Diana dropped a container of veggie sticks into Tara's hands, slipped on a disposable glove, and touched several mini tarts with delicate fingers. "The lemon meringues are good to go. So are the vanilla custard."

"Which mean the jam ones will be perfect. What about the salted caramel and choc?"

Diana hummed. "Perfect."

I transferred the last of the cupcakes onto a beautiful white platter I had purchased for my new business. I had included all of Matt's favourite cupcake flavours and combinations, and had forced myself to concentrate on the catering instead of the reason we catered.

Less crying in the kitchen was a good thing.

"When're you coming out to mingle?" Vicki's voice snapped me from my reverie.

"Soon?" I glanced at Diana and watched her slice lovely, thick slabs of brownie.

"Everyone's asking about you." Vicki slipped past and grabbed the huge plastic container of chocolate croissants.

"I'll be out when the sweet stuff goes out." I plated the mouthwatering chocolate brownie squares onto another platter.

"Where'd you want these?" Vicki asked.

I pointed to two large, shallow bowls resting on her kitchen buffet.

"What next?" Tara stepped into the kitchen and grinned. "I'm gonna fall into a food coma tonight."

"I suspect everyone will waddle out of here." Diana grinned. "What a great way to advertise your business, Aunt Bee."

"Keanu's loving it, tasting everything so he knows what to order for Benanu's." Tara chuckled. "Pretty sure he's already had requests for the menu."

Nothing like a boost in business. "Remind him I still have six weeks to go before I can increase production."

"I forgot to ask. Did your interview go well yesterday?" Vicki plonked a pastry-filled bowl on her kitchen table.

"Interview?" Diana added the dirty knife and cutting board to the wash pile.

"Is this for an employee?" Tara raised a brow.

"Yeah, my second-in-command."

"Oooh," Tara said.

"Leif recommended someone who's worked in the catering industry for over a decade, but wasn't happy in her current job role."

"And was she any good?" Tara crossed her arms over her chest.

I smiled at the memory of meeting Skye Stewart, Leif's effervescent cousin. She was competent, sweet, and overflowing with knowledge and fresh ideas. A good thing for me her current employer treated her like rubbish.

"That good, huh?" Tara asked.

"Skye's a lovely girl. She's Leif's cousin—"

"Nepotism," Tara and Diana said, chuckling.

"How could this be nepotism when Bee and Leif aren't..." Vicki widened her eyes. "Are you?"

"No." Maybe one day, if Leif was happy to wait a while. A good, long while. "Skye's quite skilled, so she's earned the position through merit alone."

"You're hiring her?" Vicki's eyes sparkled.

"She starts October tenth helping me pack up my kitchen and moving things into the new building. The kitchen fit out should be completed by then, or at least close to completion. The pantry store room will be ready." I could almost see the new place in my mind, with its fresh paint and gleaming stainless-steel surfaces and appliances.

"That's fabulous! Congratulations!" Vicki launched at me and wrapped her arms around my waist.

I laughed and returned her embrace, hands extended to avoid touching Vicki's clothes with my brownie-crumb-covered gloves. "It's a start."

My next task involved building teams of kitchen staff—experienced or people I wanted to give a chance—two groups for the catering side of the business, and another two focused on baking for the long list of cafes and restaurants I had gathered.

"We done now?" Diana surveyed the kitchen now covered with sweet treats.

"I shifted the savoury foods onto two plates and cleared the main table, so there's space for the sweet stuff." Tara pointed to the pile of used cutlery and crockery on the trolley near the back door.

"Okay, let's take all these out and enjoy the rest of our evening." I smiled at my wonderful friends and focused on their gorgeous faces, not the pressure building in my chest. Blasted emotions. "Thank you for doing this."

"Of course." Vicki squeezed my arm.

Diana and Tara grinned and hefted dessert platters through the back door.

"Vicki?" I touched my friend's shoulder.

"Yes?" She grabbed a platter of mixed cupcakes and turned her head.

"Have you seen Leif?" I had whispered prayers all throughout the food preparation time, hoping he would be here tonight. I understood his hesitancy, but prayed he would drop by nonetheless.

"Not yet, but I'm sure he'll be here." Vicki offered me a soft smile and carried the food from the kitchen.

I hoped so. *If you can do anything to persuade him, God, please do it.* I grabbed one of the bowls of croissants, slipped through the back door, and deposited the dish on the main table under a spray of greenery intertwined with twinkle lights.

The Jacobsen backyard glowed under soft lighting scattered in trees, along table edges, and underneath a large archway, illuminating familiar faces. Loved ones, friends, and colleagues.

Tears bit at my eyes and sinuses. "You'd have loved tonight," I whispered toward the dimmed sky with its winking stars. Could Matt see me? A quiet sob tugged at my lungs, and I wiped my cheeks. "Happy birthday, babe."

Conversations from all corners of the yard buoyed me, strengthening my resolve to keep it together. I had cried many tears over Matt, but now was the time to celebrate him and appreciate the people I still had in my life.

I brushed away the last of my tears, glanced around, and waved at a group of Tellarine Secondary College teachers.

Cindy returned my gesture, approached, and pressed a kiss to my cheek. "How're you doing, stranger?"

"Not bad."

"You look … brighter than when I last saw you."

"Must be the exercise endorphins." I had lost half a kilo since last week. Eating better and exercising had its merits.

"Feels like forever since you left the College." She tucked silky jet-black hair behind her ear. "I've missed my across-the-hall buddy."

I wiped my palms over my thighs and smiled. "What's the new Food Studies teacher like?"

Cindy wrinkled her nose. "A sh—ugar storm. She's a fluffing nightmare. Like, pluck-a-clucking-duck nightmare."

"Lots of swearing in your head?" I smirked.

"A buttload! She's a matronly old cow who's nothing like you." She opened her mouth, stuck out her tongue, and pretended to gag on her index finger.

I snorted a strangled laugh.

Cindy shrugged. "What can you do?"

"Well, I hope you're still enjoying your job despite the new neighbour."

"Yeah, the kids are fine." She grabbed a celery stick from the nearby table. "I only wanted to throat-punch one of the Year Seven yahoo's this year."

"Glad you didn't."

She giggled. "It's satisfying to imagine, though. Strangling the destructive so and so's."

"You sure you're in the right career?"

"It'll work for now." Cindy surveyed the room. "Any single guys here? Preferably rich."

I spotted Sam chatting with Jonathan, Keanu, and Andrew

underneath a large tree. I liked Cindy, but I liked Sam more. Jonathan's best mate seemed like the kind of guy who was into uncomplicated women.

Cindy nudged me with her elbow and squinted in the direction I had looked. "You holding out on me?"

"Most of my friends are married."

"But are they happy?"

"Cindy!" I hissed. "I'm not introducing you to my friend's husbands!"

"Okay. Calm it." She pursed her lips. "Who's the hot blond beefcake standing between Mr. Sexy Ango-Indian and the gorgeous Asian? Is he single? He's yummy."

"Andrew Daley?"

"Mmm-hmm." She widened her dark eyes. "Yummy."

"He's an ex-student of mine and Matt's." I shrugged. "No idea if he's single."

She waved a dismissive hand. "Andrew. Got it. Wish me luck."

"Uh."

Cindy stuck out her chest, pouted, and set off in Andrew's direction.

The poor guy.

"Hello, sweetheart."

I turned, grinned at Matt's aunt, and wrapped her in a hug. "Where'd you come from?"

"Melbourne." Aunt Crystal laughed, her dulcet voice blanketing me with peace. "I was standing nearby and overheard your friend."

"Cindy's an interesting one."

"Sounds like it."

"Is Uncle Brian here?" I glanced around the yard.

"With Phillipa and Troy." Aunt Crystal tilted my face to the right.

"You all came?" Warmth pooled in my stomach.

"Anything for you, Belinda darling." She wrapped her arm

around my waist. "Victoria offered us two rooms to sleep the night."

"Vicki's a beautiful friend, but I insist you all come back to my place. I'll cook pancakes for breakfast, and we can go to church together."

Matt would be thrilled at the idea.

"How could I turn down such an offer?" She smiled and sighed. "Matthew loved your pancakes."

"Matt loved food full stop." I pressed a hand against Aunt Crystal's back. "Thank you for being here."

"We're always here for you."

I blinked my stinging eyes.

"Mrs. B!"

I turned and spotted two familiar faces.

Madison Taylor and Grace Robinson walked arm-in-arm along the footpath leading from the side gate.

When was the last time I had seen Diana's school and youth group friends? At Diana's joint birthday-engagement party four years ago?

Madison planted a kiss on my cheek. "I'm so sorry about Mr. B."

"So sorry," Grace whispered and leaned in for a hug.

"Thanks, girls." *Keep it together.*

"He was the best teacher." Madison twisted a silver bracelet on her wrist.

"He was." My darling Matt.

"Super-hot too," Madison said. "All of the girls were totally jelly of you."

Tears shimmered in my vision, and I smiled.

"It's true." Grace squeezed my arm. "Anna had a crush on him too."

"I had a crush on whom?" Anna Beaufort, Diana's cousin, approached on the arm of a tall and strapping familiar-looking young man with brown hair and dark eyes.

"Mr. B." Madison turned toward Anna and widened her eyes.

"Oh my gosh, please don't tell me you've found love before I have?"

Anna and the young man glanced at each other and burst into fits of laughter.

"Why's that so funny?" Madison fisted her hands on her hips.

"You." Grace smirked and nodded at the young man. "Hey, Mitch. You back from Ibiza?"

I gaped. Mitchell Beaufort had filled out since I last saw him.

"Yeah, finished the Mediterranean circuit last week." The up-and-coming DJ aimed a bright smile in Grace's direction.

Madison gaped. "Good grief, what happened to the gangly teen always with a football in his hand?"

"Grew up, I guess." Mitchell shrugged and shoved his hands into his pockets.

"And how." Madison eyed him from head to toe.

"Stop drooling over my brother." Anna shuddered. "It's gross."

Mitch stepped closer to me. "I'm really sorry about what happened. Mr. Briggs reached out to me a few weeks before he passed, and we exchanged a few thought-provoking emails."

Anna slipped an arm around my back.

"I was struggling with my … tempting work environment, and his encouragement and prayers meant so much to me." Mitch's eyes sheened with moisture.

"I'm glad Matt was there for you when you needed him." I clasped his hand.

"Same." Mitch glanced at his sister. "It was a close call, but I'm okay now."

"I'm glad." I brushed away my tears.

"My condolences too." Anna pressed close, smiled, and released my back.

Something bumped into my leg.

"Sowwy, Ah-nee Bee!" Three-year-old Kai grappled with his one-year-old sister, Leilani. He furrowed his little brow. "Say sowwy for wunning, Lay."

Leilani stared up at me with her larger-than-life dark brown eyes, tilted her sweet face to the side, and raised her arms. "Up."

I stilled. A lump the size of large unchewed piece of steak jammed in my throat.

"Up!" The little girl thrust her hands toward me.

"Don be wude, Lay." Kai sounded like a mini version of his mother.

I flexed my stiff fingers, glanced around the group of people near me, and swallowed the lump. *You can do it.*

"C'mon!" Kai tugged on his little sister's arm.

"It's okay, Kai. I've got her." I reached for the little girl and rested her on my hip.

The space around me seemed to still, and sounds faded away. No more conversations or music. All I heard was the beating of my heart and Leilani's sweet giggles.

How had I never realised the beauty of an innocent child? She might not be mine, but she was worthy of my love and affection. Like everyone here tonight. I had love to give, and even if Matt was gone, I could still appreciate my friends.

I grinned at the darling little girl in my arms, kissed her cheek, and whispered, "Just because I can't have a little one like you doesn't mean I can't love on you, you precious cherub."

Leilani leaned her head against my shoulder and snuggled her face in my neck.

"You two look sweet together."

I lifted my gaze and stared at Leif's smiling face. "You're here."

"I am." He stepped closer.

"Thank you for stepping outside your comfort zone for me." I stroked Leilani's silky hair.

He rubbed the little girl's back in slow, sweeping circles. "Nick, Jon, and Keanu are stuffing their faces with baked goods."

I stepped to the side, peered toward the main table, and stifled a laugh.

The men from church, plus a few others, filled their plates and faces with sweet treats.

"Matt would've joined in." I stepped closer to Leif. "You going to get something to eat before the food disappears?"

He brushed his arm against mine. "Only if you promise to eat something."

"I didn't half kill myself to eat brownies and cupcakes, Leif. I'm serious about the weight loss and healthier diet."

"I know, and you've done so well, but you can also enjoy your hard work." He nodded toward the tables. "Some fruit and …?"

"A mini lemon meringue, please."

"What about a drink?"

Ever the thoughtful gentleman. "A glass of sparkling water, please."

"And would you like me to find Keanu or Tara?" Leif peeked at the weighty child in my arms. "I think she's falling asleep."

"Might be better in case they want to pop her inside for bed."

"Will be back soon." Leif strode away.

I rubbed Leilani's back and stepped to the quieter end of the entertainment deck, amazed at the new level of peace I now possessed.

CHAPTER THIRTY-FIVE
The Grace of Patience

Two and a half years later.

I twirled a caramel-dipped fork around the caramel and cream-puff triangular tower, my hands steady and gaze transfixed. Transparent, wispy threads of sticky amber-coloured caramel solidified around the croquembouche cone like frangible golden spiderwebs.

"Rockin' the croque, boss." Darcy, my newest and youngest recruit, stood opposite the stainless-steel workbench with wide eyes and a cheeky grin. "When do I get to do that?"

Skye cackled at her workspace to my left. "Haven't you watched old episodes of *MasterChef Australia*, Darc? There's serious skill involved to create a fabulous looking and tasting tower."

Darcy shrugged. "I'm seventeen. Why would I watch old TV show eps?"

"Because you're interested in food?" I dumped the fork into a tub of dirty utensils, wiped my perspiring brow with my gloved hand, and admired my creation. A dessert Claire Saffitz would "Mmm" over.

"It's a beauty." Skye glanced from her overseeing duties, smiled, and assisted a newbie piping chocolate-mint frosting onto chocolate cupcakes. "Unlike this mess. Start again, Neve."

"It'll be the pièce de resistance of the event." Desiree, one of my catering assistants, slid a box filled with tarts and pastries onto one of our oversized trolleys near the delivery exit.

"That's the plan." I grinned and dumped the pot of remaining caramel beside one of the sinks, turned, and surveyed the kitchen.

A small team, managed by Desiree, worked in the nearby assembly area boxing food for transportation. Skye instructed our inexperienced team members on correct food handling and several basic tasks since we needed all hands on deck to meet our deadline for tonight's fundraiser.

"How're we doing, Skye?" I tossed my disposable gloves into the rubbish bin.

"On schedule."

The back door opened, and Vicki, Diana, and Tara trundled inside.

"Thanks for coming, ladies!" I waved from the other side of the kitchen where I stacked more dishes for the team to wash.

"Goodness, I thought it was hot outside." Vicki fanned her face with her hands.

"That's the price one pays when living in a kitchen in the height of summer." Tara deposited a large flat-packed box onto the benchtop, peered into the stacked containers of sweet treats, and met my gaze. "The guys will be pleased you included your brownies on the menu."

"How could I *not* bake them?" Brownies were Matt's favourite, and he had everything to do with this evening's fundraiser.

Country Youth Rescue Victoria, a local not-for-profit organisation working with troubled youth in the community, was hosting a fundraiser at Benanu's. I had financially supported their efforts over the past eighteen months from a portion of my business profits, and I was honoured to be asked to cater the "sweet" part of the evening.

"Oh, my goodness! This is tremendous!" Diana gaped at my

beautiful croquembouche, linking her arm through her stepmum's.

"I see why you wanted to borrow my special box." Tara carried her large box across the room and placed it beside the tall cone of cream puffs. "Will this do?"

"Perfect."

My team and I slid the tower onto the box base and built the box around it.

"I've got it from here." Skye signalled for Desiree, and they carried the box to its designated trolley.

I turned to Tara. "Keanu doing okay?" I knew his responsibilities preparing the "savoury" part of tonight's menu required strict organisation, and I itched to get to Benanu's as soon as possible.

"Between Isabelle and Dominic, things are covered until your team arrives to help." Tara crossed her arms. "Dad Everton mightn't be as stress-free in scenarios like this, but Keanu's got it covered."

"I'm glad. When will the guys be here?" I helped my staff load containers onto the trolleys.

Diana glanced at her mobile phone. "Jonathan says they're about three minutes away."

I clapped four times, hard enough to sting my palms, and peered around the room.

Everyone stilled.

"Great job, guys and gals. Our delivery truck will return within minutes. Let's wheel everything into the waiting area. Team A coming with us, please double check your uniform's clean and complete." I raised an eyebrow at Darcy and hoped she would look better than the last event we catered. "Team B, once everything's cleaned up, you're free to head home."

Many voices murmured, "Yes, boss," and everyone except for my friends scurried to work.

Vicki pulled a tissue from her pocket and blotted my forehead. "Need you looking nice when the men arrive."

An hour ago, Jonathan and Leif had delivered trestle tables, chairs, and table linen to Benanu's, and seemed to have stayed for setup. Keanu had agreed to use the catering furniture than hire from elsewhere and reduce the profits from tonight's fundraising.

"Is Leif taking you out tomorrow night for your birthday?" Diana brushed something from my shoulder.

My cheeks warmed, and I nodded.

Tara and Diana cooed and giggled.

Several weeks ago, amidst the bustle of a busy evening catering a medical fundraiser, something had clicked inside my head—or maybe my heart—and I knew it was time.

I was ready to move on with Leif.

He had been a complete sweetheart for over two years, offering friendship and a unique but helpful wealth of knowledge, never hinting about deepening our relationship. Not once had he bemoaned the friend zone, or touched me in a non-platonic matter. No stolen kisses or inappropriate text messages. He had been the consummate gentlemen.

Now my thoughts overflowed with a desire to consummate in a different way. At first, I had hushed the loud voices in my head. But the more time I spent with Leif, the more I wanted life beyond friendship. Marriage and companionship seemed like a great idea.

"Where's he taking you?" Tara waggled her eyebrows.

"I'm not sure." I had suggested we go out for dinner alone, and used the excuse of last year's huge party being a requirement for a fortieth birthday, but this year could be quiet. My words, "More intimate," hit the mark where I wanted them to land.

"Will this be a *date* date?" Diana clasped her hands together and beamed.

"It sure will." I returned her grin.

"Does he know that?" Vicki furrowed her brows. "Because guys aren't great at picking up subtle clues."

"I didn't say, 'This is going to be a date', but…" I pressed my lips together.

"I agree with Vicki," Tara said. "Men can be daft, so make it plain."

"So, I should just tell him it's going to be a date?"

"With words … or actions," Tara said, her gaze bordering on mischievous.

"Actions speak louder than words." Diana chuckled.

"Push him into your office, close the door, and kiss him senseless." Tara glanced around the room and lowered her voice. "I speak from experience that desks are fabulous places to push one's man against. Perfect height for sucking face."

"Tara!" Diana hissed.

I widened my eyes. "I'm not sure I could do that."

"They can get up to that sort of mischief when the temptation to tug each other's clothes off is allowed." Diana wrinkled her forehead.

"Oh yeah." Tara sighed. "You gonna get married soon? No point waiting any longer now you're certain."

Vicki rested her hand on my arm. "Whatever Leif and Bee decide is up to them. No pressure from anyone."

"What're we deciding?" Leif's voice trailed shivers along my skin.

"Uh." I glared at my friends.

"We'll see you there." Vicki grabbed Diana and Tara's arms, and tugged them toward the exit.

"Sorry." I peered past Leif, satisfied myself the crew were doing fine without me, and studied Leif in his handsome suit. "You changed?"

"Jonathan dropped me home. Got sweaty setting up."

I pushed aside the barrage of images from our jogging sessions, the most recent when Leif tugged off his T-shirt and ran the final two kilometres shirtless.

Thank God I kept up with him these days and enjoyed the view.

"I drove my car in case you needed me to get something during the event." Leif grinned, setting off pitter-patters in my chest.

"You're so thoughtful." I stepped closer and touched his arm.

"Anything for you, Belinda."

"Thank you, Leif." I reached above his ear and slid coppery strands between my fingertips.

He expelled a sharp breath.

I met his open, fiery gaze, and unleashed my own.

His lips parted.

"Tara, Di, and Vicki say I need to be clear with you." I lowered my hand from his hair and rested it on his firm chest.

His heart drummed a rapid beat, and his blue eyes darkened.

"I'd like tomorrow night to be our first date." I tilted my head closer to his ear. "Are you okay with that?"

"Yes." He pressed his palm against my waist and wet his lips.

My skin vibrated with warmth. I leaned closer, my lips centimetres from his smooth cheek.

"We're all set to go, boss!" Skye called from across the room, her voice tinged with humour.

I startled, and my pulse thudded.

Leif's fingers pressed against my side.

Heat diffused in my face. "I'll, ah, see you there."

I drove the delivery van to Benanu's, my insides somersaulting, and focused on managing my team, communicating with Keanu's, and ensuring a successful evening for everyone involved.

From my vantage point near the bar, I watched my friends laughing and enjoying their time together. Jonathan, Leif, and Sam mingled with guests while Diana facilitated cash donations. Tara and Keanu popped out from the kitchens now and again, their keen eyes aware of every empty glass and every movement of our combined staff.

I glanced to the couch area nearest the bar where Nick and Vicki managed the kids' corner. The youngsters ate, played games, coloured, and giggled. My face ached from grinning at the children's antics, and peace filled the pain-filled place I once carried inside.

My phone vibrated in my pocket, and I checked the screen.

A message from my sister.

Alison Davies: CAN YOU TALK?

Me: AT A WORK FUNCTION. CAN I CALL YOU LATER? IT MIGHT BE LATE, THOUGH.

Daylight Savings came in handy for late nights like these since Queensland refused to get with the times and spring their clocks forward an hour like the rest of the eastern states.

Alison Davies: SURE. I'M A PATHETIC THIRTY-SOMETHING STAYING HOME ON A FRIDAY NIGHT, SO WHAT ELSE DO I HAVE TO LOOK FORWARD TO?

I snickered.

Alison Davies: YOU GET OUT MORE THAN I DO THESE DAYS. IT'S SAD.

Me: CAN'T BE SO BAD SNUGGLING MY NIECE.

Alison and Rob had tied the knot six months ago, two months before Candice Flora Cooper arrived. I had flown up for the Magistrates Court wedding followed by a vegan afterparty where Alison lamented about the non-alcoholic champagne she was forced to drink while I sipped the real stuff.

Alison Davies: YEAH, SHE'S COOL, BUT THAT HUSBAND OF MINE WENT OUT WITH WORK COLLEAGUES BECAUSE "HE NEEDED TO GET OUT." UM, HELLO? I PUSHED HIS BABY OUT OF MY HOOHA, SO WHEN'S MY TIME TO GET OUT?

I pressed away a smile and surveyed the room. Everything seemed to be in order.

Me: IF I DON'T MESSAGE BEFORE CANDY WAKES FOR HER LATE FEED, MESSAGE ME. BETTER GET BACK TO WORK. LOVE YOU, LITTLE SIS. XX

Alison Davies: WILL DO. LOVE YOU TOO. PS WAS WATCHING "THE LITTLE MERMAID" WITH ROB'S NIECES EARLIER TODAY AND WAS REMINDED TO TELL YOU… YOU GOTTA KISS THE BOY.

Me: WORKING ON IT.

Alison Davies: ARE YOU SERIOUS? DETAILS!

Me: Working…

Alison Davies: You suck.

Alison Davies: But I love you anyway. Spill the tea later when I'm spilling the milk from my girls.

I suppressed a laugh, and a teeny snort surfaced. *Thank You, God, for restoring my family.* I had so much to be thankful for. My gaze skimmed the room, the people I worked with, and the friends I shared my life with. I smiled at Vicki, and a forgotten conversation we once shared floated to the forefront of my thoughts.

The journey from negative self-image to seeing yourself as God's masterpiece is not only possible but life-changing.

Heat prickled my eyes.

My words.

How could something I ministered to a friend over a decade ago mean so much more to me now? I blinked away tears, dipped my chin, and pretended to examine the bar countertop.

I had rediscovered God's love, and He had transformed me from the inside out. My childhood had sucked, and the first year without Matt had almost torn me apart, but by God's grace, my life had turned around. God had changed my perspective before I ate well, exercised, and shed sixteen kilograms. His love had guided me prior to my business's exponential growth. And his goodness pursued me before my heart swelled with love for my sister and her baby, my friends and their children, and Leif.

God had given me a new lease on life. I wiped away happy tears and grinned. My broken spirit had healed by the mercy of my Father.

AUTHOR'S NOTE

I've known Matt's fate since editing *Punctured Heart* in 2020 and mourned while I wrote *Wounded Soul* and *Fractured Mind*. But I apologise if his passing caught you off guard, my dearest reader, as you weren't afforded the same opportunity to process like I did. (Yes, I also realise Matt Briggs is a fictional character, but he's as real as anyone else in my mind.)

When I shared future story ideas with my editor in late 2020, she sent me crying emojis and lamented how I used to be so sweet to my characters. I laughed. Had I known what would transpire in 2023, and how gut-wrenching writing this story would be, I would never have laughed.

My beloved Mr Wonderful underwent emergency surgery in February 2023, an experience I would not like to repeat. I used our ordeal as inspiration for writing Matt's hospital scenes.

Then, in June 2023—two weeks after I wrote the scenes of Matt's death—my father-in-law unexpectedly passed away. Talk about life mimicking fiction. Mr Wonderful and I accompanied Mum to view Dad's body at the hospital, and I was in charge of everything related to the funeral.

I witnessed Mum's heartache firsthand while she lived with us the first month without Dad, and couldn't face the thought of returning to a story about a widow. I lamented how I'd survive writing the rest of Bee's tale and lifted my concerns to the Lord. Coupled with God's grace and my commitment to a publishing deadline, I climbed back on my bicycle and finished the story. Praise God, the writing and editing process became therapy for me while I worked through my grief.

So, thank you for sticking with me and reading the last book in *The Tellarine Series*. It's blessed me to write these stories for you! While I have plans for more women's fiction books in the future, I'm currently switching gears to write a lighter romantic comedy series. Keep an eye out for some familiar characters from my previous books…

BOOKS BY SHERIDAN LEE

The Tellarine Series:
Punctured Heart
Wounded Soul
Fractured Mind

ABOUT THE AUTHOR

Sheridan Lee is an Australian writer with a penchant for true-to-life characters who triumph over adversity.

When she isn't singing along to her favourite Christian artists or watching Hollywood actors named Chris in superhero and Star Trek movies, Sheridan is reading or writing—with at least one of her five daughters lounging on her—and wishing the dirty laundry would clean itself.

Connect with Sheridan:
sheridanlee.com
Amazon
Facebook
Goodreads
BookBub
Pinterest